William Wilson

Newfoundland and its Missionaries

William Wilson

Newfoundland and its Missionaries

ISBN/EAN: 9783337327453

Printed in Europe, USA, Canada, Australia, Japan

Cover: Foto ©Andreas Hilbeck / pixelio.de

More available books at **www.hansebooks.com**

NEWFOUNDLAND

AND

ITS MISSIONARIES.

IN TWO PARTS.

TO WHICH IS ADDED

A CHRONOLOGICAL TABLE

OF ALL THE IMPORTANT EVENTS THAT HAVE OCCURRED ON THE
ISLAND.

BY REV. WILLIAM WILSON,

FOURTEEN YEARS A MISSIONARY IN NEWFOUNDLAND.

———————

CAMBRIDGE, MASS.:
PRINTED BY DAKIN & METCALF.
HALIFAX, N.S.
SOLD AT THE WESLEYAN BOOK ROOM.
1866.

DEDICATION.

Dear Brethren, — With much concern and deep anxiety I, at your suggestion, took up my pen to prepare this volume on "Newfoundland and its Missionaries." It has caused me much research, and given me great labor. But, by the good providence of God, my task is accomplished, and the book is now presented to the public.

The history of Methodism in your colony, and the biographical sketches of your deceased ministers, will be read by you with deep interest. Newfoundland is the oldest Methodist mission upon the face of the earth; and this year, 1865, is the centenary year of our existence in your country. You have great cause for thankfulness for your past triumphs, and you will commence your second centenary under circumstances truly auspicious.

You now have twenty-two ministers, fourteen circuits, eight mission-stations, four thousand members, and, at least, twenty thousand friends and adherents. Glory be to God alone!

In humbly dedicating this work to you, I can, and do from my very heart, offer up, on behalf of my old friends, or their children who may survive them, and also for my brethren who still labor on the island, this prayer, once presented in reference to the children of Israel: "The Lord God of your fathers make you a thousand times so many more as ye *are*, and bless you, as he hath promised you."

With all respect, I am,

Dear brethren,

Yours affectionately,

WILLIAM WILSON.

MILL TOWN, ST. STEPHENS, New Brunswick, March 30, 1865.

PREFACE.

During the past year I published several letters on Newfoundland in the columns of the " Provincial Wesleyan," of Halifax, N. S., which letters were brought under the notice of the brethren of the Newfoundland District at its last annual meeting. This led to a communication from the chairman on behalf of the brethren and friends of Methodism in Newfoundland, requesting the publication of those letters in the form of a volume. This communication and the reply were published in the " Provincial Wesleyan," of July 13, 1864. A copy of these documents is here subjoined : —

" The following resolutions were unanimously and cordially assented to at the District Meeting held in St. Johns, Newfoundland : —

" That the Members of the District Board, on behalf of themselves and the Wesleyans of this Colony generally, do tender their sincere and grateful acknowledgment to the Rev. William Wilson for the valuable and instructive Letters on the ' Newfoundland Mission and its Missionaries,' which have appeared from time to time in the ' Provincial Wesleyan ' and do themselves the honor sincerely to thank him on account of the excellent matter they contain, and the interesting and truly Christian spirit in which they are written ; and they beg further to be allowed to recommend that the Rev. gentleman, the author, will, if agreeable to himself, publish them in a more permanent form, by collecting them together in a volume, which it is the belief of this Board would be very acceptable to the Wesleyans of this Colony, and would find a ready sale, at a reasonable cost.

" That, should the Rev. Mr. Wilson not feel inclined to publish

them as above recommended, he would kindly permit this Board
to take the liberty of doing so.

"JOHN S. PEACH, *Chairman*."

---

*Reply to the Chairman and Ministers of the Newfoundland Dis-
trict.*

"DEAR BRETHREN, — I received with much pleasure the Resolution of your District Board on behalf of ' the Wesleyans of your
Colony,' expressing their approval of certain letters which have
appeared in the ' Provincial Wesleyan,' on ' Newfoundland and
its Missionaries,' and requesting the publication of those letters in
the form of a volume.

"In reply, permit me to say, that I spent fourteen years in
different circuits of that important mission, during which time I
mixed with all classes of society, saw into all the minutiæ of its
business, as well as the religious character of its inhabitants, and
took extensive notes of all matters which came under my observation. For many years I had thought of giving the result of these
observations to the world, but delayed doing so until the Jubilee
movement of last year, when, information being collected from various sources as to the work of God on different missionary stations, it seemed clearly my duty to communicate through the press
what I knew in reference to a country where was commenced the
first Wesleyan missionary station upon the earth, and where I
spent so many of my youthful and of my happiest days. Hence
the production of those papers; and if the perusal of them has
done any good, or has in any way contributed to the gratification
of my dear friends in Newfoundland, I consider myself amply rewarded.

"As to the publication of those papers in the form of a volume,
it is only a question of cost; and I beg therefore to say, that if the
friends think the volume will pay the expense, and they can advance the sum necessary for putting it through the press, I will
direct my best attention to the work, and will prepare a volume
on ' Newfoundland, and its Missionaries,' with such corrections
and improvements as I hope will make it both attractive and
useful.

"In conclusion, I would say that I never received anything but kindness from the people of Newfoundland, the remembrance of which is still fresh in my memory, and of which I shall delight to think and speak to the latest period of life.

"With much pleasure, dear brethren, do I subscribe myself,

"Yours very affectionately,

"WILLIAM WILSON.

"SACKVILLE, N. B., *June* 29, 1864.

"N. B. If the volume is published it can be issued early next year, which will be the centenary year of Methodism in Newfoundland.

"W. W."

Being thus committed, I determined to make the book as useful and interesting as possible. The publication of the letters alone would have been meagre; something more was certainly necessary to give circulation to the volume among the general public.

Less is known of Newfoundland than of any other of the North American Provinces: it is still a *terra incognita;* and this ignorance has led many persons to form a most incorrect, and, often, the most absurd, ideas both of the country and of the people. Writing a book expressly on Newfoundland was a favorable opportunity of assisting to dissipate this ignorance, and of communicating to the public authentic information on various matters connected with the island. Hence, the miscellaneous subjects that are brought under the notice of the reader in the following pages.

The Topography is from the Government Map; the Mineralogy from "The British Colonies;" the Civil History is compiled from various sources, and the Statistics from Monro's "British North America."

The History of Methodism is compiled from the standard publications of the connection, the Biographical Sketches from the Minutes of the Conference, and the Description of the Fishery from personal observation.

The present seemed the most favorable time for issuing such a work; for all information in reference to these provinces is now called for, to lead the people to form a correct opinion as to the propriety or impropriety of a Confederation.

Methodistically, it is a centenary volume; for it was some time during the summer of 1765 that the Rev. Lawrence Coughlan commenced his ministry, which will be *one hundred years* the coming season.

The writer now submits his book to the notice of a candid public, and prays that its circulation may be the means of doing much good.

MILL TOWN, ST. STEPHEN'S, New Brunswick, March 30, 1865.

CONTENTS.

PART I.

CHAPTER I.

PART II.

CHAPTER I.

(IX)

CHAPTER II.

CHAPTER III.

CHAPTER IV.

CHAPTER V.

CHAPTER VI.

CHAPTER VII.

NEWFOUNDLAND AND ITS MISSIONARIES.

PART I.

NEWFOUNDLAND.

DESCRIPTION OF THE COUNTRY: WITH ITS CIVIL HISTORY AND STATISTICS.

NEWFOUNDLAND

AND ITS MISSIONARIES.

CHAPTER I.

GEOGRAPHICAL POSITION AND AREA — ST. JOHNS — TOPOGRAPHY OF THE COASTS — DISTANCES TO THE PRINCIPAL TOWNS.

THE Island of Newfoundland is situated on the north-east side of the main entrance to the Gulf of St. Lawrence, between 46° 40′ and 51° 40′ 20″ N. Lat., and between 52° 44′ and 59° 31′ W. Long. It is separated from Labrador, on the west and north-west, by the Strait of Belle Isle, which, in one place, is not more than twelve miles wide. Its south-western point reaches to within fifty miles of Cape Breton.

Newfoundland is the nearest land to Europe of any part of America. The distance from Port Valentia, on the west coast of Ireland, to Cape Spear, at the entrance of the harbor of St. Johns, is 1656 miles. Its figure approaches an equilateral triangle, having its apex at Quirpon Island, in the north, and its base from Cape Race to Cape Ray. Its length, from Cape Race, its south-east point, to Cape Norman, its north-west point, if measured on a straight line, is about three hundred and fifty miles ; but, if measured on a curve, it is four hundred and nineteen miles. Its width, from Cape Race to Cape Ray, is about three hundred miles; and its entire circuit is little short of one thousand miles. Its whole surface, including its peninsulas and its numerous islands, has been variously estimated from 36,000 to 57,000 square miles. The latter estimate is nearer the truth. This gives it an area about as large as England and Wales, and twice the area of New Brunswick. The population, according to the census in 1857, was 122,638.

The deep Bays of Placentia and Trinity, separated only by a narrow isthmus, form a large peninsula called *Avalon*, which, because of its extended frontage on the Atlantic Ocean, and the excellency of the fisheries on its coast, is the most thickly inhabited, and, in a commercial view, is the most important part of Newfoundland.

St. Johns, the capital, is in Avalon : it is situated in 47° 33′ 29″ N. Lat., and 52° 45′ 10″ W. Long. The harbor is very spacious and secure : it has ninety feet of water in the middle, and is accessible at all seasons of the year. It has a commodious floating dock, where vessels of six hundred or seven hundred tons may be repaired.

The entrance is called the Narrows, which, at the sea surface, is three hundred and sixty fathoms across ; but, at the Chain Rock, it is only two hundred and twenty yards to the Pancake. On the north side is a precipitous cliff of sandstone and slate rock, three hundred feet high, above which is Signal Hill, surmounted with a citadel, five hundred and ten feet above the sea level. On the south side, a hill, or mountain, rises abruptly to the height of six hundred feet, having a sort of shoulder near the water, on which is erected a light-house, and a formidable battery, called Fort Amherst. There are several batteries which command the entrance; and in war-time a strong chain can be stretched from Chain Rock to the Pancake, which would render it impossible for hostile ships to enter the harbor. The city is well laid out, on the side of a hill: it is about one mile long. It is lighted with gas, and supplied with water from a lake, called Twenty-mile Pond, distant from the city four and a half miles. The water-works are said to have cost £80,000 sterling, which was raised on government guarantee of five per cent. The population, in 1857, was 24,851, which is nearly one fifth of the population of the Island.

St. Johns is a place of great business. In summer, the harbor presents a forest of masts. The stores are handsome and well-supplied. There are nine churches in the town. The principal edifices are, an elegant Roman Catholic Cathedral, and an English Cathedral; three Protestant Academies, — the Wesleyan, the Episcopalian, and the General Protestant; also, a Roman Catholic College and Convents; Normal School; Mechanics Institute; Hospital; Lunatic Asylum; Banks; Market and Court House. The Government House is a plain but commodious stone building, which cost over £60,000 sterling. There is a handsome granite building for the Colonial Assembly. There are several institutions for charitable purposes, also for literature and science, with a public library and botanic garden.

The soil in the vicinity is silicious and rocky; but, with great expense and labor, several thousand acres have been brought into a state of cultivation; so that the once dreary "barrens," in the rear of the town, are now traversed with good roads, studded with neat cottages, adorned with fine gardens, and ample returns are received for outlay and agricultural toil.

EASTERN COAST.

Leaving the harbor of St. Johns for the south at the distance of eight miles we come to Cape Spear, the most eastern point of the Island. A light-house on its point informs the anxious fisherman of his proximity to the metropolis. Eighteen miles from Cape Spear, we arrive at Bay Bulls, and, passing Ferriland, we reach Cape Race, the south-east point of the Island. It is sixty miles from St. Johns, and lies in 46° 40′ N. Lat., and 53° 8′ W. Long. It is at this place the Cunard steamers land the mail, on their way from Liverpool to Halifax. Here the land trends to the westward; and after passing Trepassey Bay, at the distance of twenty-five miles from Cape Race, we come to St. Shotts, the most dangerous place on the whole coast; dangerous not because of either sunken rocks or shoal water, but because of the irregular current and undertow, occasioned by the two great tidal waves, one of which had rolled along from the north, and was the result of the previous tide; the other, the tidal wave that had followed the moon across the Atlantic. These great tidal waves are here confluent; hence the irregular current, so fatal to life and property.

Leaving St. Shotts, we come to the first of the great bays: it is St. Mary's Bay. Its course is north-north-east; its length is thirty-five miles; and its breadth, from St. Shotts to Point Lance, about twenty-five miles.

After passing Cape St. Mary's, the great Bay of Placentia opens to view : it is forty-five miles wide, and ninety long. It is the largest bay in the island. Placentia Harbor is on the eastern side of the bay. On the western side, near Cape Chapeau Rouge, is the Harbor of St. Lawrence ; and five leagues up the bay is the spacious Inlet and Harbor of Burin. Many islands, and clusters of islands, are found in this bay, as the Flat Islands, Paradise, Isle of Valen, Woody Island, Barren Island, Sound Island, and many others. The Ragged Islands are said to be three hundred and sixty-five in number ; and Great Merasheen Island is twenty-one miles long. At the head of the bay is Come by Chance Harbor, from whence it is only three miles to Bay Bulls' Arm, in Trinity Bay. It is this narrow isthmus which forms the Peninsula of Avalon.

Point May is the south-western extremity of the Peninsula, which separates Placentia and Fortune Bays. Fortune Bay is thirty miles wide, and seventy long. On the eastern shore are the harbors of Fortune, Grand Bank, and Great Garnish, only fit for small craft. On the western shore are the fine havens of Jersey Harbor and Harbor Britain.

At the entrance of Fortune Bay are the French Islands of St. Pierre, Langley, and Miquelon. St. Pierre is a small, rocky island, which rises abruptly out of the water to the height of near four hundred feet, on the eastern side of which is the harbor. Here is the seat of government for the French portion of New-foundland. A ship of war is here usually, and the police regulations are very strict. Langley and

Miquelon are to the north of St. Pierre. They were formerly two islands, separated by a narrow channel which is now filled with sand, but the sea still occasionally rolls over the isthmus.

From Fortune Bay there is a straight line of coast, called the Western Shore : it is upwards of one hundred miles in length, and terminates at Cape Ray.

On the Western Shore there are several good harbors and great numbers of islands, as the Western Penguins, Rameo Islands, Burgeo Islands, La Poil Bay, Port au Basque, noted as among the best fishing stations on the island. Cape Ray is the most western point on the island : it lies N. Lat. 47° 36′ 49″, and 59° 21′ 0″ W. Long.

From Cape Ray along the entire north-west coast, including the whole length of the Strait of Belle Isle to Quirpon Island, and up the eastern shore to Cape John, which is the northern point of the great Bay of Notre Dame, the coast line, extending more than four hundred miles, belongs to the French, and is usually called the French Shore. The French Shore is the " Garden of Newfoundland," as its soil is well adapted to agriculture. Moreover, it has the most prolific fishing-grounds ; and what is of great importance in connection with the fishery, it has no fog, so that its climate is far more suitable for " *making* fish " than are those portions of the country that belong to the Crown of Britain.

How the French came to occupy so large a portion of the Island, will be understood from the treaties made at different times between England and France. The first treaty between these nations, in reference to New-foundland, was the Treaty of Utrecht, made in the year 1713. In this treaty, it was agreed, that " New-foundland, with its adjacent islands, shall, from this time forward, belong of right wholly to Great Britain; nor shall the Most Christian King, his heirs and successors, or any of their subjects, at any time hereafter, lay claim to any right to the said island or islands, or any part of it or them." The Treaty, however, gave permission to the French to catch and cure fish on the northern coast, from Cape Bonavista to Point Rich, but forbids their erecting any buildings except those that were necessary for the prosecution of the fishery. Article 13 reads, " Moreover, it shall not be lawful for the subjects of France to fortify any place in the said Island of Newfoundland, or to erect any buildings there, besides stages made of boards, and huts neces-sary and usual for drying fish ; or to resort to the said Island beyond the time necessary for fishing and drying fish. But it shall be allowed to the subjects of France to catch fish, and dry them on land in that part only, and in no other besides that, of the said Island of Newfoundland, which stretches from the place called Cape Bonavista, to the northern point of the said Island, and from thence, running down by the west-ern side, reaches as far as the place called Point Rich."

For fifty years, the only right the subjects of France had was the privilege of fishing on the northern coast, and drying their fish on the shore ; but they were not allowed to erect any permanent buildings, or even to remain there during the winter season. But in the year 1763, a second Treaty was made, called the Treaty of Paris, which concedes to the French the liberty to fish in the Gulf of St. Lawrence, within three leagues of the British coast ; and it also cedes

to France the Islands of St. Pierre and Miquelon, as
a shelter for their ships, and to keep a police guard,
but it forbids the fortification of those islands, or any
erections except for the fishery. We extract the following from the Treaty of Paris, 1763 : —

"ARTICLE 5. The subjects of France shall have the liberty
of fishing and drying fish on a part of the coasts of the Island of
Newfoundland, such as is specified in the Thirteenth Article of
the Treaty of Utrecht, which article is renewed and confirmed
by the present treaty; and His Britannic Majesty consents to
leave to the subjects of the Most Christian King the liberty of
fishing in the Gulf of St. Lawrence, on condition that the subjects of France do not exercise the said fishery but at the distance of three leagues from all the coasts belonging to Great
Britain, as well those of the continent as those of the islands situated in the said Gulf of St. Lawrence.

"ARTICLE 6. The King of Great Britain cedes the Islands
of St. Pierre and Miquelon, in full right, to his most Christian
Majesty, to serve as a shelter to the French fishermen; and his
said most Christian Majesty engages not to fortify the said islands,
to erect no buildings upon them but merely for the convenience
of the fishery, and to keep upon them a guard of fifty men only
for a police."

From the Treaty of Paris, in 1763, the French have
had possession of the Islands of St. Pierre and Migue-
lon, except in time of war.

In the year 1783, a third treaty was made, called
the Treaty of Versailles, which changed the French
line of coast from Cape Bonavista to Point Rich.
This treaty fixed the south-east point of the French
coast of Cape St. John, which is to the north of
Notre Dame Bay; and conveying the line north,
round Quirpon Island, thence down the Strait of
Belle Isle and the Gulf of St. Lawrence, it terminated at Cape Ray, which has ever since been

its south-west boundary. We make the following extract from the Treaty of Versailles, 1783 : —

" Article 5. His Majesty, the most Christian King, in order to prevent the quarrels which have hitherto arisen between the nations of England and France, consents to remove the right of fishing which belongs to him in virtue of the aforesaid article of the treaty of Utrecht, from Cape Bonavista to Cape St. John, situated on the eastern coast of Newfoundland, in 50° N. Lat.; and His Majesty the King of Great Britain consents, on his part, that the fishery assigned to the subjects of his Most Christian Majesty, beginning at the said Cape St. John, passing to the north, and descending by the western coast of the Island of Newfoundland, shall extend to the place called Cape Ray, situated in 47° 50′ N. Lat. The French fishermen shall enjoy the fishery which is assigned to them by the present article, as they had the right to enjoy that which was assigned to them by the Treaty of Utrecht."

Having given the information as to the way in which the French came to possess such a large part of the country, we shall proceed with our geographical survey.

Cape Ray, or rather a neighboring cape called Cape Anguille, is the southern point of the spacious Bay of St. George, which is near forty miles wide at the mouth, and seventy miles long. In this bay there are several fine streams of water ; there is a salt spring on the south shore ; the soil is rich ; and coals have long been found at the head of the bay. A number of Micmac Indians generally are found residing on this fine bay ; and those who have made explorations into the interior from hence, report it as mountainous, abounding in small rivers, extensive lakes, and grassy plains.

A few miles to the north of St. George's Bay, and separated from it by a narrow isthmus, is the magnificent double harbor of Port-au-Port, said to be sufficiently ·

spacious to afford good anchorage and perfect security
from storm to all the ships in the British navy.

Passing Port-au-Port, and steering north-east, at the
distance of twenty miles we reach the Bay of Islands;
so called, because of some clusters of islands at its entrance.   It is about twelve miles wide; and passing up
the bay it is seen to divide into three arms, and the
south-east arm is called the Humber Sound.   This is
the *embouchure* of the River Humber, the largest
river known in the Island.   The land is good and well
wooded.   The region around St. George's Bay, and
the Bay of Islands, is the richest and best part of Newfoundland.   We shall therefore pause here to give the
reader some further information in reference to this
interesting district.

Mr. Jukes landed near Crab's River, on the south
side of St. George's Bay, on the 11th of September,
1839.   He describes the country in that vicinity " as
gently undulating, with a fine short turf, not unlike
some English landscapes."   The place of his debarkation
was the mouth of a brook, which he describes as " a very
pretty spot, with green meadows on each side of the
brook, and a few neat houses clustered under the
shelter of a rising bank, covered with green turf.
Geese were feeding on the grass, ducks and poultry
were scattered about, and a few cows and some sheep
gave it all the appearance of a pastoral scene at home.
From the rising ground in the rear of the houses, the
view was very beautiful.   A tract of low, undulating
land, covered with a rich sea of wood, stretched away
into the interior for fifteen or twenty miles, and was
backed by a range of blue hills in the horizon, that rose
toward the south-west, while toward the north-east
they died away, and coalesced with the hills at the head

of the bay. The wood was not of that sombre hue so
generally seen in Newfoundland, but was patched with
the light green of the birch, and what the colonists call
the *witch hazel*, the *barm*, and the *aps*, and probably
the ash was present there." Mr. Jukes considered the
rich-looking valley of the brook, with its bright waters
winding away into the woods, as " completing a most
lovely and most English picture."

But unfortunately this fine country is on the
French Shore; and while the French are not allowed by treaty to make any permanent settlement,
the British Government think the same treaty forbids
them appointing magistrates among the English settlers.
The people, therefore, are lawless. From the official report of Captain Granville Lock, R. N., we make the
following extract, which will show the condition of
the British settlement in St. George's Bay. The
report is dated October 2, 1848 : —

" The inhabitants consist of English, a few Irish, and a number
of lawless adventurers, the very outcasts from Cape Breton and
Canada ; and it is very distressing to perceive a community, comprising nearly one thousand inhabitants, settled in an English colony, under no law or restraint, and having no one to control
them, if we except what may be exercised through the influence
shown by the single clergyman of the Established Church, who is
the only person of authority in the settlement. I am told the
reason why magistrates are not appointed is in obedience to direct
orders from the Home Government, it being believed against the ·
spirit of the treaty with France."

The Bay of Islands has been called *a great timber
station*. There are some British settlers on its shores,
among whom an anarchy reigns similar to that existing
at St. George's Bay.

Proceeding along the French Shore, from the Bay

of Islands seven leagues, we come to Bonne Bay,
which is a good harbor, but of difficult entrance.
Seventy miles further is Ingornachoix Bay, which
contains three good harbors, the chief of which is Port
Saunders, a spacious inlet, so landlocked that ninety or
one hundred vessels may lie in perfect security in every
wind ; yet not inhabited, because it is not a good fishing
station. A few miles to the north of Ingornachoix
Bay is Point Rich, which was the terminus of the
French Shore on Belle Isle Strait, until the year
1783. Round Point Rich is St. John's Bay, into
which a considerable stream, called Castor River, discharges its waters.

We now enter the Strait of Belle Isle, which is
fifty miles long, and in some places scarcely twelve
miles wide. The Newfoundland coast, along this
Strait, is rough, and contains no harbor of importance.

Cape Norman is the north-west point of the Island :
it lies 51° 39' 5" N. Lat., and 56° 2' 0" W. Long.
Twenty-eight miles north-north-east from Cape Norman
is Belle Isle Island, from which the strait derives its
name. This island is a good fishing station, and is
claimed as part of the French Shore. Quirpon Island
is the northern point of Newfoundland : its position is
51° 40' 20" N. Lat., and 55° 27' 50" W. Long.

The course is now nearly south to Hare Bay, a gulf
which intersects the land for two thirds of its breadth,
and which, near the head, branches off into numerous
arms and coves, sheltered by lofty hills, which pour
their torrents into the bay.

Proceeding south, we next reach White Bay, after
passing several good and much frequented harbors.
White Bay is about twenty miles wide, and runs into
the land south-west for sixty-five miles. The next

prominent land south of White Bay is Cape St. John, the present limit of the French Shore, on the eastern side of the island. It lies north-east, in N. Lat. 50°, W. Long. 55° 38'.

After leaving Cape St. John, the great Bay of Notre Dame opens to view. This bay is more than fifty miles wide, and is studded with islands. Here is Long Island, Sunday Cove Island, Pilley's Island, Triton Island, Twillingate Island, New World Island, the Black Islands, the Burnt Islands, Change Island, Togo Island, Indian Islands, Duck Islands, Wadham Islands, the Penguin Islands, and very many others, most of which are good fishing-stations, and afford good shelter for vessels. From the great bay, smaller bays, or arms, run into the land for many miles. Green Bay runs up near twenty miles, and Hall's Bay is about the same length. Both these bays are famous hunting-grounds, from whence the trappers not unfrequently cross the country to the French Shore in their hunting excursions, and sometimes go over the straits to the Labrador. To the south is the Bay of Exploits, into which is discharged the water of a considerable river bearing the same name. It was from the neighborhood of the River Exploits, that MARY MARCH, a Red Indian female, was brought to St. Johns in the year 1819.

From Notre Dame Bay, the course is south-east to Cape Freels, which is the north point of Bonavista Bay. On the north side of this bay are also many small bays and numerous islands. Here is Green Pond Island, Fair Islands, and Gooseberry Islands. Here also are Indian Bay, Trinity Bay, Locker Bay, Fresh-water Bay, and Bloody Bay ; so called because of the frequent rencounters between the aborigines and the Europeans who first visited these shores. On the south is Clode

3 *

Sound, which indents the land for twenty-five miles. Here also is Goose Bay and Indian Arm. On this shore likewise are the harbors of Keels, King's Cove, and Bonavista. Bonavista is not a harbor for large vessels; and, in heavy storms, it is only an indifferent shelter for fishing-craft. It, however, contains a population of 2000 souls, and has always figured in the history of the country. Cape Bonavista was the southern limit of the French shore on the eastern coast, until the treaty of Versailles in 1783.

A few miles south of Cape Bonavista, is the Harbor of Catalina; so named from the fact that Jacques Cartier, the French navigator and explorer of lower Canada, landed there in 1534. .Trinity Bay commences at Catalina, and is about twenty-four miles wide, and seventy long. Trinity Harbor is twenty miles above Catalina. It is a spacious haven, easy of access, safe for large vessels, and is pronounced by nautical men one of the best harbors in the island.

The town of Trinity is situated on a level spot of land, under Rider's Hill. It is small, but neat, and the inhabitants are respectable and intelligent. On the north shore of the bay, above Trinity Harbor, are the harbors of Bonavinture, Ireland's Eye, Random Sound, Heart's Ease, and Bay Bull's Arm, from the head of which it is only three miles to the head of Come by Chance Harbor, in Placentia Bay. It is this narrow isthmus that connects the peninsula of Avalon with the main land. It was in Bay Bull's Arm the Atlantic Cable was landed, which, by some unknown cause was broken in the deep sea. On the south side of the bay, are New Harbor, Heart's Delight, Heart's Desire, and Heart's Content; the last named, a good harbor, and is the place where, it is said, a second Atlantic cable will have its terminus. Below Heart's Content, are New Perlican, Hant's Harbor, Old Perlican; and near the south point of the Bay is Great's Cove.

About two leagues east from Great's Cove, is the north end of Baccalao Island, the most famous landmark on this part of the coast. This island rises abruptly out of the water to the height of some four hundred feet. It is bluff, barren, and rocky, without inhabitants, save the turs, the gulls, and other sea-birds which build their nests in its clefts, and are found there in countless numbers. They are generally called "Baccalao birds" by the Newfoundlanders. The island is six miles long. It is said to have been the land first seen by Cabot in 1497, and by him called Prima Vista; but it was afterwards called Baccalao, which means "codfish," because of the immense shoals of cod which are found near its base.

At the south point of Baccalao Island, commences this spacious bay, which is twenty miles wide, and fifty miles long. The shore around Conception Bay is generally bold; the clifts are often perpendicular; the water is deep near the land, while, in the middle of the bay, the bottom cannot be reached with ninety fathoms of line. On the north shore, every cove and inlet is inhabited. A line of fishing-stages, fishing-flakes, and oil-houses is erected along the shore, behind which peer numerous neat-looking villages, with school-houses and churches; and, in the rear, a succession of lofty hills tower above each other until they reach an elevation of five hundred feet, often terminating in conical peaks, and all more or less covered with shrubby or stunted forest. The numerous cascades which pour over the high sea-wall, the multitude of fishing-boats in the distance, and the shoals of fish, causing an agitation of the water for miles, presents to the beholder an appearance that is both grand and majestic, and, withal, truly picturesque and beautiful. There are several rising towns of importance on this shore, where there is much wealth and intelligence among the people.

Carbonear contains a population of some four thousand souls. It is not a very safe harbor at all times, being exposed to an easterly wind. It, however, has several large mercantile establishments, and is famous for the spirited resistance it made against the French forces in the year 1696, and again in 1708.

Harbor Grace is three miles above Carbonear, with a population about equal. The town is built on a level spot of land. Many of the houses are very good, which, with the churches and other public buildings, give an impression to the stranger of elegance and comfort. The harbor is good; and vessels may ride there in all winds with perfect security.

Above Harbor Grace, are Spaniard's Bay, Bay Roberts, Port De Grane, and Brigus. The two last-named places are of much importance, and have large populations.

Harbor Main and Holy Rood are at the head of the bay.

On the south shore are the settlements of Topsail, and Portugal Cove, so called, because the Portuguese first landed there in 1525. It is only an open roadstead, in which even small craft are not always safe in an easterly wind.

In approaching Portugal Cove by land from St. Johns, the scenery is strikingly picturesque. A succession of high hills on each side tower over the road, and shut out every other object except the village, which, from this stand-point, appears very beautiful.

Opposite to Portugal Cove, at the distance of four miles, and twelve miles from Harbor Grace, lies a lovely little island, called Belle Isle, from a large bell-shaped rock at its western extremity. The island is six miles long, and is perhaps the most fertile spot in Newfoundland. The soil is a deep, rich, black earth, and seldom requires manure. Wheat grows well, and will yield twenty-fold. Oats, potatoes, and hay also thrive well; and culinary vegetables of all kinds grow luxuriantly.

Conception Bay is the most populous and the most important district on the island. Its population is estimated at 25,000. Here reside some of the most wealthy merchants and planters. From its harbor, every spring, hundreds of vessels sail for the ice in quest of seals; and, on their returning from their sealing voyage, sail again in the month of June to prosecute the cod-fishery on the Coast of Labrador; while the shore fishery is followed with great diligence by those who have not the means of fitting out for Labrador; and the coast is everywhere dotted with the tiny masts of their fishing craft.

Cape St. Francis is the southern boundary of Conception Bay. Its position is given as 47° 56′ 45″ N. Lat., and 52° 30′ 0″ W. Long. It is high bluff land, covered with stunted forest.

Four leagues south-south-east from Cape St. Francis, we arrive at Torbay, where there is a considerable population, but it is a very exposed harbor. A number of fishing-boats, however, find shelter behind its points and its bluffs.

Nine miles from Torbay, we arrive at Quidy-Widy Cove and the harbor of St. Johns.

The appearance of the sea-coast is generally rough and uninviting to the stranger. Still there is much fine scenery, and many fertile spots; while British skill and industry has made tracts of land, formerly barren, to become fruitful gardens, and laid the foundation of many towns and villages, which, from their position, must in time become places of importance.

The eastern coast, from Cape Freels to Cape Race, and the southern coast, from Cape Race to St. Pierre's Island, is generally bold, and the water is deep, with comparatively few shoals and sunken rocks; but to the north-east and also on the western coast, those terrors to the weather-beaten mariner are met with much more frequently.

Around the shores of Newfoundland, besides a number of small bays, there are nine magnificent estuaries, varying in length from forty to near one hundred miles, and are from twenty to sixty miles in width at their entrance, which deep recesses entice the finny tribes to seek their food in shoal water; by which simple arrangement, a kind Providence has placed the boundless wealth of the ocean within the grasp of man.

The whole coast is rocky and frequently quite precipitous; occasionally, however, a rough, pebbly beach forms a barrier to the further advance of the ocean billows. Bold capes and lofty headlands are constantly in view; and the streams (brooks, as they are called) falling from these lands form many beautiful cataracts; several of which, miniature imitations of the great Niagara, may be seen on the bluffs of Belle Isle Island in Conception Bay.

The action of the tide is little felt on the northern

and eastern coasts; but, on the western coast, the tidal wave comes with considerable power, and in St. George's Bay the water rises nine feet at spring tides.

The distances to the principal towns are as follows:

From St. Johns to the head of Conception Bay, thirty miles; to Harbor Grace, sixty-three; Carbonear, sixty-seven; Salmon Cove, seventy-two; Bic de Verds, one hundred and five; Great's Cove, one hundred and thirteen; Bonavista, one hundred and forty-three; Twillingate, two hundred and twenty. From St. Johns to Portugal Cove, nine miles; to Topsail, twenty. Southern route — to Great Placentia, eighty; Burin, one hundred and fifty-two; Harbor Britain, one hundred and ninety-seven; Burgeo, three hundred and eight; and Cape Bay, four hundred and six miles.

CHAPTER II.

THE interior of Newfoundland remained unexplored and unknown until the year 1823, when Mr. Cormack, an amateur traveller, accompanied by some Micmac Indians, traversed the country from Random Sound in Trinity Bay, and going nearly west, reached the head of St. George's Bay. The account of his journey, with a map, is found in the Edinburgh Philosophical Journal for January 1st, 1824. He reported the country he passed, which was a line of at least two hundred miles, as barren and rocky, generally covered with moss; much intersected with streams and lakes; and thinly wooded, except on the banks of the streams and on the margins of the lakes. He gave names to a number of lakes and prominent hills on his route, and many of those names were after his particular friends; thus the first lake he called Bennet's Lake, after a respectable merchant in St. Johns, and Carson's Lake, from an eminent physician, of that name, residing in the same town. One hill he named Mount Sylvester, another, near the centre of the country, he called Serpentine Mountain; a few miles to the north of which he called a solitary hill, Red-Indian Mountain; and one near Jameson's Lake, Mount Misery.

Mr. Jukes, the geologist, made a survey of various

(36)

parts of the island in 1839-40; since which time, particular localities have been travelled and surveyed, so that we are enabled to form a tolerably correct opinion of the general appearance of the interior.

THE COAST.

The shore is everywhere grooved with valleys and ravines, bounded by hummocky knobs, with precipitous and rocky hills, many of which are sufficiently lofty to preclude all view of the interior from the sea. The woods skirt the shore, and are very stunted near the water; but the timber increases in size as you advance toward the interior. Passing these ravines and belts of woods, we arrive at an open country, called The Barrens, which are an immense waste, consisting of barren rock, or rock covered with moss. Also extensive marshes or savannas, and ponds of of all sizes and figures, around which patches of woods vary the scene, and give evidence of a more healthy subsoil. On the barrens, huge boulders are met with, and masses of loose stones, as though put there by human hands. The top of Bonavista Ridge is a place where these loose stones are found, and have been strangely called, Noah's Ballast. In the hollows are the tuckermore bushes, which is a dwarf juniper, with strong branches at right angles to the stem, and closely interlacing each other: the tops of these bushes are level, as if they had been clipped. To walk upon these tuckermores, or penetrate their branches, is equally impracticable.

HILLS AND MOUNTAINS.

The district of Avalon is hilly,— we would say mountainous, if that term may be applied to elevations of land not exceeding 1000 or 1500 feet.

4

Besides an untold number of isolated rough hills, there are two remarkable ranges of hills in Avalon. Each range is about thirty miles in length. The first commences at Renews, fifty miles south of St. Johns, and running north-north-west, terminates at Holyrood, in Conception Bay. This mountain range is known at Renews by a number of rough hummocks, called The Butter Pots : they are 1000 feet high, and is the land first seen when approaching the eastern coast from sea. Passing north from the Butter Pots, we come to more hummocks, which are called The Bread and Cheese Hills ; and on the west side are the Green Hills. Near Holyrood are several other hummocks, which also are called The Butter Pots.

About twenty miles west from the Butler-Pot range, is a second range of hills, which commences at Cape Dog, in St. Mary's Bay, and terminates near Chapel Arm, in Trinity Bay. This chain has in some places an elevation of one thousand five hundred feet : it is less broken than the former, has a more continuous outline, and many of the hills are rounded and flat at the top. Connected with this range, are Mount Scapie, near Cape Dog ; Sawyer's Hill, to the south of Great Placentia ; Cap Hill ; and North-east Mountain, to the east of Little Placentia.

The main land is equally mountainous with the peninsula. A range of mountains commences at Cape Chapeau Rouge, in Placentia Bay, and occupies a large part of the peninsula between Placentia and Fortune Bays. It runs the entire length of Placentia Bay from the cape, and sometimes it approaches the water, and forms a rough, hummocky sea-wall ; its direction is north-north-east to Piper's Hole. On the opposite side of that harbor, its bluffs again appear ;

and running the same course, it strikes Goose Bay, in Bonavista Bay : here an offshoot curves eastward to Trinity Bay, and past Random Sound to Trinity Harbor. Taking its whole length, it is at least one hundred miles. This range is often much broken, abrupt, and precipitous, with frequent table-lands and marshes in its hollows and on its summits. In width it is irregular ; but sometimes it is several miles wide. It is a peaked, wild, and serrated mass of hills. One isolated peak, called Powder-Horn Hill, or Centre Hill, near Bay Bulls' Arm, in Trinity Bay, has an elevation of more than one thousand feet ; and from the top of it, nearly the whole of Placentia and Trinity Bays can be seen, as well as portions of Conception, Bonavista, and Fortune Bays. The land in the vicinity of this range consists of undulated ridges, rising from three hundred to five hundred feet above the sea, and is often covered with dense woods.

A few miles to the westward of Green's Pond, is an isolated ridge, called Fox Harbor Hills, of about ten miles in length. A chain of hills running north-north-east and south-south-west, the south part of which is called The Heart Ridge, and the northern part known as the Blue Hills, is between Bonavista Bay and the River Exploits. The length of this chain is thirty miles, and some of its peaks have an elevation of one thousand feet.

On the south side of the River Exploits, and about thirty miles from its mouth, are the Shute Brook Hills ; and on the north side of the river is Hodges Hill, to the north-east of which is the Western Tilt Hill. Several of these hills have precipitous sides, are almost of a square form, and are flat at their summits. Some of them have an elevation of one thousand feet.

THE LONG RANGE.

Near Cape Ray, a distinct chain of mountains commences with three conical or sugar-loaf hills, and runs north-east and north-north-east, for nearly sixty miles, until it reaches the head of St. George's Bay, where it expands to the west, and forms Hare Hill. It then turns to the north-east again, and forms the north-west bank of Grand Pond, and the south-east bank of Deer Pond; and, allowing the Humber River to flow through its chasm, it runs north for sixty or seventy miles further, then resumes its north-east course, until it reaches the north-east coast, and forms a sea-wall, in White Bay. It is called the Long Range, and its entire length is upward of two hundred miles. Offshoots from the Long Range tend to the west until they reach the sea, in that direction, where they form bluffs on the Gulf Shore. These hills are steep toward the north-west, but the ascent is more gradual toward the south-east. There is a belt of level land between this chain of hills and the sea, of considerable width, through which the rivers drain the country. Hare Hill, already noticed, is very conspicuous from St. George's Bay, and is twenty miles north-east from St. George's Harbor. The Blow-me-down hills, on the River Humber, which also belong to this chain, have an elevation of eight hundred feet.

Many other isolated mountains, or mountain ranges, have been reported; but too little is known of their extent or position to justify any notice in reference to them.

What may be called the table lands, have a general elevation of three or four hundred feet. On these table lands grow quantities of wild grass, and berries in great variety. There are many tracts of good wood-land, and occasionally may be seen a spot of arable land that would repay the labor of the agriculturist ; but the general appearance of the interior is wild, rough, and barren.

LAKES AND PONDS.

Lakes, or ponds, are met with all over the country, and in every possible position : they are found in the valleys, on the higher table-lands, in every mountain gorge, in the hollow of every ridge, and on the tops of the highest hills. They vary in size, from small pools to extended sheets of water, fifty or sixty miles in length. The water is often of great depth. Their banks are well-wooded. Islands, sometimes several miles in length, covered with dense forests, give their aid to cause an appearance to those inland lakes, surrounded as they are by dreary wastes, that is romantic and beautiful. From the top of North-east Mountain, near Little Placentia, sixty-seven ponds were counted, none of which were less than one hundred yards, and some of them two or three miles in length ; and all were within ten miles from the base of the hill. From the top of Powder-Horn Hill, one hundred and fifty ponds are said to have been counted.

Of the lakes to the north of the Island, little is known, and so of many in the interior ; but, of those which are known, and of which at least a rough survey has been made, the following are the principal : —

RED-INDIAN POND.

So called because the aboriginal inhabitants were formerly known to have their encampments on its margin. It is more than forty miles in length, and five or six in width, and contains a number of islands. Its north point is about thirty miles from Hall's Bay, at the head of Notre Dame Bay; and, ten miles from that point, it is crossed by the 49° of north latitude. Ten miles from its southern point is Croaker's Lake, several miles long, and crowded with islands. The water from Croaker's Lake runs into Red-Indian Pond. These ponds are the head waters of the River Exploits.

GANDER-BAY POND.

This lake is twenty-three miles long, but is narrow, and has a ribbon-like appearance: it lies a few miles north-west from Bonavista Bay. At its south-west point, a river brings the waters from a great number of small ponds. Its outlet is north to Gander Bay; and, by its numerous brooks, it drains the land for seventy or eighty miles.

TERRA-NOVA POND

Is twelve miles long, and discharges itself into Bonavista Bay.

The ponds on Avalon are equally numerous with those on the main land; but they are not so large, because the water-sheds are less extensive. Twenty-mile Pond, near St. Johns, is a fine sheet of water; and the Hundred-Island Pond, at the head of St. Mary's Bay, is remarkable for the number of its islets.

BARROW'S LAKE

Lies a few miles south of McCormack's track, and the 55° of longitude, and passes nearly through its centre: it is about fourteen miles long, and discharges its waters into the north-west arm of Fortune Bay.

JAMESON'S LAKE

Was exactly in Cormack's track, and he crossed it: it is about twenty miles in length, and four in breadth. Serpentine Mountain is to the north-east of Jameson Lake, and Mount Misery on the south-west.

LAKE BATHURST.

A little to the south of Mount Misery commences Lake Bathurst, and lies nearly north-north-east and south-south-west. The 57° of longitude passes down the lake, which is about seventeen miles long, and five wide. It has a number of islands. A brook runs from its south point, which, after passing through a number of small ponds, discharges its waters into the ocean, on the western shore.

GEORGE IV. LAKE.

This lake lies west from Jameson's Lake, distance twenty-five miles : it is about eighteen miles long, and six wide, and contains a number of islands. Between Bathurst Lake, and George IV. Lake, there are several smaller lakes, as Wilmot's Lake, Waltee's Lake, Wilson's Lake, and Montserois Lake. These lakes, with a great number of lakelets, discharge their waters into White-Bear Bay, on the western shore.

GRAND POND, OR BAY OF ISLANDS' LAKE.

This is the largest sheet of water known on the island. It is nearly sixty miles in length, and five in width. It lies in the same direction as Red-Indian Pond, and only fifteen miles to the west of it.

This fine lake commences about fifteen miles north-east from the head of St. George's Bay. The chain of mountains called the Long Range forms the great water-shed of this part of the island; and down its gorges flow the streams which originate this noble lake. It first runs east-south-east, seven miles, and is about two miles wide, bounded on each side by the lofty hills of Long Range. Here commences an island, more than twenty miles long, and five wide. At the end of this long island, the lake curves to east-north-east, and then nearly north for a further distance of some twenty-five miles. The high hills at its south-west extremity form precipitous banks on the lake, and the depth of water corresponds with those steep bluffs; for, in some places, no bottom could be found with ninety fathoms. Numerous brooks flow into it, through its whole course; and, near its north-east extremity, it receives the waters of a considerable river, called The Main Brook, which is fifty yards wide, and several feet deep. The Main Brook drains the country from the north-east to within twenty miles from the head of Notre Dame Bay. To the north of the lake, a river quite as large as Main Brook flows out of it. This river is called Junction Brook, because it unites with the waters of the Humber, and forms another lake, at the distance of seven miles, called Deer Pond.

DEER POND

Is about fifteen miles long, and three or four wide. It lies north-east and south-west; and, at its south-western extremity, the waters are again narrowed to fifty or a hundred yards, and flow into the Bay of Islands, where they are known as the River Humber.

The Indians say, that, by means of a chain of ponds, they can navigate to Grand Pond, from St. George's Bay, and from thence to the Bay of Islands; while it is evident, that, with only a few short postages, the island can be crossed with a canoe, from the Humber River to the Exploits.

RIVERS.

The largest river on the island is the Humber. The Humber takes its rise in some gorges of the Long Range, in about the fiftieth degree of latitude, and sixty miles from the Bay of Islands. Its course has been traced for one hundred and fourteen miles. Its first rill issues at no great distance from Cow Head, on the Gulf Shore. It runs east, through a number of lakes, one of which is eight or ten miles long. It then curves to the south and south-west, and at sixty miles becomes quite a river, sufficiently deep for a small boat to glide on its surface. Up to this point, Mr. Jukes made a personal survey of the river ; but here he met with a number of rapids, which prevented his further progress up the stream. A little below these rapids, its volume is increased by a tributary quite as large as the original stream. This tributary is Junction Brook. These confluent streams form the Humber River, which rolls its waters through the Humber Sound and the Bay of Islands, into the Gulf of St. Lawrence. There is sufficient water in the Humber River, as also in both Deer Pond and Grand Pond, to float a schooner ; still it cannot be navigated, because of its rapids. There is one rapid only three miles from the mouth of the river : it is three quarters of a mile long. A second rapid, and more dangerous, although not so long, is found nearly a mile below Deer Pond, and eleven miles from its embouchure ; and that fine stream, Junction Brook, Mr. Jukes found to be so impeded with rapids, at only one mile from the main river, as to render his further progress in a boat quite impracticable.

EXPLOITS RIVER.

This river is about sixty miles long. It commences in Red-Indian Pond, whence it flows east for thirty miles, when it receives several tributaries, as Little Rattling Brook, the Three Brooks, Great Rattling Brook, and the Tilt Brook. These streams drain the country for fifty miles, and considerably enlarge the Exploits, which rolls on about north-north-east, and discharges its waters into a bay bearing the same name. The Exploits abounds in salmon ; but, like the Humber, its navigation is much impeded by rapids.

There are two considerable rivers near Cape Ray, called the Great Codroy and the Little Codroy, both of which originate in the south-west of the Long Range ; and, rushing down its gorges, discharge their waters into the Gulf of St. Lawrence, at the western extremity of the island. Mr. Jukes ascended the Great Codroy twelve miles, in a boat ; but how much further it is navigable, we have no information.

The fresh-water streams are generally small ; hence the term brook is mostly applied to them. The lack of navigable rivers is, however, in a measure, compensated for by the manner in which its splendid bays, and their numerous arms, pierce the land. But it may be stated, after all, that Nova Scotia has no rivers like the Humber, or even the Exploits ; and, while those rivers will not bear a comparison with some rivers in New Brunswick, — as the Miramichi, or the majestic St. John, — yet they will compare favorably with the St. Croix, not only as to the stream itself, but also in the number and extent of its lakes, as well as in the quantity, the quality, and the size of its timber. But while the St. Croix is, in different places, spanned by dams and studded with saw-mills; also powerful machinery is moved by its waters; logs crowd its bed for miles; the whistle of the locomotive is heard on its banks; its woods are everywhere alive with lumbermen; and its towns and its villages abound in wealth obtained from its forests, — the forests of Newfoundland, many of them equally rich, with equal facilities for bringing the timber to market, are still primeval. The woodman's axe has never felled a tree there; and, with only a few exceptions, the crank of the mill has never been heard there. The rapids murmur, and the waters glide, as they always did; for only in a few places have they been made to subserve the purposes of man. Speaking generally, no sound is heard in its wilderness, save the plunging of salmon in its streams, the screech of the wild-goose on its lakes, or the howling of the wolf for its prey.

MINERALOGY.

The survey of the island has yet been only partial and imperfect; but enough is known to satisfy scientific men that many valuable minerals exist there, which, in time, will become a source of wealth to the industrious inhabitants.

COAL.

It has long been known that coal could be found in the south-west part of the island. Forty years ago, a fisherman informed the writer, that, in St. George's Bay, where he had spent several winters, he had seen coals near his "winter tilt;" and that when there was not much snow, he used to bring in large lumps of coal, which had rolled down from the cliff, and therewith replenish his fire. Since that time, the public have been made acquainted with the fact, that there are extensive coal-fields in that region, as well as in the vicinity of the Grand Pond. Mr. Jukes saw coals when he surveyed that country in 1839. The seams he saw were of no great thickness; but he says, "More important seams will probably be found." At eight miles from the Gulf Shore, a bed of coals, known to the Micmac Indians, was seen, of three feet thickness, and of excellent quality; and equally valuable beds were known to exist in the same parallel, near the Codroy River. Mr. Jukes says: "I was informed by some Indians of Great Codroy River, that they had seen a bed of coal two feet thick, and of considerable extent, some distance up the country. Their account of the distance, however, varied from ten to thirty miles; and I could not induce them to guide me to the spot. I proceeded up the river, about twelve miles from the sea, and some distance beyond the part navigable for a boat, without seeing anything but beds of brown sandstone and conglomerate, interstratified with red marls and sandstone, gradually becoming more horizontal, and dipping toward the south-east. I believe, however, that a bed of coal had been seen by an Indian, on the bank of a brook running into Codroy River, about thirty miles from its mouth; but the person who saw it was not in the neighborhood at the time of my visit." The extent of the St. George's Bay coal-field has been estimated at twenty-five miles long and ten wide; and the total thickness of the coal for-

mation, Mr. Jukes estimated at from one thousand to
fifteen hundred feet. The coal-fields of Newfoundland are evidently a continuance of the coal strata in
Nova Scotia, New Brunswick, and Cape Breton : their
strata dip under the sea, then rise and crop out at the
south-west of the island. In the government map of
Newfoundland, coal formations are marked on the
south-east shore of St. George's Bay, running north-
north-east, from Crabb's River to the Second River.
A stream, twelve or fourteen miles to the southward of
the Bay of Islands, is called Coal River ; and another stream, to the north-east of Grand Pond, is
called Coal Brook. As the population increases,
facilities will be afforded for bringing Newfoundland
coal into market ; thus giving employment to hundreds
of people, and paying ample returns for the investment
of capital.

SILVER.

A silver mine is being worked on a small scale in
Placentia Bay.

COPPER.

A small vein of sulphuret and green carbonate
exists in Signal Hill, St. Johns ; and a copper mine
was actually opened in Shoal Bay, in 1775, by some
English miners. It, however, did not pay working ex-
penses, and was therefore, after a time, abandoned.
There is a rich mine of copper, called the Terra
Nova mine, to the northward, on what is called the
French Shore.

IRON.

Chalybeate springs exist in different parts of Newfoundland, which prove the existence of iron. One of
these springs is in Logie Bay, near St. Johns. There

5

is a substance in the harbor of Catalina, which the
people call " Catalina Stone." It is sometimes called
" horse gold ; " and was mistaken for gold by those
who first saw it. It is iron pyrites, or sulphuret of
iron. It is found in graywacke, or slate rock. Iron
ore is found in Conception Bay, and particularly on
the northern side of Belle Isle.

LEAD.

At La Manche, in Placentia Bay, there is a rich
lead mine, of which Professor Shephard, in a recent
report, says: " I saw three thousand five hundred
pounds of clean, pure galena thrown from the vein by
a single blast. From my explorations, made with
great care and circumspection, I feel confident that you
may safely calculate on one hundred feet of the vein in
depth, above water level, extending twelve hundred
feet inland, at least. I have estimated four inches of
solid galena as an average thickness therein ; but believing it better to be under estimate, rather than exceed, I will call the average thickness three inches, for
twelve hundred feet from the landmark, and one hundred feet in depth above the sea level. This will give
thirty thousand cubic feet of solid galena ; which is a
little more than seven times as heavy as the same bulk
of water ; which gives a product of upwards of thirteen millions of pounds, together with the additional
chances of quadrupling that amount by sinking below
the sea level, and extending inland. The mining is
the easiest thing imaginable." He places it on a par
with the greatest lead deposits in the United States ;
and adds, " This mine is accessible, not only by small
boats, but even by the smaller class of ocean steamers." On analyzation, a sample was found to contain

83.64 of lead, 13.87 of sulphur, and the remaining 2.49 parts consisted of silver, copper, zinc, carbonate of lime, and silica. This valuable mine has fallen into the hands of a New York company. Another has been discovered in the same vicinity.

Mining, in Newfoundland, is still in its infancy: future researches, and application of skill and capital, have on this island a favorable field for operation.[1]

GEOLOGY.

A large portion of Newfoundland is granite. Mr. Cormack, when crossing from Random Sound to St. George's Bay, saw immense tracts of granite, and from the hills at the head of that bay to near the centre of the island, he mentions no other rock than granite; but near the longitude of 56°, he found abundance of serpentine; hence he named a hill in that district Serpentine Mountain, and a small pond, near Jameson's Lake, he called Serpentine Lake. Between the Bay of Despair and Jameson's Lake, he saw sienite, granite, quartz, gneiss, fine clay slate, alum slate, with indications of coal and iron.

Nearly the whole of Avalon is composed of the *lower slate formations*. The country west and north-west of Avalon is composed chiefly of variegated slate, coarse sandstone, and conglomerate. The neck of land between Placentia and Fortune Bays is composed of sienite, porphyry, and mica slate. The Island of St. Pierre is sienite or porphyry. A large part of the western shore is granite; but quartz is found in the neighborhood of La Poile Bay. The Long Range is mostly mica slate, with granite. On the south side of St. George's Bay are the coal formations; also near

---

[1] See " British North America," by A. Munro, Esq. p. 129.

the Grand Pond. On the north side of St. George's Bay, the magnesian limestone dips at a slight angle to north-north-west. At Grand Pond are cliffs of gneiss and mica slate. A calcareous formation stretches across the mouth of the Humber River, in hills of four or five hundred feet high. About three miles up that river are lofty precipices of pure white marble. Mr. Jukes says that mica slate, gneiss, and their associated rocks, with occasional patches of primitive limestone, • extend along the whole west side of Newfoundland, and thinks from the Humber they form an unbroken ridge to Cape Quirpon.

The strike throughout the island rarely varies from a north-north-east and south-south-west course: hence all the other prominent features of the country, as hills, valleys, lakes, and all the large bays, lie in nearly the same direction.

Granite boulders, frequently very large, are found on the tops of hills four or five hundred feet high, composed of grit-stone, slate, or sienite; and in positions so isolated that there is no rock like them within twenty or thirty miles. Drift, sometimes to the depth of several feet, is found over a great part of the island.

Near the River Exploits was found a fine bed of unctuous clay, perfectly plastic, fifteen or twenty feet thick, and lying in thin layers, usually of a slate color, with a reddish band here and there; and above the clay rests a bed of fine sand two or three feet thick. Thus it is evident that marble, limestone, with all kinds of building and roofing materials, can be obtained in Newfoundland in great abundance.

SOIL.

Around St. Johns, and along the east coast, the soil

is shallow, poor, and hungry, formed of decomposed slate-rock, mixed with silicious and luminous matter, and requires much manure to make it productive. This district is but a poor specimen, and must not be taken as a criterion wherewith to judge as to the general fertility of the island. It is probable that the person who wrote the article in Morse's School Geography on Newfoundland had seen only the eastern coast; for we are told, " the island itself is rugged and uninviting, producing little beside stunted trees and shrubs." Now, while we admit that the sea-coast appears to the stranger, "rugged and uninviting," yet that it produces " little beside stunted trees and shrubs," is manifestly incorrect.

All over the country there is a thick coating of moss, which Mr. Jukes calls the "curse of the country," as it prevents the nature of the soil from being known. When this moss is cleared away, as it has been in many places, and particularly on the south side of St. George's Bay, the soil is found to be fertile, and often very rich. The wild grasses afford excellent and abundant food for cattle and sheep. There are rich alluvia along the banks of rivers, and on the margins of the lakes; and although on the coast the forests are stunted, in the interior the trees are large, and prove that there is a rich subsoil, which, if cultivated would amply repay the agriculturist.

Sir John Harvey, who was governor of Newfoundland in 1844, in a dispatch to Lord Stanley, gives his opinion of Newfoundland in the following words: —

" With respect to this island, hitherto undervalued as it appears to me to have been, there can be no doubt that the whole of those tracts designated (and depreciated by that designation) by the appellation of

5 *

' *barrens,*' merely because denuded of trees, are among
the most fertile soils in British America, the sec-
tions almost everywhere presenting to the eye from
four to six feet of fine, gravelly soil, capable of producing luxuriantly every species of crop, except, perhaps, *wheat,* and requiring only the aid of artificial
manures, and careful and judicious culture, to give good
returns, even in that species of grain ; while in respect
to all others, more especially grasses of every kind,
including clover, vetches, and I will add flax, in oats
and barley, turnips, potatoes, and in fact every species
of green crop, I have seen no country out of England
and Egypt superior to it." [1]

CLIMATE.

The climate of Newfoundland and Nova Scotia is
similar, and the seasons about equal in length.   On
the north-east coast, there are exceptions when the
northern ice is kept on the coast by a north-east wind
until late in the spring.   The spring of 1832 was one of
those exceptions.   The great jam of ice from the north
remained on the coast until late in June ; and the harbor of Bonavista, where the writer then resided, was
not clear of ice until the 21st day of June.   Such instances are of rare occurrence ; generally, the spring is
not later than in the other Provinces of British America.   The winter is not so cold as is sometimes experienced in the other Provinces.   Seldom, on the severest days, does the thermometer fall more than eighteen
or twenty degrees below zero.   One of the severest
winters ever known was in 1818, when the thermometer often sunk from twenty to twenty-one degrees below

[1] Speech of Sir John Harvey before the Agricultural Society, St.
Johns, in 1844.

´zero. The summers are warm, often hot, and a fog hangs on the eastern and southern coast for months, as it does also on the coast of Nova Scotia and New Brunswick; but to the north of Bonavista Bay, and to the west of Cape Ray, fog is seldom seen. The fog, however, is not unhealthy: the longevity of the people is remarkable, and perhaps in no country is old age attended with greater bodily and mental vigor than in Newfoundland. The climate may be pronounced very healthy.

VEGETABLE KINGDOM.

The forests which skirt the shore on the eastern and southern coasts are generally small; but, as you advance toward the interior, along the streams and around the lakes, the forest expands, and the trees are larger. The timber on the western shore in the same parallel is larger than that which is found on the Atlantic coast. St. George's Bay and the Bay of Islands are the great timber districts; and the country about the Humber River and Grand Pond is densely covered with fine woods; and Ingornachoix Bay is not less wooded. Neither the beech nor the maple is found near the shore; it is said, however, that the beech is sometimes met with in the interior; and the elm is a tree equally rare. Trees of the *conifera* family are in great variety, and some of them are large. The fir (*pinus balsamea*), or the Canada balsam, the black spruce (*pinus nigra*), and the white spruce (*pinus alba*), also the red pine (*pinus rubra*), are in great abundance, and grow well. They are from six to eighteen inches in diameter, and some are met with two feet in diameter, and from thirty to fifty feet high. The spruce is generally used for building boats; also for oars, fences, spars of various descriptions, planks, and hand-barrows.

A very large quantity is consumed for fuel. From the branches of the black spruce, that wholesome beverage, "spruce beer," is made. The fir is used for the framework of buildings, as dwelling-houses and stores; sawed into clap-boards; also for oil hogsheads, salmon and herring barrels, casks for screwed fish, shingles, and firewood.

The branches of the stunted spruce, on the verge of the barrens and savannas, are usually fringed with a yellow parasite, called in the island, *molldow*. It is the *alectoria subarta*, or negro-hair, of botanists. This lichen is the chief food of the deer during the winter season. The black, white, and yellow birch are found in great abundance, and occasionally birch trees are met with three feet in diameter. The *Ostrya Virginica*, iron or lever wood, is sometimes found. Varieties of the poplar called *popel*, particularly the aspen called *aps*, grow well. But the black larch, or juniper (*pinus penidula*), is among the most useful trees of the New-foundland forest. It is sometimes called the oak of Newfoundland, as it is the hardest, the strongest, and the most durable of all its timber. It is used extensively in ship-building; also for making cart-wheels, and other purposes requiring great strength. The top of the larch, or juniper, when growing, generally bends toward the east, and has oftentimes directed the traveller in his course. Notwithstanding the extent of wood found in many parts of the island, it is remarkable that, until late years, the only means of preparing it for use was the "pit saw;" but now there are saw-mills in different places. There are two or three saw-mills in Hall Bay, cutting up the splendid timber in the direction of Red-Indian Pond. There are seven or eight in the neighborhood of Smith's and Random Sounds,

and two or three more are met with in other parts of
the island, all of which are doing well ; and perhaps
no country affords a greater number of excellent sites
for mills, and better opportunities for damming. With
streams sufficiently large and convenient to float down
the lumber, if good localities were selected, and
science and capital employed as in New Brunswick, the
lumber trade in Newfoundland would for many years
be equally remunerative.

WILD FLOWERS.

The wild rose, of which there are three species, grows
in rich profusion ; and among them the *rosa blanda*,
with its slender purple-red branches, flourishes beside
the gentle, purling streams. " In the tribe of lilies,"
says Sir R. Bonnycastle, " Solomon in all his glory exceeded not the beauty of those produced in this un-
heeded wilderness." *L. Philadephicum* is almost the
same in appearance as the common orange lily. *L. Su-
perbum* ornaments some of the ponds, and in color is
orange with dark blue spots. *L. Canadense* also grows
in wet places, and has a collection of yellow or reddish
flowers darkly maculated.

Violets are common, but inodorous. The *Iris*, or
wild flag, a superb flower, is very common ; and, in the
flowering season, its rich blue petals dot every marsh.
The " pitcher plant," or " lady's side-saddle," with its
large, handsome, purple flowers is the natural production of the swamps. The moose wood, or heather wood,
shrub produces yellow flowers, and looks gay, as does
the *sisyrinchium anceps*, or the blue-eyed grass. Natural red and white clover, and a great variety of other
grasses, cover the plains and savannas ; and a beautiful little trailing-plant, called " maiden hair," is found in abun-

dance, It bears a small white fruit, like the egg of an ant, which contains a saccharine matter, lusciously sweet. The reed tribe is numerous; while the mosses, lichens, ferns, and fungi will furnish a wide field for the research of the skilful botanist.

CULTIVATED FLOWERS.

Roses are found in gardens in great variety. The moss rose, the damask rose, and the maiden's blush, thrive well. Dahlias grow in sheltered places; the lily of the valley, Solomon's seal, the convolvulus, Jacob's ladder, the lupin, sweet-William, fox-glove, cowslip, columbine, honeysuckle, and most of the flowers which adorn the gardens of other parts of British North America, will also grow in the gardens of Newfoundland.

WILD FRUITS.

Among the wild fruits, we mention the bak-apple, so called because its taste is something like a baked apple. It is a compound berry, in form and size like the raspberry; but when ripe, it is a deep yellow color. It is very rich, and makes a fine preserve. It is abundant. The wild raspberry is found in all parts of the island. Wild currants and gooseberries are plenty in some parts. The cranberry in several varieties is found in great quantities, and sometimes the marshes are red with this most delicious fruit. The wild strawberry is here; and the whortleberry, called hurts, which is the blueberry in the other Provinces, grows in Newfoundland in quantities that seem fabulous.

GARDEN FRUITS.

Among the exotic fruits is the apple, which, although not abundant, is found in some gardens to grow well. Some varieties of the plum, particularly the damson, is grown in Conception Bay and St. Johns ; and the Kentish cherry flourishes in those localities. The pear will grow, but does not come to great perfection ; but cabbage, cauliflowers, broccoli, lettuce, spinach, cress, beets, parsnips, carrots, peas, Windsor beans, French beans, celery, thyme, mint savory, and all the British culinary vegetables, arrive at great perfection. Potatoes yield abundantly, and are very farinaceous.

ANIMAL KINGDOM — QUADRUPEDS.

The deer of Newfoundland is the *caribou*, or reindeer. The usual height of this species of deer is about four feet, and its length, from the head to the insertion of the tail, is nearly the same. The antlers of the male are large, with numerous branches ; but those of the female are smaller, with fewer divisions. It is gregarious, and roams the country in large herds. In the summer, these herds are seen feeding on the plains and savannas far to the north. As the autumn comes on, they migrate to the south, when the open country is literally covered with their countless numbers. In their journey, they swim the inland lakes and small bays, and seem regardless of their enemies. A hunter informed the writer that he once saw the great herd " *beating* " to the south, when the open country, as far as he could see, was one living, moving mass of deer. Numerous wolves were following the herd, but seemed afraid to attack, because the deer would strike at them and kill them with their hoofs. Another man in the same district, in company with three others, once fell in with the great southern herd, when the party killed ninety-six deer. Beside this, when the writer resided in Burin, he knew one hundred and forty carcasses of deer to be brought into that harbor in one day. These deer were killed in their prime, and would average, at least, one hundred and forty pounds each carcass. A writer in the " British Colonies " gives the following information : " Former-ly, the herds that came to the south coast are stated to have been enormous. Mr. Bagg, of La Poile, says he has seen ' thousands ; ' and has killed seven at one shot with heavy slugs from a large sealing-gun." [1] Their paths are like sheep-walks ; but their footmarks are larger than those of a cow. Their food in summer is principally moss. In winter, it is the negro-hair ; but sometimes they will break the frozen snow with their hoofs, in order to get the moss. Early in the spring, they " *beat* " to the north ; and in the summer, they sep-arate into pairs, and hide themselves in the thick woods.

BEARS.

The white or Polar bear occasionally lands on the eastern coast from the ice ; and one came ashore at Bonavista, walked to Bird-Island Cove, where he again took the ice. He did no damage, and was evi-dently chary of the habitations of man. The black bear is often seen. It is the long-legged variety, and is very large. They live mostly on berries ; but late in the fall have been known to enter the lone " winter tilt " of the woodman, and devour all the pork and molasses they could find. They will run from man ; and are not savage except they are wounded, or have young. Their flesh is esteemed by the hunters.

WOLVES.

The wolves still roam in packs in the interior, and are seen in the track of the deer ; but they will not

[1] British Colonies, article Newfoundland, chap. IV.

attack a man, or approach within gun-shot. A hunter informed the writer, that he, in company with another man, was once on the open barrens looking for deer; when at a distance, they espied *three wolves*, apparently following them. The men halted, and advanced toward the wolves; soon the wolves stopped for a moment, and then ran away. The men now pursued their journey, when the wolves again turned and followed the men. Again they halted, expecting the animals would come within range. But not so; when they halted, the wolves stopped; and when the men advanced toward them, they always ran, and kept out of harm's way. This continued for hours, the wolves keeping about the same distance. In the end, the men left the hungry canine prowlers of the desert to pursue their wolfish course. They will, however, sometimes approach quite near the dwellings of man, and destroy both sheep and cows. In the year 1842, these animals were troublesome near St. Johns. A trap was set, and one was caught by the fore-leg. The trap cut off his leg, and he escaped. He was afterwards shot; and the following were his dimensions:

	ft.	in.
Length of the body, from the nose to the insertion of the tail	5	0
Length of the tail	1	6
Total length	6	6
Height of the fore-shoulder	2	9
Height at the haunch	2	8

In the winter of 1834, the wolves were troublesome near Trinity, and killed several sheep and cattle. On the morning of January 20th, the writer was returning from English Harbor to Trinity, when he suddenly came upon the track of a large wolf, which, from the

appearance in the light snow, he judged could have
passed only a few minutes before. Shortly the track
again crossed his path, and continued to cross his path at
every fifty or hundred yards, until he came up with a
man at work in the woods, who said the wolf had certainly crossed less than ten minutes before ; and was
sure the animal was in the thicket close by. We now
went in pursuit ; but soon perceived that the wolf was
aware of his danger, and made his escape. Observing
the footprint to be very large, I took a piece of paper,
and, with my pencil, traced it exactly as it was spread
on the snow. The form of the track, as then taken, is
now before me. It measures seven inches by nine.
The animal was afterwards shot in a trap ; and the
skin, when stuffed, measured, to the insertion of the tail,
five feet, three inches, and its height a little over three
feet.

The species of fox usually taken is the red or
yellow. It is taken in a trap. They are numerous. The patch, or cross fox, also the black, the blue,
the white, and the silver fox, are natives of the island ;
but the black and the silver fox are but seldom seen,
and their skins are valuable.

The beaver is plenty in some parts ; and the beaver-
house and beaver-dam are often met with near the
lakes in the interior.

The hare is very plentiful. It is brown in the summer, but becomes perfectly white in winter.

The otter is met with on the streams to the west
and the north of the island.

The musquash, or muskrat, is abundant. Its habits
are like the beaver, in building its house near the
streams.

The martin is found in many parts.

REPTILES.

There are no reptiles. Neither frog, toad, snake, nor lizard has ever been seen in any part of Newfoundland.

BIRDS.

The woods are certainly not jubilant with the songs of its feathered tribes; yet its ornithology is worth the attention of the natural historian.

Among the known birds are the osprey, or sea-eagle; owls, in great numbers, and of several varieties; the raven, the crow, and the blue-jay; two kinds of woodpeckers, one of which is speckled. A bird, supposed by Sir R. Bonnycastle to be the rose-colored ouzel, is called a robin. The martin stays about ten weeks in summer. The yellow-willow wren is very common; and the little wren is seen. The ferruginous thrush, the fly-catcher, the yellow-breasted chatterer, little black-cap, titmouse, the grossbeak, the snowbird, and the sparrow are also found. Here, also, is the ptarmigan, called the partridge. It is of a reddish-brown color in summer; but, like the hare, it becomes white in winter. It is a fine bird, and very plenty. The plover, the bittern, curlew, snipe, wimbrel, and sandpiper are found in the woods, or on the barrens and marshes.

Of water birds, there are the Canada and snowgoose, blue-winged teal, shoveller or great brown duck: the widgeon and the mallard are met with in the ponds. Of sea birds, there are the gull, lazy cormorant, twe or baccalao bird, pin-tailed duck or sea-pheasant, eider duck, kittiwake, tern, ice-bird or sea-dove, goosander, noddy, loon, puffin, and razor-bill. The Newfoundland goose is a large and elegant bird, and very plenty in the interior. It is of a swan-like form, with a black ring round its neck; can easily be domesticated, but does not then breed. Half a century ago, the penguin was very plenty. It is a handsome bird, about the size of a goose, with a coal-black head and back, a white belly, and a milk-white spot under the right eye. They cannot fly well; their wings are more like fins; they have on their bodies short feathers and down. The penguin is now but seldom seen: such destruction of the bird was made for the sake of its feathers, that it is now all but extinct.

Insects, such as mosquitoes, stinging midges, and flies, are in myriads.

The ponds and streams abound in trout; smelt inhabit the large lakes; and great quantities of fine salmon are taken in or near the mouths of the larger streams.

During the summer season, the sea is alive with herring and mackerel; but above all are its inexhaustible shoals of codfish, which are its great source of wealth and commerce.

CHAPTER III.

THERE is a twofold tradition in reference to the discovery of Newfoundland by Europeans. One is, that it was discovered by Biarne, or Biorn, a sea-king, or pirate, from Ireland, who, being driven on the coast by contrary winds, is said to to have taken shelter in Port Grace, or Harbor Grace, about the year 1000. The other, that the island was first visited some time in the eleventh century, by some Northmen from Scandinavia or Norway, who called it *vine-land*, or *wine-land*, or *wine-berry-land*, because of the vast quantities of hurts, or blueberries, which are everywhere found, and of which these Northmen are said to have made wine. For these traditions, there is little or no foundation, and they are now considered as entirely fabulous; and Newfoundland appears to have been unknown to Europeans until near the close of the fifteenth century.

The discovery of America by Christopher Columbus, in the year 1492, had delighted the men of science, astonished the ignorant multitudes, and excited the ambition and cupidity of the reigning monarchs of Europe; each of whom was anxious to gain possession of countries now known to exist west of the great Atlantic Ocean. Besides, as the true figure of the earth now began to be understood, a short way might be found to India and China; moreover, countries

6 * (65)

might be visited, whose auriferous soils would amply
repay the cost of their discovery and conquest.

In these occidental advantages, Henry VII. of England determined to share. He accordingly commissioned Giovani Gaboto, generally called John Cabot, a
Venetian, to sail toward the setting sun, in order to
make discoveries in his name. Two light ships, called
caravels, were placed under his command, and five
ships laden with goods for traffic supplied by the merchants of London. With this little fleet, Cabot sailed
from Bristol in the month of May, 1497. His destination was Cathay, or China; to reach which he was to
sail a west course. On the 24th of June, he saw land.
It was not China, but land on which no European eye
had yet gazed: it was the promontory since called Cape
Bonavista. To this land he gave the name of *Terra
primum vista*, the "Land first seen;" from which, by
some alteration in the words, but preserving the sense,
was derived the name NEWFOUNDLAND.

Intent upon reaching China by this new route, he
sailed to the north as far as lat. 67° 30′, when he must
have sighted some part of Greenland; but, finding no
north-west passage to the Pacific, he steered to the
south, and entered the Gulf of St. Lawrence, thus sailing round Newfoundland; and, taking with him ten of
the natives, he returned to England in the month of
August, and was knighted by the king. Sir John
Cabot made three subsequent voyages; but no settlement of the countries he visited then took place, as the
tide of European adventure flowed south, to Mexico
and Peru.

In 1500, Gaspar Cortereal, a Portuguese captain,
visited the coast of North America, and, following the
track of Sir John Cabot, he kidnapped several of the

natives, and sold them for slaves. In 1502, Hugh
Elliot and Thomas Ashurst, English merchants, were
authorized by Henry VII. to establish colonies in the
countries discovered by Cabot ; but they do not appear
to have availed themselves of this permission.

The discoverers of Newfoundland must have carried
back to Europe a surprising account of the quantity of
fish on its coast, and of the advantage of prosecuting a
fishery there; for in 1517, which was only twenty
years from the time that Cabot first saw Cape Bonavista, there were about fifty vessels, under the English,
French, Spanish, and Portuguese flags, engaged in the
fisheries.

Seventeen years later, that was in 1534, Jacques
Cartier, a navigator, and who had been engaged in
fishing on the banks of Newfoundland, received a
commission from Francis I., and with two small
vessels, of sixty tons each, sailed from St. Maloes' on
the 20th of April, and arrived at Newfoundland on the
10th of May. He remained there ten days ; then
sailed north, passed through the Strait of Belle Isle,
and, taking with him two natives, he returned to
France on the 25th of July, and was received with
honor by the. French king.

About this time, several attempts were made to colonize Newfoundland, and we read of a " Master Robert
Hore," a merchant of London, who, "with divers
other gentlemen," sailed in 1536, intending to remain
on the island through the winter ; but the crew of the
vessel were almost starved to death on the passage, and
would have perished, had they not fallen in with a
French ship, laden with provisions, which they seized
and brought to England. Henry VIII. of England satisfied the French claim for idemnity, and thereby pre-

vented any misunderstanding between the governments.

Down to this period, and for more than forty years after, Newfoundland did not properly belong to any nation, but was a disputable territory, — a place where fishermen and traders of different countries resorted ; and, what was far worse, it became a rendezvous for pirates, who could here follow their nefarious practices with impunity.

Britain was at that time just beginning to develop her naval strength ; and her ambitious Queen Elizabeth could allow no naval superiority in any foreign power, or permit the British flag to dip, except in compliment, to any nation, or suffer any nation to have more extensive colonies than were under her control.

Accordingly, in 1579, Her Majesty, desirous of obtaining advantage from the discoveries which Cabot had made eighty years before, but which as yet had been of little benefit, granted to Sir Humphrey Gilbert, half-brother to Sir Walter Raleigh, a patent for the "discovering or occupying and peopling such remote, heathen, and barbarous countries as were not actually possessed by any Christian people."

After many disappointments and much delay, this noble and intrepid man, having sold his estate in England to realize pecuniary means, sailed from Plymouth on the 11th of June, 1583, with five ships and two hundred and fifty men.

On the 11th of July, the fleet arrived off Newfoundland, and on Monday, August 5th, proceeded in state to St. Johns, to take formal possession of the island. A tent was pitched on the shore, the people were assembled, and the commission of the Queen of England was read. A twig from a bush was then delivered

to Sir Humphrey, who declared the island of Newfoundland to belong to his sovereign and to the dominion
and Crown of England. The people, with loud ac-
clamations, promised obedience. There were thirty-
six vessels of foreign nations then in St. Johns, the
masters of which, and the merchants connected with the
trade, all acknowledged the supremacy of the British
Queen. A pillar was erected, upon which, in a plate
of lead, was engraved the arms of the queen; and
from that time has the Island of Newfoundland belonged to the Crown of England. A tax was also im-
posed upon all ships who visited that port; and the
three following laws were promulgated for this new
colony :

1. That public worship should be celebrated according to the Church of England ritual.

2. That anything which might be attempted preju-
dicial to the Queen of England was, according to the
laws of England, treason.

3. That uttering of words to the dishonor of Her
Majesty was to be punished with loss of ears and the
confiscation of property.

It was very right for Sir Humphrey Gilbert to say
something about " public worship ; " yet it was more
than one hundred years after this, that divine worship
was performed in Newfoundland (except, perhaps, very
occasionally) according to the " Church of England
ritual," or in any other way, and more than one hundred and fifty years before public worship, to any extent, was observed by the settlers.

This gallant man, Sir Humphrey Gilbert, was lost
on his return voyage to England. On the 20th of
August, Sir Humphrey sailed from St. Johns, with
three of his ships, the " Golden Hind," the " Little

Squirrel," and the " Delight," for Sable Island, to
search for swine and cattle, said to have been landed
there some thirty years previous. The " Delight" was
lost on a sand-bank ; and no swine or cattle being found
on the island, he determined to proceed to England,
declaring that he " would fit out an expedition royally,
and return next spring." The " Golden Hind " and
the " Little Squirrel " left for England, Sir Humphrey
taking passage in the smaller vessel. Repeatedly did
his friends urge him to leave that nut-shell, and go on
board the " Golden Hind." His reply was, " I will
not forsake my little company, with whom I have
passed so many storms and perils."

The two vessels reached the Azores in safety, but
there encountered a storm of so terrible a nature that
made all hearts quail, except Sir Humphrey, who retained his courage and self-possession to the last. The
" Golden Hind " kept as near the " Little Squirrel "
as the mountain waves would permit. In the midst of
the storm, the noble admiral was seen sitting calmly on
the deck reading, and was heard to cheer the men on
board of the " Golden Hind," as well as his own crew,
with " Be of good cheer, for we are as near heaven by
sea as on the land." But night came on ; it was fearfully dark ; the lights of the " Little Squirrel " were
seen for a time, but they suddenly disappeared : the
" Little Squirrel," with all on board, foundered.

Thus perished one of the bravest of the adventurers,
who, in the glorious reign of Elizabeth, sought to extend the dominion of England in the western world.[1]

In 1585, two years after the death of Sir Humphrey
Gilbert, Sir Bernard Drake made a voyage to Newfoundland, who now claimed the sovereignty of the

[1] See Bonnycastle's Newfoundland in 1842.

island, and the sole right of its fisheries, in the name of Queen Elizabeth. He found several Portuguese ships, laden with fish and oil and furs; these he seized as lawful prizes, and with them returned to England.

A terrible war now raged with Spain ; and all England was in terror and consternation, because of the "Invincible Armada," that was to land upon her shores, conquer her armies, punish her sovereign for her heresy, and forever blot out the hated name of Protestant from the face of the earth. But divine power frustrated this wicked design ; the winds of heaven scattered and destroyed part of this invincible force ; Drake, Hawkins, Frobisher, and Howard, captured several ships: the rest took flight. And thus was humbled the haughty monarch of Spain, and the God-honored Island of Britain was allowed to enjoy all the privileges of her reformed religion. Her dominion was preserved in its integrity ; while she was destined to rise in such political importance, as to cause her counsels to be respected, and her power to be feared by every nation upon earth.

The trouble in which the parent state was involved prevented her from paying much attention to a new colony so distant and unimportant as Newfoundland. It was, therefore, twenty-five years after Sir Bernard Drake's visit, that another voyage was made there under royal authority.

The island had been considered as belonging to England from the time of its discovery by Cabot, now more than one hundred years, and twenty-seven years had passed since it had been formally claimed in the name of the British Queen ; yet no effort had hitherto been made to colonize it, or preserve order among the rabble that visited its shores.

In 1610, its colonization was first attempted ; for in that year James I. granted a patent to the Lord Chancellor Bacon, Lord Verulam, the Earl of Northampton, Lord Chief Baron Tanfield, Sir John Doddridge, and forty other persons, under the designation of the " Treasurer and Company of Adventurers and Planters of the Cities of London and Bristol, for the Colony of Newfoundland." This patent granted the lands between Capes St. Mary's and Bonavista, with the seas and islands lying within *ten* leagues of the coast, for the purpose of securing forever the trade of fishing to British subjects.

In virtue of this patent, the first party of English settlers came out under the direction of Mr. Guy, an intelligent and enterprising merchant of Bristol. Mr. Guy and his party settled in Conception Bay. His reports of the island and its capabilities were very favorable ; and, after nearly two years' residence there, he returned to England, leaving the infant colony in charge of William Colston, whose views and reports of the island were not so favorable. It is not improbable that Mr. Colston, at least in part, formed his opinion of the island, from the serious fact that twenty-five of the settlers were seized with scurvy, six of whom died. The nineteen who recovered are stated to have owed their lives to the use of turnips as an article of food. Had that powerful antiscorbutic, *spruce beer,* — now so generally used in Newfoundland, — been then known, possibly those cases of scurvy would not have happened. Mr. Guy went back to the island, in the summer of 1612, when he made a survey of the coast, and exerted himself in every way for the arrangement of the colony. The aborigines, or Red Indians, were then lords of the soil. They knew nothing of the white

man's gun, and therefore came, and held friendly intercourse with Guy, as he coasted along their shores.

. In performing his survey, he met " with two canoes
of Red Indians, with whom he held friendly intercourse." In what part of the island this took place,
we are not informed. It might have been in Conception Bay ; for there is a place on the north shore of
that bay, called " Ochre-Pit Cove," where, tradition
says, the aborigines used to get red ochre, wherewith
to paint their bodies.

Little more is known of this man than what we
have related. He, it is supposed, soon after abandoned
the settlement, which in consequence quickly lan-
guished.

The first settlers had no government, or police, or
power of any kind, to restrain evil, or punish delinquencies ; anarchy, therefore, soon prevailed among
them ; and the motley groups of lawless bands in St.
Johns and other places, who had come there for the
purpose of fishing, perpetrated crimes with impunity.
To remedy these evils, and to reduce this moral chaos
to order, in 1615, Captain Whitbourne, — a contem-
porary of Sir Humphrey Gilbert and Sir Bernard
Drake, — who had himself made many voyages to Newfoundland, was sent there, with a commission from the
admiralty, to establish order, investigate the abuses
complained of by the fishermen, and repress the fla-
grant dishonesty too generally manifested. Immediately on his arrival, one hundred and seventy masters
of vessels submitted themselves to his jurisdiction ; and
he endeavored to empanel juries in the most frequented harbors. It was not long that Captain Whitbourne exercised his judicial powers ; for, two years
after, we find him as chief of a body of Welch settlers,

7

sent out by Doctor Vaughan to form a settlement in a harbor in Fortune Bay, which was then called Cambriot, now Harbor Britain, on land purchased from the patentees.

In 1623, another party of settlers came out, under the direction of Sir George Calvert, afterward Lord Baltimore.

This has been called the first settlement of Newfoundland. There had been two attempts to colonize it before this time, as we have related : one in 1610, under Guy, the other in 1617, under Captain Whitbourne ; and, although some of the settlers remained, yet in neither of these cases was the plan successful ; therefore the year 1623 is considered as the time when the island was settled.

Sir George Calvert was an Irishman and a Roman Catholic. He obtained a large tract of land on the eastern coast, between Bay Bulls and Cape St. Mary's, where, with a number of his countrymen and co-religionists, he took up his residence, making Ferryland his head-quarters. To his Newfoundland estate he gave the name of Avalon, from the ancient name of Glastonburg, the place where tradition says Christianity was first preached in England.

Lord Baltimore built a handsome residence in Ferryland, erected a strong fort, formed salt-works, and gathered around him a prosperous settlement. He resided there about twenty years, when he returned to England ; when, through the favor of Charles I., he went out to colonize Maryland, from whence arose the fine city, in that state, which still bears his name.

By the year 1640, fifteen or sixteen settlements had been formed in different parts of the coast, including about three hundred and fifty families.

In 1635, the king granted permission to the French to cure and dry fish on the land, on condition of paying five per cent. of the produce. Encouraged by this, the French afterwards formed a settlement in Placentia Bay, which they long continued to occupy, and which was a source of trouble to the British settlers.

In 1633, the king issued a document, directed to the Lord Treasurer and others, commanding them " to erect a common fishery, as a *nursery for seamen;*" and, at the same time, exempting the British fisheries from " tax or toll." In this same year the first laws were promulgated by royal authority, and called " regulations for the governing of his majesty's subjects, *inhabiting Newfoundland, or trafficking in bays.*" The purport of these laws was, first, that all persons who committed murder, or theft above forty shillings, should be taken to England for trial ; second, that no buildings, erected for prosecuting the fishery, should be destroyed at the end of the voyage ; third, that the master of the first fishing-vessel, arriving at any port, *should be admiral of the same during the season.*

The two first laws were good; but the third, or government by the fishing admirals, was perhaps the most monstrous law that ever disgraced any free colony of the British nation. These fishing admirals were arbitrary men, and grossly ignorant. They were all either traders or common fishermen ; and, in time, they improved upon the law ; for the first captain of an English vessel, who arrived in port in the spring, would be admiral, the second rear-admiral, the third vice-admiral, and the fourth post-captain.

These admirals were empowered to " settle all disputes among the fishermen, and enforce due attention to certain acts of parliament." In their judicial character, they would decide cases, according to their caprice, over a bottle of rum ; and frequently would inflict summary punishment, by flogging the culprit with a rope's end.

This iniquitous system continued for nearly one hundred years. It began, indeed, to decline in the early part of the last century ; but it was only about the time of the revolutionary war that it entirely ceased. In the year 1823, the writer made a voyage to the westward, in the ship Duck, Captain Nicholas, who was then about seventy years of age. He well remembered the fishing admirals ; and he himself had once chanced to be a post-captain.

CHAPTER IV.

SOON after the discovery of the island by Cabot, the
fishery gave employment to a number of British
ships; and it was seen that those fisheries would prove
beneficial not only to commerce, but would become a
nursery for seamen, to man the royal navy. As far
back as the year 1549, an act of parliament was passed
for the " better encouragement of the fisheries of Newfoundland." In the reign of Queen Elizabeth there
were two hundred and sixty ships employed in the
fisheries; and it was mainly from the fishermen of these
vessels that she manned her fleets which defeated the
powerful Spanish Armada.

Charles I., in a commission for " well governing his
subjects in Newfoundland," says: " The navigators and
mariners of the realm have been much increased by the
Newfoundland fisheries."

Beneficial, however, as these fisheries were to the
mother country, yet they met with serious opposition
in England; and, what was worse, the government
gave its aid in the persecution of the people, and for
the destruction of this important and rising colony,
which it had employed so much effort, and expended so

much money on, to bring to its then prosperous condition. The cause of this opposition was the jealousy between the two parties engaged respectively in the bank and in the shore fisheries.

In the commencement, the fishery was mostly carried on by vessels which came from England in the spring, fished on the banks, and returned in the fall, visiting the land only to *make* or cure their fish. This was called the " bank-fishery." But when settlers came, and made the island their home, they built fishing-boats, and fished near the land. This was the " shore-fishery." There was really no conflicting interest here, for there was fish enough for both parties.

Nevertheless, a bad feeling existed between them. Sir Josiah Child had vessels engaged in the bank-fishery, and, in the year 1670, he published a pamphlet to prove that the bank-fishery, which employed those seamen who so often had manned the ships of war, was seriously injured by the boat or shore fishery, and that it had declined to a great extent ; for while, in the year 1605, it employed two hundred and fifty vessels, it at that time employed only eighty. He imputed this decline to the shore fishery carried on by the settlers; and said, if the shore-fishery were permitted to increase, it would in time " engross the whole business, and thus the nursery for seamen would be destroyed." He therefore advised that no more emigration should take place to Newfoundland, and that those persons and families, who had already settled there, *should be displanted.*

In our day no civilized government would pay any attention to such advice ; while a proposition like that offered by Sir Josiah Child would be universally denounced as absurd, unjust, and barbarous. It was not so regarded in those days. Three years before the

above-named pamphlet was issued, the settlers had
applied for a governor; but the merchants and ship-
owners engaged in the bank-fishery opposed the application, and it was rejected. In the year 1674, the
application for a governor was renewed, when it was
not only again rejected, but the advice of Sir Josiah
Child was adopted by the " Board of Trade and Plantations ; " and, at its instance, the government issued
what was called the " Western Charter," by which,
while encouragement is given to the fisheries, yet the
bank-fisheries are only intended by that expression ;
for all persons are in that charter prohibited from " settling on the shores or coasts of the island ; " and " no
inhabitant allowed to live *within six miles of the sea ;*
and that any person transgressing this law might be
driven out of the country.

This foolish and wicked law was actually put in
force ; and Sir John Berry was sent to Newfoundland,
with orders for the deportation of the inhabitants, the
destruction of their houses, and the entire uprooting
of that thriving colony. Berry was a humane man :
he sent home strong remonstrances against the law,
and very reluctantly carried out his commission. Still
much misery was occasioned : many houses were
burned, many outrages committed, and a number of
persons were innocently expelled from the land of their
adoption. This persecution lasted for two years, when
Mr. Downing, one of the residents, obtained an order
from the king, Charles II., to prevent any further persecution of the people. But this order, while it prevented the further deportation of the settlers, also contained strict injunctions, forbidding " any vessel to
take out emigrants, or any person to settle in Newfoundland." This occurred in 1676.

For twenty years did the prohibition of emigration to Newfoundland continue, during which time, constant complaints were made to the government that the laws in this case were evaded; while counter representations were made by those who were favorable to the settlement of the country. It is satisfactory to know that no further rigorous measures were taken; and, in 1697, the " Board of Trade and Plantations " published a report, that " a number of inhabitants, not exceeding one thousand, might be usefully employed in constructing boats, stages for drying fish, and other matters connected with the fisheries."

The permission that had been given to the French, " to cure and dry fish," and the connivance at their settlement in Placentia, caused the English much trouble in the reign of William III. One cause of war with France, at this time, was set forth in these words : " That of late the encroachments of the French upon Newfoundland and His Majesty's subjects' trade and fishery there, had been more like the invasions on an enemy than becoming friends, *who enjoyed the advantages of that trade only by permission.*"

During the war with France, which raged in this reign, Newfoundland was several times the scene of fearful conflicts between the contending hosts. The French, having had possession of Placentia for more than half a century, had strongly fortified it ; so that when it was attacked by a squadron under Commander Williams, it so far resisted the attack, that the British succeeded only in destroying the works on Point Vesti, at the entrance of the harbor. The garrison still remained in the hands of the French. This occurred in September, 1692.

In 1696, four years later, Chevalier Nesmond arrived with a French squadron, and, aided by the force on the island, attacked St. Johns, but failed, and returned to France. Before the close of the year, another French squadron, under Brouillon, arrived, who, in concert with Ibberville, the military commander, again attacked St. Johns, which being short of military stores, and in a defenceless state, was compelled to surrender; upon which the town and garrison were burned, and the troops sent to England on parole.

Ibberville, having captured and destroyed St. Johns, proceeded along the coast, and with sword and fire he destroyed all the British stations, except Carbonear and Bonavista, which were successfully defended against his attacks. "The dogs of war" were now fairly let loose or that unhappy island, to possess which, both England and France determined to contend to the uttermost. The news of this French invasion reached England, when a British squadron, with fifteen hundred men on board, was dispatched to recover the lost territory; but unfortunately, either ignorance or cowardice, or both, prevented the British commanders, Admiral Nevil and Sir John Gibson, from retrieving the honor of their country's flag.

For two years did the homes of the persecuted Newfoundlanders lie waste, until the peace of Ryswick, in 1697, put an end to hostilities, and placed matters in that country in a similar position to what they were before the war commenced.

By this time, the government saw the folly of deporting the people from the island, and not only discontinued all persecution in that way, but declared Newfoundland *"free* to all his majesty's subjects." Several acts of parliament were now passed, regulating the fisheries; and the importation of fish, taken by

foreigners in foreign vessels, was strictly prohibited.
The preamble of the act 10th and 11th William and
Mary declares, that " the trade and fisheries of Newfoundland is a beneficial trade to the kingdom, in the
employing of a great number of seamen and ships, to
the increase of her majesty's revenue, and the encouragement of trade and navigation."

Thus far, there was neither gospel nor law in Newfoundland; and the fishing admirals were the only
executive then known. The money-loving merchants
of that day were favorable to this system, because these
admirals were their paid servants, or the captains
of their own ships, and they could fee, or control their
decisions, and thus govern the people at their will.

In 1702, war again broke out between England and
France, when Sir John Leake was dispatched by
Queen Anne, with a British squadron, to take possession of the whole island; and although he did not fully
succeed, yet he captured twenty-nine sail of French
ships, and with this booty he returned to England
in the autumn.

In 1705, the French garrison of Placentia was rein-
forced by five hundred men from Canada, when they
destroyed several British settlements, and carried their
devastation as far north as Bonavista. The following
year, a British force under Captain Underdown destroyed a number of French ships, and drove the enemy
from their recent conquests. The British parliament,
now alive to the importance of Newfoundland as a
colony, earnestly entreated the queen to " use her
royal endeavors to recover and preserve the ancient
possessions, trade, and fisheries of Newfoundland."

But little attention was paid to this address of parliament, and the French, aware of the inadequate British

force, determined to expel all the English from the island. Accordingly, St. Ovide, the French commander at Placentia, was despatched with a 'force against the British. He landed at Bay of Bulls without being discovered, marched over the frozen ground, and attacked and completely destroyed St. Johns on the 1st of January, 1708. After which, the French seized almost every English station on the island except Carbonear, which again nobly defended itself against their attack.

Newfoundland was now virtually in the power of the French, and would have continued so but for the brilliant success of the British arms on the continent of Europe. This war terminated with the celebrated Treaty of Utrecht, by which the French were compelled to concede the exclusive sovereignty of Newfoundland and the adjacent islands to Great Britain ; reserving only a right to the subjects of France to cure and dry fish on the coast, lying between Cape Bonavista on the eastern side, and Point Rich on the western ; also to occupy the small islands of St. Pierre and Miquelon, with a police force of fifty men.

Both the English and the French settlements now prospered, so that in the year 1721, eight years after the peace, the French employed four hundred vessels in the trade ; and not only supplied France with fish, but rivalled the British in the fish-trade in the ports of Spain and the Mediterranean. The British settlements also, notwithstanding all the disadvantages under which they labored, continued rapidly to advance in population and in interest, so that in the year 1729, the island, which had hitherto been under the nominal administration of Nova Scotia, was now withdrawn from that position, and constituted into a separate province.

But the government of this new province was a great difficulty. In many parts, the people were completely lawless: they fought, quarrelled, and committed all kinds of crime without restraint; and rule by the fishing admirals was anarchy itself. To remedy this, Captain Henry Osborne, of her majesty's navy, was appointed governor and commander-in-chief; but, by his commission, was required to obey the instructions of Lord Vere Beauclerc, the naval commander stationed at Newfoundland.

Governor Osborne divided the island into districts, appointed justices of the peace and other officers in those districts; and copies of " Shaw's Practical Justice of the Peace " were given to those newly-appointed officers, to guide them in their decisions. He also levied a rate of a half a quintal of fish on all fishing-rooms and fishing-boats, for the purpose of building jails and putting up stocks, that the justices might have the means of punishing offenders. He likewise appointed a new class of magistrates, called "*floating surrogates.*" These were captains of ships of war, who were empowered to hold courts in the different harbors they visited, and "determine in a summary way all suits and complaints of a civil nature within the island of Newfoundland." In time, besides the floating surrogates, resident surrogates were also appointed, with equal powers; and for nearly one hundred years the laws in the out-harbors were administered either by the magistrates, who had jurisdiction in cases of a civil nature not exceeding forty shillings, or by the surrogates, who had power to decide all cases not exceeding forty pounds.

The surrogate court was certainly an improvement upon the court of the fishing admirals, which now began to decline, and in time became extinct. The surrogate courts continued down to the year 1826, when the charge of " partial and corrupt administration of justice " having been preferred against them to the imperial government, and particularly in the case of flogging a civilian by the joint order of a clerical and a floating surrogate, the surrogate courts were abolished by royal authority.

But to return : the new state of things made by Governor Osborne was violently opposed by the fishing admirals, and some of the new-made justices were quite as ignorant as they were ; while others of them thought their office as justice of the peace interfered with them in the way of trade, and brought upon them the ill-will of the people.

In 1741, a court of vice-admiralty was established ; and in 1751, a court of oyer and terminer for the trial of felons, instead of sending them to England for trial.

Newfoundland, although it had been ceded to England for fifty years, yet lacked sufficient force, both naval and military, to protect her coasts in the time of danger. It was so in 1762, when a French squadron arrived in the Bay of Bulls, proceeded overland as it had done in 1708, and finding the small garrison in St. Johns unable to defend itself, they were made prisoners of war, and the town, for the third time, fell into the hands of the French. From St. Johns, the French proceeded to Carbonear and Trinity, where they committed all sorts of depredations. Intelligence of this occurrence was communicated to Lord Colville, the British commander-in-chief, then stationed in Halifax, who immediately sailed for Newfoundland. When the British admiral arrived off St. Johns, he

8

found a superior French force, under Admiral de Ternay, lying at anchor within the harbor.   Previous to
the arrival of Lord Colville, the settlers had themselves made arrangements for assisting in an attack
upon the French.   Robert Carter, of Ferryland, and
Mr. Brooks, of Bay of Bulls, had, at their own
expense, collected a number of bank-fishing or western
boats, cut them down, and had made them into row-
galleys, ready for an emergency.   His lordship availed
himself of these Newfoundland galleys: he manned
them with fishermen, and placed them under the command of Mr. Carter and Mr. Brooks.   He embarked
a number of the military on board of this little fleet,
and in the evening despatched them to Torbay, which
is seven miles to the north of St. Johns.   The expedition arrived at Torbay the next morning, and the
troops, under command of Colonel Amherst, immediately marched for St. Johns.   In the meantime, Lord
Colville, who was now off St. Johns, made a feint of
landing his troops at Quidy Widy, when a sharp contest
ensued.   The English fought desperately up Signal
Hill, but for a time seemed likely to fail.   Just then
the troops from Torbay arrived, and the victory was in
favor of the British.   The French admiral, seeing his
danger, took advantage of a thick fog, ran out of the
harbor, and passed the British fleet without being
observed.   On the 10th of February following (1763),
was signed the famous Treaty of Paris, which again
put an end to hostilities, and gave Newfoundland back
to Great Britain, as settled by the Treaty of
Utrecht in 1713.

In the year 1763, Labrador was annexed to the
government of Newfoundland.

In 1764, under Governor Sir Hugh Palliser, a

custom-house was established in St. Johns ; and, the year following, the "Navigation Laws" were extended to Newfoundland.

During the American revolutionary war, the trade of Newfoundland suffered severely by privateers, and also for want of provisions, which used to be extensively supplied from the New England States : in consequence, flour rose to twenty-five and thirty dollars, and pork to fifty dollars, per barrel. But money was plenty, for the fishery was good ; and merchantable fish was worth nine dollars per quintal.

While Newfoundland was suffering in her commerce, in consequence of the American struggle for independence, she suffered more by a most terrible gale of wind, which covered her coasts with wrecks. Heavy storms and wrecks are of frequent occurrence ; but the tornado of 1775 has, in Newfoundland, caused that year to be emphasized as " the year of the great storm." An unprecedented furious gale of wind sprung up from the east, which caused the ocean waves to lash the shore with awful power; the sea rose twenty feet above its usual height, carrying away fishing-stages, fish-houses, flakes, and dwelling-houses : while the wrecks of *seven hundred* vessels and fishing-boats were scattered along the shores, the greater part of whose crews had perished in the water.

In 1783, a brief peace was restored, and the Treaty of Versailles, signed on the 3d of September, once more brought tranquillity to the island, and fixed the boundaries of the British possessions, and the French Shore, which are the boundaries in the present day. In 1785, the resident population was estimated at about 10,000, with near 8,000 acres of land under cultivation.

In 1789, a Court of Common Pleas was established

by the then Governor, Admiral Milbank. In 1792, a
Supreme Court was established, designated the " Supreme Court of Newfoundland," of which John Reeves,
Esq., was the Chief Justice. Surrogate Courts were
also established in the principal districts of the island.
On the breaking out of the French revolution, war
was again declared between England and France.
This time, Newfoundland suffered but little of the
horrors of war ; for the British squadron on its coasts,
was sufficient to protect it from all the power of
France. France, indeed, did not want the will to
annoy the inhabitants of the island, but her naval
force was not sufficient to do much damage. She,
however, made an attempt once more upon St. Johns,
which, in this case, proved a complete failure.

In the year 1796, on the morning of the 1st of
September, a formidable French fleet appeared off St.
Johns: it consisted of seven sail of the line, two
frigates, and several small vessels of war, under the
command of Admiral Richery. The flag-ship and
one frigate was all the British naval force then in the
harbor ; but Admiral Sir James Wallace was then
governor, — a man of sound judgment, and indomitable
in war.   Beside, the defences of the harbor had been
greatly improved since the French invasion of 1762.
A large platform had been built on South Point, called
the Duke of York's Battery, on which were mounted
eight twenty-four pounder guns, three or four eighteen
pounder carronades, and two ten-inch mortars.   Fort
Amherst, on the south side, was in a good state,
and preparations were made for throwing red-
hot shot.   Every possible arrangement was made
by the British Admiral to meet the emergency.
The flag-ship and the frigate were placed at · proper

distances, so as to command the Narrows ; the large
chain was stretched across, from the Chain Rock
to the Pancake ; and three schooners, filled with com-
bustibles, and intended to be used as fire-ships, were
placed in readiness. " The Royal Newfoundland
Regiment," which had been formed during the summer, was then considered in an efficient state :
volunteer companies of artillery, besides the regular
troops, were in the garrison. Martial law was proclaimed in the town ; and all the men fit to bear
arms, whether merchants, clerks, store-keepers, sailors,
or fishermen, were mustered and ready for action.
The French fleet stood off and on for three days, without
attacking, or making any attempt to land. On the third
day, they formed a line of battle, and stood in for the
Narrows. Every one now expected a terrible conflict to
commence ; but not so. The van ship of the enemy came
within long range of the guns at Fort Amherst, and a
shot was fired at her from Signal Hill, which was not
only not replied to, but most unexpectedly did the
whole fleet put about, and stood off to sea. They
continued in sight for several days, then bore away to
the south, to Bay Bulls, which, in a most cowardly
manner, they burnt, and drove the poor, defenceless
people into the woods. Shortly after this dastardly
act, the fleet sailed entirely away, since which time no
foreign enemy has ever attempted to invade the island.

During the remainder of this long French war, the
colony suffered but little from its effects, as her coasts
were well guarded by British ships ; and her markets,
which were principally the different ports of Spain and
Portugal, were generally kept open by the British navy.
A career of steady prosperity now attended her, and
rapidly did she increase in wealth and influence. In the

8 *

year 1814, at the close of the war, her exports are said to have reached the large sum of £2,831,528 sterling.

The first newspaper was issued in 1807. It was called " The Royal Gazette : " its publisher was Mr. John Ryan. This was the dawn of literature upon that dark and long-neglected island. It was a weekly publication, and continued to be published in the same family for near half a century. For thirteen years, " The Royal Gazette " was the only issue from the Newfoundland press; but in 1820, Mr. Henry Winton issued the " Public Ledger," a well conducted, and a very respectable paper. The third paper was " The Newfoundlander ; " then " The Newfoundland Times ; " and several others followed. The number of papers issued on the island in 1864 was eleven.

In 1815, the prosperity of Newfoundland received a check, when, at the close of the American war, the great price of fish suddenly fell from five or six dollars to two : this, with a partial failure of the fisheries, which happened at the same time, caused the ruin of several commercial houses, and involved many families in want and suffering. Besides this, on the 12th of the following February (1816), a most fearful conflagration laid a great part of St. Johns in ashes. The property destroyed was estimated at more than £100,000 sterling ; and 1,500 human beings were left homeless and penniless, in the midst of the frost and storms of a Newfoundland winter. To the honor of the citizens of Boston, let it be recorded, that, as soon as the news of this calamity reached them, they at once loaded a vessel with provisions, and clothing, sent her down to St. Johns, in that inclement season, and there gratuitously bestowed those provisions and necessaries upon the suffering and starving poor.

But other calamities followed in succession. The next year, 1817, on the 7th of November, a second and more destructive fire broke out in the same town. Upon this occasion, in the short space of nine hours, thirteen large mercantile establishments, well stocked with provisions for the coming winter, with one hundred and forty dwelling-houses, were entirely consumed. The loss in property this time was estimated at £500,000 sterling. And a third fire occurred on the 21st of the same month, when fifty-six more houses, besides wharves and stores, were consumed.

These calamities spread a deep gloom upon the minds of the people; and for a time it seemed as though the entire abandonment of the Colony would take place at no distant period.

The winter that followed — that is, the winter of 1817-18 — was a time of great distress, both in St. Johns and in the different harbors of Conception Bay. The people wanted food, and in their desperation broke open several stores and dwelling-houses; but they committed other depredations besides their search for food, and generally would use the word *Ral*, as a watch-word to their companions in crime. Hence, this winter was called by the people of Conception Bay, " *The winter of the Rals.*"

A few years after, the fishery improved; the fish commanded a higher price in the foreign markets, and a brighter day dawned upon the island. But the system of jurisprudence was defective, and against the floating-surrogate system loud complaints were heard from all parts of the island. The Imperial Parliament took up the matter: it abolished the Surrogate Courts, and established a Supreme Court, consisting of a chief justice and two assistant judges. The island was divided into three " Circuits," Northern, Central, and Southern, in which three separate courts were held, each presided over by one of the three judges. The Supreme Court was empowered to admit qualified attorneys to practice in the different courts, and to grant letters of administration and probates of wills. An appeal is permitted from the Circuit Courts to the Supreme Court, and from the Supreme Court to the Queen in Council. Courts of Quarter Sessions were now also established, and a sheriff appointed from year to year.

In 1825, Sir Thomas Cochrane, R.N., was appointed Governor. Newfoundland was then in a transition state, passing from lawlessness into order, and from ignorance, arising from an almost destitution of schools, to that of education and position among the Provinces of the British Empire.

To promote this change, Sir Thomas gave all the weight of his influence and his constant personal atten-tion. He completed the first road in the country, which was from St. John to Portugal Cove, and the second, from Harbor Grace to Carbonear. He sailed along the shores, entered many of the harbors, and conversed with all sorts of people on the affairs of the island. He travelled miles in the country, through its bushes and bogs, to form for himself a judgment of its soil ; and he sent circulars into all the out-harbors to get the opinion of the people in reference to a Colonial Parliament. His most decided opinion was, that much of its soil was capable of a high state of cultivation ; that it had come to a state when it ought to have a local legislature ; that such a constitution would be greatly for the benefit of the people ; and that it ought at once to be granted by the Imperial Government.

The opinion of Sir Thomas was severely criticised and held up to ridicule; and pamphlets, both in defence and in opposition to his judgment, issued from the press, both in the colony and in England. From a pamphlet written in opposition, by a writer who called himself "A Poole Merchant," we make the following extract :—

" That the climate is uncongenial to cultivation is well known, and is confirmed by the fact, that in this present year (1828), so late as the beginning of May, the snow laid on the ground, and the frost was so intense, that the common operations of domestic gardening could not be commenced. The winter commenced early in December, and the frost was intense and continued, the thermometer often standing at 15° below zero."

This writer showed his utter ignorance of a North-American winter, and its influence upon the cultivation of the soil. In Nova Scotia, New Brunswick, and Prince Edward Island, the winter usually commences in December : the thermometer *often stands for weeks* at about 15° below zero, and sometimes falls more than 30° below. The snow also continues on the ground, so that " domestic gardening " is rarely commenced before the month of May. Yet who that has ever seen the beautiful corn-fields of Prince Edward Island, the productive orchards of Annapolis Valley, or the rich uplands on the St. John's River, will say the climate is uncongenial for cultivation ?

Sir Thomas was successful; for, in the year 1832, His Majesty William IV. granted a Representative Constitution to Newfoundland; and on the 1st day of January, 1833, the first session of the Colonial Parliament was opened by Sir Thomas Cochrane in person.

In a very few years, the benefit of this measure became apparent. At the time of its colonization, except in the vicinity of St. Johns, scarcely a house, a gar-

den, or a potato-field, was to be seen one mile from the
shore. Now, good roads were opened in various directions; the land was cultivated; carriages of every form
rolled along the roads in the summer, and the jingle of
the sleigh-bells was heard in winter. Education was
promoted; the arts and sciences were encouraged;
temperance societies and other philanthropic institutions were organized. In fact, all those adjuncts to
civilized life were introduced, which are calculated to
elevate the mind, and make the inhabitants of Newfoundland an intelligent and an enlightened people.

In 1840, on the 5th of November, the town of St.
Johns was enlivened by the appearance of the first
steamer that ever visited her harbor. It was H. M.
Steamer *Spitfire*, which had come with a detachment of
men for the Royal Veteran Companies. The sight was
novel, and many persons went on board to examine
the machinery.

In the same year, a company was incorporated by
the Newfoundland Legislature, to run a steamboat
between Halifax and St. Johns, toward the expenses
of which, the Nova Scotia Legislature granted £500
per annum for three years.

Before the measure contemplated by this company
was carried into effect, a second steamer came upon
the coast. It was the John McAdam, which had previously been employed between Cork and Liverpool,
and was now offered for sale. She arrived at St.
Johns on the 4th of August, 1842.

Two or three days after her arrival, she made a trip
to the north, with about fifty ladies and gentlemen on
board. She passed Cape St. Francis, ran up the south
shore of Conception Bay nearly to Portugal Cove, then
round the western end of Belle Isle to Brigus, in the

harbor, of which she made a sweep, and stopped her engines a few minutes, so as to gratify the curiosity of the people. She then proceeded to Port De Grave, and made a similar sweep. She passed next to Carbonear, and, leaving that harbor, she entered the port of Harbor Grace, where she remained for the night.

Very early the next morning, she weighed anchor, and, proceeding down the north shore, she passed between the Island of Bacalieu and the main land ; then crossed the spacious Bay of Trinity, and entered the beautiful and picturesque Harbor of Trinity, where she remained for a time, then returned to St. Johns. This was the first opportunity the people of Newfoundland ever had of making a steamboat trip on their own shores.

The first royal mail-steamer ever employed in Newfoundland was the North America, Captain R. Meagher. She arrived in St. Johns at eight o'clock on Monday morning, April 22d, 1844 ; since which time steamboat communication has been regular between that harbor and Halifax.

In the year 1860, on the occasion of the visit of His Royal Highness, the Prince of Wales, to America, his first landing was at St. Johns, on the morning of July 4th. The city was handsomely decorated with triumphal arches, flags, and evergreens, and the multitude was so great, that it seemed as if the whole population of the island had gathered in that city to welcome their future king. Amidst the thunder of cannon, the ringing of bells, and the cheers of thousands, His Royal Highness was received by Governor Bannerman, and a guard of honor, formed by the Newfoundland corps, and escorted to Government House by a long and splendid procession. After the presentation of addresses by different bodies, the Prince held a levee, at which were introduced to His Royal Highness the principal gentlemen of the island. He then reviewed the Royal Newfoundland and Volunteer corps, visited Waterford Bridge, Topsail Rood, and other points affording good views, and returned to a state dinner. In the evening, the city was brilliantly illuminated, and there was a fine display of fireworks. The next day, a noble Newfoundland dog was presented to the Prince, by Chief Justice Sir Francis Brady, on behalf of the people of the colony. The Prince accepted the dog, and called him *Cabot*, after the discoverer of the island. After a short visit, His Royal Highness embarked for the continent amidst the renewed cheers of the loyal and noble-hearted people of Newfoundland.

We shall here close our historical sketch, and present the reader with the following statistics.

A Table showing the Civil Divisions, Population, and Representatives for each District.

1857. Names of Districts.	No. of Inhabitants.	No. of Representatives.
St. Johns, East	17,352	3
St. Johns, West	13,124	3
Harbor Main, Conception Bay	5,386	2
Port-de-Grave, " "	6,489	1
Harbor Grace, " "	10,067	–
Carbonear, " "	5,233	1
Bay-de-Verds, " "	6,220	1
Trinity Bay	10,736	3
Bonavista	8,850	3
Twillingate and Fogo	9,717	2
Ferryland	5,228	2
Placentia and St. Mary's	8,334	3
Burin	5,529	2
Fortune Bay	3,492	1
Burgeo and La Poile	3,545	1
TOTAL.	119,304	28

To the population of the Elective Districts . . 119,304

We must add the population (British) on the French
    shore 3,334

Therefore, the total population of 1857 was . 122,638

Of this population, the Roman Catholics are estimated
at 55,309

Protestants 63,995
                                                ———
    Total 119,304

The Protestants are thus divided : —

Episcopalians . . .	42,608
Wesleyans	20,144
Presbyterians . . .	822
Congregationalists . . .	344
Baptists	77
TOTAL . .	63,995

No. of Clergymen : —

Roman Catholics . . .	36
Episcopal	40
Wesleyan	22
Presbyterian	3
Congregational . . .	0
Baptist	0
TOTAL . . .	101

N.B.—No Return of Religious Profession from the French Shore.

A Tabular Statement of Academical Institutions in Newfoundland.

NAME.	Situation.	No. of Profrs.	No. of Studts.	Government aid.	Voluntary aid.
Academy, Epis'palian	St. Johns	2	44	$2,000	$21
Bonavista Coll., R. C.	"	4	79	4,384	2,748
Academy, Wesleyan	"	2	69	1,000	500
Academy, Gen. Prot.	"	1	30	750	750
TOTAL. . .		9	222	8,134	4,019

In the year 1857 there were two hundred and fifty-seven Day Schools, as shown in the following table:—

Tabular View of Protestant Day Schools in 1861.

Denomination.	No. of Schools.	Pupils.	Cost.
Church of England . . .	2	108	
Wesleyan	8	593	
Presbyterian	1	61	
OTHER SCHOOLS.			
Colonial Church Society .	24	2524	
Elementary Schools . . .	108	4968	
Commercial Schools . .	4	159	
TOTAL . . .	147	8413	$26,500

Catholic Schools in 1861.

	No. of Schools.	Pupils.	Cost.
Commercial Schools . . .	7		
Convent Schools . . .	10	1360	
Elementary	93		
	110	5028	$20,495

Thus the total number of schools in the island, in 1861, was 257; of pupils, 13,441; and the total cost, $46,995.

The teachers' salaries vary from twenty to sixty pounds sterling; and are made up partly by government and partly by school fees.

The government contributes one-half the cost of erecting school-houses.

There are in the Province forty-one school-districts, twenty-five of which are under a Protestant Board of

Education and Inspection, and sixteen under the control of a Catholic Board and a Catholic Inspection. The government appropriates annually £400 toward the training of Protestant teachers, who may be trained in either of the Protestant Academies; and £350 for Catholic teachers, who are trained in the Catholic College.

THE FISHERIES.

The fisheries of Newfoundland are known as the "bank-fishery," and the "shore-fishery."

THE BANK-FISHERY.

This is carried on in large vessels on the Banks of Newfoundland, a vast submarine elevation, lying in the Atlantic Ocean, and between five and six hundred miles in length, with a breadth of about two hundred miles. In the year 1775, about four hundred sail of vessels, of from eighty to one hundred and forty tons burthen, were engaged in the bank-fishery, of which about one hundred and forty were fitted out from St. Johns, and the remainder from various out-harbors. These employed from eight to ten thousand fishermen and shoremen. This fishery is now almost abandoned by the British, but is carried on with great vigor by the French and Americans, who together are said to employ one thousand vessels, with some thirty thousand men.

SHORE-FISHERY.

This is now *the fishery* in Newfoundland: it is carried on in small craft, as skiffs, jacks, punts, and gallopers, who fish near the shore.

In 1857, the number of boats employed was eleven thousand six hundred and eighty-three; the number of nets and seines, two thousand three hundred and fifty-four; the number of men, twenty-four thousand.

We shall now present two tables : the first will show the quantity and value of *codfish* exported each year, for ten years; the second table will show the quantity and value of *all kinds of produce* exported, each year, for four years.

A Tabular Statement of the Quantity and Value of Codfish exported from Newfoundland each year, for ten years.

Years.	Quintals.	Value in Dollars.
1853	922,718	2,805,500
1854	774,118	2,589,090
1855	1,107,388	3,400,415
1856	1,268,334	3,945,620
1857	1,392,322	5,030,645
1858	1,038,089	3,825,505
1859	1,105,793	4,474,830
1860	1,138,544	4,231,190
1861	1,021,720	3,341,315
1862	1,074,289	3,760,010

Tabular Statement of all kinds of Produce exported from Newfoundland each year, for four years, with the total Value in British sterling.

PRODUCE.	YEARS.			
	1836	1845	1858	1861
Codfish, dried, quintals,	860,354	1,000,233	1,058,059	1,021,720
" pickled, tubs, .	. . . . .	442	1,688	cwt. 372
Salmon, tierces, ...	1,847	3,545	2,726	2,924
Herring, barrels, ...	1,534	20,903	82,155	64,377
No. of Seal Skins, ...	384,321	352,702	507,626	375,282
No. of Furs, ...	2,959	2,037	2,004	3,886
Seal and Cod Oil, tuns, .	. . . . .	8,408	. . . . .	8,375
Other Oils, gallons, . . .	41,872	. . . . .	323,241	tuns 23
Total value, £, ...	807,829	907,112	1,280,343	1,269,546

In the year 1862, there were 26 vessels built on the island, the total tonnage of which was 2,786 tons, and cost $3,580.

The imports for 1862 were $5,035,410; exports, $5,858,615; which is a balance in favor of exports of $823,205. Number of vessels employed, 1,386; tonnage, 87,030.

The mines and minerals, just now coming into notice, are likely to increase the exports.

The revenue of 1862 was $581,638; the expenditure, $690,290. The public debt is stated at $720,000.

BANKS.

There are three banks: the Union Bank circulated notes in 1861 to the extent of $472,520; the Commercial Bank, $213,628. The assets of the Savings Bank, in 1860, amounted to $744,504; and its liabilities were $671,792.

It has been customary to speak of Newfoundland, with its commanding position, its numerous fine harbors, and its salubrious climate, as a barren and inhospitable island, totally unfit for the habitation of man. Such misrepresentations could only have been made from sheer ignorance, or by interested parties, who sought the monopoly of the entire trade. It is now evident that many parts of the island are capable of a high state of cultivation; and its fisheries are an inexhaustible source of wealth; while its mines and its minerals are likely soon to attract at least a portion of the European immigrants, to seek their *pile* upon the mountains, or in the dells of its rock-bound shores. The inhabitants have always been loyal, brave, kind, and respectful; and, if the charge of ignorance or rudeness could be sustained, it was because they had been neglected, misgoverned and oppressed. A brighter day is dawning; and that land will yet rise in wealth, intelligence, and influence, equal to any of her sister Provinces in the Western hemisphere.

END OF PART I.

PART II.

/

THE CENTENARY;

OR, THE HISTORY OF WESLEYAN METHODISM DURING THE
HUNDRED YEARS OF ITS EXISTENCE IN NEWFOUNDLAND;
WITH BIOGRAPHICAL SKETCHES OF ALL THE DECEASED
WESLEYAN MISSIONARIES AND MINISTERS WHO HAVE
LABORED IN THAT COUNTRY.

.

(103)

CHAPTER I.

STATE OF RELIGION IN ENGLAND — ENGLISH CLERGY — RISE OF METHOD-
ISM — LAY PREACHERS — PERSECUTION — JOHN NELSON — FIRST CON-
FERENCE.

THIS year, 1865, is the centenary year of Methodism in Newfoundland. It was introduced there in 1765: it is, therefore, now in the hundredth year of its existence, and was the first mission ground ever occupied by the Wesleyan Church.

The rise of Wesleyan Methodism in England, during the first half of the last century, was in a pre-eminent sense providential, and showed, in all its outlines and general operations, the constant presence of the Great Head of the Christian Church.

The reformation from Popery had done much, both on the Continent and in England, to dissipate those dense clouds of moral darkness with which that corrupt system had cast all Europe in a deep gloom ; and in the latter country, in the eighteenth century, at its very commencement, it had nearly annihilated all the influence of Romanism ; it had established a Protestant monarchy on the throne ; it had formed a national protestant church, with a most admirable scriptural liturgy ; it had given the Bible to the people in their own language ; it had required the observance of the Christian Sabbath by law ; it had recently *tolerated* dissenters from the established church, who worshipped God according to the dictates of their own conscience ; and

while the astronomical and other discoveries of Sir Isaac
Newton had filled the world with astonishment, philol-
ogy, philosophy, and *belles lettres* were cultivated to an
extent that caused that period to be distinguished as
the " Augustan age of English literature. ' Giant
minds and champions for the truth lived in those days ;
and among them we might name Archbishop Secker,
Bishops Burnet, Gibson, Butler, and a little later, that
great expositor of Scripture prophecy, Bishop Newton ;
also Dean Prideaux, Dr. John Guyse, Dr. Isaac Watts,
Rev. John Hurrion, Rev. Abraham Taylor, and many
others, who faithfully preached the gospel in their several pulpits, and fearlessly assailed the carelessness, the
infidelity, and the licentiousness of the age. But England was not evangelized : far from it. Infidel books
were extensively circulated, and infidel principles were
entertained by masses of the British people ; the wicked
and blasphemous writings of Hobbes, Toland, Blount,
Collins, Mandeville, Tindal, Morgan, Woolston, Chubb,
and a little later appeared among the foes of Christianity,
that keen philosopher and eloquent writer, Lord Bol-
ingbroke ; and the moral poison these men scattered
abroad had effected the minds of the upper classes of
society to a great extent. Within the pale of the church,
and acknowledged as its ministers, were Dean Swift and
Lawrence Sterne, whose writings, so full of burlesque,
ribaldry, and licentious humor, tended fearfully to corrupt the morals of the nation. Deadly heresy was also
tolerated in the pulpits of the establishment. The very
learned Dr. Samuel Clarke, rector of St. James, Westminster, was a decided Arian, and so was the erudite
William Whiston ; and Bishop Hoadley is said to have
given up all that is peculiar to Christianity, in compliment to the Deists, and to have espoused substantially

the Socinian heresy, while at the same time he retained his office and preferment. Little was heard from the pulpit of the cardinal doctrine of "justification by faith," or gospel holiness. Many of the clergy were ignorant of the Scriptures, and seemed to think the instruction of the people in the truths of Christianity was not their work ; that they held their position merely as *a living ;* and that they could indulge in the wine-cup, in the chase, at the card-table, at the ball-room, or in almost any other way, providing they could go through their round of official duties on the Sabbath day. With such unscriptural teaching in the pulpits, such formality and often immorality in the clergy, it were vain to look for true religious feeling, to any extent, among the laity ; hence the people, while they called themselves churchmen, and attended to all the services and ceremonies enjoined in the Book of Common Prayer, were yet grossly ignorant of the Holy Scriptures, and immoral and vicious in the extreme. Men of rank and fashion laughed at religion, and the common people literally wallowed in sin. Johnson once said to Boswell: " I remember when all the *decent* people in Lichfield used to get drunk every night, and were not thought the worse for it." [1]

That we have not overdrawn the picture, the reader will admit, if he carefully peruses the following statements, made and published by different eminent bishops in the establishment, who lived in those times.

The first evidence we shall give is from a work by Gilbert Burnet, Bishop of Salisbury, called " The Pastoral Care," first published in the year 1692, a third edition of which was issued in 1713. In the preface

---

[1] Boswell's Johnson, vi. p. 340.

to this edition, Bishop Burnet gives the following description of the clergy of his own diocese: —

"I am now in the seventieth year of my age, and, as I cannot speak long in the world in any sort, so I cannot hope for a more solemn occasion than this of speaking with all due freedom, both to the present and to the succeeding ages.   Therefore I lay hold on it to give free vent to those *sad thoughts* that lie on my *mind both day and night*, and are the subject of many secret mournings. I dare appeal to that God, to whom the secrets of my heart are known, and to whom I am shortly to give an account of my ministry, that I have the true interests of this church ever before my eyes, and that I pursue them with a sincere and fervent zeal.

"If I am mistaken in the methods I follow, God, to whom the integrity of my heart is known, will not lay that to my charge.

"I cannot look on without the deepest concern, when I *see imminent ruin hanging over this church*, and by consequence, over the whole Reformation.   The *outward* state of things is black enough, God knows; but that which *heightens* my fears rises chiefly *from the inward state into which we are unhappily fallen.   I will confine myself to the clergy.*

"Our Ember weeks are the burden and grief of my life.   The much greater part of those who come to be ordained are ignorant, to a degree not to be apprehended by those who are not obliged to know it.   The easiest part of knowledge is that to which they are the greatest strangers: I mean the plainest part of the Scriptures, which, they say in excuse for their ignorance, that their *Tutors in the Universities never mention the reading of to them;* so that they can give no account, or at least a very imperfect one, of the contents even of the Gospels.   Those who have read some few books, yet never seem to have read the Scriptures.   Many cannot give a tolerable account even of the Catechism itself, how short and plain soever.   They cry, and think it a sad disgrace to be denied orders, though the ignorance of some is such that, in a well-regulated state of things, they would appear *not knowing enough to be admitted to the holy sacrament.*

"This does often tear my heart.   The case is not much better in many who, having got into orders, come for institution, and cannot make it appear that they have read the Scriptures or any one good book since they were ordained; so that the small measure of knowledge upon which they got into holy orders not being improved, is in a way quite lost; and they think it a great hardship if they are told they must know the Scriptures and the body of divinity better before they can be trusted with the care of souls.

"These things pierce one's soul, and make him often cry out, 'Oh, that I had wings like a dove! for then would I fly away and be at rest.' What are we like to grow to? In what case are we to deal with any adversary, Atheist, Papist, or dissenter, or in any sort to promote the honor of God, and carry on the great concerns of the gospel, when so gross an ignorance in the fundamentals of religion has spread itself so much among those who ought to teach others, and yet need that one should teach them the first principles of the oracles of God.

"Politics and party eat out among us, not only study and learning, but that which is the only thing that is more valuable, a true sense of religion, with a sincere zeal in advancing that for which the Son of God both lived and died, and to which those who are received into holy orders have vowed to dedicate their lives and labors. Clamors of scandal in any of the clergy are not frequent, it is true, and God be thanked for it; but a remiss, unthinking course of life, with little or no application to study, and the bare performing of that which, if not done, would draw censures when complained of, without even pursuing the pastoral care in any suitable degree, is but too common as well as too evident."

If any writer in our day had given such a description of the Episcopal clergy of England at any time, or had declared that young men were accustomed to make application for holy orders, who were " ignorant of the contents of the Gospels," and " even of the Catechism," and who appear as not " knowing enough to be admitted to the holy sacrament;" and that after ordination, they continued in such a state of "gross ignorance in the fundamentals of religion," as themselves to need being taught the " first principles of the oracles of God;" such statements would be considered as untrue and slanderous: but coming from the pen of the great and good Bishop Burnet, who lived at the time, and wrote only what he knew, its truth cannot be questioned.

10

Of the morals of the people in the British metropolis, at that time, Bishop Gibson, in his " Pastoral Letters," published in 1728, gives the following account : —

" They who live in these great cities (London and Westminster), or have had frequent recourse to them, and have any concern for religion, must have observed, to their great grief, that *profaneness and impiety are grown bold and open ;* that a new sort of vice of a very horrible nature, and almost unknown before in these parts of the world, was springing up and gaining ground amongst us, if it had not been checked by the seasonable care of the civil administration ; that, in some late writings, *public stews have been openly vindicated,* and *public vices recommended to the protection of the government,* as *public benefits ;* and that great pains have been taken to *make men easy in their vices,* and deliver them from the restraints of conscience, by undermining all religion, and promoting atheism and infidelity."

Bishop Butler, the learned author of the " Analogy," in the advertisement to that work, published in 1736, speaks of the infidelity of his time, as follows : —

" It is come, I know not how, to be taken for granted by many persons, *that Christianity is not so much as a subject of inquiry ;* but that it is *now, at length, discovered to be fictitious.* And, accordingly, *they treat it as if, in the present age,* this were *an agreed point* among all *people of discernment,* and nothing remained *but to set it up as a principal subject of mirth and ridicule,* as it were *by way of reprisals,* for its having *so long interrupted the pleasures of the world."*

Archbishop Secker, in 1738, wrote the following sentence : —

" We cannot be mistaken, that *an open and professed disregard to religion is become,* through a variety of unhappy causes, *the distinguishing character of the present age ;* that this evil is grown to a great height in the metropolis of the nation, is daily spreading through every part of it, and, bad in itself as any can be, must, of necessity, bring in all others after it. Indeed, it hath already brought in such *dissoluteness* and *contempt of principle* in the *higher part* of the world, and such *profligate intemperance* and *fearlessness of committing crimes*, in the *lower*, as must, if this *torrent of impiety stop not*, become absolutely fatal."

We shall give one more quotation; and it will be from the pen of an eminent dissenting minister, whose name is known to every one, and whose praise is in all the churches. The writer is Dr. Isaac Watts, 1731:—

" Among the papers published last year, there hath been some inquiry made whether there be any decay of the 'dissenting interest,' and what may be supposed to have been the occasion of it. So far as I have searched into that matter, I have been informed, that, whatsoever decrease may have appeared in some places, there have been sensible advances in others. And without entering into any debate about the particular reasons of its declension in any town whatever, I am well satisfied that the great and general reason is the *decay of vital religion* in the *hearts and lives of men*, and the little success which the ministrations of the gospel have had of late for the conversion of sinners to holiness, and the recovery of them from the state of corrupt nature, and the course of this world, to the life of God by Jesus Christ.

" Nor is the complaint of the *declension of virtue and piety* made only by the Protestant dissenters. It is a general matter of mournful observation amongst all that lay the cause of God to heart; and therefore it cannot be thought amiss for every one to use all just and proper efforts for the *recovery of dying religion in the world*." [1]

Such was the state of England and the English church, sinking into infidelity and ruin, when God, in his providence and mercy, raised up the Wesleys to reform the nation; to rescue the masses from their viciousness and moral degradation; to confront the infidelity of the times; and by preaching the plain doctrines of the New Testament, and of the Reformation, be the means of diffusing spiritual life through the churches, both of the Establishment and of the Ortho-

[1] Preface to An Humble Attempt towards the Revival of Practical Religion, edition, 1735.

dox Dissenters.   Justification by faith, regeneration, the witness of the .spirit, and gospel holiness were the great truths these men proclaimed.   They were not new doctrines, though many thought they were.   They were precisely what the apostles preached, what the Reformers preached, and are found in every article, in every homily, and on every page of the English Liturgy ; yet such was the ignorance of many of the clergy that they closed their pulpits against those who preached these doctrines, denounced them as heretical, the preachers as heretics, " enemies to the church," " Papists in disguise," " rebels to the government," and men whom they might malign, ridicule, insult, and persecute at their pleasure.

But the common people " heard " them gladly.   They were first astonished at what they heard ; then wondered why they had not heard the same things from their own ministers.   They pondered these doctrines in their minds ; they found they were scriptural : deep conviction of sin followed ; and men in multitudes were turned " from darkness to light, and from the power of Satan to God."   " In the latter end of the year 1739 eight or ten persons came " to Mr. Wesley " in London, who appeared to be deeply convinced of sin, and earnestly groaning for redemption.   They desired (as did two or three more the next day) that I would spend some time with them in prayer, and advise them how to flee from the wrath to come, which they saw continually hanging over their heads.   That we might have more time for this great work, I appointed a day when they might all come together, which, from thenceforward, they did every week, viz., on Thursday evening. To these, and as many as desired to join with them (for their number increased daily), I gave those advices from time to time which I judged most needful for them ; and we always concluded our meetings with prayer suited to their several necessities."

This was the origin of the Wesleyan societies all over the world. The term *church* was not used for many years after to any association connected with Method-ism. They were simply *societies* connected with the Church of England, from which they possibly might never have been separated had it not been for the persecuting spirit evinced by the ministers of that church.

What was called " lay-preaching," that is, preaching by men who had not been Episcopally ordained, was the means of extending Methodism in those early times. This was contrary to Mr. Wesley's early prejudices and fixed opinions ; and he at first set his face against such an innovation upon the office and dignity of the Chris-tian ministry. But the force of circumstances, with the wise and Christian counsel of his most Christian mother, overcame his prejudices, and caused him to submit.

" The first lay-preacher was Thomas Maxfield, a young man who had been converted under Mr. John Wesley's preaching, at Bristol, in May, 1739. He became deeply pious ; prayed, ex-horted, and expounded the Scriptures, with uncommon power. He was appointed to assist in the society in London, in the ab-sence of the Wesleys; and there he began to preach. Complaint of this was forwarded to Mr. Wesley, who hastened to London, with all speed, to stop this irregularity. His mother then lived in London. On his arrival, he said to her : ' Thomas Maxfield has turned preacher, I find.' She looked attentively at him, and re-plied : ' John, you know what my sentiments have been ; you can-not suspect me of favoring readily anything of this kind ; but take care what you do with respect to that young man ; for he is as surely called of God to preach as you are ! Examine what have been the fruits of his preaching, and hear him also yourself.'

He took her advice, and submitted to what he believed to be the order of God." [1]

Soon after, other persons were employed in the same way, as Thomas Richards, Thomas Westell, and John Nelson, the famous Yorkshire stone-mason.

The employment of lay-preachers was soon sounded through the kingdom, was a high offence against high churchmen, and involved the Methodists almost everywhere in persecution and danger.

Every passing event was taken hold of that could in any way excite prejudice against the Methodists. The Pretender was raising a rebellion in the North, and England was threatened with an invasion from France and Spain. Reports the most absurd, and calumnies of all sorts, were now circulated against Mr. Wesley and the Methodists. It was said they were in collusion with the Pretender; that John Wesley had been seen with the Pretender, in France; he had been taken up for high-treason, and was in prison, awaiting his just doom; that he was a Jesuit, an agent of Spain, and received large sums from that country, in order to raise a body of twenty thousand men to aid a Spanish invasion; that he was an Anabaptist, a Quaker; that he had been prosecuted for unlawfully *selling gin;* and, to complete the whole, it was said that John Wesley had hanged himself, was dead and buried; that the present man was not the genuine John Wesley, but an impostor.

Outrageous as these stories were, they were believed; and persecution of Methodist preachers and Methodist people was the consequence. Charles Wesley was

[1] Moor's Life of Wesley, vol. i. p. 507.

actually indicted before the magistrates, in Yorkshire, because, in public, he had prayed that the Lord " would call home his banished ones." [1]

In Staffordshire, the Methodists were assailed, not only in their assemblies, but in their homes and in the public streets. In Dorlston, women were knocked down, and abused in a manner, says Mr. Wesley, " too horrible to be related." [2] Houses were broken into, furniture broken, and thrown into the street; and one person was denied shelter in his own father's dwelling, for fear the house would be torn down.

In Wedensbury, the disorders were frightful. The mob assaulted all the houses of those who were called Methodists. They broke the windows, suffering neither glass, lead, or frame to remain. They entered the houses, and dashed in pieces tables, chairs, chests-of-drawers, and shop-goods. They cut up feather-beds and strewed the feathers about the room.

One poor woman was confined at the time. No matter: they pulled away her bed, and cut it in pieces. Wearing apparel and valuables they took away: men and women fled for their lives. The mob divided into several companies, and marched from village to village, within a range of four or five miles, until the whole region was in a state of tumult.

These disgraceful proceedings were instigated by the *gentlemen* of the place, who drew up a paper, requiring persons to sign it, importing that they would never again invite a Methodist preacher to their dwelling; and they were assured that if they signed that paper, the proceedings of the mob should at once be checked; otherwise, they must take what might follow. This,

---

[1] Life Charles Wesley, vol. i. p. 378.   [2] Journal, 1745.

the persecuted Methodists refused with indignation, and replied : " We have already lost all our goods, and nothing more can follow but the loss of our lives, which we will lose too, rather than wrong our consciences."

At Dudley, a lay preacher was cruelly abused, at the instigation of *the parish minister*, and would probably have been murdered, had not an honest Quaker enabled him to escape, disguised in his broad-brimmed hat and plain coat.[1]

At Wedensbury, none of the magistrates were willing to protect the Methodists : on the contrary, one of these functionaries declared that their treatment was just, and offered five pounds to have them driven out of the town. Another refused to hear a Methodist who came to take oath that his life was in danger ; and a third *delivered a member of the society up to the mob*, and waving his hand over his head, shouted, " Huzza, boys ! Well done ! Stand up for the church."

The storm raged in Cornwall ; and in St. Ives the chapel was nearly destroyed. Mr. Wesley went there, and on arriving at the house of one of the Methodists, where the society was waiting for him, he was received " with a loud though not a bitter cry ; but they soon recovered, and we poured out our souls together in praises and thanksgiving." As soon as the people went out, they were saluted with huzzas, stones, and dirt. Mr. Wesley was surprised at the Christian meekness and patience with which these converted miners, once degraded and violent men themselves, now endured persecution " for righteousness sake." Some who had been the worst of the rabble had become the most exemplary sufferers. The Methodists of St. Just had

---

[1] Jackson's Life of Charles Wesley, chap. ii.

been the chief of the whole country for hurling, fighting, drinking, and all manner of wickedness; but many of the lions had become lambs, and were continually praising God, and calling their old companions in sin, to come and " magnify the Lord together."

On a public fast day, appointed to pray for the safety of the nation, against the threatened invasion, Mr. Wesley listened to a sermon in the Church of St. Ives, in which the Methodists were denounced as enemies of the church and state, Jacobites and Papists.

John Nelson was a man of good sense, cool courage, sound piety, and apt in speech. He spread. Methodism extensively in Yorkshire, Cornwall, Lincolnshire, Lancashire, and other counties, laboring at his trade by day, and preaching every night. As might be expected, he was severely persecuted. At Grimsby, the parish clergyman hired a man to beat the town drum; and himself went before it, gathering together the rabble, giving them liquor to go with him, and "fight for the church!" When they came to Nelson's lodgings, they gave three huzzas, and their clerical leader cried out to them to pull down the house; but no one offered to touch it till Nelson had done preaching, when they broke the windows, leaving not one whole square in the building. The people were assailed as they went out; but the mob began to fight one with the other, by which the preacher and his hearers were allowed to escape. Soon the minister gathered the rioters again, and gave them more drink, when they broke the stanchions of the windows, pulled up the paving in the street, threw stones into the house, demolished the furniture : and after five hours of tumult, they dispersed. But the next morning the clergyman was again at his work, when he hired the town drummer to

disturb Nelson while preaching. The man, after beating
his drum for three quarters of an hour around the congregation, threw away the drum, and stood listening
with tears running down his cheeks.

He went to Epworth, where both the clerk and the
clergyman of the parish were drunkards. The former
ran, as Nelson was preaching in the open air, and cried
to the congregation to make way, that he might reach
the itinerant, and carry him before his master, who was
at the village ale-house. The people stood up for the
eloquent stone-mason, and bade the clerk go about his
business. Still he continued his interruptions, until a
sturdy man took him up and threw him upon a dung-
hill.

At Birstal, which was his home, he was warned that
he should be impressed for the army if he did not
escape immediately. His reply was, "I cannot fear,
for God is on my side, and his word hath added
strength to my soul this day." He was seized the
next day, while preaching at Adwalton, and was
marched off to Halifax, where the Birstal vicar was on
the bench as one of the commissioners, who reported
Nelson as a " vagrant, without visible means of living."
He replied, " I am as able to get my living by my
hands as any man of my trade in England is, *and you
know it.*" But he was taken to Bradford, and plunged
into a dungeon, into which flowed blood and filth from
a slaughter-house above it, "so that it smelt," he says,
" like a pig-stye; but my soul," he adds, " was so filled
with the love of God, that it was a paradise to me."
There was nothing for him to sit on, and his only bed
was a heap of decayed straw. The people handed him
food, water, and candles through a hole in the door,
and stood outside joining him in hymns most of the

night. He shared their charities with a miserable fellow-prisoner, who might have starved had it not been for his kindness.

We will here mention the heroic conduct of Nelson's excellent wife. The next morning after his imprisonment in Bradford jail, she came to see him. She had two young children to provide for, and soon expected another. Addressing him through the hole in the door, " Fear not," she said, " the cause is God's for which you are here, and he will plead it himself. Therefore, be not concerned about me and the children, for he that feeds the young ravens will be mindful of us. He will give you strength for your day ; and after we have suffered awhile, he will perfect what is lacking in our souls, and bring us where the wicked cease from troubling and where the weary are at rest." " I cannot fear," he responded ; " I cannot fear either man or devil, so long as I find the love of God as I now do."

Nelson was compelled to go into the ranks as a soldier, and, after suffering in various ways, at the end of three months he was released through the influence of Lady Huntington.[1]

But the persecution of Methodism in no way retarded its progress : it was the work of the Lord, and it prospered against all opposition. Many thousands were converted from the error of their ways ; many societies were formed in different parts of the kingdom ; and many who had once been its opposers now became its friends, believing it to be a revival of primitive Christianity. " So mightily grew the word of God, and prevailed."

---

[1] See History of Methodism, by Abel Stevens, LL.D., book ii. chap. vi.

On Monday, June 25th, 1744, the first Methodist conference met at the Foundry, in Moorfields, London. This place was called the Foundry, because it had been used by the government for founding cannon. The building had been repaired, and altered into a place of worship, and was the first Methodist chapel in England. Its site was only a short distance from City Road Chapel, the present head-quarters of Methodism.

The first conference consisted only of clergymen who had been especially ordained, and were six in number. Jackson says, in his life of Charles Wesley, vol. i. p. 387 : " No layman was present in that assembly."[1] The six clergymen were, John Wesley, Charles Wesley ; John Hodges, Rector of Wenro ; Henry Piers, Vicar of Bexley ; Samuel Taylor, Vicar of Quinton ; and John Meriton.

Mr. Hodges was the Rector of Wenro, in South Wales, whose heart and house were always open to receive the Wesleys, when they visited the Principality. Mr. Piers, Vicar of Bexley, and his wife, were both brought to the knowledge of the truth by the instrumentality of Charles Wesley. Mr. Samuel Taylor, Vicar of Quinton, near Evesham, in Worcestershire, is said to have been a descendant of the celebrated Rowland Taylor, who was burned alive for his Protestantism, in the reign of Queen Mary. Of Mr. John Meriton little is known, only he is spoken of as " a clergyman from the Isle of Man."

---

[1] Dr. Stevens thinks this is an error, because a pamphlet has been found by Rev. J. Hargreaves, entitled the " Disciplinary Minutes," which gives information not found in regular minutes of conference. It, however, is a fact, that all the official records only name *six clergymen* as connected with the first conference. Dr. Stevens thinks that Maxfield, Thomas Richards, John Bennet, and John Downes, were also present.

This conference sat five days, during which time the doctrines of Methodism were thoroughly examined by the test of Holy Scriptures ; and a basis laid down, upon which its whole disciplinary superstructure has since been raised.

This little band, of only six men, was the nucleus of the great Wesleyan Church, which since, and in the space of a century and a quarter, has spread, not only through every part of the British Empire, but on the Continent of America, where it wields a mighty influence : its missionaries are in all lands, and its adherents are numbered by millions. " What hath God wrought ! "

> " Saw ye not the cloud arise,
>   Little as a human hand ?
>   Now it spreads along the skies,
>   Hangs o'er all the thirsty land."

11

CHAPTER II.

THE first Methodist conference being over, three of
the clergymen who composed it, namely, Messrs.
Hodges, Piers, and Taylor, returned to their respective
parishes, there to preach those soul-saving doctrines
which, in conference, they had so thoroughly examined; while the Wesleys, now accompanied by the
Rev. John Meriton, scattered the same heavenly seed
broadcast, as they itinerated through every part of the
United Kingdom. True, persecution raged fearfully;
many suffered in their property or in their persons;
and some actually died through the violence of lawless
mobs; yet they bore insults and injuries patiently, or
" took joyfully the spoiling of their goods," because
God was honored by the preaching of his word. " And
the hand of the Lord was with them, and a great number believed, and turned unto the Lord."

The rapid success of Methodism, and the influence
it has acquired, has astonished the world. The cause
of that success is, under God, attributable to its doctrines, its discipline, and the various agents it employs.
Its doctrines are only those of the New Testament:
they have often been assailed, but have never been dis-
proved. Its discipline has preserved its institutions;
and its agents have been so diversified, as either directly

or indirectly, to act upon all classes of society. And as the rays of the sun, when they come in contact with our atmosphere, are reflected and refracted, until the whole earth is illuminated ; so with the early Methodist preachers, some were directly instructed by them, others indirectly ; but, in whatever way, light was thereby diffused abroad until it has permeated every evangelical church in Christendom, and produced a great moral effect, unparalleled in the whole history of the church, since apostolical times.

In the year 1747, three years after the formation of the first conference, Methodism found its way to, and took its stand in, Ireland. Sometime in the month of July, Thomas Williams, one of Mr. Wesley's lay-preachers, came to Ireland, and preached in Dublin. He was a zealous man, and both a useful and a popular preacher. His labors were blessed, and a small society was soon formed. Three weeks after, Mr. Wesley visited Dublin, personally examined the society, and pronounced them " strong in faith." He also said the Irish were the politest people he had ever seen. This was the first visit of the founder of Methodism to the sister isle. The first preachers there had great persecution to endure, but their labors were attended with much success.

About five years from this time, two young men were awakened, and brought to a knowledge of the truth. Neither of them was particularly distinguished either for learning or talents in any way ; yet were they to be the means, in the hand of Divine Providence, of giving birth to Methodism in the Western Hemisphere. These young men were Lawrence Coughlan and Philip Embury. The former planted

Methodism in Newfoundland ; and the year following the latter did the same in the city of New York.

Methodism was introduced into Newfoundland in the year 1765, and into New York in 1766. One year is the only difference; but the seniority must be *claimed for Newfoundland.* In both cases, the agents were Irishmen.

Although Methodism in New York was the second in order of time, yet we shall first give a synopsis of its early history there, to avoid interruption in our narrative of Newfoundland.

In the reign of Queen Anne, a number of German Protestants left the Palatinate, their native home, with the view of settling in America, but were driven by stress of weather on the western coast of Ireland. Lord Southwell was there; and, feeling for their distress, he offered them land on reasonable terms, if they would settle on his estates in the County of Limerick. They accepted his offer. Twenty families settled at Court-matris ; twenty more at Killeheen, a mile off; fifty at Balligarane, two miles eastward ; and twenty at Pollar, four miles farther, — all in the County of Limerick. These Germans had no minister of their own, and no religious ordinances among them ; and " they soon became eminent for drunkenness, cursing, swearing, and utter contempt for all religion." [1] For more than forty years did these people live in this state. " No man cared for their souls." But sometime in 1749, Thomas Williams preached in the street in the town of Limerick, when he showed that " Christ crucified " is the only foundation of the Christian's faith, and hope of eternal salvation. Several of the Palatines were

---

[1] Wesley's works, vol. iii. p. 336. See also Methodist Magazine for 1825, p. 597.

there. After the sermon they said to each other,
"*This is like the preaching we used to hear in Ger-
many*." The result was, they invited the preacher to
visit their settlements. He did so, and so likewise
did that distinguished and holy man, Robert Swindells. The next year Mr. Wesley visited Court-
matris, when he found the people had built a Methodist chapel, and that many of them had been awakened
and converted to God.

Among the converts was Philip Embury, a carpen-
ter by trade, and a young man in the twenty-second
year of his age. Soon after his conversion, Mr. Embury began to act as a local preacher, in which capacity
he continued to exercise his talents for several years.
Among those who emigrated from Ireland to New
York in the year 1760 was this same Philip Embury,
who, in the land of his adoption, became the honored
instrument of introducing Methodism into the United
States of America, and in laying the foundation of that
mighty organization, now known as the Methodist Episcopal Church.

It must, however, be related, that Mr. Embury did
not commence preaching immediately on his arrival in
America ; so far from it, that he was then a backslider
from God. America was not only a strange land to him,
but it was then morally a dark land ; and he allowed
six years to roll over, ere he bore his public testimony
against sin, or undertook to point sinners to the " Lamb
of God, which taketh away the sin of the world."

Some five or six years after Mr. Embury arrived, two
other German-Irish families came, of the names of
Heck and Dean, who seem to have retained more of
that religious influence which they had experienced in
Ireland than any of their emigrant brethren who had

preceded them. Some time in the year 1766, a party of these emigrants had so far forgot the teaching they had enjoyed under John Wesley, Robert Swindells, and Thomas Williams, as to be found playing at cards; and when they were so engaged, Mrs. Heck entered the house, and with holy indignation, she swept the cards into the fire, and warned her friends of their guilt and danger. She then went to Mr. Embury, and said to him, " Brother Embury, you must preach to us, or we shall go to hell, and God will require our blood at your hands."

This reproof was effectual in arousing the latent zeal of this, at least partially, fallen man; for, in a few days afterwards, he commenced preaching in his own house, to a congregation of *only five persons.* This was the first Methodist sermon ever preached on the *continent* of America.

The number of hearers soon increased; some back-sliders were restored; sinners were awakened and converted to God, and, before the close of the year 1766, a society was organized in New York, which was the first fruits of Methodism in the then " far West."

Soon Embury's house was found too small, when a room was hired near the military barracks; but this was also too small. A rigging-loft was next procured, which was still small for the constantly increasing congregation. The open fields were then taken, where to proclaim the words of life and salvation. About this time, Captain Webb arrived in New York. He was a British military officer, and had been in the campaign in Canada, in 1758; was at the conquest of Quebec with General Wolfe, where he received a wound in his arm, and lost his right eye. He returned to England with his regiment; and, under the preaching of

Mr. Wesley in Bristol, he was converted, and shortly after he began to preach. He was sent to New York on military duty. He at once united himself with the little Methodist society there, and began to preach in his uniform. The cause now prospered, so that a regular Methodist chapel was designed, — a building sixty feet by forty, with galleries on three sides. This chapel was opened for divine service, by Mr. Embury, on the thirtieth of October, 1768. This was the first house of worship the Methodists ever owned in America. It was called Wesley Chapel; but afterwards it was named "The John Street Methodist Church."

Captain Webb and his friends now applied to Mr. Wesley, to " send them an able and experienced preacher, a man of wisdom, of sound faith, a good disciplinarian, and whose heart and soul were in the work." This strong appeal was followed by a second letter, in which occurs the following sentence : " With respect to money for the payment of the preacher's passage over, if they could not procure it, we would sell our coats, and so procure it for them."

At that time the conference was pressed down with a heavy debt, which crippled its energies, and induced much privation among the preachers. This debt was caused mostly by payments for building chapels and preachers' houses. In 1766, the total amount of debt was £ 11,383. It was at this conference, that Mr. Wesley said: " We shall be utterly ruined, if we go on thus. How may we prevent the increase of debt ?

" Ans. 1. Let no other building be undertaken, till two thirds of the money are subscribed.

" 2. We will allow nothing to any house which

shall be begun after this day, till the debt is reduced to
£ 3000.

" 3. Let every preacher labor with all his might, to
increase the collection next year."

By very strenuous efforts, the two following years,
the debt was considerably reduced ; yet, at the conference of 1769, the remaining debt was between five and
six thousand pounds. Notwithstanding this financial
difficulty, the magnanimous and Christian heart of
John Wesley was moved by the powerful appeals from
America : he knew the men, he knew their wants, he
knew the country ; and he determined to send them
help.

He therefore brought the matter before the conference.   The manner in which he did this was remarkable.   There appears to have been no canvassing or
discussion of the matter previously, but it came up as
an ordinary conference question.   The following is the
simple statement in the minutes : —

Ques. 10. What is contributed towards the debt ?
Ans. £2,458 19s. 7d.
Ques. 11. How was this distributed ?
Ans. As follows : [Then a list of appropriations is given, by
which the whole amount is expended.]
Ques. 12. What is reserved for contingent expenses ?
Ans. Nothing.
Ques. 13. We have a pressing call from our brethren at New
York (who have built a preaching-house) to come over and help
them.   Who is willing to go ?

It is said, that when Mr. Wesley proposed this question, " *Who is willing to go?*" the conference was
silent; not a man spoke. The preachers were probably
taken by surprise ; besides which, the voyage to
America was then a formidable affair. The following
morning, Mr. Wesley preached at five o'clock, and

took for his text Isaiah i. 2: " I have nourished and brought up children, and they have rebelled against me." After this sermon, the question was again proposed, when the conference had assembled, and it was then that Boardman and Pilmoor offered their services; hence the answer to the question in the minutes: Richard Boardman and Joseph Pilmoor.

Ques. 14. What can we do further, in token of our brotherly love?

Ans. Let us now make a collection among ourselves.

This was immediately done; and out of it fifty pounds were allotted toward the payment of their debt, and about twenty pounds given to our brethren for their passage.[1]

This was the first missionary collection ever made in England; and, taking the number of men and their means into account, it was perhaps never exceeded. For, 1st. The Methodist preachers at that conference were poor men; or, if any of them had money, they would cheerfully give it to pay the enormous conference debt. 2d. None were at the conference but the assistants, or, as they are now called, superintendents of circuits. 3d. The number of assistants that year was, according to the minutes, thirty-seven; and supposing all the assistants in England were present at conference, which is not probable, the collection would average near eight dollars for each preacher.

It is a remarkable feature in this transaction, that, while the English conference had a debt of their own of between five and six thousand pounds, they yet sent fifty pounds to pay the debt of their brethren in New York.

Forty dollars to each of these missionaries was all that could be paid: a small amount, indeed, for an outfit

---

[1] Minutes, 1769.

and a passage to New York. Yet with this small sum did these intrepid servants of the cross leave their native shore to preach the gospel of Christ in that distant land. Soon after the close of conference, the Brothers Boardman and Pilmoor embarked for New York. They left on the 22d of August, and, after a tedious passage of nine weeks, landed at Gloucester Point, New Jersey, about six miles below Philadelphia, on the 24th of October; from whence they soon reached their place of destination, and immediately entered upon their missionary work.

On the 31st of October, one week after their arrival, Joseph Pilmoor wrote to Mr. Wesley, from which letter we make the following extract: —

"PHILADELPHIA, Oct. 31, 1769.

"REV. SIR, — By the blessing of God, we are safe arrived here, after a tedious passage of nine weeks.

"We were not a little surprised to find Capt. Webb in town, and a society of about one hundred members, who desire to be in close communion with you. This is the Lord's doing, and it is marvellous in our eyes."

Two years these missionaries labored; preaching alternately in New York and Philadelphia, when their hearts were cheered by the arrival of two more missionaries sent over by Mr. Wesley. These were Francis Ashbury, and Richard Wright. The Methodist itinerancy was now commenced in America. Mr. Pilmoor was appointed to travel south; and Mr. Boardman formed his circuit eastward. He introduced Methodism into the state of Massachusetts, and proceeded as far as the city of Boston, where he remained for a short time, preached with success, and formed a small society; when he returned to New York.

Such was the origin of Methodism in America, which,

notwithstanding the war of independence that soon
followed, struck deep into the American heart, so as to
influence its inhabitants to form the Methodist Episcopal Church, — a body of Christians which has spread
itself in every part of the United States, which numbers its ministers by thousands, its members by hundreds
of thousands, and its adherents by millions. It has its
colleges and its halls of literature in every State; it
has its several book-rooms, from whence issue its num-
berless publications to instruct the people in religion
and general knowledge, as well as to confront the dangerous sentiments sent forth to the world by a licentious
press; it has its divines in its pulpits, its judges on the
bench, and its statesmen in its senate. Moreover, it has
become, like its parent, a great missionary church. It
has its missions in almost every part of the earth,
speaking in many tongues the wonderful works of
God. It takes an important and very prominent part
in the affairs of the Bible Society, in the circulation of
tracts, in the temperance movement, and in every
other Christian, benevolent, and philanthropic object.
In fine, it seems one of the great organizations which
our heavenly Father will employ for the illumination
of the darkened minds of men, and for bringing the
nations of the earth to knowledge and experience of
evangelical truth.

Richard Boardman labored in America five years.
He returned to Europe in the beginning of the year
1774, and was appointed to the Londonderry Circuit.
He labored in different circuits in England and Ire-
land for eight years, and was suddenly called to his
reward on the 29th of September, 1782. He died in
Cork of an apoplectic fit. His last sermon was from
Job xiii. 15 : " Though he slay me, yet will I trust

in him." It was preached the evening before his death. He was said to have been a good preacher, and a man of great simplicity and sincerity of character. In the minutes of 1783, Mr. Wesley says of him : " He was a pious, good-natured, sensible man, greatly beloved of all who knew him."

Joseph Pilmoor was admitted on trial as a Methodist preacher at the conference of 1765. In his southern tour, as an American missionary, he preached in different parts of Maryland, Virginia, North and South Carolina, and Georgia as far as Savannah ; in which extensive circuit he spent four years, and returned with Richard Boardman to England. Thus the two first missionaries sent out by Mr. Wesley both went on their mission and returned in company, — a circumstance that has rarely, if it has ever, happened since. Mr. Pilmoor continued, for a few years, to travel and labor in connection with Mr. Wesley, as a Methodist preacher. But he afterwards returned to America, took orders in the Protestant Episcopal Church, and spent the remainder of his life in the cities of New York and Philadelphia, as an acceptable and efficient minister of that church. He lived to a good old age, and, it is believed, was beloved and respected by the people to whom he ministered to the end of his life ; and was instrumental in the conversion and salvation of many. The truly evangelical spirit produced through his instrumentality in the congregation over which he presided, and a correspondent attention to some of the peculiar means of grace which he introduced among them, continued to manifest themselves for a number of years after his death.[1]

_____

[1] Wesley's Missionaries to America, p. 28.

It would not be in accordance with our plan to extend our remarks on American Methodism. Suffice it to say, that we rejoice in its great prosperity. May it prosper yet more and more! Whatever difference national usages or peculiar localities may have made in the administration of Methodist discipline, Methodist doctrine is universally the same. The proper essential divinity of the Redeemer, the atonement of his precious blood, the universality of his salvation, justification by faith, the witness of the spirit, entire sanctification, with the everlasting beatification of the righteous, and the equally eternal punishment of the finally impenitent, are constantly heard from every Methodist pulpit upon earth. It is by the faithful preaching of these great truths that such multitudes have been " turned to the Lord ; " and if these same doctrines continue to be preached with faithfulness, with scriptural simplicity, and Christian zeal, they will continue to be blessed, and be the means of salvation of myriads of the present and of unborn generations.

12

METHODISM commenced in Newfoundland in the year 1765, under the ministration of the Rev. Lawrence Coughlan, who was connected with The Society for the Propagation of the Gospel in Foreign Parts.

This society was formed in the reign of King William III., and incorporated on the 16th of June, 1701. The design of its founders was to supply the British Colonies " with Episcopal ministers, catechists, and school-masters." [1] This society, from its commencement, was " High Church ; " yet it numbers among its originators and promoters the honored and pious Bishops Burnet, Beveridge, and Tennison. It opened a school in New York in 1704 ; and, the year following, it appointed a missionary to Newfoundland, whose parish, it is said, was the " whole island." We are not in possession of the name of this missionary, or any notation of his labors, or of the labors of his successors, if he had any, before the arrival of Mr. Coughlan.

Mr. Coughlan was an Irishman, and, like Philip Embury, was among the first fruits of Methodism in his native isle. After his conversion, he was called to the work of the ministry, and labored ten years as a trav-

---

[1] Propagation of Christianity by Brown, vol. ii. p. 657.
(134)

elling preacher in connection with Mr. Wesley. It is
no argument against this to say, the name Lawrence
Coughlan is not found in the Minutes of Conference,
for there is a chasm in our early minutes of sixteen
years.   "The doctrines and principal parts of the discipline of the Methodists being agreed upon, Mr. Wesley, it appears, discontinued publishing the minutes annually from 1749 till 1765 ; at least, if any were published, we cannot find that a single copy of them is extant." [1]   It was during ten of those years that Mr.
Coughlan was a Methodist preacher, and therefore his
name could not appear. Mr. Myles, in his " chronology,"
expressly says: " From 1755 to 1765, Mr. Lawrence
Coughlan travelled in the connection, and then separated from Mr. Wesley. [2]

We shall here insert two letters from Mr. Coughlan
to Mr. Wesley, while he was a travelling preacher, in
both of which we see the high state of his religious experience the second, in particular, shows that at the
time of writing it he lived in the enjoyment of perfect
love.

FROM MR. COUGHLAN TO REV. MR. WESLEY.

"January 26, 1762.

" REV. SIR, — I bless God, I do hold fast whereunto I have attained. Christ is all and in all to my soul. In all his works my
God I see, the object of my love. Two or three years ago, you
wrote the following words with a diamond pencil on a window in
Whitehaven : ' God is here.' Those words have often since been
a great blessing to my soul. I am often so filled with gratitude
that I can let silence speak his praise. Sometimes it is drawn out
in sweet holy mourning for those who are as sheep without a shepherd. At other times, God shows me what a poor, helpless creature I am. And the sense of this always abides with me, so that I
am often amazed at my own ignorance ; and whatever good I feel

[1] Minutes of Conference, vol. i. p. 46.   [2] See Myles, p. 170.

or do, I can truly say, it is the Lord. I now hear a voice say, in
a few years thou wilt turn out worse than ever. But, blessed be
God, I hear and follow *his* voice : therefore I take no thought for
the morrow. This day is put into my hands, and I have only to
make the best of it. I have need to watch against my own will.
But is there not what we may call an *innocent* will ? For instance, I *will* to be in London, from this motive only, that I may
hear more of the praises of God. So I choose or refuse this or
that kind of food, that I may be more fit to serve God. But I am
not uneasy about it. If I were, I apprehend it would be a sinful
will. No : I am entirely resigned, knowing God will cause all
things to work together for good.

"I am, Reverend Sir, yours,

"LAWRENCE COUGHLAN."

"April 12, 1762.

"REV. SIR, — I staid two nights at Chester after you: and indeed it was a time of love. In the meeting of the bands, several
of our friends spoke. Old Mr. Pritchard was the first. He said:
'For some time I have been longing for a clean heart, yet I
thought God would not give it to so vile a sinner. And the first
night Mr. W. preached, I felt something across my heart, like an
iron bar, cold and hard. But hearing Mr. W. insist on the word
now, I said, Lord, here I am, a poor sinner. I believe thou canst
save me *now*, and give me a clean heart. In that moment Jesus
said to my soul, *I will: be thou clean.* Immediately that bar was
broken, and all my soul was filled with love; nor could I doubt
but Jesus had made me clean, through the word which he had
spoken to my soul.' And three more were enabled, before we
parted, to declare the same.

"I find Christ to be exceeding precious to my soul, and it is my
one desire to do his will. My soul is like a watered garden; my
life is hid with Christ in God; and I believe, when Christ, who is
my life, shall appear, I shall appear with him in glory.

"I am, Reverend Sir, yours truly,

"LAWRENCE COUGHLAN."

Mr. Thomas Marriott, in an article entitled "Methodism in Former Days," which is inserted in the Wesleyan Methodist Magazine for 1851, page 869, says: "In 1768 he (Mr. Coughlan) was ordained, and sent to Newfoundland by the Society for the Propagation of the Gospel." As far as the year is concerned, this was a mistake; for a letter is given in another page, written by Mr. Coughlan in 1772, in which he says he had been seven years a missionary. This will make the year 1765 the time when he went to Newfoundland.

The destitute state of the settlers in Newfoundland was made known to Mr. Wesley; but no missionary society then existed, and he had no funds at his disposal. Yet there was a man in his connection, whom he considered as every way fit to become the evangelist of that country. That man was Lawrence Coughlan. He therefore applied to the Bishop of London to ordain Mr. Coughlan, and send him to Newfoundland; with which request his lordship thought proper to comply, and sometime during the summer of 1765, Mr. Coughlan accordingly came out as a missionary to Harbor Grace, in Conception Bay.

Although now a clergyman under the auspices of the Society for the Propagation of the Gospel in Foreign Parts, he was still a Methodist preacher, both in doctrine and discipline; and to his evangelical labors Methodism owes its origin in Newfoundland. The people were in a fearful state. True, there was then a governor, in the person of Captain Palliser, R. N., and magistrates had been appointed in different places; yet law was little known in the out-harbors, except as administered by the fishing admirals, which infamous system had not then entirely passed away. The merchants ruled the people at their pleasure: not a school was known in the island, nor was a single temple raised

there to the worship of Almighty God. Men who had
come from England had never seen a minister since
they left their native shore; and those who had been
born on the island had never seen one in their lives.
The Sabbath was unknown; there was none to celebrate marriage, and the marriage vow was little regarded. Oppression, violence, swearing, debauchery,
profanity, licentiousness, and every crime that can de-
grade human nature, sink civilized man to a savage, or
even reduce him below the brute, was practised without a check; in a word, the people were demoralized to
an extent that could scarcely have been exceeded by
the thunder-smitten inhabitants of Sodom's plain.
Surely there was no place that stood more in need of
a missionary than did Newfoundland; and few men
were better adapted for that work than the man now
sent.

In this far distant land, without a Christian friend,
and surrounded by every vice, did this faithful servant
of God bear his testimony against sin, and proclaim,
" Behold the Lamb of God, which taketh away the
sin of the world."

His style of preaching was plain and simple, yet
faithful, affectionate, and kind. Forty-four years ago,
when the writer was laboring on the Island Cove and
Perlican circuit, he knew a few aged persons who had
sat under the ministry of Mr. Coughlan, and who
knew him well. Particularly, would he mention a
venerable Christian woman, Mrs. Elizabeth Lock, of
Lower Island Cove, then in the seventy-fifth year of
her age. She always mentioned the name of Mr.
Coughlan with respect. She would tell of his faithful
preaching, and of its effect upon the hearers. " You
cannot think," she would say, " what a state New

foundland was in, when that man of God came among us. Imagine any sin you will, and you cannot think of anything too bad. He would sometimes describe the sins of the land in language that polite people would seem to be shocked at; yet they knew he was speaking only the truth. One expression he would use, when earnestly enforcing the command of God, — 'Cry aloud, spare not, lift up thy voice like a trumpet, and shew my people their transgressions, and the house of Jacob their sins,' — was, 'You fishermen, you New-foundland fishermen,' he would say with great empha-sis, 'I tell you, if you repent not, your sins will sink you into hell.' "

This was a kind of preaching not one of his congre-gation had ever heard before. They were astonished. Some laughed at it; others were disgusted to think that the parson should say such strong things, and interfere with their pleasures; but some were awakened and converted. These persons were at once united in class. This was the first Methodist society on the west of the Atlantic, and it was formed before the close of the year 1765.

The society increased, and the class was divided; when the married men and the married women met apart, and the Methodist discipline was introduced among them. Our missionary now became a faithful pastor, visiting the people from house to house, and ex-pounding the word of God.

He kept up a correspondence with Mr. Wesley, and received consolation and help from his replies. From a letter, written by Mr. Wesley to Mr. Coughlan while in Newfoundland, we make the following extract : —

" DEAR LAWRENCE, — By a various train of providences, you

have been led to the very place where God intended you should be ; and you have reason to praise him that he has not suffered your labor there to be in vain. In a short time, how little will it signify whether we had lived in the summer islands or beneath ' the rage of Arctos and eternal frost !'

" How soon will this dream of life be at an end ! And when we are once landed in eternity, it will be all one whether we spent our time on earth in a palace, or had not where to lay our head."

Persecution soon began. The English settlers, or their fathers, had mostly come from the neighborhood of Poole, or other parts of Dorsetshire, where the Methodists were then but little known, and were all churchmen ; and now in the land of their sojourn, as they had obtained a minister, they expected he would be like the ministers they had known in England, — read prayers to them, and preach on Sunday, and, if he did not join with them, he would at least let them alone in their " innocent amusements." What right had a church minister, in a distant dependency, to introduce heresy and schism into the church, or in any way connect himself with the hated John Wesley, who had been refused several pulpits for preaching salvation by faith, and who, by his preaching, had turned the " world upside down."

He was opposed and insulted by some of his parishioners, but he disregarded it ; then he was prosecuted in the chief court of the island, but his enemies were unsuccessful ; next he was summoned to appear before the Governor, but His Excellency declared in his favor, and made him a justice of the peace. Foiled in all their attempts thus far, they thought of another plan, which, if successful, would forever silence his warning voice against their sins. This plan was to poison him ; and they actually engaged a physician to poison any medicine he might administer to him; but, before any opportunity offered for carrying that murderous design into effect, the physician was converted to God, and revealed the plot. Lastly, they sent abusive and slanderous letters to England, to injure him with his friends at home. But all was in vain, for God was with him; his enemies were reduced to silence; the work prospered; and, when he left the island after seven years' labor, there were two hundred communicants, all awakened and brought to a knowledge of the truth through his instrumentality.

The ministrations of Mr. Coughlan were mostly confined to Harbor Grace, or within the radius of a few miles, yet the benefit was felt all down the north shore. The character of his labors while on the Newfoundland mission, as well as his views and success, will be best understood by a perusal of the following letter, written to Mr. Wesley a few months before he left the island, and published in the Arminian Magazine for September, 1785, page 490.

FROM REV. L. COUGHLAN TO REV. JOHN WESLEY.

" HARBOR GRACE, NEWFOUNDLAND, Nov. 4, 1772.

" REV. SIR, — I bless God, my poor labors in this land have been attended with some little success: some precious souls are gone to glory, and a few more are walking in the fear of the Lord, and in the comforts of the Holy Ghost.

" I am now in the seventh year of my servitude as a missionary, at the end of which I hope to return to England. Could I travel up and down in this land, so as to be useful any longer, I would gladly stay; but, as I cannot, except by water, in small boats, I am not able to stand it.

" I am, and do confess myself, a Methodist. The name I love, and hope I ever shall. The plan which you first taught me, I have followed as to doctrine and discipline. Our married men meet apart once a week; and the married women do the same. This has given great offence, so that repeated complaints have been made to the governor. But truth is mighty, and will prevail.

"In winter, I go from house to house, and expound some part of God's word. This has also given great offence; 'but God is above men, devils, and sin.' The society,[1] I make no doubt, have many complaints against me; but in this I shall commit all to God, for I am conscious to myself that what I do is for the glory of God, and the good of souls. We have the sacrament once a month, and have about two hundred communicants. This is more than all the other missionaries in the land have; nor do I know of any who attend our sacrament, who have not the fear of God, and some are happy in his love. There are some also whose mouths God hath opened to give a word of exhortation. I hope he will raise up more.

"About this time twelve months I hope to be on my passage to England. If I come by the way of Ireland, I should like to see my old friends there. I shall be glad to know if it will be agreeable to you for me to speak in your societies. I beg leave to ask you one thing more. Having served the society seven years, as their missionary, upon my return to England, with a strong testimonial from my parish, is the society obliged to find me a living? And if I could get a place in the church, would you advise me to accept of it? If I know my own heart, I would be where I can be most useful. To be shut up in a little parish-church, and to conform in every little thing for sixty or a hundred pounds a year, I would not; no not even for a thousand. My talents, you very well know, sir, are but small; so that to be shut up here any longer will not do. I am sure that it is high time that I should be removed. Who God will provide for this people, I know not. But he opens, and none can shut. I have informed good Lady Huntingdon of my coming next year. Her plan is somewhat agreeable to me; that is, in going from one place to another. Yet there is one thing wanting, viz., discipline; which I look upon, under God, has been the preserving of my society. My preaching in this land would do but little good, were it not for our little meetings. A line from you next spring will be very acceptable to, Rev. and dear sir, Your dutiful son in the gospel,

"L. COUGHLAN."

---

[1] The Society for Propagating Christian Knowledge.

Mr. Coughlan returned to England the next spring, after which we have but little information respecting him. It would seem, however, that in some way he wandered from God, and brought guilt upon his conscience; yet it is satisfactory to know that he again found the favor and m·rcy of God. In a letter written to Mr. Stretton, of Harbor Grace, dated Feb. 25, 1785, which the writer saw in the hand-writing of Mr. Wesley, and which was afterwards published in the Wesleyan Methodist Magazine for 1824, p. 307, occurs the following sentence:—

"The last time I saw Mr. Coughlan, he was ill in body, but in a blessed state of mind. He was utterly broken in pieces, full of tears and contrition for his past unfaithfulness. Not long after I went out of town, God removed him to a better place."

Little did Mr. Coughlan think, when he expressed so much concern for his "two hundred communicants" whom he was about to leave in Harbor Grace, that, beside their conversion, he had also kindled a fire in the land that should never be extinguished; that a large Wesleyan community should arise therein, as the result of the seed which he had sown; that the little church which he had planted should be cared for, watched over, and edified; that, in after years, its members should be counted by thousands; that its influence should be felt in the government, and its representatives should sit in the councils of the country; and that, by the preaching of his successors, multitudes should be "turned unto the Lord," and be saved forever.

We here pause in our narrative, to make a remark upon the introduction of Methodism into the Norman Islands and into France, which can be traced back to a religious awakening first felt in Harbor Grace. The facts are these:—

Pierre Le Sueur, a native of Jersey, and several other persons from the same island, were engaged in trade in Newfoundland, while Mr. Coughlan was exercising his ministry there. Some of these persons, and among them Le Sueur himself, attended the ministry of Mr. Coughlan. He became seriously impressed, and returned to Jersey with an awakened conscience, and told his friends and neighbors the blessed effects that had been produced upon his mind, by the faithful exhortations of the Newfoundland preacher. The neighbors of Mr. Le Sueur thought him mad ; his wife also opposed his views ; and, without counsel or sympathy from any one, for some time he felt the guilt of his sins upon him, without a friend to direct him to the cross of the Redeemer. At length, a man named John Fenton returned from Newfoundland, and gave him the guidance he needed ; and Le Sueur, after weeping and searching the Scriptures through whole nights, received the peace of God while prostrate in secret prayer. His wife, convinced by his example, began to pray, and, after great mental suffering, received, while upon her knees by his side, the consolation which he had obtained. The conversion of Le Sueur and his wife soon produced no little excitement ; and in about a week twelve persons were awakened, and joined in their devotions, while others violently discussed and opposed their supposed fanaticism. This occurred in 1775, soon after which Le Sueur became a local preacher, and his friend, John Fenton, gave exhortations, and prayed with the people.[1]

[1] See memoir of Mrs. Elizabeth Arrive, of Guernsey; Methodist Magazine, 1820, p. 239. Also, History of Methodism, by Abel Stevens, LL. D., vol. ii. p. 329.

The little Methodist Church in Jersey was kept together by M. Le Sueur for several years.

The first conference appointment to Jersey was in 1786, when those two distinguished men, Robert Carr Brackenbury and Adam Clarke, were sent to that then mission station.

Mr. Brackenbury was a gentleman of fortune, but became a Methodist preacher; and the fame of Dr. Adam Clarke has gone through the world.

By the labors of M. Le Sueur, as a local preacher, a person by the name of Peter Arrive, from the Island of Guernsey, was brought to a knowledge of the truth; at whose instance, Mr. Brackenbury went to that island, and was instrumental in the conversion of an excellent young man named John De Queteville, who entered the ministry in 1786, and labored more than fifty years.

M. De Queteville carried Methodism into France in the year 1790; and although it had everything to contend with during the horrors of the French revolution, and the war that ensued, yet it still survived, and, after the peace, it was resuscitated, and continued to prosper, so that, in the year 1852, French Methodism was organized into a separate conference. "In the morning sow thy seed, and in the evening withhold not thy hand; for thou knowest not whether shall prosper, either this or that, or whether they both shall be alike good."

Two years before Mr. Coughlan returned to England, his heart was cheered by the arrival of Mr. John Stretton, a local preacher from Limerick, who at first settled in Carbonear. With the relict of this gentleman, the writer was very well acquainted; and although, at the time, she was upwards of seventy years of age, yet she was in the full strength of her intellect, a woman of in

13

telligence, a great reader, and for half a century had lived in the enjoyment of perfect love. Mr. Stretton was a respectable merchant; had often, with his excellent wife, sat under the ministry of the Rev. John Wesley. He was a truly pious man, and for many years exercised his talents as a local preacher, with great acceptance to the people, both in Ireland and in New-foundland. He frequently corresponded with Mr. Wesley.

Carbonear is four miles from Harbor Grace; and, at the time of which we are writing, there was no road between these harbors, so that it was only when the ground was frozen that the Harbor-Grace missionary could visit Carbonear and the coves down the bay. Of these places, Mr. Stretton writes, Oct. 29th, 1770 : —

"Religion is scarce to be found in this country; a few professors are scattered through the different bays, that were awakened by the labors of Mr. Coughlan, who still keeps up meetings among them in the winter season, — the only time they have to spare."

Among those who had been brought to God by the ministry of Mr. Coughlan, was Mr. Arthur Thomey, a respectable Irish merchant, of Harbor Grace, who became a local preacher. The relict of this gentleman was also known to the writer ; but only at the time when she was imbecile from age. She had been a mother in Israel.

Mr. Stretton having removed from Carbonear to Harbor Grace, in 1771, he, with Mr. Thomey, took charge of the society when Mr. Coughlan left. The magistrates, who had been the enemies of Mr. Coughlan, thought to neutralize the labors of the brethren Stretton and Thomey, by opening the church on Sabbath, and one of themselves reading the church prayers. Of this matter, Mr. Stretton writes : —

"After Mr. Coughlan's sailing for Europe, the justices took upon them to read prayers in the church, and labored with all their might to introduce the dullest formality in the room of the pure gospel which he had preached. They partly succeeded: those who had received the truth under him had been wont to meet as a class on Sabbath evenings; but now their worships would not suffer it. Mr. Arthur Thomey and I, being disquieted with this mode of action on the part of the justices, resolved to oppose the torrent of iniquity. We gathered a few together who loved the Lord Jesus, and found among them a poor fisherman, who was not ashamed of his heavenly Master, but boldly stood up, and spoke in his name. Mr. Thomey also exhorts, and is endowed with both gifts and grace. We drew up rules as like Mr. Wesley's as we could, consistently with local circumstances. Our number is about thirty, who, I believe, are sincere in heart."

For many years these faithful men labored in the cause of their Master. They preached three times a week, in private houses, during winter: in summer, the business of fishing prevented them from having any meetings except on Sabbath. They met the classes, they visited the sick, they prayed with and expounded the Scriptures from house to house; they travelled the whole length of Conception Bay on foot, from Holyrood to Bay de Verd, preaching in every harbor and cove, wherever human beings were found, many of whom had never heard a sermon preached, a chapter read, or a prayer offered up to God; and, not satisfied with a sixty-mile circuit in their own bay, they extended their circuit, by crossing the dreary country, sixteen or twenty miles, over to Heart's Content, in Trinity Bay. Of his visit to this place Mr. Stretton says: "My labors seemed in vain; the people there being scarcely removed from savages. Yet I have since felt as if God would bless the seed sown."

These brethren travelled in company to St. Johns, where, to their joy, they found a few pious men, who were Congregationalists, and only eight in number; "yet have they built a neat meeting-house," and Mr. Stretton adds: " They are Calvinists, but have 'the genuine mark of love,' and, wherever that is found, we joyfully give the right hand of fellowship."

> "Let names and sects and parties fall,
> And Jesus Christ be all in all."

These eight poor men laid the foundation of the Congregational church in St. Johns, — a body of Christians, who, in after years, numbered among its members, some of the most intelligent, the most respectable, and the most influential in the city.

For about thirteen years did Messrs. Stretton and Thomey labor together, when Mr. Thomey, having to go to Portugal on business, landed at Oporto, retired to his lodgings, and was found dead in the morning.[1]

Mr. Stretton survived his friend several years. He built a Methodist chapel at his own expense, and gave it to the connection; and he lived to see the object of his prayers and his labors, as well as the great desideratum of his heart, which was, that Newfoundland should be permanently occupied as a mission-station, and appear regularly on the minutes of the conference. After Mr. Coughlan, no man in Newfoundland was ever more useful among, or more beloved by, the Methodist society, or more respected by the general public, than was John Stretton, of Harbor Grace.

[1] Wesleyan Methodist Magazine, 1852, p. 87.

CHAPTER IV.

OLD PERLICAN is on the south shore of Trinity Bay, and about twenty-four miles from Trinity Harbor. It had been settled mostly by Englishmen, from rural districts, but few of whom could read. They were poor men, and had left their native land to better their circumstances, in collecting wealth by the fishery on the wild but far-famed coasts of Newfoundland. Only a few of them realized the object for which they crossed the ocean. Their circumstances were not much bettered. They indeed obtained a living, but for that they toiled incessantly, both night and day, for six months of the year, and then, after an unsuccessful voyage, would often, during the winter, suffer severely from the pinching hand of poverty. In both a mental and a moral sense their case was wretched. Having no books, their children were brought up in ignorance; being situated many miles from any mercantile establishment, their families could not profit by mixing with better informed people; they had no place of public worship, and the name of God was not heard among

them, except in an oath: but drunkenness and profligacy
of every form was there; and society in that place was
fast verging to a state of downright savageism. They
called themselves churchmen, because their forefathers
had attended the Episcopal Church in England; and,
however depraved the parents had been, the children
made it their boast: "I am of the religion of my
father."

Nothing could better the condition of these people
but the gospel. This, and this alone, could raise them
from their fallen state; and, in the providence of God,
this gospel, which is

"A sovereign balm for every wound,"

was carried to them by John Hoskins, a private individual, a poor man, and who, like the people among
whom he labored, had left the shores of Britain to improve his temporal circumstances. He purposed to go
to New England, and keep a school for a livelihood, but
called on his way at Newfoundland, where he remained,
became the instrument in the conversion of many,
and was the founder of Methodism in Old Perlican and
Island Cove.

John Hoskins was brought to God when about fourteen years of age, and joined the Methodist society in the
city of Bristol, England, in the year 1746, which was
only two years after the meeting of the first Methodist
Conference. He was personally acquainted with Mr.
Wesley and the first Methodist preachers; he had seen
them mobbed and persecuted; but he believed Methodism
was of God. It had saved him, and therefore he loved
it; and when, in the order of Divine Providence, he was
led to seek a home in the New World, he brought his
Methodism with him, which was made an incalculable
blessing to the community among whom he came to

reside. Wicked men hate religion, because it opposes their vices, and lays restraint upon their evil passions; hence the first preachers of gospel truth, in every country upon earth, no matter what may be the character or talent of the preachers themselves, are sure to suffer persecution. It was so with John Hoskins, in Trinity Bay.

Mr. Hoskins left London in the month of March, 1774: he went down to Poole, and embarked for Newfoundland.

The object of this good man, in leaving his native land, is clearly expressed in a letter to Mr. Wesley, dated Old Perlican, Newfoundland, October 15, 1781.

" REV. SIR, — My design was to work there (in Newfoundland), till I got money enough to pay my passage to New England, where I intended to keep a school for a living, to work out my salvation, and to spend my little remains of life (being in my fifty-sixth year) with the people of God, and, as far as I was able, to help forward the salvation of others." [1]

After five weeks' passage from Poole, he landed in the Harbor of Trinity, which he called a " barren and uncultivated country." A poor woman received him into her house; and he says : " She gave me some seal and bread to eat, and some coffee to drink, the best the house afforded." After partaking of this poor woman's hospitality, he went in quest of employment, and was recommended to cross the bay to Old Perlican, to which place he now directed his way, and there commenced his career of usefulness.

There were then about fifty families in Perlican; but there was no school for the children, and no kind of religious service whatever. Many of the people had never seen a church or minister; but their fathers had

---

[1] Arminian Magazine, 1785, p. 25.

come from England, and had called themselves churchmen, and now they had got a school-master in their
midst, they thought he might become a parson as well,
and do for them what they had been told parsons did
in England. This was just what Mr. Hoskins wished.
He therefore says : " I accepted the invitation to read
prayers, as a call from God, knowing it was my duty
to do all the good I could to the souls as well as the
bodies of my fellow-creatures." His congregation was
grossly ignorant, so that they did not know how to conduct themselves : they would neither join in singing nor
kneel with him in prayer, but stand and gaze at him as
though he were some other being than a mortal man.
On this he says : " My congregation did not know
how to behave in divine service, no, not to kneel in
prayer, or sing at all ; but would stand at a distance, and
look at me, as if I had been a monster; and yet they
call themselves of the Church of England."

In conducting divine service, he read the Church of
England prayers, he sang Mr. Wesley's hymns, and he
read Mr. Wesley's sermons. After a time, he began
to explain some parts of the Prayer-Book, then to
speak to the people about experimental religion, as repentance, remission of sins, and holiness, and insisted
on the necessity of conversion. Some were soon awakened, began to kneel in prayer, and help him to sing,
and evinced " a desire to flee from the wrath to come,
and be saved from their sins ; " and with sixteen such
persons, did Mr. Hoskins form the first Methodist society in that part of Newfoundland.

In the year 1778–9, a great revival commenced in
Old Perlican, when many were awakened, many were
brought into the favor of God, and a religious influence
was felt through the whole population. The next year,

1780, the work spread over to Island Cove. Hearing what had taken place in Perlican, five or six persons came to see for themselves. While there, they were awakened, found religion, and went home to tell their friends in Island Cove what great things the Lord had done for them. Many listened to them, and sought the Lord; so that a society was formed, also, in Island Cove, consisting of thirty members, who soon commenced the erection of a Methodist church. But now came persecution.

In Island Cove, our society sent up the bay for Mr. Thomey, who cheerfully complied with the invitation, and came down to preach to the people. But one evening, while he was preaching in our unfinished church, a party of men, armed with clubs, entered, and swore they would kill him. One of the party went directly up to Mr. Thomey, and made a blow at his head: he missed the man, but struck the candlestick. The friends now got between him and his enemies, and put them out of the building. After the meeting was over, they followed him, and again attempted his life; but his friends again interfered, and he escaped unhurt.

In Perlican, a young man in the employment of the firm of Lester, of Trinity, found "peace with God;" but this was a crime, and his superior dismissed him from his employment, and sent him to England. In the month of August, Mr. Hoskins went to Trinity, with an intent to preach to the people; but the merchants there, all of whom called themselves churchmen, would not allow a house to be opened for him to preach in. He, however, visited several families, prayed with them, and gave them some little books. Tracts, as we now call them, were not then known. After remaining in Trinity some days, and not being allowed to preach there, he prepared to return, and went to ask one of the merchants for a passage in one of his boats to Perlican. The clerk told him that his employer was on board one of the ships. Mr. Hoskins went to the vessel, and, as soon as he got upon the deck, one of the sailors said to him, sarcastically, " Will you preach us a sermon ? " and immediately daubed his face with a tar-brush full of tar. Some more sailors laid hold, and held him, while others almost covered him with tar. The captain of the vessel and the *honorable* Trinity merchant were in the cabin at the time, and the only notice they took of it was a remark from the Trinity nabob to this effect : " If they had asked me, I would have given them feathers to have feathered him all over," — a memorable saying for a Newfoundland mer-chant. Thank God, there are no such merchants there now. When Mr. Hoskins left the vessel, one of the men threw a stick of wood after him, which missed him ; but it was accompanied with an oath, " When we see you ashore, we will make an end of you." The next day some of the sailors went ashore to look for him, one of whom had a knotted rope in his hand to beat the preacher or any of his converts. The man with the knotted rope, probably under the effects of liq-uor, lay down and fell asleep, and, while he was in that state, Mr. Hoskins passed him unhurt. Not so with an individual, who, to the man on his awaking, was pointed out as one of the Hoskinites. The drunken sailor took hold of the poor man, and beat him severely, although he assured him that he was not a convert, nor was he from Old Perlican, but from English Har-bor ; and as though they wished to destroy his life, the merchants interdicted their skippers of boats from taking Mr. Hoskins out of the place. A friend, however, from

Old Perlican, came, as by stealth, and took him over the bay from the hands of his persecutors.

But our Christian hero was not thus to be terrified into silence; for the next summer he visited Trinity again. At that time there was a church in Trinity, but no clergyman. One of the readers of the Society for the Propagation of the Gospel in Foreign Parts, who was a fisherman, sometimes read prayers on Sabbath afternoon. Mr. Hoskins now visited the people from house to house, and on Saturday afternoon put up a notice, that, if there were no service in the church, he would preach in the church-yard on the Sabbath at eleven o'clock. To annoy him, the flag was hauled up, and about six persons came, but there was no one to read prayers. He went outside, gave out and sung a hymn, then kneeled down to pray, when a constable came and took him before the magistrate, who demanded, " By what authority do you go about preaching ? " He took out his Bible, and said, " That is my authority." The magistrate said he did not wish to hinder him from preaching on Rider's Hill, or anywhere else in the harbor, providing there were no riots. He spoke kindly to him, told him to take care of himself, for there were some sailors and other rude fellows, who proposed to abuse him ; and added " I would have punished the men who abused you last year, if you had lodged your complaint to me." A house was now opened for him to preach in, and he was henceforth protected from lawless mobs. In Trinity, as in other places visited by John Hoskins, did the word preached " profit them that heard it ; " and while we admit that in that harbor it has not had the same leavening influence that it had in Old Perlican, yet it has been the means of salvation to many in that place, and, by the grace of God, Methodism still lives there and prospers. Mrs. Elizabeth Lock, whose name we have mentioned before, well remembered when Mr. Hoskins arrived: she heard his first sermon, and was present at his first class-meeting. Several other persons were known to the writer, who were acquainted with Mr. Hoskins; and among them we might name those then aged disciples, Messrs. Gooby, Snelgrove, and Green. Mr. Green possessed some poetical genius. He had been converted under the preaching of John Hoskins: he cherished his memory, and would often speak of his labors, his persecutions, his success, and his peaceful end. To his spiritual father he would apply the following lines: —

> "From softest boyhood to extreme old age,
> Pursued the way that led to endless rest;
> And, ripening to his exit,
> Left in peace."

The society which Mr. Hoskins formed in Old Perlican was called *Hoskinites* by their enemies; and sometimes the cognomen Swaddler, imported from Ireland, was shouted, as the members went or returned from their religious meetings.

Although Mr. Hoskins was very careful to read all the prayers appointed in the Rubric, yet singing hymns, reading Wesley's sermons, and talking to the people about "repentance and faith and pardon and holiness, were, they understood, subjects that the *parsons* in England seldom or never named! This man, therefore, could not be a churchman; and hence they would curse him as an enemy to the religion of their fathers. But God continued to bless his labors, and many sinners were converted, both in Perlican and in Island Cove. In the former place, in particular, the

congregation increased, so that no house in the harbor
was sufficiently large to contain the people. A small
Methodist chapel was therefore erected,—a plain, rough
building, in which the congregation continued to worship God for nearly fifty years. The ruins of this old
chapel the writer well remembers to have seen when
on the circuit in 1821. At that time, the son of Mr.
Hoskins was living, who was about fifteen years old
when he came with his father to Perlican ; and from
him several particulars in this narrative were obtained.

Thus there were two bodies of Methodists in different parts of the island, — one in Harbor Grace, under
the care of John Stretton and Arthur Thomey ; the
other in Old Perlican, under the care of John Hoskins. The distance of these places from each other is
about fifty miles.

The emigration of Philip Embury to New York,
with every particular connected with the introduction
of Methodism into the United States, is detailed in
every Wesleyan history extant ; but Newfoundland,
which has a prior claim as Methodist ground, receives
only a passing notice. Lawrence Coughlan is sometimes named ; John Stretton, very seldom ; but John
Hoskins, the humble, pious, and faithful school-master
and local preacher, who first taught the children in
Old Perlican to read, and who first preached the gospel to the destitute fishermen on the rough shores of
Trinity Bay, seems to have been unknown to our historians and annalists.

But these were the pioneers of Methodism ; and the
honor which the Great Head of the Church thus conferred upon them shall not pass away : it shall be last-
ing as eternity ; for, " they that be wise shall shine as

14

the brightness of the firmament, and they that turn many to righteousness as the stars forever and ever."

Mr. Stretton was engaged in his mercantile affairs, which required his whole attention during the week; and Mr. Hoskins could not leave his school to itinerate beyond the village. Beside which, Popery was establishing itself in Harbor Grace and other parts of Conception Bay; and there was great danger of the Protestants being drawn away by its mummeries. After thinking, and doubtless praying, over these matters for some time, Mr. Stretton determined to put himself in correspondence with Mr. Wesley, and, if possible, get a regular preacher sent out as a missionary to Newfoundland. In this letter, he said: "The work is at a stand here, and superstition and profaneness increasing; we want one given wholly to the work. A preacher should not be entangled with the affairs of this life. It has not been the desire of getting rich that has kept me here; but I have been waiting to see the motion of the incumbent cloud, and dare not desert my post until lawfully discharged. Single and alone, the Lord has enabled me to withstand the whole place where I dwell; and I am still preserved by the power of God."

Again he says: "Whoever seeks ease or comfort is not likely to meet much of it in this island. Blessed be God, who has so wonderfully kept and supported me for many years in this dreary region! When I have been weak, then was I strong." [1]

The above was partly written to Mr. Wesley direct, and partly to a friend who seems to have made known the contents of the letter to him.

[1] Wesleyan Methodist Magazine, 1851, p. 872.

A reply was sent by Mr. Wesley, the autograph of which the writer had the pleasure of reading. It was shown to him by Mrs. Stretton, in Harbor Grace, in 1826. It reads thus:—

"LONDON, Feb. 25, 1785.

"MY DEAR BROTHER,—You did well in breaking through that needless diffidence: if you had wrote sooner, you would have heard from me sooner. Although I have not been at Limerick for some years, yet I remember your father and mother well. They truly feared God when I conversed with them. Be a follower of them, as they of Christ.

"If that deadly enemy of true religion, Popery, is breaking in upon you, there is indeed no time to be lost; for it is far easier to prevent the plague than stop it. Last autumn, Dr. Coke sailed from England, and is now visiting the flock in the midland province of America, and settling them on the New Testament plan, to which they all willingly and joyfully conform, being all united as by one spirit, so in one body. I trust they will no more want such pastors as after God's own heart. After he has gone through these parts, he intends (if God permit) to see the brethren in Nova Scotia, probably attended with one or two able preachers, who will be willing to abide there. A day or two ago, I wrote and desired him, before he returns to England, to call upon our brethren also in Newfoundland, and perhaps leave a preacher there likewise. About food and raiment, we take no thought. Our heavenly Father knoweth that we need these things, and he will provide. Only let us be faithful and diligent in feeding his flock. Your preacher will be ordained. Go on, in the name of the Lord, and in the power of his might. You shall want no assistance that is in the power of your affectionate friend and brother,

"JOHN WESLEY.

"To Mr. JOHN STRETTON, in Harbor Grace, Newfoundland."

Dr. Coke did not call at Newfoundland on his way to England, as he had no preacher to leave there; but, at the conference, Mr. Wesley fully redeemed his promise to Mr. Stretton; for Newfoundland was placed on the minutes, and John McGeary and James Cromwell were appointed as the preachers. James Crom-

well never came; but John McGeary left England soon
after the conference, and arrived early in the autumn.
Of this event, Mr. Stretton takes the following notice
in a letter to a friend :—

"In October, 1785, a preacher arrived here from London, sent
by Mr. Wesley. His name is John McGeary, — a good man and a
good preacher: I hope he will prove a blessing to this place."

Synchronical with the preaching of Philip Embury,
Richard Boardman, and Joseph Pilmoor to the sparse
and destitute settlers on the American continent, and
the labors of Lawrence Coughlan, John Stretton, and
John Hoskins, on the shores of Newfoundland, some of
the mightiest minds that our own or any other church
has ever produced were actively engaged in investigat-
ing the theory of, and organizing a system of discipline
for, Methodism, that should place it in a high position
among Protestant churches, and give it a stand and a
reputation that no one had imagined.

John Wesley, our venerable founder, was then in his
prime, and in the full strength of his mature judgment,
He was evidently raised up, by the providence of God,
to enlighten the nations of Christendom, and to revive,
enforce, and defend the pure apostolic doctrines and
practices of the primitive church. In learning and
sincere piety, scarcely inferior to any. In zeal, ministerial labors, and extensive usefulness, superior, perhaps,
to all men, since the days of Saint Paul. Regardless
of fatigue, personal danger, and disgrace, he went out
into the highways and hedges, calling sinners to repentance, and publishing the Gospel of Peace.

He was
sixty-five years
in the ministry, and
fifty-two an itinerant preacher.
He lived to see, in three kingdoms only,
about three hundred itinerant and one thousand
local preachers, raised up from the midst of his own people,
and eighty thousand persons in the societies under
his care. His name will be ever had in grateful remembrance by all who rejoice in
the universal spread of
the Gospel of
Christ.

SOLI DEO GLORIA.[1]

As Mr. Wesley lived, so he died, in the favor of God. One of his dying expressions, repeated again and again, was, "The best of all is, God is with us!" "How necessary," said the dying saint, "it is for every one to be on a right foundation."

"I the chief of sinners am;
But Jesus died for me."

A little while before he expired, he broke out in a manner which astonished all present, in these words: —

"I'll praise my Maker while I've breath;
And when my voice is lost in death,
Praise shall employ my nobler powers:
My days of praise shall ne'er be past,
While life, and thought, and being last,
Or immortality endures."

Charles Wesley, the poet of Methodism, who composed six hundred and twenty-five out of the seven hundred and sixty-nine hymns found in the Methodist hymn-book. The poetry of these hymns is pure: the theology is perfectly evangelical. Dr. Watts was a good poet, and many of his compositions are fine, and

[1] Epitaph upon a marble tablet in the City-Road Chapel.

truly devotional; but in the richness of evangelical
sentiment, in deep religious experience, as well as in
variety of metres and in the general construction of
verse, he must yield to Charles Wesley. That this is
the view of the Christian public is evident, from the
fact, that scarcely a collection of hymns is used by any
evangelical church wherever the English language is
spoken, but a considerable number of his compositions
are embodied, and are admired by the spiritually
minded.

Every important doctrine of Holy Scripture, every
degree of spiritual experience, almost every shade of
religious thought and feeling, and nearly every ordinary relation and incident of human life, are treated in
his abundant and ever-varying verse. No poet sur-
passes him in the variety of his themes. Rarely can
any man open his volumes without finding something
apposite to his own moods and wants.

" The soul of Charles Wesley was imbued with poetic
genius. His thoughts seemed to bask and revel in
rhythm. The variety of his metres (said to be
unequalled by any English writer whatever) shows
how impulsive were his pathetic emotions, and how
wonderful his facility in their spontaneous utterance.
There are twenty-six different metres in the Wesleyan
Hymn-Book. They march, at times, like lengthened
processions, with solemn grandeur; they sweep, at
other times, like chariots of fire through the heavens;
they are broken, like the sobs of grief at the grave-
side; play like the joyful affections of childhood
at the hearth, or shout like victors in the fray of the
battle-field. No man ever surpassed Charles Wesley
in harmonies of language.

" He never seems to labor in his poetic compositions.

The reader feels that they were necessary utterances of a heart palpitating with emotion and music. No words seem to be put in for effect; but effective phrases, brief, surprising, incapable of improvement, are continually and spontaneously occurring, like lightning, revealing for a moment the whole hemisphere. His language is never tumid; the most and the least cultivated minds appreciate him with surprised delight: his metaphors, abundant and vivid, are never far-fetched, and his rhymes are never constrained."[1] The Methodist Hymn-Book is an invaluable treasure.

The passing events of life, and even social gatherings, were improved by him in his soul-stirring lyrics. We shall give, as an example, that beautiful hymn found on page 455, composed and sung by him at a *tea-party* : —

> " How happy are we,
> Who in Jesus agree,
> To expect his return from above !
> We sit under his vine,
> And delightfully join
> In the praise of his excellent love.

> " How pleasant and sweet,
> In his name when we meet,
> Is his fruit to our spiritual taste !
> We are banqueting here
> On angelical cheer,
> And the joys that eternally last.

> " Invited by him,
> We drink of the stream
> Ever flowing in bliss from the throne :
> Who in Jesus believe,
> We the spirit receive
> That proceeds from the Father and Son.

[1] Stevens' History, vol. ii. p. 497.

> " Come, Lord from the skies,
> And command us to rise,
> Ready made for the mansions above ;
> With our Head to ascend,
> And éternity spend
> In a rapture of heavenly love."

Poetry was in the soul of Charles Wesley until his heart ceased to beat. When so ill that he could not use a pen, he called Mrs. Wesley to him, and dictated the following lines : —

> " In age and feebleness extreme,
> Who shall a sinful worm redeem ?
> Jesus, my only hope thou art,
> Strength of my failing flesh and heart ;
> Oh, let me catch one smile from thee,
> And drop into eternity."

John Fletcher, the pious vicar of Madeley, was at that time engaged in his defence of Wesley on Theology. The peculiar teaching of Calvinism is to limit the blessings of gospel salvation to part of the human race ; and to say of the other part, that, from eternity, they were doomed to eternal death ; or, as it is sometimes modified, they are *passed by* in the plan of redemption, and left to perish in their sins without any hope. On the other hand, it is the mission of the Methodist Church to declare that the Son of God assumed human nature, " that he, by the grace of God, *should taste death for every man ;* " and to preach a free and a full salvation to all. These opposing views were sure to come in contact, which they did, in a remarkable manner, by the publication of the conference minutes of 1770. These minutes contained the views of the preachers on this subject, presented in the form of a series of detached propositions drawn up for their use and guidance. That the reader may understand this matter, we will make the extract from the minute in question. In the conference of 1770, it was asked : —

QUEST. 28. "What can be done to revive the work of God where it is decayed ?

"ANS. 6. Take heed to your doctrine.

"We said, in 1744, 'We have leaned too much toward Calvinism.' Wherein ?

"1. With regard to *man's faithfulness.* Our Lord himself taught us to use the expression ; and we ought never to be ashamed of it. We ought steadily to assert, on his authority, that if a man is not 'faithful in the unrighteous mammon,' God will not give *him the true riches.*

"2. With regard to *walking for life.* This also our Lord has expressly commanded us. 'Labor (ergazesthe) literally, work for the meat that endureth to everlasting life.' And, in fact, every believer, till he come to glory, works *for* as well as *from* life.

"3. We have received as a maxim, that a man is to do nothing in order to justification. Nothing can be more false. Whoever desires to find favor with God should 'cease from evil, and learn to do well.' Whoever repents should do 'works meet for repentance.' And if this is not *in order* to find favor, what does he do them for ?

"Review the whole affair.

"1. Who of us is *now* accepted of God ?

"He that now believes in Christ, with a loving and obedient heart.

"2. But who among those who never heard of Christ ?

"He that feareth God, and worketh righteousness according to the light he has.

"3. Is this the same with he that is sincere ?

"Nearly, if not quite.

"4. Is not this salvation by works ?

"Not by the *merit* of works, but by works as a *condition.*

"5. What have we then been disputing about for these thirty years ?

"I am afraid, about words.

"6. As to merit itself, of which we have been so dreadfully afraid : we are rewarded 'according to our works ;' yea, 'because of our works.' How does this differ from, *for the sake of our*

works? And how differs this from *secundum merita operum?*
as our *works deserve?* Can you split this hair? I doubt I cannot.

" 7. The grand objection to one of the. preceding propositions
is drawn from matter of fact. God does, in fact, justify those who
by their own confession neither feared God nor wrought righteousness. Is this an exception to the general rule?

" It is a doubt whether God makes any exception at all. But
are we sure that the person in question never did fear God and
work righteousness? His own saying so is not proof: for we
know how all that are convinced of sin undervalue themselves
in every respect.

" 8. Does not talking of a justified or a sanctified *state* tend
to mislead men, — almost naturally leading them to trust in what
was done in one moment? Whereas we are every hour and every
moment pleasing or displeasing to God, ' according to our works,' —
according to the whole of our inward tempers and our outward
behavior."

Had Mr. Wesley been writing at this time an article
on Methodist theology, for popular use, he would have
been more particular, and expressed his meaning more
at large. But that was not the object of the minutes:
they were drawn up to guard the evangelical doctrine
of salvation by grace, as preached by the conference,
from Antinomian abuses. It was unkind to pervert
them. But so it was. Lady Huntingdon was the
leading mind, and was said to be the head of the Calvinistic clergy of the day. She was a good woman;
and she employed her influence, her talents, and her
fortune in the cause of religion. A little before this,
six students of St. Edmund's Hall, Oxford, were cited
to appear before the proper authorities, for *holding Methodistic tenets, and taking upon them to pray, read, and
expound the Scriptures, in private houses.* Dr. Dixon,
principal of St. Edmund's, defended the accused students from the Thirty-nine Articles, and spoke in the

highest terms of their piety and exemplary lives; but his motion for their acquittal was overruled, and they were expelled.

This monstrous act of expelling young clergymen from college, for reading, praying, and expounding the Scriptures, produced a great sensation among religious people throughout the country.

Her ladyship, who was a church-woman, felt this most keenly; and she opened her college at Trevecca, in Wales, for young clerical students, where it was not expected similar circumstances would ever transpire. Of the Trevecca college, the Rev. John Fletcher was president, and the Rev. Joseph Benson was head master.

The minute of conference did not accord with the hyper-Calvinistic views of Lady Huntingdon; and, notwithstanding her former respect for Mr. Wesley, she raised a terrible storm against him and the whole conference. Not very unlike the affair of St. Edmund's Hall, she declared that whoever did not wholly disavow the obnoxious minutes should leave Trevecca College. Her wrath first fell upon Mr. Benson, who, although his piety was unquestionable, and his classical talent of superior order, yet, because he avowed his concurrence with Mr. Wesley, he was forthwith discharged, but with a certificate, stating that no complaint lay against either his personal character, his scholarship, or his ability to teach. Mr. Fletcher, whose services as president of the college were gratuitous, now sent in his resignation, which was promptly received.

Not satisfied with expelling the Methodists from Trevecca College, her ladyship determined to get up an anti-Wesleyan demonstration in the city of Bristol, where the next conference was to be held, to effect which she got a printed circular, signed by the Hon.

and Rev. Walter Shirley, who acted as her ladyship's agent. This circular read as follows : —

" SIR, —Whereas Mr. Wesley's conference is to be held at Bristol on Tuesday, the sixth of August next, it is proposed by Lady Huntingdon, and many other Christian friends (real Protestants), to have a meeting at Bristol, at the same time, of such principal persons, both clergy and laity, who disapprove of the underwritten minutes ; and, as the same are thought injurious to the very fundamental principles of Christianity, it is further purposed that they go in a body to the said conference, and insist upon a formal recantation of the said minutes; and, in case of a refusal, to publish their protest against them. Your presence, sir, on this occasion, is particularly requested; but if it should not suit your convenience to be there, it is desired that you will transmit your sentiments on the subject to such persons as you think proper to produce them. It is submitted to you, whether it would not be right, in the opposition to be made to such dreadful heresy, to recommend it to as many of your Christian friends, as well of the dissenters as of the established church, as you can prevail upon to be there, the cause being of so general a nature. I am, sir,

" Your obedient servant,

" WALTER SHIRLEY."

All this flourish of trumpets ended in mere sound as far as injury to Methodism was concerned; for the whole thing was so perfectly ridiculous that neither man, woman, nor child obeyed this summons, or repaired to Bristol for any such purpose as named in the circular.

But this affair brought on the great Calvinistic controversy, which, while a number of persons on both sides entered into it, yet, on the Arminian side, was mostly taken up by Mr. Fletcher. His " Checks," written with so much thought and logical acumen, and, withal, in such a devotional and heavenly spirit, have put multitudes right on this point of theology. They still control the minds of evangelical ministers everywhere ; they have softened down the asperities of those

who advocate a limited salvation ; they have given a
clearness and perspicuity to Methodist preaching, that has
caused its doctrines to be listened to by vast multitudes,
and given it a great amount of influence and of power.

Joseph Benson, dismissed from Trevecca College for
his Methodism, then refused orders in the establishment
for the same reason, now went forth in the highways
preaching Jesus.

His knowledge of the Greek Testament was profound ; his grasp of mind on theological subjects was
most extensive ; his voice, although weak, was heard
by listening thousands ; when the depth and range of
thought, the fervor of his zeal, his clear expositions of
Scripture, and his frequent bursts of eloquence, would
astonish the hearers, and cause the stoutest sinner in
their midst to tremble.

Robert Swindells, one of Mr. Wesley's first, and one
of his best, lay itinerants, did much good in Ireland,
and suffered much from Irish mobs. He began to
preach in 1741. Many were converted to God through
his instrumentality ; and among them was that distinguished scholar, Thomas Walsh. In the minutes of
1783, the following obituary is found : " Robert Swindells had been with us above forty years. He was an
Israelite indeed. In all those years I never knew him
to speak a word which he did not mean ; and he always
spoke the truth in love. I believe no one ever heard
him speak an unkind word. He went through exquis-
ite pain for many years, but he was not weary. He
was still ' patient in bearing ill, and doing well.' One
thing he had almost peculiar to himself : he had no enemy ; so remarkably was that word fulfilled, ' Blessed
are the merciful ; for they shall obtain mercy.' "

Thomas Walsh was awakened while listening to a

15

sermon from that text, " Come unto me, all ye that labor and are heavy laden, and I will give you rest,"
preached on the parade-ground. at Limerick, in 1749, by
Robert Swindells. He had been educated, and was designed for the Roman Catholic priesthood. He was a
young man of most extraordinary talent and learning
as well as piety. Mr. Wesley once said, respecting this
Irish youth : " I knew a young man who was so thoroughly acquainted with the Bible, that, if he was questioned concerning any Hebrew word in the Old, or any
Greek in the New Testament, he would tell, after a
brief pause, not only how often the one or the other occurred in the Bible, but what it meant in every place.
Such a master of biblical knowledge I never saw before, and never expect to see again. His name was
Thomas Walsh." In the pulpit, there was a saintly
dignity and a moral grandeur about him that struck
his hearers with solemn awe. While preaching Jesus,
" he seemed to be clothed with the ardor and majesty
of a seraph." For depth of piety, for fervent zeal, for
diligence in his studies, and for extensive and constant
labor, he has had no superior in the whole Methodist
itinerancy. He died a martyr to his work. His constitution was feeble, but he labored as if it had been
strong. He preached constantly twice, sometimes
thrice a day, beside visiting his people from house to
house ; yet his studies were pursued as if they were his
only occupation. He rose at four o'clock every morning, and pored over his books until late at night.
When he walked the streets of great cities, he seemed
absorbed in contemplation and prayer, entirely unob-
servant of surrounding objects. He began his ministry at twenty years of age, and closed his life at the
early age of twenty-eight.

Thomas Olivers was a wonderful example of the power of religion on the sinner's heart. He was one of the trophies of early Methodism, rescued as he was by its influence from a state of almost hopeless reprobacy. He was a Welshman, and by trade a shoemaker ; hence his enemies have sometimes called him the " holy cobbler." He used, before his conversion, to travel over the country, sometimes working at his trade, but plunging in all kinds of vice, contracting debts, and congratulating himself on his adroitness in fraud. He was converted under the preaching of Mr. Whitefield ; when he purchased a horse, visited his old haunts of vice, paid his debts with interest, and begged pardon from all persons whom he had in any way injured. He connected himself with Mr. Wesley, and became a zealous and very useful Methodist preacher. He was a laborious and indefatigable student, so that Mr. Wesley made him corrector of the press in London. He took part in the Calvinistic controversy. He composed that beautiful hymn, page 609, beginning : —

> " The God of Abraham praise,
> Who reigns enthroned above."

Of this hymn, Montgomery says : " There is not in our language a lyric of more majestic style, more elevated thought, or more glowing imagery." He also composed the tune called " Helmsly," for the hymn on page 68 : —

> " Lo ! he comes, with clouds descending."

He died in 1799, and the minutes of that year contain the following obituary notice : —

" Thomas Olivers, who died advanced in years. In his younger days, he was a zealous, able, and useful travelling preacher ; but for a considerable part of his life, he was employed by Mr. Wesley as the corrector of his press. His talents were very considerable; and his attachment to Mr. Wesley and the cause of Methodism was fully evinced by several masterly publications."

Samuel Bradburn, the Demosthenes of Methodism, was received on trial, as a travelling preacher, at the conference of 1774. He was a man of uncommon wit, and much given to humor. As a preacher, his grasp of thought was amazing. His discourses were rich, sublime, and mighty; and his eloquence was overpowering. Dr. Adam Clarke, who knew him well, being once asked to describe his eloquence, replied: "I have never heard his equal. I can furnish you with no adequate idea of his powers as an orator. We have not a man among us that will support anything like a comparison with him. Another Bradburn must be created, and you must hear him yourself, before you can receive a satisfactory answer to your inquiry." He died in 1816; and the minutes make the following record: "His ministry was owned of God for the salvation of many; and for several years he was considered, not only as one of the first preachers in the land for all the higher powers of persuasive eloquence, but as a faithful laborer in the vineyard of the Lord." It was the privilege of the writer in his youth to sit under the ministry of this then aged, but still wonderfully eloquent, Christian minister.

We mention last, but not least, Thomas Coke, LL. D., a Welshman by birth, a gentleman by fortune, an Episcopal clergyman, and a man of extensive learning. He was the founder, the advocate, the champion, and to a great extent the supporter, of the first Methodist mission. He employed his talents, he spent his ample fortune, and devoted his life, to the cause of missions, and, having founded the West Indian mission, and organized the Methodist Episcopal Church in the United States, watched over, and repeatedly visited, the missions in the West. He essayed to go to India with a small band of missionaries ; but, ere the ship reached the end of her voyage, he was called from his labor to his reward.

Such were the talents, such were the character, the labors, and the success of the early Methodist preachers ; and the men who were so greatly honored in being instrumental in laying the foundation of Methodism in Great Britain and Ireland were also the spiritual fathers and tutors of the first missionaries in Newfoundland. We need not, then, wonder at the devotedness of those missionaries, or the result of their labors. They preached, on the shores of Newfoundland, Methodist doctrines fully ; they caused the people to understand them thoroughly. They taught them the soul-stirring lyrics of the Poet of Methodism ; the same which are now sung with enthusiasm in their public congregations, and are to be heard in " duet " or " solo " as the vessels glide over the ocean billows, and melodi ously sung by their females while engaged in their domestic work, or while toiling in the dreary hours of night ; by the sublime and heaven-inspired strains of our hymns are they edified in their religious meetings, and comforted in sickness and in death ; and the gospel heard by that people from Methodist missionaries has proved to thousands of them " the power of God unto salvation."

15 *

CHAPTER V.

JOHN McGEARY is the first name which appears
on the minutes of conference as a missionary to
Newfoundland. In the same year was commenced the
West Indian mission ; and Antigua was the island where
Methodism was planted in that important field of labor.

Newfoundland was then truly missionary ground.
The country was not colonized ; the forests were in
their primitive simplicity ; there were no roads, but
few horses, and no vehicles of any kind ; no bridges ;
and the weary traveller, with his knapsack or nunny-
bag at his back, would climb the rocks, and wade every
stream in his way. The children without education,
the people without religious instruction, and the land
without Bibles, demonstrated the wisdom of our founder
and the conference in 1785, in selecting that country
as one of the first spots on the earth's surface where
British missionary operations should commence ; where
the first rays of evangelical light should shine into the
dense darkness that had overspread the British Provinces, as well as other lands, which, like the rays from the
morning sun, should continue to penetrate the moral
gloom ; and the Sabbath school, the Bible Society,

(174)

and other adjuncts of the gospel, soon then to be brought into existence, should, like our atmosphere, reflect and refract that light, until "the earth shall be full of the knowledge of the Lord, as the waters cover the sea."

Mr. McGeary was a plain, laborious Methodist preacher. His circuit was an immense one : it extended from Port de Grave, in Conception Bay, to Old Perlican, in Trinity Bay, — a distance of between fifty and sixty miles ; all of which distance he travelled on foot, except a chance time when he might get down the shore in a fishing-boat.

He was often discouraged in his work, but he had much cause for rejoicing. Persecution and lukewarmness had indeed scattered the flock in Harbor Grace ; but he gathered another flock in Carbonear, about four miles distant, and built a Methodist church there : from which time, Carbonear continued to be, and is still, the head-quarters of Methodism in the island. Here we have ever found some of our best friends and most liberal supporters. The people are kind to a proverb. Our church is a noble structure. Our congregation is very large and respectable ; and our members there are now almost one-sixth of the whole membership of the district.

In the minutes of 1787, two years after Mr. McGeary went to Newfoundland, one hundred members are returned for that mission. This was the first time the number of members on the mission stations was published. From 1785 to 1791, Mr. McGeary continued to have the whole island as his circuit ; but in the minutes of 1791, appears the first circuit appointment, and the name of this pioneer of Methodism is put down for Carbonear. The number of our members was one hundred and fifty. This was the year the Rev. John Wesley was called to his reward.

During the summer of 1791, the solitary life of our missionary was relieved and cheered by the arrival, on a visit, of the Rev. William Black, the apostle of Nova Scotia. Mr. Black landed at St. Johns on the 10th of August, where, after remaining one day, he walked to Portugal Cove, and there, in an open fishing-boat, crossed Conception Bay to Carbonear, a distance of seven leagues, where he met Mr. McGeary. The meeting of these laborers from different fields of labor is thus described by Dr. Richey, in the " Life of the Rev. W. Black." Mr. McGeary hailed Mr. Black with the liveliest emotions of gratitude and joy.

"I have been weeping before the Lord (said he) over my lonely situation and the darkness of the people, and your coming is like life from the dead."

Sabbath, August 14th, Mr. Black preached his first sermon in Carbonear : several were awakened, and several backsliders were restored. In the evening of that day thirty-seven persons gave their names to meet in class.

Wednesday, 17th, he preached again in Carbonear Church. He says : —

"While I was preaching, some began to cry aloud. I ceased preaching, and began to pray. My voice was nearly drowned. Weeping on every side. I left the pulpit, and passed through the church, exhorting those who were wounded to cry for mercy. All over the chapel, three or four were to be seen in almost every pew thus affected."

August 18th, Mr. Black writes : —

"I accompanied Brother Stretton, a judicious and upright man, to Harbor Grace, and preached in the evening in the church he had built at his own expense."

Sabbath, 21st, he writes : —

"After preaching in the morning to about three hundred people at Port de Grave, I addressed nearly the same number in Bay Roberts in the afternoon. Here I found twenty-six who met in class, but not regularly : of these, few only enjoy the consolations of experimental godliness. I added four to their number, furnished them with a class-paper, explained the rules of the society, and left them in charge of George Vey, the leader, a pious young man, who I trust will be a blessing."

The anticipations of Mr. Black, in reference to George Vey, were fully realized. Thirty years after the above entry was made in Mr. Black's journal, the writer became acquainted with George Vey, not then indeed a young man, but an infirm old man ; and during that long time had this good man been faithful as a class-leader and as a local preacher. He lived in the constant enjoyment of the favor of God ; he was beloved by all who knew him ; he was a blessing to the neighborhood where he resided ; and at length, full of years and honor, he went triumphantly home to God.

Mr. Black travelled down the bay to Freshwater and Blackhead. In both places the same gracious influence was felt among the people.

To chronicle all the occurrences of interest that transpired during this eventful visit, or even to advert to the numerous cases of conversion, in which Mr. Black gives the names of individuals, would draw out these details to a disproportionate length. Those already exhibited amply evince the extraordinary impression produced, under the divine blessing, by his ministry in Newfoundland, " the result of which," in the words of the Rev. Richard Knight, seventeen years of whose highly useful missionary life were spent in the same scene of labor, " was a large accession to the

Methodist Society, and the dawn of that brighter day
which has since shone upon our mission in that island.
No less than two hundred souls were converted to God
during his brief sojourn in Conception Bay.   Nor are
the fruits of that visit to be estimated by its immediate
results.   He organized Methodism, settled the mission
property, and secured it to the connection, increased
and inspirited the society, and obtained them the help
they needed." [1]

Of Mr. Black's visit, Mr. Stretton makes the following record :—

"November, 1791. The Lord was pleased to revive his work
in a most remarkable manner last August, through the instrumentality of Mr. William Black, of Halifax, in Nova Scotia. He came
hither on a visit, spent about six weeks among us, and then returned. Many were converted, chiefly young people; and since
Mr. Black's departure, I have gathered near sixty young persons
and many little children, that have serious impressions on their
minds. This work was the most extraordinary I have ever seen.
This is the day my soul has longed for. I could almost take up
Simeon's exclamation ! Surely, He who has begun this glorious
work in the dreary wilderness will carry it on, until this dark
region is illuminated with gospel light, knowledge, and love." [2]

Mr. McGeary, after laboring seven years, returned
to England, when the number of members reported for
Newfoundland was two hundred and seventy.

In 1792 and 1793, Newfoundland is omitted in the
minutes of conference ; and, to the great loss of our societies, no preacher was sent there during those two
years; but, in the year 1794, it received a second conference appointment, in the person of that excellent
man, George Smith, who had been two years an assistant
with R. C. Brackenbury, Esq., a wealthy layman who

¹ Methodist Magazine for 1851, p. 873.
² Life of Rev. William Black, by Dr. Richey, p. 274.

gave himself to the work of the ministry, and paid all his own expenses.

Mr. Smith commenced his itinerancy in 1792. He was a Methodist preacher of the John Wesley type; a man of strong constitution, a good preacher, deeply pious, and of great zeal in the cause of Christ. He extended our mission to Bonavista, where he had much fruit of his labors; and, among many others, Charles Saint experienced converting grace. Mr. Saint afterward became a local preacher, and preached with much acceptance, and led a class with great fidelity. He lived many years, an ornament to our church; and at length, after much suffering, which he bore with Christian patience, he went to the land of rest. His son James now fills an important position in our church; and his children, both male and female, seem determined to meet their honored grandsire before the throne in glory. Our church in Bonavista has never declined; and our minutes for the year 1863 show our membership there to be two hundred and ninety, and fifty on trial. Mr. Smith subsequently was stationed in various circuits in England, in all of which his ministry was greatly owned of God. He died, Jan. 25th, 1832, aged sixty-six years.

The year before Mr. Smith left, William Thoresby was appointed; and 1796 was the first year when two preachers were allotted to that extensive and important mission. The entry on the minutes reads thus: " NEW-FOUNDLAND, WILLIAM THORESBY, GEORGE SMITH." Mr. Thoresby remained on the island two years. He was a man of excellent pulpit talent, and, wherever he preached, he had crowded congregations. He returned home in 1798, at which time our membership was five hundred and ten. He died in 1809. In 1799, Wil-

liam Bulpitt came to Newfoundland, and continued
there until 1807, when he removed to Nova Scotia.

Our next missionary was John Remmington, a native of Ireland. He was converted to God in 1790,
entered the ministry in 1802, and was appointed to
Coleraine. He came to Newfoundland in 1804, where
he labored with great success. In 1810, he returned to
Ireland, and labored until 1834, when he was compelled
by infirmity to become a supernumerary.

Mr. Remmington was a " man of unquestionable piety, of sterling uprightness, of great simplicity of manners, and enjoyed uninterrupted communion with God."
He was a lover of music, and a good singer. He
taught our people a number of old English tunes, and
would enliven the prayer-meetings with some revival
melody. In a manner truly enchanting, he would sing
that now almost obsolete hymn : —

> " Come, saints and sinners, hear me tell
> The wonders of Immanuel ;
> Who saved me from a burning hell,
> And brought my soul with him to dwell,
> And gave me heavenly union."

He extended our missions to the Harbor of Trinity,
where for many years his name was a household word,
and, in the hearts of all who knew him, his memory
was imperishable. No man ever left the shores of Newfoundland more deeply regretted than was John Remmington. He sailed from Trinity at midnight, and
that evening was a sorrowful vigil with his friends.
Just as he was about to leave the house, amidst the
tears and sobs of many, he sung : —

> " Here's my heart and here's my hand,
> To meet you in that heavenly land,
> Where we shall part no more.".

He died, Nov. 11, 1838, in the sixty-sixth year of his age, and the fortieth of his ministry.

A little before his death, he said to his family, " Oh, be a family of prayer ! Come, come, I want you all in heaven." His sorrowing wife replied, " You will soon have the victory." She inquired, " Is the Saviour precious ? " " Yes," said he, " very, very precious." His last words were, " Farewell, all is well ! "

In 1808, three missionaries appear in the minutes, — John Remmington, William Ellis, Samuel McDowell, — all Irishmen, and noble and faithful men.

Mr. McDowell labored six years in different parts of the island to the north of St. Johns. He was a native of Dromore, and was born in 1780. He was brought to God in early youth, entered the ministry in 1808, and was appointed to Newfoundland. He was a kind man, and had an untiring zeal in the cause of his Maker. His ministerial talents were very respectable, but he shrank from everything like popularity. He was respected and beloved by all who knew him. He spent six years on this mission, when, his health becoming somewhat impaired, he went to England, and spent one year in the Ipswich Circuit, after which he returned to his native land, and labored many years as an Irish missionary. He became a supernumerary in 1848, and died in August, 1855, in the seventy-sixth year of his age and forty-eighth of his ministry.

William Ellis was the other colleague of Mr. Remmington. With this excellent missionary, the writer was well acquainted, and was his fellow-laborer for fourteen years.

Mr. Ellis was born in the County Down, in the North of Ireland, in 1780 ; and was converted to God in the sixteenth year of his age. When about eighteen,

the Irish Rebellion broke out, and to some of its fearful
scenes he was an eye-witness.   At the battle of Bally-
nahinch, his parents, with all the family, had to leave
their house, and hide themselves in the field as best
they could, where the crying of one of the children exposed the place of their concealment, and, but for the
timely arrival of the troops, they would have been mas-
sacred.   The providence of God preserved him in the
midst of danger.   He afterward filled several important positions in the church in his native land, — in particular, those of a class-leader, and a local preacher.
He came to Newfoundland as a missionary, in 1808,
where he spent all his remaining life, which was twenty-
nine years, in preaching the word of life and salvation.
He was a kind and amiable man, of good natural abilities, and very eloquent as a speaker : he was faithful,
laborious, and successful in his work, and continued to
labor until within a few months of his decease.   He
died in peace, at Harbor Grace, Sept. 21st, 1837.   This
was the first missionary who died on the island, although
it was then seventy-two years since Mr. Coughlan came
to Harbor Grace.

In 1810, William Ward was appointed to assist
the brethren Ellis and McDowell, and was stationed
at Bonavista, — the first missionary ever stationed there.
Two years after, on making a passage to St. Johns
in a fishing-boat, he was drowned, as were all the
boat's crew.

Sampson Busby was ordained by Dr. Coke, and
came to Newfoundland in 1813.   Carbonear was his
chief station, where he continued three years ; and, in
1816, he removed to Prince Edward Island.   He was
afterward stationed in Nova Scotia, and spent twenty-
nine years of his useful life in some of the most impor-

tant circuits in that Province and New Brunswick. He died, March 31st, 1850, in the sixty-first year of his age and the thirty-eighth of his ministry. In his last illness, he was sustained by the presence and grace of God, and was enabled to rejoice in that " perfect love " which " casteth out fear." The name of Sampson Busby was long cherished in Carbonear ; and the name of his excellent wife ought not to be forgotten. She it was who commenced the first female school in that part of the island. When she arrived, it could scarcely be said there was a school of any kind either in Harbor Grace or Carbonear, or anywhere on the North Shore ; and if any respectable person wished to give their children an education, they were obliged to send them to England. Mrs. Busby was an accomplished and deeply pious lady. She opened a school for young ladies, which was numerously attended, and thereby gave the impetus to female education in Carbonear now so generally observed by the inhabitants of that important town.

The year 1813 was when the Wesleyan Methodist Missionary Society received its *present form and constitution.* Not that the Wesleyan Church then for the first time sent missionaries abroad, to preach in distant lands the same great truths which had produced such mighty effects in every part of the United Kingdom ; for it will be seen, from the preceding pages, that she had done this near fifty years before : or, to speak more correctly, it was then forty-eight years since Lawrence Coughlan had commenced his mission in Newfoundland. In 1769, two missionaries were sent to America ; and, in 1785, Newfoundland was regularly entered upon the minutes ; and also the West Indian mission then commenced. And this last date (1785) was earlier, by several years, than any other evangelical church in England entered the mission field. During these years, Mr. Wesley and the conference had fostered the missionary spirit, and had sustained and extended their missions to the utmost of their means. But hitherto the labors of the missionaries had been desultory, the management of the missions informal, and the Wesleyan Church, as well as the evangelical church in general, was only very partially imbued with true missionary zeal. A different feeling was to influence the church ; a different state of things was to exist ; Christian liberality was soon to develop itself to an extent that would silence gainsayers and infidels ; and British Christian missions, instead of being local in their efforts, or limited to the provinces of the empire, were to expand in every direction, until the gospel of the Redeemer should be preached in every nation upon earth.

In 1785, our mission stations were only Nova Scotia, Newfoundland, and Antigua ; our missionaries only four, and they stood thus : —

> NOVA SCOTIA — Freeborn Garrettson.
> NEWFOUNDLAND — John McGeary
> ANTIGUA — J. Baxter, J. Lambert.

Our membership : —

Nova Scotia, including Newfoundland,			.	.	.	.		300
Antigua, Whites .	.	.	.	.	.	.	.	8
Blacks .	.	.	.	.	.	.	.	1,100
		Total	.	.	.	.		1,408

The supervision of these missions was not then a very difficult task ; but it was very difficult to raise the small pecuniary means for their support. Both these duties were cheerfully undertaken by Dr. Coke.

He was treasurer, secretary, and collector, and made his report *viva voce.* He begged the money from benevolent persons who felt an interest in the mission cause; and among these first contributors were several peers of the realm, ladies of rank, and Episcopal clergymen.[1]

In 1793, the doctor presented his first written statement to the conference. It was the receipts and disbursements of six years, from August, 1787, to August, 1793. The largest amount in any one of these years was £ 1,167 12s. 6d.; and the smallest was only £ 339 15s.; this was in the year 1790. When the account was presented, a balance was due to the doctor of £ 2,167 17s. 2d.; when, with his noble Christian benevolence, he said, '" The large balance due to me will never again be brought into account; *it is my subscription to this great work."*

On the reading of this report, the following question was asked in conference : —

" QUEST. 36. The fund for the support of the missions in the West Indies being exhausted, yea, considerably in debt, what can be done for its relief?

" ANS. A general collection shall be made for the missions, in our congregations, for this year."

· During eight years, mostly by the unwearied efforts of the doctor, our mission stations were increased from

[1] " Among the pious and benevolent, the names of Whitbread, Wilberforce, and the Thorntons are invariably found, together with the Right Hon. the Earl of Dartmouth, Lord Elliot, Earl of Belvidere, Lady Mary Fitzgerald, Lady Maxwell, Sir Charles Middleton, afterward Lord Barham, Sir Richard Hill, Sir John Carter, Sir William Forbes, Lady Smythe, Hon. Mrs. Carteret. and the Hon. Mrs. Bouverie. Of the clergy who aided the doctor, were Rev. Mr. Dodwell of Lincolnshire, Melville Horne of Madeley, Berridge of Everton, Abdy of Horsleydoun, Dr. Gillis of Glasgow, Simpson of Macclesfield, Pentycross of Wallingford, Easterbrook of Bristol, Kennedy of Teston, &c." — Methodist Magazine, 1844, p. 222.

16 *

three to thirteen, our missionaries from four to twenty-two, and our missionary membership from 1,408 to 7,840.

At the conference of 1797, the foreign missions were again directed to be brought to the notice of our people, by one of its miscellaneous regulations.

"V. CONCERNING THE WEST INDIES.

"1. Let a collection be made in the course of this year, for the support of the missionaries, in every congregation where it is practicable.

"2. The district committees, in the month of May, are to inquire, whether any preacher is willing to go to the West Indies; and the chairmen of those districts, in which any preacher offers himself, are to inform Dr. Coke of it before the meeting of the Irish Conference."

There is no published statement of the amount of missionary collections as the result of these special applications; but the appeal for missionaries was nobly responded to; for our men in the West Indies were increased next year from fourteen to twenty-two.

These were times of great trouble and suffering throughout both England and Ireland. The French war then raged fearfully; commerce was seriously affected by the war; a short harvest caused a famine to a great extent; England was threatened with a French invasion; and Ireland was in a state of rebellion. But in the midst of all, the mission cause was not forgotten; for at the conference of 1798 it was asked : —

"QUEST. What can be done for the support of our foreign missions?

"ANS. Dr. Coke is desired to make private collections, as far as possible, among our societies and among strangers, for the missions, and the preachers are to assist him in this business; and in those societies which the doctor cannot visit, the preachers are to do what they can by private applications for this purpose. And this is to be considered as a substitute for a public collection, on account of the temporal circumstances of our connection."

The next year, 1799, recourse was again had to public collections ; and the mission work, which had hitherto been solely under the control of Dr. Coke, the conference now took under its own direction, and appointed the doctor its agent. We quote the minutes on this subject : —

" QUEST. 44. Are there any further directions or regulations in respect to the West India missions ?

" ANS. 1. We, in the fullest manner, take those missions under our own care, and consider Dr. Coke as our agent.

" 2. We agree, that a general collection be made, as soon as possible, in all our Sunday congregations in Great Britain, for that blessed work.

" N. B. The collections are to be sent up to London, and lodged in the hands of Brother Whitefield."

George Whitefield, our book steward for that year, was the first missionary treasurer in the connection.

In 1802, the first general instructions were issued to the West Indian missionaries, by which were arranged their time and service in that Archipelago, which was as follows : —

" 1. That preachers who had been previously in full connection should remain four years.

" 2. Preachers who had travelled on trial in Europe should remain five years.

" 3. Preachers who had not travelled at all in Europe should remain six years."

In 1804, Dr. Coke was " re-appointed to the office of general superintendent of all our missions." 2. " A committee of finance and advice is appointed, consisting of all the preachers stationed in London." 3. " Dr. Coke is appointed president of this committee, Mr. Entwirle the secretary, and Mr. Lomas the treasurer." This was the first missionary committee.

Thus far missionary collections were only occasionally taken ; and donations only occasionally solicited ; but in 1805, a more systematic method was adopted to raise pecuniary means. At this conference it was

"*Resolved*, Let annual subscriptions be taken in by the general superintendent of the missions, or the superintendents of the circuits.

"2. Let the collection, which has been frequently made for their support in our congregations, in town and country, be annual."

This was the first movement to raise a regular income for missionary purposes.

A few more entries in reference to foreign missions are found on the pages of our minutes ; but nothing is recorded there calculated to awaken a dormant spirit of the connection to its duty, as to the important part it was designed to take in giving the gospel of salvation to the world, until the year 1813. At that time our number of mission stations, exclusive of Ireland, was twenty-two. We had twenty-seven missionaries in the West Indies and Bermuda, thirteen in Nova Scotia and New Brunswick, and three in Newfoundland, — total number of missionaries forty-three ; and our missionary memberships sixteen thousand seven hundred and forty-two. So that our increase from 1791, the time Mr. Wesley died, a period of twenty-two years, was only twenty-three missionaries and ten thousand two hundred and seventeen members.

The year 1813 will be famous in all time to come, in all Wesleyan annals, by whomsoever written : — 1. As the time when the important mission to India was inaugurated. 2. Because the Wesleyan church then became missionary in earnest.

As early as the year 1781, Dr. Coke had looked upon India with deep interest, and desired to occupy it
as a mighty field for missionary enterprise. But India was then hermetically sealed against all efforts to
Christianize her teeming millions.

Great Britain seems, in the order of Divine Providence, raised to her present high position among the
nations, to destroy slavery everywhere, and to carry
liberty, knowledge, civilization, and evangelical truth
to every nation under heaven. But in India, for many
years, she was recreant to her trust.

After a series of brilliant conquests, on the twenty-
third of June, 1757, occurred the battle of Plassy, by
which the whole Peninsula of India was placed under
British control, and the standard of our empire waved
over every fortress of that vast country.

But, strange, we assumed the government there as a
nation of Atheists! We ignored Christianity, and
professed no religion at all. We dallied with and we
fondled and nursed every system of idolatry and crime,
by which the people had been enslaved and cursed for
three thousand years. And so determined were the
East India Company, who then held the reins of government, that Christianity should not be known there,
that when Robert and James Haldane, two Scotch
gentlemen of fortune, offered to establish a mission at
Benares, which is the " Maynooth " of India, at a cost
of £ 10,000 sterling, the offer was insultingly refused ;
and one of the directors of the East India Company
is reported to have said : " I would rather see a band
of devils land in India than a band of missionaries."

The doctor's plan for the conversion of India, therefore, of necessity stood for several years in abeyance.
But he never lost sight of this great object. He con-

stantly mentioned it to his friends ; and year after year
he earnestly sought the sanction of the conference
for this philanthropic measure.   In the year 1813, he
was president of the Irish Conference.   He brought
his plan before that conference, and asked for its official sanction.   It was voted with enthusiasm.   He
next appeared before the British Conference, to plead
for India.   Some of the brethren opposed his plan,
when he burst into tears, and exclaimed : " If you
will not let me go to India you will break my heart."
The brethren now withdrew their opposition, and six
missionaries were appointed to accompany him to
India, and one was to be left at the Cape of Good
Hope.

The doctor and his missionary band left the British
shores in the month of January, 1814 ; but he died in
his cabin, on the night of May 2d, when the ship
was within eighteen days' sail of Bombay, where she
was bound.   The brother of the writer was on board
the ship Cabalva at the time, and assisted in lowering
the body of the doctor into the sea.

While Dr. Coke lived, the responsibility of the missions mostly rested on him.   The great part of the
missionary subscriptions and collections was raised by
his effort, and he supplied large sums, sometimes to ·
the extent of £ 1,800 or £ 2,000, from his own private purse.   Now that he was taken away, many
thought the missionary work would soon come to an
end.   But not so ; " God can bury his workmen and
still carry on his work."   Thus it was in this instance.

FORMATION OF THE WESLEYAN METHODIST MISSIONARY
SOCIETY.

As soon as the conference of 1813 was over, and

some months before the doctor left England, some of its members began to feel that the responsibility of providing the means, as well as the men, must be thrown upon the church ; and that some new and more productive plan for raising funds for missionary purposes must be adopted. That year Jabez Bunting was chairman of the Leeds District, and there were associated with him in that field of labor, besides several eminent men, George Morley, James Buckley, and Richard Watson.

The Rev. George Morley was the Superintendent of the Leeds Circuit ; and when he returned from conference, the stewards waited upon him, to mention a fact that had occurred during his absence, and to ask his judgment respecting it. The fact was this : some of the agents of the London Missionary Society had adopted a weekly subscription, like our class money, to raise funds for their missionary society, and had requested several of our class-leaders to accept collecting-books for that purpose. Mr. Morley pondered over this circumstance. It struck him, "this is the very thing that is wanted in the Methodist connection ; and such weekly contributions would form a valuable source of income to our mission fund." He thought, however, that the raising of such contributions should not be confined to members of the church, but that missionary collectors should be employed to solicit from benevolent persons subscriptions either weekly, monthly, quarterly, or annual ; and that public meetings should be held, at which missionary information should be given, and the claims of the missionary enterprise set forth both by ministers and laymen.

He consulted his chairman and colleague, the Rev. Jabez Bunting, whose comprehensive mind at once saw the immense advantage of such a measure. After further consultation with the ministers and several intelligent laymen, it was determined to call a public meeting, in order to carry the plan into effect. The meeting was appointed for half past two o'clock, on the 6th of October, in the old chapel at Leeds. A preparatory missionary sermon was preached on Tuesday evening, Oct. 5th, at Armley, in the Bramley Circuit, by the Rev. James Buckley, from Isaiah lv. 10, 11, and the services of that important day, Oct. 6th, 1813, were commenced by a most solemn prayer-meeting, held at six o'clock in the morning, in the old chapel. At half past ten o'clock in the forenoon, the Rev. Richard Watson preached his memorable and never to be forgotten sermon on the " dry bones," Ezek., chap. xxxvii. 9, " Come from the four winds, O breath, and breathe upon the slain, that they may live." The sermon was delivered with great power, with much pathos, and with a persuasive eloquence that deeply affected his whole audience. Of the heathen in general, he remarked : —

" The heathen have turned the truth of God into a lie. Their religious opinions are absurd fables ; and the principles of morality being left without support, have all been borne down by the tide of sensual appetite and ungoverned passion. Ignorance the most profound, imaginations the most extravagant, and crimes the most daring, have ever characterized the world which lies in the power of the wicked one."

Of Asia, where Dr. Coke was now going, he said : —

" If we turn to the East, there the peopled valleys of Asia stretch before us ; but peopled with whom ? With the dead. That quarter of the earth alone presents five hundred millions of souls, with but few exceptions, without a God, save gods that sanction vice ; without a sacrifice, save sacrifices of folly and blood ; without a priest, except a race of jugglers, impostors, and murderers ; without

holy days, except such as debase by their levity, corrupt by their
sensuality, or harden by their cruelty."

At the time mentioned, half past two o'clock, the
public meeting was held. The meeting was large, and
the gallery was wholly occupied with ladies. The resolutions passed at that meeting were the basis upon
which "The Wesleyan Methodist Missionary Society"
was afterward formed; a society which, during fifty
years of its existence, has sent many hundreds of missionaries to labor in distant lands; has collected and expended many hundreds of thousands of pounds in
spreading the gospel; has been instrumental in saving
hundreds of thousands of souls; and, at this day, is
one of the most important and most extensive missionary organizations upon the face of the earth.

The benefit of this organization was soon felt, both at
home and abroad; at home, by the increase of the true
missionary spirit and the augmentation of funds;
abroad, by the addition to our missionary staff, and the
extension and influence of our missionary churches.
In Newfoundland, down to this time, our missionaries
were without any fixed abode, or fixed salary. They
itinerated up and down the north shore of Conception
Bay, receiving what the people thought proper to give
them, and drawing for their remaining necessities upon
Dr. Coke, or upon their kind friends in England, who
deeply and constantly felt for the long neglected inhabitants of that rock-bound island. But this irregularity
was now soon terminated by organizing the missions into
a district, forming circuits in that district, and originat-
ing a plan of finance and expenditure. We shall, therefore, from this time, have to speak of the missions in
Newfoundland by the Methodist phrase, "The Newfoundland District."

17

BY the conference of 1815, the missions of Newfoundland were formed into a district, and stand
thus on the minutes : —

> CARBONEAR, — Sampson Busby,
> BLACKHEAD, — William Ellis,
> PORT DE GRAVE, — John Pickavant,
> ISLAND COVE, — John Lewis, Sen.,
> ST. JOHNS, — Thomas Hickson,
> BONAVISTA, — James Hickson,
> WILLIAM ELLIS, Chairman of the District.

This year the conference gave a plan for the management of our missions, the substance of which
was : —

" That the missions and missionaries shall be superintended, during the intervals of the sittings of the conference, by an " Executive Committee.

" The spiritual concerns of the missions shall be under the exclusive superintendence of the conference.

" A general report of the state of our missions shall be annually
prepared by the Executive Committee, and, if approved, shall be
published and circulated."

In the year 1818 this plan was fully matured ; our
missionary society was organized ; and the " Laws and
regulations of the General Wesleyan Methodist Missionary Society," as they appear in our " Annual Missionary Report," were enacted by the conference.

(194)

Carbonear, Blackhead, Port De Grave, and Island Cove are situated on the north shore of Conception Bay, and are the places where our earliest missionaries labored, and where the inhabitants generally had never heard any other than Methodist preaching; so that they almost considered Methodism the "established religion;" and, whether they were "born again" or not, would often say, "I was born a Methodist." The only opposition our missionaries met with here was the depravity of the human heart, which, by the grace of God, was frequently overcome, for very many went to heaven who had been converted on the north shore.

These circuits had all to be travelled on foot, as there were few horses, and no roads; and the houses being all built by the sea-shore, and around the different coves and harbors, the paths were of necessity rugged, difficult, and laborious. And how dexterously he ascended the "sculpin highlands," climbed up Job's Cove Droke, toiled through the sands at Northern Bay, waded the Northern Gut, or plodded through Short's Marsh, would furnish a theme for conversation to the weary traveller, as he sat by the cheerful evening fire, and partook of the kind hospitalities of these proverbially hospitable people.

St. Johns now, for the first time, appears on our list of stations. For several years after our mission was commenced in the bay, we had but little interest in the capital, and the missionaries could only pay it an occasional visit. But some of our people, who had resided in Harbor Grace, removed to St. Johns, and among them we might mention Messrs. Jonathan Parsons, William Freeman, and James Lilly; also Mr. Mark Coxen, who had been in the army, and had heard Methodist preaching in different places, and Mr. James

Bailey, who had been a member of our society in England.

The only two Protestant places of worship were the Episcopal church, where no pretensions were made to teach experimental religion, and a Congregational church, where the teaching was ultra Calvinistic. Such theology did not suit the little Wesleyan band there. They, therefore, invited the preachers from the bay, who, on coming to St. Johns, were received with much kindness, and preached with much success.

St. Johns is the fifth place on this station sheet, because that was its Methodistic " status " at that time. Our people this year put up a neat, substantial chapel, and our cause seemed likely to prosper in the metropolis. In the town, during the autumn, everything appeared encouraging; trade was brisk, money was plenty, provisions in abundance, and all anticipated a pleasant winter. How vain are our hopes of happiness when built on earthly things!

In the month of February a fire broke out, which speedily laid two-thirds of the town in ashes. It raged from River Head, which is the upper part of the harbor, to Magotty Cove, destroying private buildings, shops, merchants' stores filled with provisions, wharves, some ships, the custom-house and court-house, and our own chapel, not yet completely finished. By this dreadful conflagration hundreds of people were turned into the street, houseless and penniless, where they erected sheds, or raised canvas tents, and dwelt there for the remainder of that severe winter, until the sun's return toward the summer solstice should enable the ships from Britain to bring their " spring supplies," and cause the fish to return to the shore to give employment and food to the starving multitude.

We here mention with very great pleasure the benevolence and great Christian kindness of our American friends in the city of Boston, in affording prompt
relief to the sufferers in St. Johns, but for which relief
many persons must have died. In those days there
were not only no steamers, but there was no post-office
or regular mail from St. Johns to any part of the
world. Letters were sent by private conveyance, or
given to captains of vessels, who charged " a postage,"
and sometimes a heavy one. The writer has often paid
3s. 6d. sterling — 82½ cents — for a letter from England.

To let their distress be known, and to bring a little
relief, the merchants of St. Johns despatched a private
vessel to Boston ; and as soon as the news of this awful
calamity had spread in that city, a public meeting was
called, a vessel was chartered and loaded with provisions and clothing, a crew of men nobly volunteered to
navigate the vessel, at that dangerous season, to the
rocky shores of the sea-girt island, to carry this splendid donation to those who were perishing from hunger
and from cold. A kind Providence safely brought the
ship into the harbor, where her entire cargo of provisions, clothing and blankets, were distributed *gratuitously*.

Many of the citizens of Boston, who gave their contributions to the sufferers by fire in St. Johns, in February, 1816, are now gone the " way of all the
earth ; " yet their kindness is not forgotten, and we
would say, all honor be to their memory. There
were two other severe fires in St. Johns, which followed
this great conflagration, by which the town was almost
ruined, and it was several years before it recovered its
former prosperity.

17 *

In the summer of 1816, Mr. Pickavant went to England to beg for means to rebuild our chapel in St. Johns, which the losses our people had sustained by the fires rendered impossible for them to accomplish unassisted.

Near the time of the " great fire " in St. Johns, a new chapel, nearly finished in Carbonear, was also accidentally destroyed by fire. Mr. Pickavant, therefore, included both cases in his appeals to the British public. When he arrived in England, the Rev. George Smith, who, as we have seen, was formerly a missionary in Newfoundland, rendered great assistance to Mr. Pickavant in soliciting subscriptions for this important object.

Our Missionary Committee, in their first annual report (1816), which is entitled, " The Report of the Executive Committee for the Management of the Missions," thus speaks of this matter : —

" The destruction of the newly erected chapel at St. Johns, by fire, in February last, was an event which not only left the congregation without a place of worship, but the trustees charged with a debt of £500, which remained on the premises, after a very liberal subscription among the inhabitants had been made. This calamity excited the compassion of many persons in this country to contribute toward the re-erection of the chapel, and as the sum already obtained is still greatly inadequate, should any benevolent persons wish to assist a poor but pious people to rebuild their chapel, the committee will gladly receive any sums for that specific purpose."

The result of this appeal was a noble subscription from the English people of £ 2,017 5s. 7d.

The committee, in their report for 1819, make this statement : —

" The chapels in St. Johns and Carbonear, formerly burnt down, have been rebuilt, chiefly by the kind sympathy and exertions of the friends in England, who, in collections made for this purpose by Mr. Pickavant and Mr. G. Smith, contributed the sum of £2,017 5s. 7d."

A portion of this sum was paid to Carbonear, but the greater portion was paid to St. Johns; and by the help of these moneys the friends in both these towns were enabled to rebuild their sanctuaries, and also to erect substantial residences for the ministers who from time to time should be stationed amongst them. Since those times, God has blessed our people with much temporal prosperity, by which they have been enabled for many years to pay their ministers handsomely and contribute to the missionary cause, and to all other Christian and benevolent objects to which they are invited.

Bonavista is last on this list of stations. The distance of this place from St. Johns is about one hundred miles. In consequence of the distance of Bonavista from Conception Bay, and the paucity of missionaries, it was impossible to visit it, except occasionally. Our little church there, however, had been kept together by the faithful labors of two local brethren, Messrs. Saint and Cole, who in turn preached every Sabbath, and met the classes; but the appointment of a regular missionary to the Harbor was hailed by our people with great delight.

The population of Bonavista was estimated at about fifteen hundred souls, of whom three-fourths were Protestants; and the Episcopalians and Wesleyans were the only religious bodies among the Protestants.

The Episcopalians at that time never had a minister stationed among them; but they had a layman, who had formerly been a fisherman, authorized to read prayers on the Sabbath. He also baptized the children, and married the people.

As all the Protestants had been Churchmen, the introduction of Methodism was first looked upon with contempt; then it was opposed, and afterward persecuted as far as the parties had the means. Opposition began most undisguisedly to show itself when a Wesleyan church was about to be erected, and a Wesleyan missionary stationed in the place. Our people, intent upon their object, braved all opposition, and put up their church, when the first open act of persecution occurred. It was in reference to the flag-staff placed in front of the building. The reader must be informed that, as there were no bells in the out-harbors, the signal for divine service was to haul up a flag in the front of the church, one hour before service began; drop it half-mast at the end of thirty minutes, and haul it down as the minister entered. As the Wesleyan church was nearly opposite to the Episcopal church, the officials of the latter intimated that it would be considered a gross insult, if the Methodists should *dare* to hoist a flag in the presence of their Episcopalian brethren; and that such an audacious act should not be permitted. No notice was taken of this kind of talk, and when the church was fit for occupancy, our people proceeded to erect a flag-staff. The worthy magistrate, who was a zealous son of the Church, thought this was too bad, and he must put forth all his power and authority to prevent such an outrage. Was it not as much his business to stop the progress of Methodism as to keep the king's peace? Believing this to be his duty, he came over to the mission ground, and with much emphasis demanded: —

" What are you Methodists doing there? "

Ans. " We are putting up a flag-staff."

Magistrate. " What do you want of a flag-staff there? "

Ans. " To hoist a flag as a signal for divine service."

Mag. "What, directly opposite the church?"

Ans. "We are not aware that we are doing any wrong."

Mag. "I tell you it shall not be, and I forbid it."

Ans. "We think you have no right to interfere with us, and we shall not regard your prohibition."

Mag. "Well, I will allow you to hoist your flag on any day but Sunday."

Ans. "That is the day on which we intend to hoist our flag."

Mag. "If you dare to hoist your flag on next Sunday, I will certainly cut it down."

The Sabbath came, and, regardless of his worship, the flag was raised at the appointed hour. As soon as our justice heard that the Methodist flag was up, he came in great wrath to punish such manifest contumacy. He was accompanied by his son Jared, who was constable, and who brought an axe to cut down the obnoxious flag-staff. Considerably excited, and a little out of breath, he said to the people who were now assembling for worship : —

"Did I not forbid your hoisting your flag on Sunday?"

Ans. "You did; but we have not regarded your order, in this case, as we thought you had no right to interfere with us."

Mag. "I will let you Methodists know that I have power, and I will cut down the pole." Calling to his son, he said, "Jared, cut down that flag-staff." The axe was raised, but ere the blow impinged the wood, Mr. Saint said, "Sir, take care what you do, for I have taken advice, and find we have done nothing wrong. If you will 'dare' to cut down the pole, I will give five pounds." At the sound of the word "advice," his worship was startled, and instantly called to his son to "stop;" and then addressing the people who were now assembled in considerable numbers, he said, "I will not cut down your flag to-day; but mind you never raise it again on Sunday."

His worship retired amidst the jeers of the people, and himself afterward taking "advice," he ascertained that he had gone too far, and therefore left the Methodists to hoist their flag whenever they thought proper.

17 *

The strange conduct and persecuting spirit of this Bonavista magistrate were afterwards satirized in a piece of poetry, from which we extract the following : —

> " Some few years ago, to our harbor there came
> Some preachers from England ; they're Methodists by name;
> They opposed our whole conduct, and said, ' Ye are wrong ;
> ' Repent, or ye'll perish,' was the theme of their song.
>
> A chapel and flag-staff they soon did erect,
> Though 'gainst *Bonavist law* it was levelled direct ;
> ' I'll cut down your flag-staff,' said one then in power,
> ' If you raise up your flag at the specified hour."

This petty persecution did Methodism no harm, and the labors of Brother James Hickson were greatly blessed. Our church was quickened and consolidated, and it has continued to prosper ever since. Other persecution, however, our people afterward had to experience, which shall be related in proper time.

As the Cod Fishery was almost the only occupation in which the people of Newfoundland were engaged at the time of which we are now writing, the reader will not be displeased with the following account of the manner in which that important business was conducted : —

Arable spots are found all round the shores of Newfoundland, which, when cleared of stone and cultivated, produce luxuriant grass and culinary vegetables, the latter unsurpassed for richness of taste by the productions of the best cultivated gardens in Europe. Whole districts may be found to compensate the agriculturist for his toil and expense ; yet sterility is the character, and not the exception of the country at large ; but this sterility of soil is more than counterbalanced by its submarine wealth, gathered and brought to land by the skill and ceaseless industry of her hardy fishermen.

As soon as stern winter has passed away, and the powerful influence of Sol's rays has loosened the icy fetters by which the streams were bound and the land was covered, prodigious shoals of fish come upon the coast to give food to the hungry, and replete the exhausted stores of the now anxious inhabitants.

It was the large quantities of fish that excited the astonishment of the discoverers of the island. There is still extant a document published by Captain Hayes (the second in command to Sir Humphrey Gilbert, who made a voyage to Newfoundland in the year 1583, in the reign of Queen Elizabeth), relating to the fish with which its waters abounded. I will give an extract from this curious document, or report, in the antique language and orthography in which it was written : —

" Touching the commodities of this countrie, serving (answering) either for sustentation of inhabitants, or for maintenance of traffique, there may be diuers : so and it seemeth nature hath recompensed that only defect and incommoditie of some sharpe cold, by many benefits : viz., with incredible quantitie, and no less varietie of kinds of fish in the sea and fresh waters, as Trouts, Salmons, other fish to us unknown : Also Cod which alone draweth many nations thither, and is become the most famous fishing of the world. Abundance of whales, for which also is a very great trade in the bayes of Placentia, and the Grand Bay, where is made trane oils of the whale. Herring, the largest that have been heard of, exceeding the Alstrond herring of Norway : but hitherto was neuer benefit taken of the herring fishing. There are other fish very delicate, namely the Bonito, Lobsters, Turburt, with others infinite not sought after : Oysters hauing pearle, but not orient in colour : I took it by reason they were not gathered in season."

The above was written near three hundred years ago, and with the exception of the " oysters having pearle," nearly the whole can still be predicated of the fish and fishery, on the coast and in the streams of

Newfoundland. Whales are often very numerous, but the whale fishery is not now prosecuted. In some parts herring, salmon, and mackerel fishing is carried on to a considerable extent; but cod-fish is the staple of the country, and its fishery occupies almost the entire labor of the people. The systematic and universal practice of the cod-fishery has necessarily produced three classes in society, — merchants, planters, and fishermen.

The merchants of Newfoundland are a respectable and wealthy class of men. There are a number of small merchants, but the principals of the large firms mostly reside in England or Scotland, and have agents in one, sometimes in several parts of the island. Agencies of these large firms are also in different parts of the continent of Europe, as Hamburg, Oporto, Lisbon, Malaga, and other ports up the Mediterranean. The merchants' premises are called merchants' rooms, and are always by the water-side. Spacious wharves for landing goods extend sufficiently far for ships to lie alongside. On their wharves are fish stores, salt stores, and provision stores; and at the head of wharves are dry goods' stores, all of which are generally well supplied. Connected with the merchants' room is a staff of clerks and mechanics, as coopers, carpenters, and blacksmiths, for very few of these reside at the fishing stations.

The second class is the planters. The word planter at once conveys to the mind the idea of cultivation, and would lead the reader to suppose that planters were farmers, or were in some way engaged in agricultural pursuits. But this is not the meaning of the word in this country. The word was applied, when America was discovered, to all settlements west of the Atlantic, which were called " plantations." The term " planter," in the Newfoundland vocabulary, means the owner of the fishing-room, who is himself a fisherman, and not a farmer. A few potatoes, but seldom sufficient for the use of his family during the year, was the whole amount of his plantation.

The planters were not an educated body of men, in the times of which we are speaking; there were bu few schools, and their constant employment in reference to the fishery rendered education very difficult for them to acquire. But their kindness cannot be excelled by any people upon the face of the earth.

By the word fishing-room is meant the planter's premises, where the fish is made or cured. On the fishing-room is the fishing-stage. This is a long shed, built out sufficiently far in the water for the fishing-boats to lie at the stage-head. The stage is supported by posts fixed in crevices of the rocks, against which the sea often beats, and sometimes with sufficient violence to throw down the building. These stage-posts are of different lengths, but usually from ten to fifteen feet, and are braced with shorter posts or shores, which rest against the perpendiculars, at an angle of about forty-five degrees. Upon these posts are nailed the stage-poles horizontally, which are the only floor of the building. The sides are rough-boarded, and covered with rinds, or the bark of the spruce-tree, procured as afterwards described. The length of the stage is sometimes fifty feet; but it is shorter or longer according to circumstances. Five or six feet of the building near the water is left uncovered as a place to throw the fish from the boat. This space is called the stage-head. Entering the stage from the stage-head, we first see the splitting-table. This is usually on the right hand, as being most convenient for handling the fish. The splitting-table is that whereon the fish is split and prepared for salting. It has a trunk-hole for dropping the heads and offal of the fish into the sea; and a gully through which to drop the liver, which forms the cod-oil, into a barrel placed under the table. Near the middle of the stage is a large vat for washing the fish after it has been sufficiently long in salt. At the upper end of the stage is the green fish, or fish under salt. Near this end of the stage is, also, " the water-horse," that is, the fish after it has been washed from the salt in the vat, and left to drain, preparatory to its being taken out of the stage to dry.

We now leave the stage, and, passing an oil-house and a fish-house, a small house to keep the dry fish, we come to the fish-flake. This is a scaffolding more or less extensive, according to the business of the planter. The fishing-stages along the north shore are always re-moved in the fall, unless, perchance, the sea knocks them down and carries them away; but the fish-flake remains during winter. The flake is from eight to ten feet high, built like the stage, with perpendicular posts and shores. Upon these posts are laid the longers, which are slight poles at a few inches' distance from each other, and these longers are covered with spruce boughs, upon which the fish are laid to dry. The fish-ing-boats and all the apparatus for the fishery, as nets, hooks, lines, &c., are also the property of the planter.

The third class are the fishermen. These are prop-erly the laborers, and their ranks are supplied from the youngsters brought from Europe by the merchants. The merchants were accustomed, early in the spring, to bring a number of young men from England or Ire-land, who are engaged, or shipped in their native land for the fishery; and the time for which they are shipped is two summers and one winter. These young men, when they arrive, as are all strangers when they first land, are called youngsters. When they have spent one summer and one winter, they receive the title of *white nose;* but when their full time of service is expired, they receive the honorable appellation of *oldsters.*

As soon as the frost is out of the ground in the spring, the planter does all his planting, which consists simply of putting a few potatoes in the ground. The manure used is mostly kelp, gathered from the seashore, and brought on men's backs, in bags. The potatoes are planted in long beds, about four feet wide. They are put into the ground with a narrow spade ; trenches are dug on each side of the bed, and the earth thrown upon the seed. The remainder of cultivation, both of potatoes and the kitchen garden, is left to the women.

This done, the planter, very early in the month of May, proceeds to ship both his boat's crew and his shore crew. He generally commands the boat himself, and his title is skipper. He requires two men with him. One is called midshipman, because his station is the middle of the boat ; the other man is called the fore-shipman, because his station is forward. The foreshipman is sometimes called captain ; but the captain of a fishing-boat is the cook. The captain is frequently a youngster.

The shore crew are mostly females. The planter's wife is generally skipper of the shore crew. If she has no daughters sufficient for the work, she hires or ships (for the same word is used) what help she may require. In the case of the girls, as well as the men, a written agreement is made which defines the work each person is to perform. This agreement is called the shipping-paper. Thus, one is shipped to tend table and cut throats; which means to put the fish on the fishing-table from the stage-head, and cut the throats of fish. Another female is shipped as splitter, and a third as salter. These shipping-papers, after stating the work to be performed, usually close with this sentence, " And I am to do anything else for the good of the voyage."

The crew shipped, the first thing is to " come in collar," that is, to commence the spring work. It takes its name from part of the mooring of the boat, in the form of a horse-collar, which is passed over the stem of the boat, and holds her without an anchor. On coming in collar, the boat's crew go rinding. The warm sun in the month of May causes the sap of trees to flow, and forms a large quantity of cambium under the bark, by which it is easily removed from the tree. About the tenth of May, the rinding parties go into the woods and strip the rind or bark from the spruce-trees for about four feet of their height, tie it in bundles, and bring it out on their backs (their only means of transport) to the fishing-room, where it is used for covering the fish when nearly dry, and also for covering their stages and small houses.

Rinding being over, they next rebuild their fishing-stages, and repair their flakes; then go to the merchant's store for their spring supply. For the boat, is wanted canvas, cordage, hooks, lines, and small anchors ; for the general purposes of the fishery, salt, nets, lines, twines, knives, pues, provisions, bread, which always means sea-biscuit, flour, pork, butter, tea, and molasses. Thus prepared, the fishery commences about the middle of May. The first bait used is herring. These are taken in herring-nets; but the cod has not yet struck in for the shore, and is therefore only taken in small quantities. About the first of June, the caplin strikes in, and then is the Newfoundland harvest. This small fish, about the size of a smelt, comes to the shore to spawn, followed by the larger fish in the most inconceivable shoals. This is called the " caplin scull." The caplin is sometimes taken by hand with a dip-net; at other times, it is hauled in a caplin seine. A certain number of men are appointed in each place, to attend the seine, and supply the boats with bait. The toil of the fisherman is now incessant, so that he is scarcely out of the boat for the whole week.

Soon after twelve o'clock on Monday morning, he is away after bait, in order to be on the fishing-ground, which is some leagues off, by the dawn of day. He continues fishing all day, and returns perhaps at sunset with his *put* of fish, throws it upon the stage-head, and immediately leaves for bait, in order to get to the fishing-ground again by daylight on Tuesday morning; brings in his second put in the evening, and so on through the week. The fisherman's clothes are seldom off, except on Saturday, and Sabbath evenings. I once heard a fisherman, on Friday evening, say, " I will now pull off my boots, as I have not had them off since Monday morning." The caplin scull lasts for six weeks, and is followed by the squid scull. The squid comes upon the coast in the beginning of August, and continues until the middle of September. It is a small, round fish, about five or six inches long. Its color is a greenish-red, and it is luminous in the dark. It has from eight to ten arms or suckers, by which it fastens itself to different substances, and with which it grasps its prey. It also has a bag, containing an ink-like matter, which is its means of defence. It ejects this black liquid when pursued. Some writers call it the ink-fish. The squid is taken by jigging, and is the best bait after the caplin. With the departure of the squid, the fishery begins to lag; but another small fish, called the lance, supplies bait for a short time longer.

Let us now look at the labor of the "shore-crew," and we shall see that the labor of the females is quite as incessant, and even more exhausting, than the labor of the men. When the men have thrown the fish upon the stage-head, it is put upon the splitting-table, by one of the females, with a *pue*. The pue is an instrument having a long handle like a hay-fork, with only one prong, which is fixed in the centre of the stick. This prong is stuck in the head of the fish, and thus, with great ease and rapidity, it is thrown from the boat to the stage-head, and from thence to the table. The throat is now cut, and the fish passed to another female, who pulls off the head and the offal, drops it through the trunk-hole into the water; takes out the liver, and drops that into the gully; then pushes the fish across the table to the splitter, who, with one stroke of her knife, takes out the sound-bone, and drops it into the water, and slides the fish into a drudge-barrow. The women at the splitting-table have each a leather apron, called a barvel, which fits to the neck and covers the dress. When the drudge-barrow is full, it is dragged to the upper end of the stage, where the fish is taken out and salted. The mistress is generally the salter. The stage-work commences in the evening, as soon as the fishing-boat arrives, and if the put of fish is large, will occupy the whole night. As soon as the sun is up next morning, the females have to carry the last water-horse from the stage to the flake, a distance of some fifty yards, in a hand-barrow. The hand-barrow is

made by nailing a few short pieces of board on two
small poles, about eight feet long ; and is carried between two persons. The quantity of fish in the water-
horse is indefinite ; it simply means one put or trip of
fish, that had been washed from the salt the day before,
and left to drain ; sometimes it is not more than two or
three quintals, sometimes it is ten or twelve ; but each
quintal of fish, in this green state, is calculated to
weigh two hundred and forty pounds. Breakfast over,
all hands away into the stage, to prepare another water-
horse for the next day. A put of fish, sufficiently
salted, is thrown into the vat ; water is then drawn up
with a rope and block, put in the vat, and the salt
is washed off; the fish is taken out of the vat and
left to drain. This is the water-horse. The water-
horse being thus prepared, the fish spread in the morning has to be turned ; after which, perhaps an hour is
taken to trench the potatoes or weed the garden. In
the afternoon the dry fish has to be put in piles or large
round heaps, and covered with rinds. And as evening
approaches, the fish spread in the morning has to be
taken up and put in fagot, or little heaps, and left on
the flake until next day, when it is again spread. The
sun is nearly down by the time the fish is in fagot,
when the out-door work necessarily ceases. But the
poor, exhausted females have scarcely sat down in the
dusk of the summer evening to take a little refreshment, before the voice of one of the boat's crew is
heard : " Come, missis, a fine put of fish." The re-
sponse to this is, " Come girls, finish your tea, and let
us get to work." There is then the same work the
second night as the first, and the same routine of labor
the next day as has been already described ; and thus
it continues during the week, until Saturday night ; so

that the women, no more than the men, get a night's
rest. Often have I heard the women complain for
want of sleep, and say, " If I had but two hours'
sleep in twenty-four, I could stand the week's labor;
but to do without rest for nearly a week is too much
for my strength." This state of things continues only
during caplin scull, and then only when the fishing is
good, and the weather fine. If it rains, or is damp,
nothing can be done on the flake. When a rainy day
comes, some of the girls will almost leap for joy, and
exclaim, " Oh, how it rains! we shall have rest to-day;
the more rain the more rest."

To the west the case is something different, as the
boats are larger and go a greater distance; so that the
fish are split at sea by the boat's crew.

In the month of August, the merchant's large boat,
or galloper, goes to the planter's fishing-room, to select
the first " dry fish." A culler usually goes in the
boat, to select the mercantile fish. The culler makes
three qualities of fish, — merchantable, madeira, and
West Indian. The merchantable goes up the Mediterranean, to Roman Catholic countries; Halifax and
the United States are markets for the madeira, and the
inferior fish find sale in the West India Islands.

The fishery on the north shore ends either on the
twentieth or on the last of October, when, the voyage
being over, those shipped in the spring receive their
wages and a clearance. Some of the fishermen are
not engaged for wages, but are on shares, and are said
to *cut their tails*; which means that they cut a piece
from the tail of the fish as soon as it is taken out of
the water, by which the man's fish is known from the
rest. Of this fish one half is his, as wages, and the
other half belongs to the planter for the supplies. Such

a person is said to " have half his hand." The " lay "
is less than " half the hand."

All the fish-oil belongs to the planter. The liver of
the fish, as said above, is dropped through a hole in
the splitting-table, into the gully or barrel beneath;
when the gully is full of liver it is emptied into a vat
or hogshead outside, and exposed to the weather; the
heat of the sun melts the liver, and it becomes oil.
The rain helps to purify the oil, which in the autumn
is drawn off into barrels, and at once is fit for expor-
tation.

The fishery over, a few days are required to dig the
potatoes, and put them in the cellar. The cellar is
simply a hole dug in the ground and planked up,
against which a quantity of earth is thrown to make it
frost-proof; it has a double door, and a southern
aspect, so as to be entered on a mild day during
winter.

About the last week in October is the time for the
planter to settle his yearly account with the merchant,
and get his winter supplies. The winter supplies are
similar to the spring supplies, minus the articles requisite for the fishery. If the fishery has been good,
or the planter independent, the winter supplies are
always ample, the family live well; but if the fishery
is poor, or the planter dependent upon his merchant,
his winter stock of provision and clothing are very
scant, and often, after the exhausting toil of the summer, on his part, and the almost superhuman labor of
his wife, his family have to eke out an existence,
during a long winter, upon fish and potatoes; and
even these articles of food fail before the arrival of
spring.

When the winter supplies are brought home, the

fishing-boats have to be hauled up or taken into some safe harbor, the fishing-stages which are exposed to the action of the sea have to be taken in, and the dwelling-houses to be secured against the cold as much as possible.

THE WINTER SEASON.

In many harbors to the west, it is a custom for a number of families to go to the woods during winter, to do a winter's work, as building boats, cutting hoop-poles, or making staves for barrels. Sometimes they migrate for the sole object of catching fresh meat, — that is, of killing deer during winter, and wild geese in the spring, with both of which the country abounds. But going into the woods is not so generally a practice in Conception Bay.

The men in general do little else during winter, than get "room-stuff" and firewood. A man's wages in winter are very low, and a strong man can be hired for the season for his board, with his cuffs and buskins. The cuff is for the hand, made like a mitten, but the substance is a stout, white cloth, called "swanskin." It is doubled on the back of the hand, and stitched until it is almost impervious to water. The buskin is for the leg, to keep out the snow. It is also made of swanskin. While the men can be hired for this small remuneration, the wages of the females are nearly as much in the winter as in the summer.

As winter approaches, the carriages have to be repaired or made for getting out the firewood. These are of two kinds, the slide and the catamaran. The slide was a segment cut out of plank, the convex side to move on the snow. The catamaran was made like a hand-sled. To these carriages two dogs were harnessed in tandem, and a man on the left side, to guide the carriage and its load with his right arm, while a " hauling rope would pass over his left shoulder, with which he would assist the dogs in dragging their burden. This was the Newfoundland team. In some few places, there was an occasional horse, but this was the team generally used all over the country, in those days, for getting out firewood. The load that this team would drive for miles out of the woods was surprising. In Bonavista, the man and his two dogs would sometimes drag eight or ten " turn " four miles. A turn is what a man can carry a short distance without resting. The Newfoundland dog is famous all over the world. They are usually fed on the offal fish.

The slide, or catamaran, can only be used on the snow. If wood be wanted before the snow fall, it must be " spelled out," that is, carried on men's shoulders ; and when some snow has fallen, but not sufficient to make a good path, the stick of wood is nobbled out. To nobble is to drag on the ground.

When the snow has fallen sufficiently deep, the snow path is formed. This is done by a number of men walking with pot-lid rackets. The word racket means a snow-shoe, but the racket of the Newfoundland woodsman is made by nailing strips of board on a small hoop about eight inches in diameter. The pot-lid rackets are fastened to the feet, and, by using these several times, the snow is pressed solid, and a smooth path is thus formed.

The preacher, some time during winter, would have a " haul of wood," when all the men in the village would turn out, double man the slides, and take four dogs to each slide, and bring, in one day, wood enough for the whole year. In Burin, this can not be done, owing to its insular position, but the wood has to be brought in a boat.   One year, the writer failed in getting wood in the fall; he had therefore himself to " haul the slide," accompanied by his " winter man," and thus drag from the woods all the fuel his family required for the season.   But God gave him strength for his day, and he felt it no dishonor, as the circumstances of his missionary work rendered such labor necessary.

The winter houses are called tilts.   The Newfoundland tilt can lay no claim to any ancient order of architecture, but is in its style perfectly original.   The walls are formed of rough spruce sticks, called studs, of about six inches in diameter, the height of the sides six feet, and of the gables about ten or twelve feet.   The studs are placed perpendicularly, wedged close together, and the chinks or interstices filled with moss.   This is the only defence against the cold.   A ridge-pole passes longitudinally from the gables on which the round rafters are notched.   These are covered with rinds, or the spruce bark which had been used during the summer as covering for the fish-piles.   These rinds make the tilt water-tight.   A hole is left in the rinds, about four feet square, which serves the double purpose of a vent for the smoke and an aperture for the solar rays to permeate the dwelling.   The tilt has seldom any window.   The floor is made with round studs like the walls, which are sometimes hewed a little with an adze.

A few stones, piled five feet high, form the fireplace. These stones are placed close to the studs, which, being thus exposed to great heat, will often ignite.   A vessel full of water was always at hand to extinguish the kindling spark; and it required no small skill to throw the water from that vessel up the chimney in such a manner as to prevent its return, surcharged with soot, upon the head of the unfortunate operator. A rough door, a few shelves, and a swinging-table fastened to the side of the building, exhausts nearly all the boards usually allowed for such structures.

In a tilt like the above, with the only addition of a rough, boarded floor, and two windows, brought from the mission-house, did the writer, with his family, spend the winter of 1827–1828. In the mission-tilt, however, we had three apartments, two sleeping apartments, and one large room, nearly twenty feet square, which was our kitchen, our parlor, my study, and also our chapel where we held public service and class-meetings during the winter. The carpets from the mission-house we put to a new use, for, instead of wearing them under our feet, we tacked them overhead, to keep away the dust and the cold. This event occurred in the Burin Circuit. Our tilt was erected upon the bank of a large lake, called Fresh-water Pond, and, as we were surrounded by some twenty Wesleyan families who had migrated there from Burin Harbor, we called the locality of our winter residence Wesley Vale.

CHAPTER VII.

THE great sin with which the early missionaries
had to contend was Sabbath-breaking. Hauling
caplin and jigging squids for bait were generally practised on that sacred day. Catching fish, sometimes;
but taking seals and making fish on the Sabbath were
universally practised. The seal-hunter would say, " If
the seals come near my vessel on the Sabbath day, it is
Providence sends them, and it would be tempting Providence not to take them." The skipper of the boats
would say, " I must get bait on Sabbath, in order to be
early on the ground on Monday morning, or I shall
miss the scull;" and the skipper of the shore crew, " I
must spread my fish, or it will spoil, if the weather be
fine." And this constant breach of the holy day would
be justified in the estimation of the parties by quoting
Luke xiv. 5, " Which of you shall have an ass or an
ox fallen into a pit and will not straightway pull him
out on the Sabbath day?" Such were the force of
habit and the influence of bad example that many
persons, after they professed religion, seemed to think
that some of these things might be done guiltlessly.

One of the first, if not the very first person in Newfoundland, who made a stand against spreading fish on the Sabbath day, was Mrs. Elizabeth Lock, of Lower Island Cove, whose name has probably now become somewhat familiar to the reader.

She was skipper of the shore crew. She had remonstrated with her husband on the evil of working on the Sabbath ; but he insisted upon it that fish should be spread if the weather was fine ; and such an act would be no violation of the fourth commandment. She thought differently, and determined, by the grace of God, come what would, she would not spread her fish on the Sabbath day. A time came when her faith was to be put to the test. Her husband was from home, and the responsibility of the voyage rested upon her. The weather had been foggy for several days, but it cleared up on the Sabbath morning. All hands were on the flakes except Mrs. Lock and her crew. As soon as the neighbors had spread their own fish, they went to inquire for the absentees, when the following conversation took place : —

Neighbor. "Mrs. Lock, are you unwell, that you have not spread your fish, this fine morning?"

Mrs. Lock. "I am not unwell, thank God ; and I have not spread my fish, because it would be breaking the Sabbath."

Neighbor. "But you have always done so before, and so has every one else."

Mrs. Lock. "True, but we have all done wrong ; and it is time that we repented of our sins, and lived differently."

Neighbor. "But you will lose your voyage ; for this hot day will certainly spoil every fish that is left in fagot." [1]

Mrs. Lock. "I would rather lose my voyage than lose my soul, which certainly will be the case if I live in sin."

Neighbor. "We will spread your fish for you."

Mrs. Lock. "The sin would be the same. If I do not go on the flake myself, I will not allow any one else to go there."

[1] "Fagot" is a small pile of fish left on the flake at night, or during rainy weather.

Neighbor. "But your husband, what will he say? He will be very angry, and justly so; for you will cause his ruin."

When this neighbor had left, our Christian heroine was, for a time, much agitated, and thought she must yield; but determined she would first lay the case before the Lord in prayer. She retired to her chamber and prayed that wisdom might be given to her to do the thing that was right; and that if she was to suffer for doing right, she might have strength and grace for the trial She arose from her knees, and resolved, " Come what will, I will never again spread fish on the holy Sabbath."

The day was very fine, and sun scorching. In the evening some of her friends came and upbraided her for her neglect; and, among other unkind things, they said, " We have saved our voyage, but all your fish will be lost." Some outside called her a Methodist fool. That night she slept but little, so great was her anxiety. As soon as daylight came, she went on the flake, to see what had happened to her fish. " I trembled," said she "as I went from the house; for I expected nothing else but that every fish then on the flake would have to be thrown away. But I looked at one fagot, then at another, and so all over the flake, when, to my utter surprise, I found my fish were not injured. My neigh-bors also were soon on their flakes, and they went there with a smile at me. But that smile was soon changed into a deep seriousness; for it was evident at once that every fish which had been spread on the Sabbath was scorched and destroyed by the very pow-erful rays of the sun. It was sunburnt, but my fish were not exposed, and, with the exception of a few on the top of the fagot, none were injured, and my voy-age turned out well.[1]

[1] The above particulars were detailed to the writer by Mrs. Lock, in a conversation on the evil of Sabbath-breaking.

This was a great triumph for religion, and the effect was soon seen in Island Cove and along the North Shore; and while it is now an admitted principle that the Lord's day should be kept holy, yet it is to be feared that many persons, contrary to their convictions, do still violate the sanctity of the Sabbath by doing work connected with the fishery.

A few years later, a similar case occurred at the ice to one of our Methodist captains from Carbonear. A young man, master of an ice-hunter, had lately found the pardoning love of God, when duty called him to go on a sealing-voyage. He resolved he would not take seals on the Sabbath, and told his men so before he left the harbor.

One very fine Sabbath, a floe came near his vessel, on which was a great number of seals. The men, notwithstanding what he had told them, prepared to take the seals. He forbade them; still they persisted. He however stood in the gangway and declared, "Not a seal shall be put on board my schooner this day." Presently another schooner saw the floe, bore down upon it, and immediately commenced taking the seals on board; and by night she had taken about five hundred. The day was very fine, and the reflection of the sun's rays, from the snow and ice, greatly affected the eyes of the men. The Monday morning came, the floe was still there, and more seals upon it than were seen on the Sabbath. Our Methodist captain now directed his men to go to work, which they did with a good will, and in three days they captured sixteen hundred seals; while the men on board the other schooner were all ice-blind, and, after the Sabbath, they never took another seal for the season.

The first Newfoundland district had only six members. Of William Ellis and Sampson Bushby, the two first names on the list, we have given some account in our brief biographical sketches. A few notices of the other brethren we shall now lay before the reader.

John Pickavant was a native of Lancashire, born in 1792. He was brought to God when in his sixteenth year, and when quite young, he began to exercise his talents as a local preacher. In the year 1814, he was called into the regular work, and appointed to Newfoundland. He filled the office of chairman of the district for many years, and labored on the island for about thirty years. He was a good preacher; his address was easy, engaging, and dignified; and his views of evangelical truth were clear and comprehensive. His health was not generally good. In the year 1843, he returned to England, with his health greatly impaired. He, however, so far recovered as to take some important circuits in his native land. He died, while Superintendent of the Third Leeds Circuit, on the 27th of March, 1848, in the fifty-sixth year of his age, and the thirty-fourth of his ministry.

John Lewis, Sen., was a native of Wales. He was called out into the ministry by the conference of 1814, and appointed to Newfoundland, where he labored for six years. He was one of the first missionaries to the westward of St. Johns. In the autumn of 1817, an opening for Methodism occurred in the harbor of Burin, in Placentia Bay. The brethren sent him there; a place where a Methodist preacher had never set his foot, far away from any communication with his brethren, and where he had not one Christian friend with whom he could converse. Moreover, the leading merchants were opposed to Methodism, and the wickedness

of the people was proverbial.   He went, however, in
the true spirit of a Christian missionary, firmly trusting
that the Great Head of the church would open his
way, and give him success in his work.   He was not
disappointed.   The people received him with all con-
ceivable kindness; they opened their houses to him;
they built a church, and contributed largely to his support.   God blessed his preaching, so that many were
turned from their evil ways.   A society was formed,
and Methodism took firm hold of the people, which
hold it still retains.   For many years, the name of John
Lewis was remembered with much affection and esteem;
and his removal from the circuit was deeply regretted.
In the spring of 1820, brother Lewis left Newfoundland, and labored in England two years, when he was
appointed to Yell, one of the Shetland Islands, where
he remained three years, and then returned to England.
In the minutes of 1863, his name is still recorded as
living.   He is down as supernumerary for Nottingham
North Circuit.

Thomas Hickson, an Englishman, entered the itinerant work at the conference of 1815.   His first appointment was St. Johns, Newfoundland.   He labored
in different circuits on the island for nine years, with
very great acceptance and usefulness; and in every circuit, God honored him in the conversion of souls.
The summer before he left, he went on a mission to
the Labrador Indians, of which notice will be taken
in the proper place.   He returned to England in 1824.
In the minutes of 1863, his name is down as supernumerary on the Northampton Circuit.

James Hickson, brother of Thomas Hickson, was
born in the year 1791.   In his sixteenth year, he was
brought to an experimental acquaintance with the " truth

as it is in Jesus," and soon afterward he employed his talents as a local preacher with much acceptance. After being so employed for several years, he believed it to be his duty to give himself wholly to the ministry; and although he had a widowed mother, whose soul seemed bound in his, yet the cause of Christ was, in his estimation, paramount to all human affections and ties. He therefore, painful as it was, broke off from her embraces, and offered himself as a missionary at the conference of 1815. He was sent to Newfoundland, where he labored with great zeal and faithfulness for nine years. He was not what people call a great preacher, but he was a sound theologian, and preached with much earnestness and solemnity. His voice was clear, but of a low bass pitch; so that, in singing, he could sound double C with ease. His walk before the people was always uniform and circumspect; and in the circuits where he labored, particularly in Island Cove and Perlican, Bonavista and Trinity, he was made very useful, and many were converted to God through his instrumentality. Every one spoke of James Hickson with reverence. He returned to England in 1824, where he continued to be eminently successful, both in the conversion of sinners and in the edification of believers. He died in peace, on the 3d of September, 1837, in the forty-sixth year of his age, and the twenty-third of his ministry.

The conference of 1815 resolved to send two additional missionaries to Newfoundland; but the missionary committee increased those two to six; and, before the conference of 1816, the following six additional missionaries were sent out: Ninian Barr, George Cubit, Richard Knight, John Walsh, John Bell, John Haigh.

The station-sheet for 1816 reads thus : —

NEWFOUNDLAND.

St. Johns — John Pickavant, Ninian Barr.

Carbonear — George Cubit, Richard Knight.

Blackhead — John Walsh, Thomas Hickson.

Port de Grave — John Lewis.

Island Cove and Perlican — John Bell, John Haigh.

Bonavista — James Hickson.

John Bell, Chairman of the District.

N. B. William Ellis was omitted by mistake, so that the number of missionaries was now eleven, and our membership five hundred.

The above is the list of stations as they appear on the printed minutes ; but the committee gave a discretionary power to the district to make any alteration in the appointments that they might deem necessary.

The following were the stations for that year, as altered by the district meeting, and as they appear in the minutes of 1817 : —

St. Johns — George Cubit.

Carbonear — John Walsh.

Harbor Grace — Ninian Barr.

Blackhead — John Pickavant.

Western Bay — John Haigh.

Island Cove and Perlican — John Bell.

Port de Grave — James Hickson.

Bonavista — Thomas Hickson.

Trinity Harbor — William Ellis.

Fortune Bay — Richard Knight.

Hants Harbor — John Lewis.

The additional circuits are Harbor Grace, Western Bay, Trinity Harbor, Fortune Bay, and Hants Harbor.

Harbor Grace, the scene of Lawrence Coughlan's labors, and where Methodism was first planted on this side the ocean, had for a number of years been less frequently visited than some other places on the shore, because of the determined opposition made against us

there; yet the missionaries had never abandoned the
ground, and there was always "a faithful few" in that
interesting town, some of whom had been converted
under the preaching of Mr. Coughlan; and now, in
their old age, were enabled to rejoice that at length
their prayers were heard, and the desire of their hearts
realized by the permanent appointment of a Methodist
preacher to their circuit.

Western Bay. — This place is on the north shore,
and about three miles from Blackhead. It has often
formed a part of the Blackhead Circuit. It contains a
considerable population, and was a place often visited
by our first missionaries, as they peregrinated up and
down the shore.

TRINITY CIRCUIT.

John Haigh was the first Wesleyan missionary stationed here, which was in 1816. He remained one year,
and was succeeded, in 1817, by William Ellis. These
brethren were very kindly received by the people; and
the court house was opened for them, as a place of
worship on the Sabbath. There was, however, much
gayety in the town, and the court-house was used,
when wanted, as a ballroom. Our people were but
few in number, yet they soon commenced a church,
which was carried to its completion chiefly by the exertion of our firm friend, Dr. George Skelton, to whose
means, influence, and talent Methodism owes its origin
in Trinity. We have had much to contend with here,
and we are yet but few; nevertheless, by the blessing
of God, after half a century, our cause still lives and
prospers, and has been the means of salvation to many,
both in Trinity Harbor, and also in English Harbor, a
part of the circuit distant six miles.

Fortune Bay is next on our station-sheet. The entrance of Fortune Bay is two hundred forty miles west from St. Johns ; it is about thirty-five miles wide, and eighty in length. It contains a number of harbors, and a considerable population.

Information reached Fortune Bay that several Methodist missionaries had arrived from England, and a vessel going from thence to St. Johns, application was made for one, for Grand Bank and Fortune Bay ; and Richard Knight, afterward so well known in these Provinces, was the first Protestant minister, of any denomination, stationed in that part of the island. Mr. Knight remained two years on the station, during which time he collected congregations in Grand Bank and Fortune Bay, formed the first class, and was instrumental of much good among that interesting people. Hickman, Forsey, Evans, and Chilcot, are names well known as among the first fruits of Methodism in that remote part of the Newfoundland mission.

The head of the circuit is Grand Bank, a small harbor, only fit for fishing-boats and small schooners. It is dry at low water. The land is level, the place is pleasant, the inhabitants are not very numerous, but a more kind and affectionate people are not to be found. They have always highly esteemed their ministers, and have exerted themselves at all times to make them and their families comfortable. God has blessed them, both with temporal and with spiritual prosperity. Fortune, from whence the bay derives its name, is a small harbor four miles east from Grand Bank. The traveller, after leaving Grand Bank, first had to ford a stream, sometimes only to the knees ; at other times it would be breast high ; about one mile of land he next passed, but the remainder of the journey was over loose stones by the sea-side.   Through the whole of this extensive region, there was no Protestant church, or any religious service whatever, except by a man who lived some thirty miles up the bay, and who sometimes read the church service on Sabbath day.   This man was in the employment of the " Society for the Propagation of the Gospel in Foreign Parts."   He was grossly ignorant, and, like most other persons in the employment of that society, he was most determinately opposed to Methodism.   It is difficult to determine which was the most glaring, the impudence or the ignorance of this man, — this then *only Protestant teacher* in all Fortune Bay.

One day, this " Reader," who was sometimes dignified with the cognomen of " Parson," met one of our missionaries in the house of our aged friend, Mr. Blake, in the harbor of Fortune, when he thought it a good opportunity to offer an insult to the Methodist preacher, as well as to exhibit his own *wisdom*, before the preacher's friends.   He therefore most unceremoniously commenced : —

Teacher. " Aint you a Methodist preacher ? "
Missionary. " I am."
Teacher. " And you call yourself a *missionary*, don't you ? "
Miss. " I do."
Teacher. " But you aint ' a missionary ; ' our ministers are missionaries ; but Methodist preachers aint missionaries."
Miss. " What should Methodist preachers be called, if they are not missionaries ? Pray what is a missionary ? "
Teacher. " Why, you are only *mis-shine-aries ;* that is what you ought to be called, a ' *misshineary.*' "
Miss. " Pardon me, sir ; I never heard the word before ; will you please tell me what the word means ? "
Teacher. " A ' misshineary ' means, a man who is *inferior* to a missionary."
Miss. " Perhaps you will also be kind enough to say, in what respect Methodist preachers are inferior to Episcopal clergymen."

Teacher. " Why, you are not college-bred ; you don't wear a gown, and you don't observe the laws of the Church and the Bible."

Miss. " With regard to not being 'college-bred,' not wearing a gown, and not observing the laws of the Church, are all matters of small moment; but it is a matter of serious charge, not to observe the laws of God. In what respect do we not observe the laws of God ? "

Teacher. " You eat pork on Friday.'

Miss. " Does the Bible forbid eating pork on Friday ? "

Teacher. " To be sure it does."

Miss. " I do not remember to have read such a prohibition in the Bible. Will you please to tell me in what part of the holy book it is to be found ? "

Taking up the Bible, and turning over a number of leaves, he looked confused ; and, after a little while, said,

" I do not think it is in the Bible, either ; but I am sure it is in the Prayer Book."

Miss. " I do not remember to have seen anything in the Prayer Book about eating ' pork on Friday.' "

Teacher. " But I am sure it is there. Taking up a Prayer Book, he read the Rubric : ' Observe all the Fridays in the year, except Christmas-day, as days of fasting or abstinence.' "

Miss. " What is that to the purpose ? "

Teacher. " Does it not say ' Observe all the Fridays as days of abstinence ? ' and what does abstinence mean but pork ? "

Such was the intelligence of the only Protestant teacher in the bay, when the providence of God led the first Newfoundland district to send one of their number for the instruction of the people.

Hants Harbor is the least on the list of stations. It is situated on the south shore of Trinity Bay, about eighteen miles from Old Perlican. Some of the first settlers came from Old Perlican ; and several of the aged people knew the first Methodist preachers that visited that place. Methodism was the only religious system with which they were acquainted ; they loved its doctrines ; and brother Lewis was received by them

20

with much thankfulness and pleasure. Seal Cove, three miles below, and Scilly Cove, six miles above Hants Harbor, constitute the several parts of the circuit. Above Scilly Cove, three miles, is New Perlican; and about the same distance above New Perlican is Heart's Content. These places were occasionally visited by our ministers.

The appointment of Mr. Cubit to St. Johns was a great benefit to our rising cause in that important town. Mr. Cubit had been in his circuit but a short time before his learning and abilities were known to the public, and attracted large congregations to our church. The numbers who flocked to hear him were not disappointed; for few preachers, in their public capacity, were more "apt to teach," than Mr. Cubit. His store of information was inexhaustible, his manner was striking and simple, his reasoning was cogent, his expositions of Scripture were rich, and his arguments in defence of revealed truth convincing and unanswerable.

Among other fruits of his ministry was a young gentleman attached to the army, — Lieutenant, afterwards Captain Vicars, of the Royal Engineers, who came to St. Johns light and volatile in his manners, and in his mind strongly imbued with deistical principles. Hearing of the learning and fame of this newly arrived Methodist preacher, he thought he would go and hear him, and see if he could prove that the Bible was the word of God. The preaching and private conversation of Mr. Cubit discovered to him his error, and he soon became convinced of his guilty state by nature, and he sought and found the pardoning mercy of God. Shortly afterward was seen in St. Johns the great moral phenomenon of a military officer, in his uniform, preaching the gospel of Jesus, in a Methodist chapel, to the public, to his comrades in arms, and to his quondam companions in vice.

Captain Vicars married in St. Johns, and the lady of his choice was also a Wesleyan. The regiment to which he belonged removed from Newfoundland about two years after his conversion; but he and his excellent lady carried their religion and their Methodism with them; and when God gave them a family, they endeavored to bring them up in his fear.

Hedley Vicars was the son of this gentleman. He received a military education, obtained a commission in the army, and was attached to the ninety-seventh regiment of foot. During the fearful struggle with Russia, the ninety-seventh was ordered to the scene of conflict. The religious instruction that young Vicars had received, while under the paternal roof, was blessed to him; and in early life he became a subject of converting grace. Like his father, he was not ashamed of the cross, but whether on the sea-girt Island of Malta, surrounded by the mummeries of Popery, on the mountains, in the dells, or before the crumbling ruins of classic Greece; whether advancing to the front, where the booming of distant artillery showed the position of Sebastopol and its deadly heights, or doing dangerous duty in the trenches, he instructed his men in his Bible-classes, he boldly bore the gibes of his brother officers, and, in return, made known to them and to all others who would listen, the unsearchable riches of Christ. This noble youth fell in the trenches, when repelling a night attack by the Russians, on the twenty-second of March, 1855. Among his last words were, "This way, ninety-seventh," intended to direct his men as to their advance, and showing that he was a military hero, being himself in the place of danger; and words which were expressive, also, of his religious state, and directing those for whose salvation he had labored, the way to life and immortality. An interesting life of Hedley Vicars has been published; but all reference to his Methodism, or the Methodism of his pious father, has been studiously avoided.

SABBATH SCHOOLS.

In those days, there was but little education in Newfoundland. Very many large communities were without any kind of school; so that only a few persons could read, less were able to write, and to see a young married couple sign the marriage register was no ordinary event. To meet this want as much as possible, our brethren established Sabbath schools in every circuit; but the lack of persons competent to teach rendered it necessary for the preachers and their families to take the principal part in instructing the children, from the enunciation of the letters of the alphabet to that of reading the Scriptures of truth. There were no Wesleyan Catechisms then in existence; so that instruction in gospel doctrines and Bible history had all to be given verbally, which was a great additional labor for the preachers. But they were compensated in the readiness which the children showed in acquiring the art of reading, and the knowledge of those subjects to which their attention was directed. Hundreds of persons in Newfoundland obtained all their knowledge in our Sabbath schools; and the religious impressions made upon their minds, while in those schools, were never forgotten; but in many instances, in after life, were the means of their conversion.

As every person, both male and female, was engaged in the fishery, either in catching or curing the fish, we could have no meetings on week days during the summer, but all our meetings were crowded together on the Lord's day. Thus in most of the out harbors at six o'clock in the morning, a prayer-meeting would be held in the chapel; at seven, a class-meeting; at nine, the Sabbath school; at eleven, preaching; at two, the Sabbath school again; at three, preaching; after preaching, a female class; and at half-past six either preaching or prayer-meeting. At all these meetings the missionary was expected to be present; so that to him the Sabbath was indeed a day of toil. But God gave the missionaries strength for their day, and blessed them in their work.

20 *

CHAPTER VIII.

THE number of missionaries at the first district meeting, which was in 1816, was *eleven;* and the district contained the same number for twenty-four years. The number was increased to *twelve* in 1840.

The missionary committee, in their report for 1816, p. 25, say, — "In Newfoundland there are not less than twenty thousand persons without religious instruction; and the old people among the settlers, who remember this 'land of Bibles and ordinances,' often weep that the year now rolls over them without Sabbaths, without public worship and the ministry of the word!"

In this same year, our missionary income was £12,565 0s. 9½d., which paid all the expenses of the year, and left a balance in hand of £2,705 18s. The total number of missionaries was ninety, and of our missionary membership twenty-one thousand and ninety-seven.

Here let it be recorded that as Newfoundland was the first spot in our moral world cultivated by Methodist missionary enterprise, so it was the very first place, out of England and Scotland, that contributed to our mission fund. Even Ireland, with all her magnanim-

ity, and although she has given so many missionaries
to this and other countries, and long has had a Conference of her own, yet her name does not appear in the
Report of 1817 as a contributor to our mission fund;
but Newfoundland stands out in bold relief, as the first
contributor in the sum of £30 18s. 6d. sterling. There
was no Missionary Auxiliary Society then formed; but
the preachers mentioned the matter to particular friends,
who promptly poured their moneys into the treasury of
the Lord. The subscriptions were taken in the autumn
of 1816, and paid at the district meeting held in May,
1817. For the honor of the names, and the satisfaction
it may give to the children or families whose eye may
catch this narrative, I will transcribe the missionary
list from the Report of 1817, which now lies before me.

NEWFOUNDLAND DISTRICT.

Cawley, James, Esq., ...	£ 5	10	0
Chancy, L., Esq., ...	2	0	0
Cowan, Mr. James, ...	1	1	0
Cowan, Mrs., ...	1	1	0
Gosse, J., Esq., ...	5	5	0
Henderson, Mr. J., ...	1	1	0
Henderson, Mr. B., ...	1	1	0
Johnson, Mr., ...	1	1	0
Lilly, W., Esq., ...	1	5	0
McCartney, Mr., ...	1	0	0
St. John, Mr., ...	1	10	0
Thistle, Mrs., ...	1	5	0
Small sums under 20s., . . .	7	18	6
	£ 30	18	6

Such was the first missionary list, out of Great
Britain.

While Newfoundland was the first foreign contributor to our mission fund, Nova Scotia has the honor
of having formed the first foreign auxiliary missionary
society.

On the third of June, 1817, and only a few weeks after the above money was remitted to England, " the Methodist Missionary Society for the district of Nova Scotia, including New Brunswick and Prince Edward's Island," was formed in Argyle Street Chapel, Halifax. During the year, branches were formed in Halifax, Liverpool, Shelburne, St. Johns, Fredericton, Annapolis, Cumberland, Horton, Newport, and Lunenburg; and the total net amount remitted was £323 7s. 8d. sterling. The first annual meeting of this society was held in Halifax, June 2, 1818, when ten resolutions were passed, and twenty speakers addressed the meeting besides the chairman. The above amount was reported at this meeting.

From the report published by the Nova Scotia Missionary Society, in 1818, we make the following extract : —

" In Newfoundland, where so much distress has lately prevailed, and still continues to exist; where there have been such destructive fires; where so many pecuniary embarrassments have been felt; and where there are so many things to discourage and depress the minds of missionaries, — your committee are happy to inform you, that Methodist missionaries are employed in blowing the gospel trumpet, and are wandering along its barren shores to scatter the word of life. There they have necessarily to endure many trials, to labor under peculiar disadvantages; and having lately had two of their best chapels destroyed by fire, they continue undaunted and undismayed; and, relying upon the Lord God of Elijah, cheerfully prosecute their labors; and by the latest accounts from them, we learn that a gracious work is progressing in several of their stations and circuits."

The circuits to which reference is here made were Island Cove and Perlican, under Thomas Hickson; Harbor Grace, under James Hickson; Trinity, under William Ellis; and Buren, under John Lewis; in all which places, at that time, the Spirit was poured out from on high; and our societies received a character and a permanency which they still retain.

A biographical sketch of the preachers connected with the first district meeting, which have not been so noticed, will now be given.

John Bell was a native of Hull, in Yorkshire, born October 19, 1788. His parents were Episcopalians, but he was awakened to a sense of his lost state by nature when in the fourteenth year of his age, and joined the Wesleyan church. When in his twenty-first year, he began to use his talents as a local preacher; and in the year 1811 he was received as a probationer in our ministry. He travelled five years in England, when he came to Newfoundland as a missionary in 1816, and was appointed chairman of the district. He was the second man who filled that office, and he retained that position until the year 1823, when he returned to his native land. He continued to labor in his high vocation until the year 1851, when he became a supernumerary. He was very neat and precise in his person. His preaching abilities were not of a high order; still, as a preacher, he was distinguished by his perspicuity and great simplicity. He was an excellent pastor, and in the sick-chamber and by the bed of the dying his affectionate manner was often made a blessing. He died in peace, October 26, 1855, in the sixty-eighth year of his age, and the forty-fifth of his ministry.

George Cubit was born in the city of Norwich, in the year 1791. His father's family removed to Sheffield, while he was yet a boy, when he attended Carver-Street Chapel. He joined the Wesleyan church in 1808, and soon after became a subject of pardon, through faith in the Lord Jesus Christ. He now began to employ himself for the benefit of others, and it is believed that he originated the plan of tract distribution by loan. He also commenced to act as a local preacher, when the great powers of his mind became developed, and it was seen that he was no ordinary man, but gave promise of superior abilities. He was received on trial for the itinerancy, at the conference of 1813, and labored three years in England. He came to Newfoundland in 1816, and removed from thence in 1819, spending three years of his useful life as a missionary on that important island. Of the manner of his preaching, and the success of his labors as a Newfoundland missionary, we have already spoken ; and we shall now follow him to his native land.

For sixteen years, he filled some of our most important circuits, commanding large congregations of highly cultivated and intelligent hearers. In 1836, he was called to fill the editorial chair, first as assistant, and afterward as principal editor of our English Magazine, and the various other literary and religious works that constantly flow from that important establishment, the Wesleyan Book-Room, City Road, London. For many years, he presided over the literature of the connection with great judgment. It is said, however, that in his latter years he became quite a recluse, seldom mixing with society, which was a great grief to his friends, whom he had so often instructed and delighted with his boundless stores of religious, scientific, and miscellaneous knowledge. He died, October 13, 1850, in the fifty-ninth year of his age, and the thirty-seventh of his ministry.

John Walsh was born at Ormskirk, Lancashire, in the year 1795. His parents were Roman Catholics, and he was brought up in that religion. His father intended that he should be a priest, and his early education was all in reference to that object. Removing from Ormskirk to Liverpool, he was led to visit the Methodist Chapel, where, under the ministry of the Rev. Joseph Entwisle, he was brought to the knowledge of the truth as it is in Jesus. To the grief and disappointment of his popish friends, but to the honor of our Protestantism, he renounced the Papacy, and became a Wesleyan Methodist. In the year 1814, he was received on trial as a Wesleyan minister, and stationed in Lancaster, under the superintendency of the Rev. John Beaumont. After laboring two years in the Lancaster Circuit, he came, in 1814, to Newfoundland, and was appointed to Carbonear. He spent nine years on the Newfoundland mission, and returned to England in the year 1825. His manner, by some, was thought to be stiff and priestly; but, as a preacher, he was faithful and laborious; and his sermons were rich in evangelical truth, and always delivered with earnestness and power. He was called to his reward on the 19th of December, in the year 1857, in the sixty-third year of his age, and the forty-fourth of his ministry. Before he died, his speech having failed, his sorrowing wife exclaimed, "Victory!" He moved his head in token of assent, and then fell asleep in Jesus.

Ninian Barr, a Scotchman by birth. He was called into the itinerant work by the conference of 1816, and appointed as a missionary to Newfoundland. His manner was cheerful; he was a man of talent, and a good preacher. He labored on the island ten years, then returned to England. He filled several important circuits, but was compelled to retire from the active work, by infirmity, at the conference of 1854. His name is on the minutes as a supernumerary in the *Abroath and Montrose* Circuit, in 1863.

John Haigh was born in Leeds, in 1795, and was brought to God under a sermon preached by the late Mr. William Dawson. In 1816, he was received into the Wesleyan ministry, and sent to Newfoundland, where he labored twenty-one years. He occupied some of the best circuits in the district, with great acceptance to the people; and in nearly all the circuits he witnessed a revival of religion. In 1837, he was nominated chairman of the Bahama District, but his constitution would not endure a tropical clime; he therefore returned to England, and labored eighteen years in his native land. He was a man of clear perception, a good theologian, an earnest, faithful, and practical preacher. He was attacked with paralysis; and, after remaining speechless for two days, he died May 2, 1859, in the sixty-fourth year of his age, and the forty-third of his ministry.

Richard Knight, D. D., was born in Devonshire, in the year 1788. We have no information of the time and circumstances connected with his conversion to God; but we know that he was one of the young men sent to Newfoundland in 1816. His first appointment was Fortune Bay, and, as we have seen, he was the first Protestant minister of any name that resided among that people. His next appointment was Bonavista and Catalina, on the way to which the fishing-boat in which he sailed put into the harbor of Trinity. While there, he preached from Jeremiah xxii. 29, " O earth, earth, earth, hear the word of the Lord." A lady was present, then one of the gayest of the gay. She had been brought up a strict Church-of-England woman; and while she in heart despised Methodism, yet she thought she would go, for once, to the Methodist chapel; it might afford her some amusement. But her mind, that night, was powerfully wrought upon by the Holy Spirit. She became a penitent; she sought and found mercy; she united herself with our church; boldly bore the cross; became an humble follower of the Lord Jesus, employing her time and her ample means in visiting the sick and the poor; and to the utmost did she spread abroad the knowledge of religion. She was not ashamed to call herself a Wesleyan, and sustained the cause of Methodism by all means in her power. This lady was the wife of William Kelson, Esq., who also became a member of our church, and who, with Dr. George Skelton, were for many years the principal supporters of our cause in the Trinity Circuit.

Mr. Knight labored in Newfoundland for sixteen years, and in several circuits was he made eminently useful. In Carbonear and Blackhead, extensive revivals took place under him, and many persons attributed their conversion to his instrumentality. He was secretary of the district most of the time that he was on that mission. In the year 1833, he came to Nova Scotia, and was elevated to the chair of the district. He continued to occupy the chair of the Nova Scotia, then of the New Brunswick, district, and, after the formation of the Eastern British American Conference, of the several districts where he resided, until he was called to his reward. For the last three years of his life, he filled the office of co-delegate, and certainly would have been elected president had his life been spared. He made no pretensions to extensive literary attainments; nevertheless he received the honorary title of D. D. He was a good preacher, an excellent pastor, a man of firm integrity, a kind father, and, as a

21

Methodist preacher, was highly respected and useful in the various circuits in which he labored. He was the senior effective Methodist missionary in the world. He was a firm believer in the doctrine of Christian perfection; and, for years before his death, he professed to live in the enjoyment of the perfect love of God. His frame was athletic, a man of strong muscular powers, and through his whole life almost a stranger to sickness. He continued to labor until within a few days of his end. On Sabbath, May 14th, he preached in Sackville; on Monday and Tuesday, he attended the academic exercises, but was taken very ill on Tuesday evening, and, on the twenty-third of the same month, he exchanged mortality for life. He died at Sackville, on the 23d of May, 1860, in the seventy-second year of his age, and the forty-fourth of his ministry. A few days before his death, he called his family around him, and charged them all to meet him in heaven. Just before he expired, he exclaimed, "I see his glory, hallelujah!"

Such were the men who constituted the first Wesleyan District in Newfoundland, — men who, while they preached the truth to others, themselves lived under its influence, and in death triumphed in its saving power. Over a large portion of the island had these heralds of the cross carried the standard of their Great Captain, and many had they enlisted into his service. In every circuit, classes had been formed, Sabbath schools organized, and souls converted to God. Our membership in Newfoundland was then 670.

The Wesleyan Church had now begun to assume large proportions, and to appear before the world in its true light, as a missionary church. Its missions were now planted in many different and distant lands; and while the exalted talents of Richard Watson, Jabez

Bunting, Adam Clarke, Robert Newton, George Morley, and a host of other gigantic minds, were arousing the churches in England to their duty in reference to the world's conversion, at least one hundred missionaries, sent out through their influence, were proclaiming, in various languages, the solemn verities of the everlasting gospel.

In 1818, we had four misionaries in France; we had missions on the Island of Ceylon, and Continental India; in New South Wales and Africa; at Sierre Leone and Little Namacqualand; in the West Indies, in the Canadas, Nova Scotia, New Brunswick, Prince Edward Island, and Newfoundland. The total missionary membership was 23,573. The balance-sheet for the same year presented a missionary income of £20,599 17s. 7¼d. sterling. This was a large sum for our exchequer, considering that the society had only been organized five years.

The Christianity of our world is like the orbs of the solar system, which, while they all receive light from the sun, do reciprocally illuminate each other; so every evangelical church, receiving its light from the Sun of Righteousness, must and will reflect that light to the " regions beyond," and then farther into the deep recesses of moral darkness, until that darkness is entirely dissipated, and every land enjoys the light and the blessings of pure, Protestant Christianity. To the church is the injunction given, " Arise, shine, for thy light is come, and the glory of the Lord is risen upon thee."

The missionary band in the Newfoundland District continued unbroken until about the month of January, 1820, when Mr. Cubitt, on account of ill health, had to return to his native land. His brethren, however, continued to labor in their different circuits under many privations, but with much zeal and success. God was with them; the people everywhere received them with kindness, and attentively listened to their instructions. The fruit of their labors, in many instances, has already been apparent; but the entire result thereof will only be known when the Great Head of the Church shall appear in the clouds of heaven to "judge the world in righteousness."

In the year 1818, the population of the island was estimated at 90,000 souls, of whom about 40,000 were Protestants. The Protestant population were scattered over a line of coast, which, including the deep indents of the large bays, extended more than eight hundred miles. For the religious instruction of this large and scattered body of people, the agents of three missionary societies, and no more, were employed. Of these, the Wesleyans were the earliest in the field, and by far the most numerous. We had eleven missionaries, and occupied different positions in five, out of the eight, large bays of the island.

The second was the Congregationalists. These had a respectable church in St. Johns, with the Rev. Mr. Sabine as pastor. There were also a few members of this church residing in the harbor of Twillingate.

The third was the "Society for the Propagation of the Gospel in Foreign Parts." This society had five missionaries, viz.: St. Johns, Rev. Messrs. Rowland and Grantham; Harbor Grace, Rev. Mr. Carrington; Trinity, Rev. Mr. Clinch; and at Twillingate, Rev. Mr. Leigh. Messrs. Rowland and Grantham soon after removed from the island, and Mr. Leigh went to England for a time; so that in 1820 there were only two Episcopal clergymen, Rev. Mr. Carrington, who was now in St. Johns, and Rev. Mr. Clinch, in Trinity.

Beside these two ministers, they had eleven persons called school-masters, some of whom were respectable men.   These school-masters received from £10 to £20 per annum for reading prayers on the Sabbath.   This was the whole establishment of the Episcopal Church in the year 1820.

From the Roman Catholics of Newfoundland we have never met with any formal opposition ; but we regret to say, it has been otherwise with the ministers of the Episcopal Church.   The Wesleyans have never placed themselves in antagonism to the Church of England, and particularly did they in Newfoundland respect the ministers of the Church.   But that respect was returned with contempt and ridicule, and even persecution when in their power.   Did not the official publications of the " Propagation Society " tend to this? We give, as an example, an extract from the Report of the " Society for the Propagation of the Gospel in Foreign Parts," for the year 1818, published in London.   In that report, at page 46, when speaking of Trinity Bay, we have the following paragraph : —

" The whole population of the bay is estimated at one thousand souls, and within a few years they were almost exclusively members of the Church of England ; but lately some *fanatic* preachers have made considerable progress there, as well as in other parts."

The compilers of that report ought to have informed themselves better, ere they made such a statement. Before Methodist preachers went to Old Perlican, the people of Trinity Bay were neither " members of the Church of England," nor of any other church ; but were " without God," literally *Atheists* in the world ; nor did Methodist preachers obtrude upon Episcopal ground, as the above statement would show.

We could afford to smile at the expression " fanatic

preachers," when applied to such men as George Cubit, Richard Knight, and others of our brethren whose powers of intellect were no way inferior to those who wrote that sentence,— only it was a sort of watchword for the persecution of the people. The Committee of the Society denounced their seniors in this field of labor as " fanatics ; " and their agents must put down such fanaticism, whatever means they employ to accomplish their purpose. Thus one clerical gentleman, in that same Trinity Bay, would show his superiority, by occasionally wearing his surplice among the fishermen in the public path, and, with a portion of it gathered in his hand, would say, " See, I can wear a gown, but Methodist preachers are not authorized so to do." Another said to one of our friends, " How is it that you can give the preference to that Mr. Hickson (Brother James Hickson) who is ' *so much my inferior* ' ? " While a third called upon the father of two young ladies who had lately joined our church, and said to him, " It is your duty to prevent your daughters from going to the Methodist chapel, and *make them* come to the church." The kind father replied, " Sir, I will do no such thing ; my daughters are old enough to think for themselves ; and, if they wish to go to the Methodist chapel, I will not interfere with them."

But the most serious persecution occurred, a little later than this, in the Harbor of Bonavista. The autograph written at the time, and containing the details of this painful matter, now lies before me ; and, suppressing the names, I will give a condensed statement of the case.

A certain clerical gentleman came to Bonavista to reside only for a time ; but his zeal was great against the fanatics, which zeal had been greatly excited by reading an article in an English Methodist magazine which chanced to fall into his hands. Just then, God had been pleased to bless us with a revival of religion, and among many others who were awakened was a married woman who had been an attendant at the Episcopal Church. The event excited the surprise of her friends, who said she was out of her senses. The doctor was called in, who said there was nothing the matter with her; yet he thought that bleeding would do her good, so he cupped her in the back of the neck. The clergyman was sent for, and she told him she felt herself a sinner, and wished to learn the way to heaven. He said she was *hypochondriacal;* and if her friends would try and amuse her, or even take her out, and *pelt her a little with snow-balls,* it would perhaps drive away her melancholy. The Wesleyan minister went to see her, and to him she spoke freely. She said she felt herself to be a guilty sinner, and wished to learn the way to heaven. As soon as his reverence heard that the Methodist preacher had been to see the woman, he wrote rather a singular note, from which we make the following extracts: —

"I have been told you have been to visit ——. I beg to be informed if it be true, and by whom you were sent for. Had I visited one of your flock when she was hypochondriacal, I should have considered myself guilty of impertinent interference.

"With Mr. Wesley, I cannot ascribe these things hastily to God. I do not suppose dreams, voices, impressions, visions, or revelations to come from God: they may be from him; they may be from nature; they may be from the devil.

"Your obedient
"John ———."

The missionary, on the evening of the same day that he received the above note, met the doctor, and asked him, "Does Mrs. P—— labor under any bodily disease?" He replied, " No; there is nothing the matter with her body : it is all mental, and arises from *mistaken notions of religion ; and, if she was my wife, I would flog her well.*"

After this, her head was shaved and blistered ; her hands were tied ; and her cruel father actually flogged her. Still it was stated that nothing was the matter with her, but " mistaken notions of religion."

The Wesleyan minister was now peremptorily excluded from the house ; but some of our female members contrived for a short time longer to see her. One of these ladies happened to go to the house just after her father had beaten her. She was standing at the door, and addressed our friend as she entered, " Oh, how happy I am to see you ; see how I am treated, and there is nothing the matter with me, only I feel myself to be a sinner, and I want some one to tell me the way of salvation." Here the conversation was interrupted by her brother, who began to swear at her, and call her father to come again and flog her.

Upon another occasion, three of our female members went in company to see her ; and the doctor was at the door, who reluctantly consented to their admission ; but gave them them this caution, " I have one thing to say, and that is, you must not speak to her on religious subjects." When they entered the room, she had a strait-jacket on, and a blister on her head. While they conversed on common topics, all went on well ; but, the moment they introduced religious conversation, they were interrupted, and she was threatened with confinement in a dark room. With much difficulty, they succeeded in getting permission to pray with her. This was the last time they could do so ; for, in the evening of the same day, the Rev. Mr. —— came in great wrath, and absolutely forbade that any " more Methodists should be permitted to see her."

The following Sabbath, one of our local preachers determined to make an effort to see her, as he was a distant relation. He went in the afternoon, while most of the family were at church ; but her father was at home, who admitted our friend with very great reluctance. He stated that she was quite gentle, and had no appearance of gloom or melancholy ; but she still had on the strait-jacket, and a blister on her head. He inquired as to the state of her mind. She replied, " I am a poor ignorant creature ; I feel I am a sinner, and nothing but the blood of Christ can do me good." Her father overheard the conversation, and came into the room, when our friend asked permission to pray with her. The abrupt reply was, " No ! " He remonstrated, " Not pray with your daughter in her present state of mind ; that is cruel ! " The father replied, " I have a minister of my own, and I do not wish to offend him." Our friend answered, " Remember, while you are trying to avoid giving offence to your minister, you are sinning against God : the salvation of your daughter is at stake." " Well, said" he, " you should pray with her with all my heart ; but the Rev. Mr. —— was here last night, and he forbids any person praying with her ; beside, they are now praying for her in the church." The poor woman in the end was compelled to yield, and was never afterward permitted to enter a Methodist chapel.

I will make no comment on the above ; only would assure the reader, that the statement was not compiled from a series of flying reports, but was taken down from the lips of the parties, on the respective days when the event occurred.

In the year 1819, the Rev. George Cubit returned to England, and thus reduced the number of our missionaries to ten. But, in the spring of 1820, the writer was sent to make up the number to eleven. He came from the London West Circuit, then under the superintendency of the Rev. George Morley. He was ordained in Chelsea Chapel, London, April 5, 1820 ; left Liverpool on the 21st of the same month, and landed at Harbor Grace on Sabbath, May 21st. The district meeting commenced June 1st ; and his appointment was St. Johns, under the superintendency of the Rev. John Pickavant.

Newfoundland was still without any roads ; and, except in the vicinity of St. Johns, there was not a house anywhere one mile from the water-side. Three calamitous fires had reduced the town of St. Johns to great distress, from the effects of which it was now slowly recovering. The first fire has been noticed in this narrative. It occurred on the 12th of February, 1816, and desolated a great part of the town. The property destroyed was said to exceed £100,000 sterling ; beside which, some fifteen hundred human beings were left houseless and penniless amid the snow and storms of a Newfoundland winter. The second fire broke out on the night of November 7th, 1817, which, in the short space of nine hours, destroyed thirteen mercantile establishments, well stocked with provisions, one hundred and forty dwelling-houses, and property to the amount of £500,000 sterling. This was succeeded by a third fire, which happened on the 21st of the same month, when several other wharves and stores, with fifty-six other dwelling-houses, were entirely consumed.

These repeated fires produced great distress, and

prevented the merchants from ordering supplies from
Europe to the extent to which they had been accustomed. Many of the inhabitants were in great
want, and became desperate ; provision stores and
private houses were broken open, both in St. Johns
and Carbonear. The people of Conception Bay called
the winter of 1817 the " winter of the rals," from a
sort of watch-word which was used in these gatherings.

When the writer of this arrived in his circuit, the
town was being rebuilt. A new chapel and mission-
house had been erected, by the kind contributions of
the friends of missions in various parts of Great
Britain. St. Johns Circuit then comprised Portugal
Cove, Torbay, and Petty Harbor. In the town,
beside our usual services in the chapel, we, during
summer, preached in the open air once a week at
River Head and Magotty Cove. Portugal Cove
is nine miles from St. Johns. There is now a good
road to this place ; but then, for more than half way,
it was a complete bog. Here we had a small society,
and an excellent local preacher, Mr. Curtis, so that we
visited this place but occasionally. The next place
was Torbay, which is north from St. Johns, about
seven miles. The path is mostly bog; but we thought
little of the walk, as we were always rewarded with
every kindness from the people, and had the whole
Protestant population as our regular hearers. Petty
Harbor is nine miles south from St. Johns. For
three fourths of the way, the path was over a series of
high hills, many of them having an inclination of more
than forty-five degrees, with large rocks and caverns almost every step ; so that locomotion was necessarily very
slow, and the labor very great to the wearied pedes-
trian. The winter path was not so exhausting, as it

lay mostly over ponds and level marshes. This was truly mission ground, where we both had to toil and suffer. Newfoundland is justly proverbial for its hospitality ; and, in the out-harbors, every house is, or may be, the stranger's home. Petty Harbor was an exception. The people would come to hear us preach, but none would invite us to their table. We were accustomed to walk this terrible path on Sabbath morning early, preach twice, and teach a small sabbath school, remain without dinner, unless we took it with us, and return the same nine miles in the evening. Often has the writer been compelled to satisfy the cravings of hunger with a few berries plucked by the way-side. One Sabbath, Brother Pickavant walked this laborious eighteen miles, preached twice, and, having taken no food since the morning, he fainted as soon as he entered the Mission House. How merciful was the Redeemer, when he justified his disciples, who, being "an hungred" on the "Sabbath day," began to pluck the ears of corn and to eat. When the winter came on, it was not possible to return on Sabbath evening : we therefore went on Saturday, and remained generally until Tuesday morning. The writer had to sleep two, and sometimes three, nights every fortnight, during the severe winter of 1820–1821, in an open loft, on a bed of shavings, with two horse-rugs for his covering. These labors were not in vain ; great good was done both in Torbay and Petty Harbor ; and, could those places have been attended in after years, we certainly should have seen much fruit : but the paucity of missionaries rendered it necessary for the district meeting, at its next meeting, to remove the second preacher from the St. Johns Circuit, when they had to be abandoned.

CHAPTER IX.

THE first two reports were made up to February
1st ; the next four, to June 24th ; but, since the
year 1820, our balance-sheet was not made up until the
31st of December. The amounts for these years were
as follows : —

			£	s.	d.
1814,	amount of income to February 1,		6,820	2	5
1815,	"	" "	9554	4	4½
1816,	"	" to June 24,	12,565	0	9½
1817,	"	" " "	19,933	7	7¾
1818,	"	" " "	20,599	17	7¼
1819,	"	" " "	25,087	9	8
1820,	"	" to December 31,	37,221	15	9

The number of our missionaries at the conference
of 1821 was one hundred and thirty-two ; and our
missionary membership, 28,699.

The early missionary reports contain a mass of
interesting matter, at which we need not be surprised,
when we know that they are the production of the
giant mind of Richard Watson, a man who seemed
to scan the world at a glance, and thoroughly to understand its state and its wants ; who knew the talent,
the tact, and the necessities of every missionary in the

22   (253)

field ; whose pulpit oratory, unsurpassed in a century, was always employed on behalf of missions; whose pen put their enemies to silence; whose theological productions will continue to benefit mankind to the latest period of time; who did more, and with greater effect, toward the emancipation of slaves in the West Indies, than any other man in England, not in the Legislature ; whose life was a pattern of kindness, diligence, and piety; whose end was peace; and whose name will go down, with unblemished reputation, to unborn generations.

Such was the character of one of the first secretaries of the Wesleyan Methodist Missionary Society; and his coadjutors, Jabez Bunting and Joseph Taylor, were truly kindred spirits with his own.

The missionary committee, and especially the secretaries, as soon as they entered office, found that they not only had to raise money for missionary purposes, but also that it was incumbent upon them to see that the moneys so raised should be properly expended. There were three usages among our first missionaries, which would now appear extremely strange. The first was, that every missionary had a separate and individual right to draw bills for his own support, without any limit as to the amount of the bill. The conference of 1815 put its veto upon this practice, by the following minute : —

"No missionary in the West Indies, Newfoundland, Nova Scotia, New Brunswick, Canada, or Bermuda, shall be permitted to draw a bill for more than fifty pounds at one time, without previous advice and explanation of the extraordinary nature and circumstance of the case. No missionary, stationed in the East, shall be permitted to draw a bill for more than one hundred and fifty pounds at one time, without similar advice."

The second usage was, the appropriation of moneys from the sale of books, sent by the book-steward, to the personal use of the missionaries. The conference also put this right in 1816, by the following minute : —

" That all our missionaries shall be personally responsible to the book-steward for all books which they may order from him for the purpose of sale at their respective stations. But they shall be left at liberty, at their several district-meetings, to apply the produce of such sales, if they deem it expedient, to the payment of their ordinary deficiencies as missionaries, so far as it will go ; and shall pay the book-steward what they owe him, by sending him an order on the missionary treasurer in London, to the amount of those ordinary deficiencies, which they have received out of the book-money."

The third usage was, they drew bills upon other persons beside the treasurers for their support. The conference of 1817 regulated this matter by the following resolution : —

" That the missionaries shall be peremptorily prohibited from drawing bills, for missionary expenses, upon any other person than the general treasurers ; and that, in order to prevent any such irregularities, printed forms of bills shall be forwarded to each missionary station ; of which forms, and no others, the missionaries shall be required to make use, when they have occasion."

Beside the above irregularities, the missionaries had no fixed allowance for either board or quarterage ; and it was truly amusing, at the district meeting, to hear the brethren read their circuit accounts, and name each article of food and clothing that was made use of during the year. There was always something in the account which must be struck out. This we called rasping. No matter what the brother himself thought of his account, it was sure to be rasped at the district meeting. One man would have had too much beef ; another was rather too expensive in sugar; a third had a new coat when his old one would have lasted a little longer; another wore out too many shoes; and such a brother could not want so many pocket handkerchiefs as appeared on his bill. This matter engaged the early attention of the secretaries and missionary committee, who issued their first circular on March 31, 1819. This circular now lies before me, from which I will extract the second paragraph : —

" It is highly desirable that a regular and proper scale of allowances of income should be established for the various missionaries in every part of the world, so as to provide them with what is sufficient for food, clothing, &c., in those places where they reside, according to the necessary expense of living in each place. We are of opinion, also, that the allowance ought to be such as will render the missionaries and their families sufficiently comfortable, while engaged in their great and important work."

The circular bears the signature of " Charles Atmore, Chairman."

The substance of this circular engaged the attention of the brethren in Newfoundland for some two years before they could agree as to the scale of allowance they would request the committee to make for their district. Brother John Walsh took an active part in this matter. He carefully ascertained the expenses of each circuit in the district; calculated what clothes each brother would require; and, making allowances for miscellaneous and incidental expenses, he drew up a scale of allowance, and presented it at the district of 1822, which, being sanctioned by the missionary committee, formed the scale of allowance which, with some trifling alteration, has been observed to the present time.

Beside the above circular, the secretaries were accustomed, a few days after the close of conference, to send " an annual circular " to each missionary, giving a condensed view of the proceedings of the conference, the state of the connection, the state of the different funds, with instructions to the missionaries on particular topics, and other information of great value and importance to the missionaries at that time, as neither the " Wesleyan " nor the " Watchman " then existed ; and particularly were these circulars valued in the distant stations of this mission, where, for six months of the year, we never saw a newspaper, or received a letter.

The substance of these circulars was, in the year 1832, put in the form of a small volume, called " An Appendix to the General Instructions of the Missionary Committee, for the private use of the Missionaries." From this little volume, we shall make one extract, because it will always be of importance to the right working of our itinerancy. The heading is, " Solitary Stations : " —

" Several of the districts, and especially those in British North America and Newfoundland, are divided almost entirely in solitary stations, in consequence of which many circuits are unavoidably intrusted to the superintendence of young men, with little experience in the discipline of Methodism, to the great detriment of the societies, and to the hinderance of the work of God. We would recommend to the chairmen and brethren of districts so circumstanced, to turn their attention to a union or re-arrangement of their circuits, so that two preachers may, as far as practicable, be stationed together; and the young men be thus placed, as long as needful, under the direction of the senior brethren."

We shall here give a biographical sketch of our missionary secretaries, that the reader may form a judgment of the men who guided our missionary concerns in their first movements, and by whose judicious management, at that early time, is, under God, mainly

22 *

owing the present reputation and wide-spread influence of the *Wesleyan Methodist Missionary Society.*"

The secretaries were Jabez Bunting, Joseph Taylor, and Richard Watson.

Jabez Bunting, D. D., was senior secretary. He was a man of deep piety, of singularly quick apprehension of mind; while his judgment was acute, discriminating, comprehensive, and far seeing. At the first missionary meeting, which was held in Leeds, October 6, 1813, he was only of fourteen years' Methodistic standing; but, from that period, he held a prominent position in all the institutions of Methodism, — defending those institutions when attacked by their enemies, and sustaining the connection itself by his wisdom and humility, when, by some of its unfaithful members, it was threatened with division and annihilation. The " British and Foreign Bible Society," the " Anti-slavery Society," and the " Evangelical Alliance," all had the benefit of his wise counsel and advocacy. As a preacher, his sermons always overflowed with rich evangelical sentiments; his exposition of Scripture was clear and instructive; his statement of doctrine was preëminently scriptural, striking, and simple, and delivered with an eloquence, a pathos, and an effect that attracted multitudes to every place where he officiated. On the missionary platform, his speeches told upon the listening multitudes, who were thereby led cheerfully to give of their substance, in order to send the gospel of salvation to the " ends of the earth."

Upon one occasion, when our income was only moderate, he gave it as his decided opinion, that the resources of Methodism were sufficiently ample to raise *fifty thousand pounds annually* for *missionary purposes.* Some of his best friends were sceptical on this ; while to those outside, the idea of the Wesleyan Church raising fifty thousand per annum for the mission fund was treated with ridicule, or considered as only the raving of a fanatic or a madman. But time proved that his opinion was correct, and that, from his knowledge of the *means* and *minds* of our people, he reasoned, *a priori*, what they could and would do, when the wants of the world were made known to them, and their duty in the case made plain and clear. There was indeed a " massive grandeur " in Jabez Bunting, such as does not ordinarily pertain to mortals : he was a " Prince in our Israel." He died in " perfect peace," crying " Victory, victory, through the blood of the Lamb."

Joseph Taylor was the first resident secretary at the Mission House, Hatton Garden, London ; to which office he was appointed by the conference of 1818. He had been a missionary, and spent eight years of his life in missionary toil among the negroes of the West Indies. His talents were not so splendid as those of his colleagues in the secretariat ; but he was a kind, a wise, and holy man. To him pertained the duty of class-leader to the missionaries in London, before they left for their respective destinations. For the space of four months, the writer had the privilege of meeting in his missionary class, before he left for his station in Newfoundland. Mr. Taylor was most diligent and laborious in his office, and acted as a kind father to the missionaries, who loved him sincerely. After six years of faithful service in the secretaryship, he went out again in the regular work, and continued to labor until the year 1845, when, in the sixty-seventh year of his age, he was called to his reward. Just before he died, he exclaimed, " I am on the rock, and all is right : I have fought my way through, and the Saviour is with me."

Richard Watson was one of the brightest ornaments that ever adorned the Wesleyan, or any other church in Christendom. He possessed a range and brilliancy of thought, with a grasp of intellectual powers, that seldom fall to the lot of mortals. " To his understanding belonged a capacity which the greatness of a subject could not exceed ; a strength and clearness which number and complexity of its parts could not confuse ; and a vigor which the difficulty and length of an inquiry could not weary." It was the high privilege of the writer to sit under the ministry of this distinguished man for three years ; and although it is now more than forty years ago, yet the recollection of him is still clear and vivid. His person was tall, his countenance pale, and his general appearance that of a man in ill health. When he entered the pulpit, there was a solemnity in his manner that affected the whole congregation. In reading the Scriptures, he was very impressive ; his style of reading our hymns was peculiarly poetic ; and his fine musical ear required that the tune should be always devotional, and suited to the sentiment of the hymn. Upon one occasion, in Lambeth Chapel, London, he gave out the hymn on page 251 : —

> " A thousand oracles divine,
> Their common beams unite,
> That sinners may with angels join,
> To worship God aright."

The choir struck up the tune called, " Acton," in Rippon's collection. Mr. Watson thought that tune so unsuitable to the hymn, that, at the end of the first verse, he addressed the choir in these words, " I never did, and I never will, suffer a Christian congregation to be thus insulted." He closed the hymn-book, engaged in prayer, and dismissed the congregation.

In the pulpit, he stood erect, almost like a statue: his action seldom went beyond a slight motion of the right hand, or a significant shake of the head. The subjects on which he delighted to dwell were the depravity of man, the divinity of Christ, the great atonement, with the extent and freedom of the gospel salvation. To the explanation and elucidation of these great subjects, would he bring all the vast powers of his master mind. Having given the sense of his text with his usual critical acumen, by which the most familiar topics of theology would often appear in a new light, or be clothed with fresh interest, in the pure emanation of his soul, he would soar to themes lofty and sublime; grasp in the range of his thought the whole scheme of human redemption; scan the attributes of Deity with a mind almost superhuman; or seem to fathom the joys of the hymning multitude before the throne of God.

As a writer, no man since the days of John Wesley has done the Wesleyan Church greater service than Richard Watson. In the infancy of our missionary existence, 1816, Mr. Barham, M. P. for Stockbridge, in the House of Commons, attacked the Methodist missionaries in the West Indies, and said, that, " under a mask of religion, they inculcated principles of sedition." This produced from the pen of Mr. Watson, " A DEFENCE OF THE WESLEYAN METHODIST MISSIONS IN THE WEST INDIES." This silenced the slanderer, and brought a compliment from his Majesty's Government, through Lord Castlereagh, to the effect, " That there lay no charge whatever against the missionaries who had been slandered so harshly by name." In 1819, Mr. Watson wrote " The Instructions to the Wesleyan Missionaries," a copy of which now lies before the writer, which he received at his ordination, and which bears the autograph signatures of Jabez Bunting, Joseph Taylor, and Richard Watson.

These Instructions did the writer often peruse with much profit while on the Newfoundland mission. In 1820, Mr. Watson published his " Observations on Southey's Life of Wesley."

The Wesleyan Catechisms are the production of his pen, by which our children are in early years taught the principles of a sound theology, and are made thoroughly acquainted with all the leading facts of the Bible. His " Conversations for the Young " amuse and instruct our youth ; while his Theological Institutes and his Theological Dictionary supply our church with a body of divinity, which, for scriptural accuracy, distinctness of thought, and elevation of style, is unsurpassed by any theological writings the Christian Church has ever produced since the days of the apostles.

We shall close this sketch by the following quotation from the minutes of the British Conference for 1833 : —

" In his last affliction, he was greatly honored of God ; and perhaps the closing scene of no saint's life ever furnished lessons of richer instruction. On the approach of death, he viewed it as a foe, and felt it to be an evil ; he was humbled that a man should be stricken and trampled into the grave by the last enemy, and when, as in his own case, his faculties were in their prime, and his mind meditating and revolving plans of usefulness to the world. It was the glorious hope and Christian assurance of perfect bliss after death and beyond the grave that enabled him to triumph ; and his triumph was complete. Through the grace of his Divine Saviour, with his characteristic strength of mind, he grasped and applied his Christian principles ; and they sustained his faith in his walk through ' the valley of the shadow of death.' ' I am a poor vile worm,' said he ; ' but then the worm is permitted to crawl out of the earth into the garden of the Lord.'

'I shall behold his face,
  I shall his power adore;
  And sing the wonders of his grace
  For evermore.'

" Thus confident, he waited until his Master's call spoke him up
to heaven. As a man, he was of a noble mind, superior through
life to everything mean and little ; he was magnanimous, disin-
terested, generous. His form was dignified, and his countenance
bore striking expressions of his intellectual greatness. His elevated views, and the majesty of his character, impressed a dignity
on his manners which the kindness of his temper, and his general
readiness to oblige, rendered particularly easy and graceful. As
a friend, he extorted no servile homage as the price of his friendship. If there were times when he was too much engaged in
thought to exhibit more than common fervor of affection, there
were others, which occurred far more frequently, when he gave
himself freely to his friends, and then his conversation never
failed to instruct and charm. This bright luminary of the church
and of his circle set in death, to rise in glory, January 8th, 1833.
He died in the fifty-second year of his age."

In the year 1824, a change took place in our missionary secretaries.   Mr. Bunting removed to the Manchester South Circuit, and Mr. Taylor, having served
his term, also retired from his onerous position of resident secretary.   Our missionary secretaries now were
George Morley, Richard Watson, and John Mason.
All these excellent men are now recorded on our death-
roll.   While they lived, they not only performed the
various duties incumbent upon them as Christian
ministers with great faithfulness and zeal, but they
also, in other ways, labored hard for the benefit of their
fellow-men, and particularly for the spread of Scriptural
knowledge, and the extension of missions over every
part of the world.

GEORGE MORLEY.   The name of this excellent minister will be recorded in the annals of Methodism, as
long as time shall last, as the originator of a movement
which led to the formation of the present financial plan

of our missions, by which they have become so wide-
spread in their influence, and so vastly beneficial in
their results. He had been on terms of intimacy with
Dr. Coke, and had seen how that apostolic man had labored and begged from door to door to obtain means
for the support of missionaries in foreign lands; but in
the year 1813, the doctor and his little missionary band
were appointed to India; when Mr. Morley saw that
something more must be done by the connection for
the mission cause than had yet been done, or it would
dwindle and die. He was then superintendent of the
Leeds Circuit; and his colleagues were Jabez Bunting
and Robert Pilter. In Wakefield, an adjacent circuit,
were found two kindred spirits, in James Buckley and
Richard Watson. These brethren, after much consultation and prayer, appointed Mr. Buckley to preach
the first missionary sermon in the village of Armley;
and Mr. Bunting having prepared the plan, the first
public Methodist missionary meeting was held in the
old chapel at Leeds, in the afternoon of October
6th, 1813. Thomas Thompson, Esq., M. P., a most acceptable local preacher, presided upon the occasion.
Though the plan was matured by Mr. Bunting, yet it
was Mr. Morley that suggested the idea of employing
collectors to raise weekly, monthly, quarterly, and annual subscriptions, in aid of Methodist missions. Five
years after the formation of the Leeds Missionary Society, which was the year 1818, Mr. Morley was appointed to the London West Circuit, when the writer of
this article had the pleasure of having him as his superintendent; and he records with thankfulness, that to
the judicious counsels and fatherly instructions of the
Rev. George Morley, he owes his present position in the
Wesleyan connection. He was resident secretary for
our mission, six years; and those of us who had the

honor of his correspondence were always encouraged by his letters and instructed by his advice. He exchanged mortality for life on the 10th of September, 1843. A little while before he died, he said, with great emphasis, " I gave myself to God and to God's people threescore years ago, and he has never left me. He is with me now, and he will never leave nor forsake me." The minutes of conference say of him, " His life was one of perpetual sunshine. He was emphatically a happy man ; and his end perfectly accorded with the tenor of his life."

John Mason was the junior missionary secretary, which situation he filled with kindness to the missionaries for three years, when he was called to the important and responsible office of book-steward. He continued in that office for thirty-seven years, during which time he circulated an immense amount of Christian literature, from whence large profits were derived ; which profits were appropriated to the support of aged and worn-out ministers, and ministers' widows. From six to ten tons of books would sometimes be sent from the book-room in one month. Mr. Mason died in peace on the 1st of March, 1864, in the eighty-second year of his age, and fifty-third of his ministry.

The first official circular, bearing the signatures of the before-named secretaries, reached the writer in the month of October, 1824. He was then stationed in Port de Grave. We shall quote the last paragraph from this circular, which shows the deep anxiety the committee felt that their missionaries should all be able ministers of the New Testament. It reads : —

" Study to be ' workmen who need not to be ashamed.' By careful reading, increase your knowledge of the Scriptures ; distribute the truths they contain with plainness of speech, with earnestness, and affectionate feeling. He who makes preaching a mere declamation from a text of Scripture will often be barren in himself, and unprofitable to others; but he who feels that it is his business to display the truth of God in his discourses, and who confirms and illustrates what he advocates by well-chosen and clearly-explained texts, will find his preaching salutary to his own heart, and it will give spirit and life to others. ' Let the word of God then dwell in you richly; and from that fulness you will be able to minister to the wants of others.' "

The kind and style of preaching recommended by our secretaries can never fail of doing good; and it may be inferred, as a general thing, that Methodist missionaries in different parts of the world adhere to these instructions, which is the grand secret of their success in their respective stations.

The paucity of schools, and in consequence the great ignorance that prevailed among the people, was a matter of much concern and anxiety to the early missionaries in Newfoundland.

Along the whole north shore, where there were some thousands of inhabitants, there was not a school of any kind, except our Sabbath schools; and while the people would willingly have paid for the education of their children, yet no competent teacher could then be found. To select Black Head as an example: down as late as the year 1820, there never had been a day-school in that large and interesting community.

Mr. Walsh, who was then stationed on the Black-Head Circuit, brought this prominently before the missionary committee, in a letter dated Black Head, Oct. 20, 1819. From this letter we make the following extract:—

" Only a few in my circuit are able to read the Word of God. It often draws from my heart a sigh of pity, when I look round me from the pulpit, and see so many of them unable to take up a hymn or prayer book, to join in the worship of God. If you consider the circumstances in which these people are placed, you will with me conclude, that this want of common learning does not arise from incapacity, but from destitution of means and opportunity. If I am rightly informed, there never was one person or place wholly devoted to the instruction of the rising generation in this circuit. In no place, I think, could a mission day-school be established with greater probability of success than at this station. Had we a pious young man, with moderate abilities, fixed here as a school-master, under the superintendence of the missionary, I have no doubt a hundred children would be immediately collected, and their parents would contribute gladly to the support of such a master. But in this country such a person is not to be found. Could you provide this station with a person who would engage to instruct these dear children to read the Word of Life, you would bestow upon them the next great favor to those you have already bestowed, in giving them the word and ministry of reconciliation."

However much the missionary committee might wish to send a staff of school-masters to Newfoundland, such an appropriation of their funds would scarcely have been compatible with their object, which was simply to supply the country with an evangelical ministry. Beside which, the report for 1821 showed an excess of expenditure above the income of £7568 5s. 10d.

For many years had the establishment of day-schools in different parts of the land been a great desideratum, both with the missionaries and also with the more intelligent among their congregations ; and, in the year 1823, it was for a time thought their views would be met, and their expectations fully realized, by the institution of the Newfoundland School Society.

Some of the agents of this society claimed for it a liberal and evangelical character ; and while it was said the masters were expected to be members of the Church of England, yet the Wesleyans, who were the only

nonconformist body on the island, would have equal
rights with their Episcopalian neighbors in all matters
appertaining to the school. Several of the missionaries,
in consequence, took deep interest in these schools ; and
our committee paid twenty pounds a year, for several
years, toward their funds. Schools were soon established in St. Johns, Harbor Grace, Trinity, Bonavista,
and other places, in which our people heartily united.
But in time it changed its name, and took the title of
the Church-of-England School Society for Newfoundland and the Colonies. Our people from henceforth
were debarred all management or control in the schools,
which now became decidedly Church-of-England schools.
Persecution, also, was not quite kept out of the way
in the matter. In the Northern Harbor, when preparations were being made for the erection of a school-
house, some things not appearing quite clear, as to the
management of the school when it should commence
operations, one of the merchants said to the writer, "If
Mrs. A. and Mr. B. and I were determined, we could
make the people build the school, *for we have them completely under us.* I could therefore go to a family man
and say, ' Go, and haul me a stick for the school ;' and I
could order others who were handy to go to work in
putting up the building. They dare not refuse us ; and
they would say, ' We must go, or he will not let us have
a half gallon of molasses when we want it.' " The
magistrate in the same place went much farther than
our merchants, for he considered he had the power in
himself to tax the people for the school-house ; and, in
his *pro rata tax*, he sent to a poor Roman Catholic man,
and threatened to put him in jail if he did not pay ten
shillings toward this school ; and it was only when the
writer informed the magistrate that he would lay the

whole matter before the government, that he gave up his arbitrary proceedings.

This society is now professedly a Church-of-England institution, and we cheerfully yield its meed of praise. It has established schools in many destitute parts of the island; it has taught many thousands to read, who, but for it, would have been brought up in entire ignorance; it has circulated Bibles, prayer-books, religious tracts, and other books of moral and religious tendency; and its teachers, beside attending to their duties in schools, have visited the sick and the dying, and have done much good among the people. In the year 1849, it reported 40 schools and 2,734 scholars. It had also extended its operations into Canada. Its receipts for that year were £1937 14s.

Near the close of the year 1819, and at the commencement of 1820, there was a great revival in the "Island Cove and Perlican Circuit," under the ministry of the Rev. James Hickson. We will give a few extracts from the journal of this excellent missionary, as published in the Methodist Magazine for 1820: —

" Dec. 27th. We had a powerful season in the men's class: two received the blessing of pardon, and many others went away pleading for mercy. We in the kingdom of grace, and angels in the kingdom of glory, gladly sing, ' The dead's alive; the lost is found.' We have many in this society (Old Perlican), but few had received the ' spirit of adoption.' The danger of living and dying without the Spirit's witness urged me to fast, and ardently to pray for the baptism of the Spirit. Glory be to God, to-night I had an answer of prayer.

" 30th. This night, two females were born of the Spirit. It was the first time of their meeting in our society. My soul had a new baptism of the Spirit, and seemed as if it would have left the body, while agonizing for the mourners in Zion. I felt more than ever the truth of that saying, ' God is love.'

" Jan. 3d, 1820. Found much joy in visiting different families, but the greatest in meeting one of the classes. There was, indeed, a shaking among the 'dry bones.' Many were crying, from the very bitterness of their souls, 'Thou Son of David, have mercy on me.' And after continuing long in prayer, the Lord bound up four broken hearts.

"Sabbath, 9th. Island Cove. Preached twice; but the power of God was most evident at night, in the prayer-meeting. Many wept aloud. On Monday night, in the men's class, we had one more in number. I pressed them more especially NOW, not to rest without a clear sense of the pardoning love of God; and it was not in vain, for the hearts of many were broken, and they cried bitterly for mercy. We remained with them in prayer for some time. The next night many were pricked in the heart. In the class, on Thursday, there was one much tempted of Satan, and did not find deliverance; but God sent his Spirit into the heart of another, crying, 'Abba, Father.' The day following, we had an increase of another member and another believer.

"Sabbath, 30th. Old Perlican. Had much divine help, in preaching three times to this people. I had a seal to my ministry, a soul for my hire, while crying, 'Agree with thine adversary quickly.' He was seventy years old, and had been thirty years a member of the Methodist Society. He was always strictly moral, but an utter stranger to experimental godliness, till one and another were enabled to stand forth as witnesses that God has power on earth to forgive sins. This shook his sandy foundation: he had read his Bible much, and satisfied himself with that. But now it became to him as a two-edged sword: his castles in the air were all destroyed, and he had no refuge but Christ. Now Jesus filled his heart with joy, and he published it to all around. He became an 'epistle, read and known of all men.' There is a danger of our societies consisting of merely moral but unconverted characters. Hence it becomes necessary, even among our own people, to 'cry aloud and spare not;' for our mission is not to make 'almost Christian,' but Christians altogether."

This revival continued for more than two months, during which time every part of the circuit was visited with this gracious influence. In Hants Harbor alone, near fifty souls were brought to God in about a fortnight. On this Mr. Hickson writes:—

"Wednesday, Feb. 23. 'What hath God wrought. When I came to this place on the 9th, the number in society was forty; now it is ninety, seventy of whom enjoy the pardoning love of God."

It was the happiness of the writer to follow brother James Hickson in that circuit, the very next year (1821); and, were it necessary, he would bear his humble testimony to the reality and extent of that great revival.

In the minutes for 1823, the stations for the New-foundland District stand thus:—

St. Johns — John Walsh.
Carbonear — Thomas Hickson.
Harbor Grace — John Pickavant.
Black Head and Western Bay— Ninian Barr.
Island Cove and Perlican — Adam Nightingale.
Port de Grave — Richard Knight.
Bonavista and Catalina — James Hickson.
Trinity Harbor —John Boyd.
Grand Bank and Fortune Bay — William Wilson.
Burin — William Ellis.
Brigus — John Haigh.

Brother Nightingale has now (1864) spent forty-two years on the Newfoundland mission, which includes the whole of his missionary life. He has "borne the burden and heat of the day;" he has travelled its wastes and its wilderness when horses were not used, and when roads were unknown; he has had to ford its streams, and drag his weary limbs over its extensive marshes; to take his refreshment by the purling brook in the dark woods, or untie his *nunny-bag* on its bleak and snow-clad barrens; and more than once has he made his bed on the snow, and there passed a long and dreary night in the midst of a

Newfoundland winter. He has seen that country as a Crown colony; and he has seen it with its halls of legislature: he remembers the formation of its first road; and he has seen it with its macadamized highways, its studs of horses, and its beautiful carriages; with steamboats, not only for local travelling, but also for communication with other colonies and with Europe: he has seen its rocky potato-garden by the seaside, as the sole token of agriculture in a community; and he has seen its cultivated acres bowing their golden *plumes* to the passing stranger, and yielding their farinaceous substance as food for man and for beast: he has seen its communities without education, and their children without schools; and he has seen the " schoolmaster abroad," academies founded, the children instructed, the people rescued from ignorance, and their minds imbued with knowledge, religious, scientific, and general; and, above all, he has seen many souls converted to God, and Methodism increase from 973, the number of its members when he landed on its shores, to 3231, the number as returned at the conference of 1863. After being engaged in the active work for thirty-seven years, he sat down as a supernumerary in the year 1859; and he still lives, and labors occasionally. May God bless that dear brother in his old age, and may his end be perfect peace.

John Boyd labored in Newfoundland from 1822 to 1831, when he returned to England; and, in the year 1863, he was still in the active work. His station then was Glossop, in the Manchester and Bolton District.

CHAPTER X.

SEALS AND THE SEAL-FISHERY.

THREE species of seal are found upon the Newfoundland coast, — the square flipper, the hood, and the
harp. The square flipper is said to be identical with
the great Greenland seal. This animal sometimes at-
tains a length of sixteen or eighteen feet: it, however,
is but seldom seen, and must be shot before captured.
The hood is met with much more frequently, and is
called the hood from a large piece of loose skin on the
head, which it can inflate at pleasure. But it should be
stated that the male seal only has the hood. The female has no such appendage. This seal is not so large
as the square flipper ; nevertheless, it is often found
twelve or fourteen feet in length. The young hoods
are called blue-backs. They are found far to the north,
and generally near the outer edge of the ice. The
male and female are mostly found together, and the object of the hunters is to kill the dog-seal first ; if they
succeed, the female is easily killed ; but, if she should be
first killed, the dog becomes furious. He instantly in-
flates his hood, which covers his face ; his nostrils become distended like bladders ; his whole appearance is

(273)

terrific and he rushes on his assailants with great impetuosity. To strike him on the hood is useless, and he will snap the gaffs in the men's hands, and break them as though they were cabbage-stumps. A blow on the nose will kill the seal; but, if that fails, it is most tenacious of life, and, unless the heart can be reached with a musket-ball, it can scarcely be slain. Instances have occurred where the hunter has been seriously wounded, and even killed, by an old hood. I once heard an old seal-hunter give a graphic account of an encounter he and a friend had with an old hood. There were only two men in company: they came up with a pair of hoods, and imprudently killed the female. The dog-seal inflated his hood, and attacked them with tremendous fury. Escape was impossible; so they stood striking him with their gaffs until they both became exhausted. At length one of them said, we must make a desperate effort, or we shall both be killed. Keep him in abeyance as well as you can, and I will make the effort. He then opened his jack-knife, rushed upon the furious animal, and stuck the knife into the hood, when the air instantly escaped, and a blow from the gaff of his friend felled the monster on the ice.

The seal most frequent upon the coast is the harp, sometimes called the half-moon. It receives the name harp from a large black or dark spot on the back of the old dog-seal; but the female has no such mark. This seal, when very young, is called a white-coat; when one year old, it is a bedlamer; afterward, a harp. The northern seas, between Labrador and Greenland, is the home of the harp.

In the month of February, the field-ice from these seas comes in immense masses upon the north-east coast of Newfoundland. Some days before the ice is actually seen, its approach can be descried from the shore by its glim, or the reflection of light which it throws into the atmosphere when the night is dark. Upon this ice, the harps whelp, and the dams seem all to whelp about the same time, as millions of white-coats are found upon the ice, and all about the same age. From the twentieth to the last of February is the whelping time; and the ice about that time is generally in the drift of White Bay, or the Bay of Exploits.

The young cubs are called "white-coats," because they are covered with a white fur, slightly tinged with yellow. The appearance of the "white-coats" on the ice has not inaptly been compared to young lambs in a meadow; but they are far more numerous, as tens of thousands of them may be seen in every direction, basking in the sun's rays. The seal is called the sea-dog, because it barks and howls like a dog. Sometimes these young "white-coats," when weakly, will be found frozen in the ice, when the hunters call them "cats." The skins of these "cats" are not good as an article of merchandise; but they are brought home to make caps for the next sealing-voyage. The young seals grow very rapidly, and in about three weeks their white coat changes, and a darker fur comes in its place; after which they take the water with their parent, and are more difficult to catch.

In the commencement of the seal-fishery, large boats were used, which did not sail until about the middle of April. But the whelping ice had passed many weeks before this, so that no young seals could be found: their catch was therefore necessarily small, and mostly confined to the stray seals, called "rangers," which were shot in the water. The boat-sealing continued down as late as the year 1795, when the whole catch of seals for the island was 4,900; not as many as is now taken sometimes by a single vessel.

In the commencement of the present century, the sealing-boats gave way to small schooners of some thirty to fifty tons' burden; and they sailed about the twenty-first of March. They sailed thus late to avoid the equinoctial gales, or, as the saying was, "We wait until after Saint Patrick's brush;" or until "Saint Patrick takes the cold stone out of the water." But this was too late to get the young seals; yet, as they would meet with some ice at that time, the catch was greatly increased. Thus, in the year 1820, the catch was increased to 221,334.

The seal-fishery was destined to be one great source of wealth to the country, and to assume proportions which the most sanguine could never have anticipated; for its humble sealing-boats were to give place to vessels of from fifty to one hundred and fifty tons, and to be manned with crews of from twenty-five to forty men; while the interest of every individual to the north of St. Johns, from the richest to the poorest, was to be so interwoven with it, that its prosecution and results should cause more speculation, more anxiety, more excitement and solicitude, than perhaps does any other single branch of business in any part of the world.

The length of time spent in sealing-voyages is from three to eight weeks. The medium length is five weeks. The owner of the vessel supplies her with provisions, and all other necessaries, for which he claims one half the catch of seals. He also receives a certain amount from each man for his berth in the vessel. The price of the berth varies from ten shillings to two pounds. A man's share is likewise claimed for the vessel. The captain or master receives from fourpence to sixpence per seal as his wages; and the balance of the voyage is equally divided among the crew.

The monotony of a Newfoundland winter is broken during the Christmas holidays, when the young men on the North Shore go up the bay to secure a berth to the ice; which having been effected, they return to finish their winter's work.

Early in February, the women prepare the requisite supply of clothing for their husbands and sons, particularly their coarse jackets, with cuffs and buskins. About the last week in February each man goes to his doctor (for they pay the doctor by the year, whether they want his services or not), for a little medicine for the voyage. And a little it is, consisting mostly of a little salve, in case of a cut, a little friar's balsam, in case of a sprain, and, above all, a phial containing a solution of the sulphate of zinc, in case of ice-blindness. They are now ready to take their departure. But, on all the Wesleyan stations, it is customary to have a special sermon preached, and a special prayer-meeting held, for and on behalf of those about to be engaged in the perilous seal-fishery. On the part of our young men who profess religion, this is of great importance, to prepare, or rather to fortify, their minds against the temptations to which they are soon to be exposed. The swearing, Sabbath-breaking, drinking, and general profanity, in the sealing-vessels are truly fearful. They have sometimes been called floating hells. True, there are noble exceptions, and particularly in those vessels which sail from Conception Bay, where not a few pious men, and some pious captains, are to be found who set themselves to worship the God of heaven, and present a bold front to that torrent of iniquity which so constantly rolls against them. But these need much of the grace of

24

God; and the prayers of the church should be constantly offered up for them, that they may be kept faithful in the trying hour.

Our valedictory services were always interesting; particularly so was the evening prayer-meeting, when the big tear could be seen dropping from the eye of many a hardy mariner; while the hearty Amen, that would ever and anon fall upon the listening ear, from the male part of the congregation, and the silent sobs of mothers, daughters, and sisters, would indicate the divine presence, and involuntarily induce the exclamation: "This is none other but the house of God, and this is the gate of heaven."

The Sabbath being over, the sealers prepare for departure. The men themselves do not call the animal they now go to seek, a seal, but a swale, or a soil, and the occupation, swaling, or soiling. About the last of February, hundreds of ice-hunters might be seen toiling up the sculping highlands, with their gaffs, and long swaling guns on their shoulders, and bearing packs on their backs, in order to join their respective vessels on the first of March, when every man was expected to be in collar for the ice.

A few days is sufficient to fit out the vessel, which is full timbered, with false beams, to resist a side pressure from the ice; and the plank at her bows sheathed with wood and plated with iron, to bear the friction, as she presses forward. When ready for sea, the men are divided into groups, to cut their vessel out of harbor. At this time, the ice in the harbors of St. Johns, Harbor Grace, Trinity, and other places, presents a lively appearance, as hundreds of men, with their loud hurrah, and their junction song, "Ho, heave ho," work their pit-saws and wield their hatchets, to cut the ice, and then, with their gaffs and their handspikes, push it into open water; while the vessels in long line are slowly dragged down the newly made channel, to be ready to spread their snowy sails to the first fair breeze that can waft them toward their destination in the north.

In the time of which we are writing, but few of the masters or skippers of ice-hunters knew anything of navigation; and although they were excellent seamen, yet sometimes they found it difficult, after being out of sight of land for weeks, to regain their own shore.

Their method for calculating for their return was carefully to note the point of their departure, and the direction in which the ice drifted. When practicable, they took their departure from Bacalieu, which is an island in the drift of Conception and Trinity Bays, from which island they steered north-east for the ice; and as the northern ice usually drifts to the south-east, in returning, they were accustomed to steer north-west for the place of their departure. Hence it became a proverb: "Wherever you are, steer north-west for Bacalieu." But, in so doing, our skippers would sometimes miss the whole island, and bring up on some other land. An amusing incident, connected with this steering north-west, was related to the writer by a friend in Grand Bank. Our friend was fishing off the Island of St. Peters, early in the month of May, when a sealing-schooner bore down upon him, and, hailing him, asked, "Is that land Bacalieu Island?" The stranger was some three hundred miles out of his way. Our friend replied, "There is no such place as Bacalieu on this coast: the land on which the fog hangs is the French island of St. Peters." The man stood aghast! He had never heard of St. Peters, any more than our friend had heard of Bacalieu; but catching the words,

" the French Island," he seemed to think he had got somewhere on the coast of France. Pausing a moment, he said, " I do allow I am out of reckoning ! The French island! which is the way to Bacalieu ? " Our friend said, " I do not know." " Well, then," said the stranger, " what is the course to St. Johns ? " " I never was at St. Johns," said our friend ; " but you must steer north-east seven leagues to Cape Chapeau Rouge, then east half south twenty-three leagues to Cape St. Mary, then south-east about twenty-two leagues, and you will come to Cape Race, and St. Johns is on that shore." The stranger, after a sigh, shaped his course for Cape Chapeau Rouge, with a shout of " Good-by, a fair wind to you, and a good time of it," from the crew of the fishing-boat, and he was soon lost in the distance.

A day or two sail from the Island of Bacalieu will bring the vessel to the ice, which presents to the eye a boundless waste ; the ocean swell of the great Atlantic now agitates the floating mass, and heaves it in heaps of every form, which comes craunching against both sides of the vessel, as though she were between the jaws of some aquatic monster ; while the myriads of huge ice-islands from the Arctic seas sluggishly roll their ponderous weight along, threatening destruction to any craft that might chance to be in their way. It not unfrequently happens that the vessel — notwithstanding her false beams, her sheathed bows, and every other precaution that has been used, to render her invulnerable — is crushed to pieces, and her hapless crew left to wander in quest of another vessel, or perish on the ice.

But by the kind providence of that Great Being who controls all nature, and whose eyelids never slum-

ber, the men being preserved from these dangers, commence the work which had brought them from their
homes.

In the second or third week in March, the white
coats are in their prime, and the barking of the dams
and the weaker cry of their young unmistakably point
out the direction the hunter must go, to find the object
of his pursuit. His implements are a scaling-gaff, a
hauling-rope, and a knife. The gaff is a bat of wood,
about seven feet long, with a hook in one end. This
is the instrument with which the seal is killed; it is
struck on the nose, and one blow will kill a young seal.
The knife is to take off the pelt, and the rope is to haul
the load to the vessel. By the word pelt is meant the
skin and the fat; for the fat of the seal adheres to the
skin, as does the fat to the back of the hog: when,
therefore, it is said such a vessel brought home so
many seals, the reader must understand, those were
only seals' pelts, for the carcass, which scarcely contains a particle of fat, is left upon the ice.

When the man approaches the young seal, the
mother, with a howl and a bound, will leave her off-
spring, and, darting through a crevice in the ice, will
seek refuge in the water beneath. The young white-
coat will now cry like a young lamb,— some say like
a child; and the tear can be seen in the eye. But
compassion for the young seal is out of the question
on the part of the man who has labored so much and
braved so many dangers, for the sole purpose of taking
its life and seizing its skin : the gaff is raised, the stroke
falls with fatal effect, the knife is plunged into the belly
of the animal; when a few dexterous cuts will take off
the pelt, and the carcass, still quivering with life, is left
on the spot in a pool of its own blood.

The pelt of the white-coat will weigh about fifty pounds; and when the hunter has taken three pelts, it is a load; which he ties in his hauling-rope, and then returns to the vessel, where, having left his prize, he again goes to the scene of carnage, to repeat the same act of slaughter, which is thus continued from early dawn to evening shade, by all the crews of all the vessels in the vicinity of the seal-meadow, until acres of ice are stained with the blood, and strewed with the carcasses, of these unoffending victims. In this manner, when the seals are plenty, the vessel can be loaded in a few days; when she carries her cargo into port, and returns to the ice to make a second trip, ere the season shall have passed away. But the seals are not always so plenty: sometimes the voyage is a failure; and then the consequences, in a pecuniary view, are serious, both to the owner and to the crew.

When the seals are found, they are not always close to the vessel, but have to be brought a distance of some miles, when hauling a *turn* of soils over the big hummocks, or ice-hillocks, makes the labor exceedingly toilsome. Sometimes chasms occur, over which the men must leap, or move pans of ice with their gaffs so as to form a bridge; sometimes slob, or small loose ice covered with snow, intervenes between the larger ice, on which, if the hunter should chance to step, he must be extricated by the gaff of his friend, or he is ingulfed and perishes in the water; not unfrequently, when a distance from the vessel, a dense fog arises, or a snow-storm comes on, when the hunter is speedily lost, horns are blown, and guns are fired, but they are inaudible by the roaring of the wind, and the pitiless pelting of the storm. Lights are shown at night, but they are invisible in the snow-drift; deep anxiety is felt by the crew for their missing shipmate, and every exertion is made to find him : but the vessel has drifted far away, or he has wandered in an opposite direction, or fallen through the ice ; or overcome with fatigue, cold, or hunger, he lies down, and is frozen to death. Seldom does a sealing-voyage terminate without some such calamity, or the month of May arrive without the bitter intelligence being conveyed to some expectant family, that the wife is a widow, and the children are orphans.

Taking seals on the Sabbath used to be practised by all hunters ; and it must be admitted, that when, on the Sabbath morning, the ice would be alive with seals, and there was a possibility, and perhaps a probability, that by the next day they would all disappear, a powerful motive was presented to the mind to violate the sanctity of that holy day. When some members of the Wesleyan Church first made a stand against taking seals on Sunday, and insisted that that day was the Sabbath of the Lord as well at the ice as on the shore, and that its hours should be as sacred, and his worship performed with as much reverence, on board the schooner as in the stately temple in the crowded city, they were laughed at as enthusiasts, or considered as taking leave of their senses. And although it is a painful fact, that of the many hundreds of vessels that now go to the ice every spring, far the greater part of the crews of those vessels still constantly disregard the injunction of Jehovah in regard to the Sabbath ; yet there are now many noble exceptions. Many captains will not now allow a seal to be brought on board their ships ; there are many individuals, and whole crews, who will not catch a seal ; and, in some instances, not only is the Bible read, and prayer-meetings held, but a regular

public service is performed on board by the master, or
some one of the crew, during the hours of God's holy
day. As to the loss of seals by keeping the "Sabbath
day holy," that is only in imagination; for the Sabbath-
keeping captains are just as successful, and often more
so, than the Sabbath-breaking captains. But, even
were it not so, earthly gain must not be placed in
juxtaposition with the mandate of Heaven; but, in all
cases, is that divine law to be considered of paramount importance, "Remember the Sabbath day to
keep it holy."

Hundreds, and sometimes thousands, of seals being
thrown together with a portion of the blood, and the
heat of the April sun melting the fat, and changing it
into oil, causes a most unpleasant effluvia, and produces
a state of filth which is more easily conceived than
described.

The flesh of the seal is eaten largely by the hunters,
and the heart is considered by some as a dainty. On
shore, the seal is eaten when young and fresh. Boiled,
it has the appearance of mutton; but the general way
of cooking seal-flesh on land is to soak it in water, and
bake it, and bring it on the table with berry-sauce or
preserved fruit. The writer has often partaken of seal-
flesh; but, to his taste, it was not very savory.

Early in April, the sealers think of returning home,
and reach there about the middle of the month. If
they have been unsuccessful, or any calamity has happened, they enter the harbor as silently as possible; but
if they have had a prosperous voyage, the flags fly at
the masts, and a gun is fired for every hundred seals
that has been taken on board.

Formerly, when the vessel arrived, the pelts would
be counted, and sold so much for each, according to its

size; but some of the hunters were guilty of fraud, by leaving a portion of fat on the carcass, that the load might be lighter to haul. The seals are therefore now all purchased by weight. The number of seals brought into the different ports in one spring often exceeds half a million. The number taken in the year 1840 was 631,385, which would average something over one dollar for each seal. When the seal-pelts are landed, the skinners scrape the fat from the skin, and put it into large vats, where the heat of the sun during the earlier months of summer melts it, and it becomes the pale seal-oil, which is drawn off in casks, and mostly exported to Europe. The skins are slightly salted, and exported to the same countries.

Sometimes the drift-ice will come into the harbors with thousands of seals, when men, women, and children will go to get a haul. It is said that, in the spring of 1843, near 20,000 seals were thus taken by the people from the shore.

While our members are away to the ice, they are never forgotten at home. They are always remembered in public and family prayer, and prayer-meetings are specially held to supplicate a throne of grace on their behalf. It was truly delightful, on the arrival of the young men from the dangers of the ice, to hear the female portions of the family relate to them from memory the sermons that had been preached, the exhortations that had been given, the prayers that had been offered up for them, and the hymns that had been sung at public worship and at the prayer-meetings, during their absence.

A few days after the return of the ice-hunters, the preparation for the summer cod-fishery commences, when the labor, fatigue, and anxiety connected therewith, as already described, have again to be endured; and thus, in summer and winter, in spring and autumn, has the Newfoundlander a life of constant toil and of danger.

We will now present a table, by which the reader will see the progress of the seal-fishery since the year 1795. The years in the table are not regularly consecutive, but are given simply as examples.

Years.	No. seals taken each year.
1795	4,900
1814	156,000
1815	141,370
1820	221,334
1825	221,510
1830	300,681
1831	559,342
1832	442,003
1833	384,699
1834	360,155
1835	557,490
1836	384,321
1838	375,361
1840	631,385
1841	417,115
1842	344,683
1847	455,180

Number of vessels engaged in the seal-fishery in 1847.

Districts.	Vessels.	Tonnage.	Men.
St. Johns,	95	9,353	3,215
Brigus,	66	5,010	2,111
Carbonear,	54	4,634	1,672
Harbor Grace,	51	5,084	1,684
Ports to North'd,	74	5,803	2,123
Total,	340	29,884	10,805

The capture of the seal for its pelt, — that is, the skin, and fat which produce the seal-oil, — has been the practice of the inhabitants from the first settlement of the island. In the commencement of the seal-fishery seal-nets were used; and the seal-fishery, by means of seal-nets, was extensively carried on all along the north-eastern coast. Venturesome men next went to the ice in boats, when it came near the shore; and the number of seals thus taken, they considered an ample reward for their daring and danger. The success of the seal-ing-boats encouraged parties to fit out decked vessels, as they could go to a greater distance, and could better stand the roughs connected with a sealing-voyage. The boats that used to be employed in this hazardous voyage were open fishing-boats; but, in 1793, two small schooners, of about forty-five tons each, were fitted out for the ice, and sailed from St. Johns on the first week in April. They were very successful, one of them re-turning with eight hundred seals. In 1796, four ves-sels, of a similar size, sailed from St. Johns, and a few from Conception Bay, some of which were equally suc-cessful. Still, for many years, there was a prejudice against employing vessels at the ice of over fifty or sixty tons. But in the year 1825, two vessels (thought at the time too monstrous for such a purpose), of 120 tons each, were built in Conception Bay, expressly for the seal-fishery. They were both very fortunate: one returned in the spring of 1826, with 6,666 seals, and the other with 5,828. This set the question at rest as to the size of the vessels; and the ice-hunters now are usually well-built craft, of from 120 to 140 tons. As seen in the above table, the number of men employed in 1847 was near 11,000, and the estimated value of the seals taken that spring was £214,175 sterling.

CHAPTER XI.

MISSION TO THE LABRADOR INDIANS.

THE Moravians have the honor of several important mission stations on the frigid coast of Labrador, which were established only by the most indomitable Christian courage and perseverance. The first attempt of this noble object was in the year 1752, when four Moravian ministers sailed from London for the Labrador in a trading vessel, determined, by the grace of God, that, while the captain should transact secular business with the Indians, they would take the opportunity of speaking to them about spiritual things, and of making known to them the gospel of salvation. Two of the ship's crew were murdered by the natives, in consequence of which the missionaries had to return, to enable the captain to bring the ship back to Europe, and the mission, for a time, was abandoned.[1]

Twelve years afterward, or in the year 1764, Jens Haven, who had been for some years a missionary in Greenland, and who spoke the Greenland language, sailed from England in a Danish ship, with the design of again attempting to establish a mission on the Labrador coast. Whenever he landed the Indians fled, so

---

[1] Crantz's History of United Brethren, p. 404.

that he could not get an opportunity of making known to them his object. After a time, the ship had occasion to touch at Quirpon Island, on the north-east point of Newfoundland, where he met with a number of the Esquimaux, with whom he conversed freely, and taught them the worship of the true God, and the way to heaven.

The year following, accompanied by another Danish missionary from Greenland, he, with two lay-brethren, in a Danish ship of war, again visited the coast. They now met with some hundreds of the Exquimaux, and spoke to them in the Greenland language, " of the things pertaining to the kingdom of God." There is an affinity between the Greenland and the Esquimau languages; but that affinity is not so great as to enable the Indians to understand the verities of Christianity from the Danish missionaries, who could only speak in Greenlandic.

The Esquimaux thought themselves very good people; that the Greenlanders were wicked people; but that the foreigners, and particularly the Europeans who traded with them, and generally cheated them, were real *Kablunats*. A *Kablunat* means a very wicked man, or a villain. When, therefore, the missionary Drachart spoke to them about their depravity, and of the depravity of mankind, they said, " That may be true of the *Kablunats;* but, as for us, we are good people." When they told them of the Greenlanders, who had been washed in the blood of Christ, they replied, " Then they must have been very bad people." When they spoke about the Redeemer, they imagined he was some great personage, who would save them from the Kablunats, and assist them against their enemies in the north. The missionaries had a

letter of friendship to them from the Governor of Newfoundland, which, while they listened as it was read,
yet they would in no way be persuaded to take the
document into their own hands, as they thought there
must be something living in it, since it could communicate the thoughts of a man at such a distance. The
brethren, however, did not yet see their way clear, and
the establishment of the Labrador mission was again
deferred. This happened in 1765, — the same year
that Lawrence Coughlan came to Newfoundland.

In the year 1771, after nineteen years of effort, or,
rather, of efforts made at different times during a period
of nineteen years, the Moravians succeeded in establishing their mission. Labrador belongs to Great Britain ;
therefore the missionaries, Jens Haven, Christian Drachart, and Stephen Jenson, applied to, and obtained a
grant from, the British government for missionary purposes. The spot upon which they fixed as their mission
station was in 57° north latitude, about the parallel of
the Hebrides. It was at the head of a bay, or deep
indent in the land ; and from its pleasant situation, and
its commanding view of the ocean, they called their
station Nain, which means pleasant, or beauty. The
climate of Nain varies from 75° or 80° in summer, to a
degree of cold in winter where ordinary rum will freeze
like water, and rectified spirits soon become as thick as
oil.

The ignorance of the Esquimaux was so palpable
that it was difficult to make them understand the first
principles of religion. When the missionaries spoke to
them of indulging in their brutal passions, they, like
many in Christian lands, would try to make out that
they were quite as good, if not a little better, than their
neighbors. Thus the liars would console themselves

that they were not thieves; the thieves, that they were
not murderers; and the murderers, that they were not
Kablunats! which they placed in the highest scale of
criminals.

God blessed the labors of these devoted men; and in
five years, — that is, in 1776, — they formed a new settlement on a small island called Okkak, about one hundred and fifty miles north of Nain, and near Hudson's
Strait. Here they had a good haven for boats, a harbor
for ships, with abundance of fish, and a plentiful supply
of wood. Many of the savages soon felt the power
of religion, and were baptized into the Christian faith.

In the year 1782, a third settlement was formed to
the south of Nain, which the brethren called Hopedale.

The missionaries soon acquired a complete knowledge of the Esquimau language, when they translated
the New Testament and a Harmony of the Four Gospels, which were printed at the expense of the British
and Foreign Bible Society. They collected the children in schools, and translated a spelling-book, and a
catechism for the use of the schools, and a hymn-book
for the general purposes of the mission. They taught
the people to sing, and they succeeded in getting all
their converts to have family prayer, both night and
morning, and, in different ways, to edify and love
each other.

We cannot close this statement without presenting to
the eye of the reader the following very interesting
account, as found in the appendix to the report of the
British and Foreign Bible Society for 1812, p. 42.

"When the Gospel of John, which was first printed, was distributed among the converts, they expressed their sense of its
value in the most affecting manner. Some burst into a flood of
tears; others pressed the little book to their bosom, and looked as

happy as if they had enjoyed a foretaste of heaven. They used
to take it with them when they went in search of provisions; and
they spent their evenings in their tents or snow-houses, reading it
with great delight. Several of the Esquimaux at Nain, having
been informed of the nature and operations of the Bible Society,
began, of their own accord, to collect seals' blubber, with a view
of sending it as a contribution to that invaluable institution. Some
brought whole seals, or part of a seal, according to their several
ability; others brought portions of blubber in the name of their
children, begging that their offerings might also be accepted, so
that other heathens might be presented with that blessed book."

In the year 1821, a statement of the Esquimaux
mission was given to the world, showing its results;
the tabular view of which we here extract from Brown's
History of the propagation of Christianity among the
heathen.[1]

When begun.	Settlements.	No. of Adults.	Children.	Total.
1771	Nain	95	124	218
1776	Okkak	189	142	331
1782	Hopedale	102	116	218
	Total	386	381	767

In the Missionary Register for February, 1820, there
is found this statement of the Labrador mission: —

" The gospel continues to show its power in the hearts of the
Esquimaux, and of rough, wild, and proud heathen, to use the
words of the missionaries, to make repenting sinners humble followers of Jesus; while most of the members of the congregations
become more firmly grounded on the only true foundation. Great
thankfulness is expressed for the portion of the Scripture printed
for them by the British and Foreign Bible Society. The missionaries
write thus: " We rejoice in prospect of the great blessings
which our dear people, young and old, will derive from the peru-

[1] Brown's Christianity, Vol. 1, p. 594.

sal; for they value the Scriptures above every other gift, and always carry the books with them, as their choicest treasure, whenever they go from us to any distance, that they may read in them every morning and evening.' " — *Wesleyan Mission to Labrador.*

Such was the state of the Moravian mission at Labrador, when the Wesleyan Missionary Committee resolved also to establish a mission on the southern part of that dreary land, so that the Esquimaux, from Hudson's Bay to the St. Lawrence, might all be rescued from heathen darkness, and enjoy the light and privileges of Christian truth.

From Hopedale, the most southern of the Moravian settlement, to the mouth of the St. Lawrence, or the Strait of Belle Isle, there are some three hundred miles of coast, over which still roams the Esquimaux, in his heathen state and savage wildness. It was to this tract of country that our noble missionary secretaries, the Rev. Messrs. Bunting, Taylor, and Watson, contemplated sending a Wesleyan missionary, in order to reclaim the nomads of the south, as their brethren, the Moravians, had so successfully done with the same tribes in a more hyperborean district.

A young man of talent, of sterling piety, and in every way qualified for such a work, was already in the mission field, — Adam C. Avard, then stationed at Fredericton. This young missionary enjoyed the full confidence of the committee, and would have gone to Labrador the next year, but his Master called him home. He sickened and died. In the Missionary Report for 1821, page 106, the committee make a note on this as follows : —

" An excellent young man, Mr. Avard, has been called away from this mission (Nova Scotia and New Brunswick) by death, who had given great promise of usefulness. He was appointed

19 *

to establish a mission among the Indians on the Labrador coast, but was taken sick before the commencement of his voyage. That enterprise has been confided to the brethren in Newfoundland; and the instructions sent out by Mr. Avard have been transferred to the missionary who may be appointed by the chairman of that district."

About two years before this, considerable excitement had been produced by the baptism of six Labrador Indians by our missionary, Mr. Ellis, at Bearneed, in the Port de Grave Circuit. They were all of one family, and consisted of a mother, her daughter, her son, her son's wife, and two grand-children. Of their costume, Mr. Ellis gives the following description : —

" Their dress is of the skin of deer and seals, and there is no difference in the manner of wearing it, except that the coats of the women have long tails hanging down to the ground. Both men and women wear pantaloons made by the latter, and to the coat of the women is fixed a hood, in which they carry their young children. Their face is rather broad, eyes a deep black, and their color approaching that of mahogany, their teeth white and well set, hands small, and of fine symmetry. They are an interesting-looking people."[1]

The first instructions that the Newfoundland District received was in the year 1820; and are referred to in the Missionary Report for that year, p. 86. In this report, both the aboriginal inhabitants of the island, and the Esquimaux, are brought to the notice of the brethren and the public, as objects of missionary enterprise. The paragraph reads : —

"NEWFOUNDLAND DISTRICT. The accounts from this island are favorable. The attention of the public has lately been turned to the aboriginal inhabitants in the interior, and should any opening to these insulated tribes occur, the brethren are directed to avail themselves of it to attempt their instruction. They have been

[1] Methodist Magazine, 1820, p. 637.

also directed to make inquiries as to the establishment of a mission on the opposite coast of Labrador, with which there is an intercourse in the fishing-season."

Although the brethren received instructions about the Esquimau Mission in 1820, yet they did not see their way to move in the case until the year 1824, because they had not a man to spare from any of their circuits. But in this year, Thomas Hickson was about to return to England, and offered, before he left, to go on a mission of exploration to the Labrador, and report the result to the committee. Mr. Hickson sailed from St. Johns, June 18th, 1824, and reached the coast on the 23d. He sailed along the coast, visiting different harbors, and arrived at the place of his destination, which was the Great Bay of Esquimau, on the 8th of July. The geographical position of Esquimau Bay is laid down as in lat. 51°. 25' 10''; lon. 57° 32' west.

The journal of Mr. Hickson is published in the missionary notices and Wesleyan Methodist Magazine for 1825. He opened his mission in Tub Harbor, on the 11th of July, 1824. He says, " I had the unspeakable satisfaction of preaching the word of life for the first time in the Great Bay of Esquimau. The poor Indians were very serious, though they could not understand much of what was spoken." Mr. Hickson spoke in English at this time, but a few days later he found a native female who could act as an interpreter. He now collected forty Indians, and preached to them with great satisfaction. Of this sermon he says : " I spoke through the means of the above mentioned person as an interpreter, who, when she had made them to understand any truth of the gospel, manifested very pleasing tokens of gratitude. The interpreter was at loss to find a word

in the Esquimau for prayer; and the reason she assigned was, that prayer was not known among them;
they had, therefore, no word for it."

Mr. Hickson continued at the Labrador about one
month, and had to leave Esquimau Bay on the 10th
of August. He spent most of his time among the Indians, in their wigwams, or in some way instructing
them in the knowledge of the truth. He met with
some who had been with the Moravian missionaries in
the north, who frequently expressed a grateful and affectionate remembrance of their former teachers, and
sometimes while Mr. H. was preaching, would aloud
inform their brethren that they had heard the same
truths spoken by the Moravian missionaries.

Of the population of Esquimau Bay, Mr. Hickson,
as the result of his inquiries, sets down the following
figures : —

Real Esquimaux adults,	100
Real Esquimaux children,	60
Half Esquimaux children,	60
European settlers,	90
Canadian settlers,	16

Total number, exclusive of any other part of the coast, 326

Of their ideas and practices we are furnished with
the following statement : " The Esquimaux have very
confused notions of a Supreme Being, but they have an
idea of the devil, whom they suppose to be the author
of all pain. In the case of dangerous illness, the oldest
person in the place hangs all the pot-crooks or old hoops
about him, and, taking a stick in his hand, he turns
over all the skins in the wigwam in order to drive the
devil away. If his satanic majesty is not terrified by
this rumpus, they have recourse to sacrifice, which is

by killing their best dog." But human sacrifice was not then unknown. Mr. Hickson mentions a case which occurred about three years before he visited the bay. An Indian, supposing himself to be in dying circumstances, and having a notion that the devil would spare his life if he could accomplish the death of another person, fixed upon a neighbor's wife as his victim, and ordered his own wife to do the bloody deed. She was reluctant, but he seized a hatchet, and threatened her life if she refused obedience to his mandate; when, prevailing upon another female to assist her, they together murdered the poor woman by hanging. But the man died, and the wife became frantic. When an Esquimau dies, his body is wrapped in skins, and laid upon the surface of the ground, and a large pile of stones is raised over it. The canoe, darts, kettles, and other utensils are buried with him, supposing he will need them in another world.

Mr. Hickson was fully impressed with the importance and duty of sending a missionary among them. Before he left he intimated that a missionary would be sent among them, and said it was necessary that they should live as near to him as possible, in order to enjoy the benefit of his labors. To this they replied, " Wherever the missionary may be, we will not be far from him." As Mr. Hickson was leaving, the Indians stood upon the shore, and with tears in their eyes, they waved their hands and cried out " Tava, tava:" farewell, farewell.

With Mr. Hickson's Journal the missionary committee were well pleased, and their view of the matter is given in the Missionary Report for 1825, p. 133: —

" LABRADOR MISSION.—Mr. Thomas Hickson visited the Esquimau Indians, from Newfoundland, in the course of last summer. He found there a people truly ' prepared of the Lord ; ' and from his favorable report, the committee have resolved on the appointment of a missionary to that poor people in the neighborhood of Esquimau Bay."

At the district meeting, in the spring of 1825, the Labrador Mission was discussed at great length, when some of the brethren thought that Mr. Hickson was too sanguine, and the success of a mission there was very problematical. To satisfy such brethren, and to meet the views of the committee on this point, Richard Knight was appointed to visit the same coast that Mr. Hickson had visited the previous summer.

Mr. Knight was stationed in Brigus, but the following entry is found in the minutes of conference for 1825: —

" MISSION OF REV. RICHARD KNIGHT TO THE ESQUIMAU INDIANS. — *Indian Mission, Esquimau Bay, on the Labrador Coast.* Richard Knight, who is to spend the summer months on this station."

Mr. Knight's station was mostly supplied, during his absence, by the writer, who was then stationed in the adjoining circuit, Port de Grave.

Mr. Knight went to Labrador in the month of June, 1825, in a vessel belonging to, and accompanied by his friend, Charles Cozens, Esq., of Brigus. On arriving at Esquimau Bay, Mr. Knight was left to prosecute the business of his mission, while Mr. Cozens ran down the coast to visit the Moravian mission stations. He arrived off "Nain" on a Sabbath morning, and, after asking permission to land, which was readily granted by the missionaries, he, with the captain of his vessel, went directly to the Moravian Church, in which divine service had already commenced. The church was a plain, neat building, of about thirty-six feet by twenty-eight, with one aisle in the middle; all the men sitting on one side, and all the women on the other. The service was in German, which, while Mr. Cozens could not understand, yet he was struck with the order and attention of the Indians. When the English party went in, so engaged were the Indians in worship, that not an eye was observed turned toward them; and at particular parts of the sermon the countenance of the congregation showed that the word powerfully affected their hearts; but when they began to sing, it was heavenly. There were four violins accurately tuned to concert pitch, and played by the Esquimaux; the tunes were the solemn old German Church music, every person sang, and every voice was in unison, and while tears flowed down the manly cheeks of our European visitors, the dark physiognomy of these sons of the northern wilds was brightened with heavenly fire, as, with heartfelt sincerity, their lips vibrated with the praises of the great Jehovah.

The Moravian missionaries are plain but intelligent men, and their wives and children were remarkable for the neatness of their attire. The settlements are small villages, each having its church, its school-house, and its parsonage. They have fine gardens and plenty of vegetables, with some cattle. All the adults can read, and all the children of sufficient age go to school. The men still hunt and fish, but some of them have learned to be carpenters or blacksmiths; and the women have been taught by the ladies of the mission to sew and do household work. The writer has eaten a piece of bread baked on the Labrador Mission. Our Moravian brethren have labored long and hard among those Indians, but they are amply rewarded for their toil. A vessel from Europe annually visits the coast, to bring supplies to the missionaries and trade with the natives.

While Mr. Cozens was getting information from the

German missionaries, which hereafter might be of
great use to the English missionaries, Mr. Knight was
faithfully preaching to the heathen Esquimaux in the
south, and making every observation and inquiry on all
matters bearing upon the then contemplated Wesleyan
Mission, to be established in their midst.   The Indians
heard him with attention as he preached to them, through
the same female interpreter, and were in the same ec-
stasy when he spoke about a missionary being sent to
reside among them, as they were when the first intima-
tion thereof had been given to them in the previous
summer by Mr. Hickson.   Additional interest was im-
parted to the case by the arrival of several Christian
Esquimaux from the Moravian establishments in the
north, who told their brethren of the benefits which
Christianity would confer upon them in this world, besides the hope of eternal life in the world that is to
come.   These Christian Esquimaux had learned to
sing at the mission stations, and Mr. Knight, who
understood music, and had a good musical taste, said of
their performance : " I have heard good singing, and I
have heard good music scientifically performed ; but such
a perfect chorus, and such a melody of voices, never
before fell upon my auricular nerves. I gazed and
wept." Mr. Knight was cheered with the prospect, and,
with Mr. Hickson, was decided in his opinion that a
mission to the Esquimaux should at once be established.
By that opinion the committee for a time were guided.
Hence the following entry in their report for 1826,
p. 97 : —

" LABRADOR. — The Esquimaux on this coast were again visited
last summer. Mr. Knight, who was appointed to that service, reports favorably of the prospect of doing good, and measures will
be taken to establish a regular mission."

The Labrador Mission now began to excite consider-able interest in England, and the committee, with their wonted liberality and kindness, sent out articles for build-ing and furnishing a mission-house, to a large amount. Had there been no more exploring for a mission, and could we have patiently waited until the committee had found a volunteer missionary who would have taken up a permanent residence among the Esquimaux, the British Conference of near forty years ago would have had Esquimau Bay in their long list of " missions to the heathen ; " but such is not the fact. At the dis-trict meeting of 1826, George Ellidge was selected for the Labrador Mission. It was an untoward selection. Mr. Ellidge objected to the appointment and said : " I will not offer for the Labrador ; *if I go, you send me.*" From that moment a cloud began to gather over the Esquimau Indian Mission, which continued to spread until the mission was obscured in its density.

Of the appointment of Mr. Ellidge, the committee have the following entry in their Report for 1827, p. 110 : —

" LABRADOR MISSION — ESQUIMAU BAY — MR. ELLIDGE. — The visit of Mr. Knight, during several months of the last summer, to the Esquimau tribes of the Labrador coast was equally satisfactory with that of Mr. Hickson, the preceding summer. The natives of these rude shores present to the labors of the self-deny-ing servants of Christ, who may take up their residence among them, a docility and susceptibility of feeling on subjects of religion highly encouraging, and the committee therefore directed one of the brethren in Newfoundland to take steps to establish a per-manent mission among them during the present summer. Mr. Ellidge was in consequence sent by the chairman of the New-foundland district, and the committee have reason to be satisfied with the person chosen for this arduous work, and with his pros-pects. At the last account, he was building a house for a winter residence, to the great satisfaction of the natives."

By a letter from Mr. Ellidge, we find that he has fixed upon Snook's Cove, on the Labrador coast, as the place for commencing a permanent mission ; and that he left St. Johns, Newfoundland, to winter there, having made preparations for building a house, and obtaining stores for the winter. This place is considered to afford most convenient access to the Indians.

Mr. Ellidge remained at the Labrador during the winter, and returned to Newfoundland in the autumn of 1827. The writer was then on the Burin Station. Of the views of Mr. Ellidge in reference to the Labrador Mission, he knew nothing, but the Esquimau Mission had for years occupied his thoughts ; and, on the 23d of November, 1827, he wrote to the committee, and offered his services permanently to reside among the Indians as a Wesleyan missionary. This offer is noticed in the Report for 1828, p. 107. The offer was accepted ; and in the conference minutes of 1828, in the list of stations, is the following appointment: " *Indian Mission, Esquimau Bay, on the Labrador Coast,* William Wilson." He now began to make arrangements to enter upon his Indian Mission. He engaged a man to go with him, who had been several years among the Esquimaux, and who understood something of their language. From this man he obtained a number of Esquimau words, which he intended as the basis of a grammar, and an Esquimau-English Lexicon. But all was in vain. Mr. Ellidge, who had been sent, reported unfavorably. The chairman and brethren whom he consulted were astonished at the incongruity between the reports of Messrs. Hickson and Knight, and the report of Mr. Ellidge. They therefore sent another brother, Mr. Bate, to occupy the station until the pleasure of the committee be known. Upon the report of the brethren Ellidge and Bate, the committee came to the conclusion that the mission must be abandoned. The writer, although appointed there by the committee and conference, never saw the Labrador coast.

He will copy the last two notices of the Esquimau Mission, as found in the reports for 1828 and 1829. The former report on p. 10, reads : —

"LABRADOR MISSION — ESQUIMAU BAY — CHAS. BATE. — The Mission to the Esquimau tribes of the Labrador coast has been impeded by difficulties, which, though partially foreseen, could not be known in their full extent, before the mission had been commenced. Mr. Ellidge, agreeably to the appointment of the committee, proceeded to Esquimau Bay, and for several months labored with diligence and zeal, and under great privations, amongst both the natives and the settlers; but, being doubtful of success, from the scattered state of the different tribes, their migratory mode of life, and the paucity of their number, he returned to Newfoundland. The brethren on that island, unwilling to abandon the mission, immediately resolved to send Mr. Bate to occupy the station until the pleasure of the committee be known Since then, letters have been received from Mr. and Mrs. Wilson, offering, in the true spirit of Christian enterprise, to leave their present station, and proceed to the Labrador coast, if appointed by the committee. This decision they are now expecting to receive; and there is ground to hope that, under the blessing of God, their patient and persevering labors may yet cause the ' barren wilderness to smile, by the illuminating and cheering influences of the gospel light and truth.' "

In the Report for 1859, p. 132, we have the following notice : —

" The *Labrador Mission* is for the present suspended, principally in consequence of the removal of the Esquimau tribes from the coast into the interior of the country, and their general dispersion."

Thus terminated the British Esquimau Indian Mission, after it had cost some hundreds of pounds; and had engaged the attention of the Christian public for some eight or ten years.

The Conference of " *Eastern British America* " has indeed " Labrador " on the list of stations, but its mission is only to the British settlers and fishermen from Newfoundland. We hope, however, a mission to the Indians will yet be commenced on the coast, or, if need be, in the interior; that we may assist our Moravian brethren in rescuing the savages on British soil, and within our own boundaries, from their darkness and heathenism.

CHAPTER XII.

THE RED INDIANS — THEIR HABITS — KILLED BY WHITE MEN — ATTACK
A PARTY OF WHITE MEN — CAPTAIN BUCHAN — MARY MARCH —
THREE LOST INDIANS SEEN — SHANANDITHIT.

THE RED INDIANS OR ABORIGINES OF NEWFOUNDLAND.

WHATEVER continent or large island the modern navigator may visit, he always finds human
beings there; beings who, like himself, were created in
the image of God, and bought with the " precious blood
of Christ." Sometimes he finds these men in a state
of civilization that excites his astonishment, as in the
case of the inhabitants of Central America, of China
and Japan, and sometimes in a state of complete barbarism, as the natives of South Africa, Polynesia, the
Indians of the North American forests, and the original
owners and proprietors of the Island of Newfoundland.
He wonders by what educational process the one people
became so elevated; and why it was that the other
people should have been left in their native state. This
is a mistaken view; for man did not, in early times,
rise from barbarism to civilization, but he sank from
civilization to barbarism. When for the wicked attempt
of the people, on the " plain in the land of Shinah," to
build " a city and a tower whose top might reach unto
heaven," " the Lord scattered them abroad from thence
upon the face of all the earth," it is certain those people
were a civilized people, and must have been acquainted
with all the science of those times. Those of them

who colonized lands abounding in the necessaries of life,
could remain in large bodies, build cities, and employ
their leisure in instructing their children in such branches
of knowledge as had engaged their own attention and
study. But those who wandered into distant lands,
where the soil was rocky or sandy; where the forests
were inpenetrable, or the morass impassable; where
the earth yielded but a scanty supply of food; where
man was dependent upon the chase for a living; or
where a large portion of his time was engaged in preparation for the coming months of a northern winter;
where the inhabitants were but few in number, and the
families isolated; and where science was not needed, —
it would, as a consequence, follow, that their children
would be instructed in little else than what was required to gain a living; and thus future generations
would drop into that state of barbarism in which we
find them in the present day.

The aboriginal inhabitants of Newfoundland belong
to this class. They are of American origin, and seem
to be of the mountaineer type, from the interior of
Labrador. But after they had crossed the "Straits of
Belle Isle" to their island home, they assumed a national character, and in time became different, both in
habit and person, from their supposed ancestors.

They called themselves "Boeothicks;" but the settlers called them "Red Indians;" from the fact of their
painting their bodies and their wigwams with red ochre.
Red ochre is found on the north shore of Conception
Bay, and there is a small village on that shore called
Ochre-pit Cove; from a tradition that the Boeothicks of
that region used to get their red ochre from that place.

There is something fearful, and truly humiliating, in
the thought, wherever civilized and Christian people, so

called, come in contact with savage tribes, those tribes melt away, and in time become extinct. The reason is obvious: we plunder those tribes, and we give them our vices, but we withhold from them our Christianity which only can elevate, bless, and save them. Thus it was with the Red Indian race.

When John Cabot, in the year 1497, first sighted Cape Bonavista, the Red Indians possessed the entire island; their canoes glided on its streams, or fished on its shores, while they had no fear of molestation on their hunting-grounds, or apprehension of the white man's bullet, as they passed through the woods to their humble wigwam beside the placid waters of the inland lake. But the Indians had large quantities of what the Europeans called wealth: it consisted in beautiful furs, the skins of animals taken in the chase.

Newfoundland is one of the best hunting-grounds upon the earth. Its surface contains 57,000 square miles. Over this extensive range of country, not one foot was cultivated, or a building of any kind stood, save the wigwams of its Indian lords. Here was abundance of game of all kinds peculiar to northern latitudes, — as the black bear, the otter, the wolf, the beaver, the red, the black, and the silver fox; the ponds were the home of the wild goose, for that bird breeds there; while the barrens and open plains were alive with the caribou or reindeer.

With the skins of animals taken in their extensive hunting-grounds were the Indians clothed; and upon the same rich furs did they repose at night. This inflamed the cupidity of the European furriers. They might have carried on a lucrative trade with them; but no, they must have their rich furs without any compensation! They therefore shot them down in cold blood, and took possession of their property. The Indians defended themselves as best they could, but the dart and the bow and arrow were their only weapons, which were useless against the fire-arms of the whites. They were driven from the coast, and sought refuge on the margin of, or on the islands in, the great ponds in the interior. Thither they followed them, or employed the Micmacs to follow them, until the whole race was almost annihilated. No one thought any more of shooting a Red Indian than of killing the animal with the skin of which the Indian was clothed.

It was about the commencement of the present century that the government avowed itself on the side of this oppressed race, declared the Red Indians to be British subjects, and placed them under the protection of British law. But it was too late for any practical good; most of the tribe were destroyed, and it was impossible to inspire confidence in any white man, on the part of those that yet remained.

A place called Bloody Bay, on the north side of Bonavista Bay, has often been named to the writer as a place where frequent encounters had occurred with the Red Indians. When the fishermen would be looking for bait, or getting wood from the shore, they would be assailed by a shower of arrows, and be obliged either to defend themselves with their fire-arms, or escape in their boats. In a place called Cat Harbor, some Indians came one night, and took all the sails from a fishing-boat. The next day they were pursued, and when seen, were on a distant hill, with the sails cut into a kind of cloak, and daubed all over with red ochre. Two men belonging to the party, who had gone in pursuit of the Indians, were rowing along shore, when they saw a goose swimming in the harbor. It was a decoy, for, while their attention was arrested with the goose, two Indians rose up from concealment, and discharged their arrows at them, but without effect.

The government, however, now determined to defend the property, as well as the lives, of these people. In 1810, an instance of this occurred in Green Bay, at the head of Notre Dame Bay. A man named Wiltshear, and his crew, were returning from the fishing-ground, when, rounding a point of land, they came close upon a canoe where there were five Red Indians, — four men and one woman. The Indians were alarmed, pulled toward the shore, jumped on the beach, and ran to the woods. The men took the canoe and carried it home. In the fall of the year, they went to St. Johns with a boat-load of fish, and took the canoe with them as a present to the governor, but they were taken into custody, and put in prison, charged with murdering the Indians and stealing their canoe. After being in prison ten days, and no evidence being produced against them, they were acquitted. The imprisonment of Wiltshear had a good effect, for we never after heard of any depredations being committed upon the Indians.

A few years later, a lieutenant, afterward Captain Buchan, of H. M. schooner Pike, the same person who went in quest of the north-west passage, was commissioned by the governor, Sir John Thomas Duckworth, to discover, and, if possible, bring about a friendly intercourse with the Red Indians. He cruised up the Bay of Exploits, Notre Dame Bay, and at length came up with an encampment. He prevailed upon two Indians to come on board his vessel, but to effect this, he had to leave two marines with the Indians as hostages. He removed the vessel to another place with the Indians on board; and when he returned to the encampment,

he found his two marines with their heads severed from
their bodies, and all the Indians had fled.   The two
Indians that were on board the Pike also escaped, and
were never seen afterward.

In the winter of 1819, in the month of March, ten
armed men at the head of White Bay went into the
country, came up with an encampment, and brought
away the only person they found, who was a female.
She was brought to St. Johns, for the government had
offered a reward to bring a Red Indian to them, hoping
by such means to commence a friendly intercourse with
the tribe.   But it was a mistake.   This Indian woman,
having been taken in the month of March, was called
Mary March, when she came to St. Johns.   While
there, she was treated with every kindness, loaded with
presents, and then taken back to the place from whence
she came.

Red Indian Pond, at the head of the River Exploits,
was the home of Mary March.   On its beach had she
played in her childhood; over its waters had she paddled
in her canoe; she had fished in its streams, and when
she became a wife, it was on its margin; she had been
compelled to leave her husband, and her hapless infant,
her only child, to die, which rumor says, it did, two
days after the ruffian armed band of white men had
taken her captive, and carried her, her friends knew
not where.   To take a savage woman captive, and
bring her away by force, in order to open a friendly
intercourse with her tribe, was a clear absurdity.   It
therefore failed.   It were wild to say, she was better
off while in St. Johns than in her own country.   She
could not think so.   The husband and child of Mary
March were as dear to her as can be the partner and
child of the titled lady; the rough wigwam as much a

home to her as a palace is to the prince; her deer-skin dress as much admired as the costly costume of the fashionable belle; and the wood-bound banks of the Red Indian Lake were as beautiful, in her eyes, as the rich landscape and the decorated pleasure-park are to the refined taste of the courtly lord.

The manners of Mary March, while in St. Johns, were very pleasing, and there was a dignity about her which led to the conviction that she was the wife of a Boeothick chief.

How long she lived after her return, we have no means of knowing. But some years after, an exploring party visited the Red Indian Lake, and at its eastern extremity, while they saw no people, they saw evidence that the shores of that lake had long been the central and undisturbed rendezvous of the Boeothick tribe. They found a number of their wigwams, a building for drying and smoking venison, and a log storehouse. They found wooden huts which were used as repositories for the dead. One of these huts was in size ten feet by eight, and four feet high in the centre. It was floored with squared sticks, and roofed with rinds, — well secured against the weather, and the intrusion of wild beasts. Two full-grown persons, wrapped in skins, were laid on the floor. It was computed that these persons had been dead not more than five or six years. But what excited our travellers most was the discovery of a white deal coffin, containing a skeleton neatly shrouded in white muslin. This, it would seem, was the remains of Mary March. If so, the white muslin must have been among the presents she received when in St. Johns. Beside her were two small wooden images of a man and woman, supposed to represent Mary March and her husband;

and a small doll supposed to represent her child.   In
the same building were models of boats and canoes,
also a bow and a quiver full of arrows, with two fire-
stones, or radiated iron pyrites, with which the Boeothicks produce fire by striking them together.   There
were also a number of culinary utensils, neatly made
of birch bark, and ornamented.

It was the arrival of Mary March in St. Johns that
induced the Wesleyan missionary committee to make
the following entry in their Report for the year 1820,
in reference to the Newfoundland District : —

"The attention of the public has lately been turned to the aboriginal inhabitants of the interior, and, should any opening to
these long isolated tribes occur, the brethren are directed to
avail themselves of it to attempt their instruction."

Four years after Mary March was brought to St.
Johns, three others of the tribe were captured and
brought to the same place.   These were the last of the
Red Indians ever seen.   As the writer himself saw
these persons, shook hands with them, and tried to converse with them, he will give the account from his own
journal : —

"St. Johns, Newfoundland, June 23, 1823.

"Last week there were brought to this town, three Red Indians, so called, who are the aboriginal inhabitants of this island.
They are all females, and their capture was accomplished in the
following manner.

"In the month of March last, a party of men from the neighborhood of Twillingate were in the country hunting for fur.   The
party went two and two in different directions.   After a while
one of these small parties saw, on a distant hill, a man coming
toward them.   Supposing him, while at a distance, to be one of
their own party, they fired a powder gun to let their friend know
their whereabouts.   The Red Indian generally runs at the report
of a musket : not so in the present instance.   This man quickened
his pace toward them.   They now, from his gait and dress, dis-

covered that he was an Indian, but thought he was a Micmac, and therefore still felt no anxiety. Soon they found their mistake, and ascertained that the stranger was one of the Red Indians. He was approaching in a threatening attitude, with a large club in his hand. They now put themselves in a posture of defence, and beckoned the Indian to surrender. This was of no use; he came on with double fury, and when nearly at the muzzle of their guns, one of the men fired, and the Indian fell dead at his feet. As they had killed a man without any design or intention, they felt deeply concerned, and resolved at once to leave the hunting-ground and return home. In passing through a droke of woods, they came up with a wigwam, which they entered, and took three Indian females, which have since been found to be a mother and her two daughters. These women they brought to their own home, where they kept them until they could carry them to St. Johns, and receive the government reward for bringing a Red captive Indian. The parties were brought to trial for shooting a man, but as there was no evidence against them they were acquitted.

" The women were first taken to government house, and, by order of his excellency the governor, a comfortable room in the court-house was assigned to them as a place of residence, where they were treated with every possible kindness. The mother is far advanced in life, but seems in good health. Beds were provided for them, but they did not understand their use, and they slept on their deer-skins in the corner of the room. One of the daughters was ill, yet she would take no medicine. The doctor recommended phlebotomy, and a gentleman allowed a vein to be opened in his arm, to show her that there was no intention to kill her; but this was to no purpose; for when she saw the lancet brought near her own arm, both she and her companions got into a state of fury, so that the doctor had to desist. Her sister was in good health. She seemed about twenty-two years of age. If she had ever used red ochre about her person, there was then no sign of it in her face. Her complexion was swarthy, not unlike the Micmacs; her features were handsome; she was a tall, fine figure, and stood nearly six feet high; and such a beautiful set of teeth I do not know that I ever saw in a human head. In her manners she was bland, affable, and affectionate. I showed her my watch: she put it to her ear, and was amused with its tick. A gentleman put a looking-glass before her, and her grimaces were

27

most extraordinary; but when a black-lead pencil was put into her hand, and a piece of white paper laid upon the table, she was in raptures. She made a few marks on the paper, apparently to try the pencil; then in one flourish she drew a deer perfectly; and, what is most surprising, she began at the tip of the tail. One person pointed to his fingers and counted ten, which she repeated in good English; but when she had numbered all her fingers, her English was exhausted, and her numeration, if numeration it were, was in the Bœothick tongue. This person, whose Indian name is Shanandithit, is thought to be the wife of the man who was shot. The old woman was morose, and had the look and action of a savage. She would sit all day on the floor with a deer-skin shawl on, and looked with dread or hatred upon every one that entered the court-house.

" When we came away Shanandithit kissed all the company, shook hands with us, and distinctly repeated ' good-by.'

" June 24. Saw the three Indian women in the street. The ladies had dressed them in English garb, but over their dress they all had on their, to them indispensable, deer-skin shawl; and Shanandithit, thinking the long front of her bonnet an unnecessary appendage, had torn it off, and in its place had decorated her forehead and her arms with tinsel and colored paper.

" They took a few trinkets, and a quantity of the fancy paper that is usually wrapped round pieces of linen; but their great selection was pots, kettles, hatchets, hammers, nails, and other articles of ironmongery, with which they were loaded so that they could scarcely walk. It was painful to see the sick woman, who, notwithstanding her debility, was determined to have her share in these valuable treasures."

After a few weeks, a vessel was sent to take the women to the place from whence they came. The ship's boat took all their things ashore; then the women went, with great reluctance; but when they were landed, and the boat was about to leave them, they cried, they screamed, and rushed into the water after the boat; they would not be left. The captain was at a loss what to do. His orders were to put them ashore, and leave them. He felt that this would be cruel; he, therefore, determined to leave them in charge of the person who brought them away, until the pleasure of the government was known. The orders were not repeated, so the women remained. The sick daughter soon died, and the mother did not live long with civilized people; but Shanandithit survived for about two years, during which time she learned English, and became very useful as a house-servant.

From her it was understood that her tribe was reduced to a very small number; and the reason she and her relations would not be left on the beach was that they would have been killed by their own people as traitors, as they had been among the white people, whom they considered as their deadly enemies.

The writer is not aware that any Boeothicks have since been seen. Some suppose that the whole race is extinct; others that they have escaped across the Strait of Belle Isle to the main land of Labrador. But when it is remembered that there are thousands of square miles of land in the interior, on which no foot of any civilized man has ever trod; that there are numerous large "ponds," some of which might almost be called inland seas; that there are large islands in those lakes, and immense forests on their margins, that we have never seen, — it may be that some sequestered spot yet contains a few of this persecuted and injured race, who may hereafter make their appearance; which, should it be so, they assuredly will be treated differently, and with greater kindness than was ever shown toward their ancestors. What a fearful thought that we, who have Christianity and the Bible, and who boast of our high state of civilization, should have destroyed a whole people, who did us no harm, until we commenced to murder them and take their property!

The labor the Red Indians performed, in order to catch deer for their subsistence, was very great, as is evident from the remains of the deer-fences, which were standing only a few years ago. The deer is gregarious, and the herds in Newfoundland sometimes are said to contain numbers that appear fabulous.

During the summer they feed on the mountains of the north, and may be found in large numbers on the highlands near White Bay, or about the latitude of 50° or 51°; but in the autumn, or near winter, they migrate, or, as the hunters say, they " beat to the south," and go near Cape Ray or the Bay of St. George.

To catch the deer in their southern migration, and to provide food for themselves during winter, seems to have been the motive of the Red Indians in putting up their deer-fences. Inland from Notre Dame Bay, and far to the north-west of Red Indian Pond, a double line of strong fence was put up, which at its commencement diverged many miles. The southern fence ran down to the lake, so that the deer should thus come near their own encampments, and the northern line of fence was to prevent their escape near the shore. This northern fence ran down to the River Exploits, along the bank of which another fence was raised, with openings at particular places for the deer to go to the river and swim across it. These openings were called passes. A number of men now got within the fence, and from the wider enclosure they drove them to the narrower part, or to passes of the river where others were stationed, and thus killed the deer at their leisure. These deer-fences extend thirty miles on the River Exploits, and how far in the interior no white man can tell.

The present state of the Boeothick tribe, if, indeed, any of that tribe is in existence, is calculated to teach

us that civilization and education, abstracted from the
Bible and pure Christianity, can never raise a savage
people from their degradation, or place them in their
proper position among the tribes or nations of the earth.
However civilization may distinguish the nation that
has it, yet it does not possess the elements requisite for
the amelioration of the human race. It may make a
people proud and boastful, and, as knowledge is power,
it may subdue surrounding nations, and impose its laws
upon them ; but it lacks true philanthropy, and has no
disposition to impart its knowledge to other nations, or
place them in a position to rival themselves in wealth,
intelligence, or power.

The world has never heard of any civilized heathen
nation, who founded hospitals for their own sick, free
schools for the instruction of the children of their own
poor, benevolently manumitting the slaves in their own
land, sending teachers to instruct other people in their
philosophical theories, colporteurs to circulate their sacred books, or missionaries to propagate their faith or
system of theology in distant lands. All this is peculiar to Christianity.   •

Rome, in the height of her civilization and power,
conquered the savage hordes of the north ; but they
continued savage until the missionaries of the cross
went among them, and proclaimed the verities of gospel salvation. The same great nation visited the coasts
of Albion, first for commercial purposes ; next she
formed settlements there, and then subdued the country
by the number and power of her legions. But it was
the story of Gethsemane and Calvary that overthrew the
Druidism of our ancestors, gave us our civilization, our
constitution, our laws, and our liberty. Ever since the
time that Vasco de Gama found the way to India, South

27 *

Africa has been constantly visited by men of education and science; and these men of science told their brethren, in Europe, that Hottentots were so stupid and brutish, that you might as well think of making a turnpike to the moon as attempt their instruction. But Christian missionaries have instructed, civilized, and taught them the way to heaven. Scientific men visited the Polynesian Isles of the south, and were terrified with the cannibalism of the people; but the heralds of the cross went there with the Bible in their hands and the love of God in their hearts; and with these they braved the club and the oven of these worst of all savages, destroyed their unnatural appetite, taught them to read, gave them a code of laws based upon the Bible, have brought them to a knowledge of the truth, and now they are saved and in their right mind.

Had the first visitors and settlers on the shores of Newfoundland carried the Bible with them, and invited the Christian missionary to accompany them, instead of poisoning the natives with their fire-water, slaying them with their gunpowder, or making them more corrupt with their own immoralities, the noble Bœothic race would now have been a happy people, either quietly transacting their business by the sea-shore, with foreign residents, or prosecuting their hunting in the interior; while the hills and the vales, the woods and the lakes, would have resounded with their song of praise; and thus would the words of the prophet in this place have been verified: "The wilderness and the solitary place shall be glad for them, and the desert shall rejoice and blossom as the rose."

CHAPTER XIII.

THE following is the list of stations as appears in the minutes for 1825 : —

ST. JOHNS — William Croscombe, Ninian Barr.

CARBONEAR — John Pickavant.

HARBOR GRACE — John Corlett.

BLACK HEAD AND WESTERN BAY — John Haigh.

ISLAND COVE AND PERLICAN — Simeon Noall.

PORT DE GRAVE — William Wilson.

BRIGUS — Richard Knight.

TRINITY BAY — Adam Nightingale, Charles Bate.

BONAVISTA AND CATALINA — John Boyd.

GRAND BANK AND FORTUNE BAY — George Ellidge.

BURIN — William Ellis.

INDIAN MISSION, ESQUIMAU BAY, ON THE LABRADOR COAST. — Richard Knight is to spend the summer months on this station. WILLIAM CROSCOMBE, *Chairman.*

Wesleyan missions now began to excite considerable interest throughout the Christian world; and many wealthy persons contributed largely for their support and extension. In the year 1818, died that extraordinary, that saintly man, Robert Carr Brackenbury, Esq., of Raithby Hall, Lincolnshire. This gentleman gave up the pleasures of a splendid mansion for the life of a Methodist preacher. He, with Dr. Clark, became mis-

(319)

sionaries in the Island of Jersey. He gave liberally of his wealth, while he lived, to the cause of God ; and at his death, he bequeathed the sum of £1000 to the Missionary Society. The same year, a lady died in Ireland, Miss Houston, who gave a legacy of £2000 to the same cause. But the most princely sum the committee had hitherto received was a benefaction of £10,000 from the Rev. T. Dodwell, Vicar of Welby, in Lincolnshire. This gentleman had been a personal friend of Mr. Wesley, and a warm friend to our missions. While the missions were under the direction of Dr. Coke, he contributed liberally to their support ; and after the death of the doctor, he sent his contributions to the anniversary meetings of the different missionary societies held in his neighborhood.

The committee, in their circular for 1822, gave this instruction to their missionaries : " We again call the attention of the brethren to the necessity of forming missionary societies, in aid of our funds, on every foreign station where practicable ; and, where that is not practicable, at least to make a public collection annually, for this purpose, in all the congregations ; taking that occasion to inform the people of the extent, state, and prospects of our missions, and to interest them in the universal establishment of the kingdom of Christ in all the earth."

This important instruction was soon observed ; for in the year 1824, contributions flowed into the missionary exchequer from nearly all the foreign districts. The report for this year credits the Newfoundland District with £59 5s. 7d., and the Nova Scotia District with £250 15s. 2d. The latter was a much larger sum than was raised that year in any foreign district within the range of Methodism.

THE CONFERENCE DEATH-ROLL.

The fourth question asked at every conference is, " What ministers have died since the last conference ? " Immediately all business ceases, and the most solemn attention is paid while a sketch of the life of each minister, whose death has occurred since the last conference, is read.   This is called " the death-roll." Sometimes this roll is short; at other times it is very long.   The greatest number of deaths which the Eastern British American Conference has had to record in one year was four; but the British Conference, in 1860, had thirty-one deaths in Great Britain, four in Ireland, and three on the foreign stations, — making a total of thirty-eight ministers, belonging to the British and Irish conferences, who were called away in one year.

As the roll is read, while every preacher endeavors to acquiesce in the divine will, yet they are but men, and feel as men ; therefore, as each name is announced, the brethren will be more or less affected as the deceased had filled his position in the conference.   To one he was a spiritual father ; to another a special friend, a companion, and more than a brother : to one he was a kind superintendent; to another he was a zealous, faithful, and devoted colleague.   In years past he might have instructed the conference by the profundity of his thought ; directed it by the wisdom of his counsels ; defended it from its enemies by the power of his pen ; or charmed it with his eloquence.   He might have been a president, — when the junior brethren would think, with deep gratitude, of the important advice he gave to them in his ordinary charge.   Every one feels the loss; but all believe the departed was a man of God.   Many eyes will overflow with tears of gratitude at the statement that the departed successfully combated " man's last, man's latest foe ; " that he felt the supporting power of that religion which he had preached to others ; and that he died in peace ; then with hearts oppressed with sorrow, the brethren rise, and with lips still quivering, and voice still faltering, unite and sing those beautiful words of Charles Wesley, found on page 399 : —

> " Oh, may I triumph so,
>   When all my warfare's past,
>   And dying, find my latest foe,
>   Under my feet at last ! "

In addition to those already named, the death-roll records the following honored brethren : —

1. William Croscombe, who was a native of Tiverton, in Devonshire, England, and was born on the 19th of February, 1789.   In the eighteenth year of his age, he became acquainted with the Wesleyans, was deeply convinced of his guilty state, and at a Sabbath morning prayer-meeting was enabled to rejoice in the liberty of the sons of God.   A few months after his conversion, he began to exhort others " to flee from the wrath to come ; " and, having exercised his talents for a short time as a local preacher, he was received into the regular work, at the conference of 1810, and as the junior preacher, was appointed to the Shepton-Mallet Circuit, in the Bristol District.

The next year he offered for the foreign work, and was appointed to what was then called the Nova Scotia, New Brunswick, and Newfoundland District, of which William Black was chairman.   Mr. Croscombe arrived at Halifax on the 12th of April, 1812.   On the way, the vessel put into St. Johns, Newfoundland.   St. Johns was not then a Wesleyan Circuit, but the brethren Ellis and Mc'Douell occasionally preached there, and Mr. Croscombe, during his brief sojourn, also preached to that people the words of life and salvation. He was then in his twenty-third year; his hair was light, and his appearance very youthful; he preached with considerable effect, and his style and manner so arrested public attention, that they called him the "eloquent white-headed boy." He labored seven years in the lower provinces, when, his health failing, he returned to England, and travelled in Nottingham two years; after which he was appointed to Gibraltar, where his labors were greatly blessed both to the army and also among civilians. His next appointment was St. Johns, Newfoundland. The reminiscences of the friends in that place called to mind the "white-headed boy," who had, twelve years before, preached there with so much acceptance. His appointment as their minister, therefore, was hailed with pleasure, and a crowded house greeted him on his arrival. He remained in St. Johns three years, during which time he filled the office of chairman of the district. He did not occupy any other circuit in Newfoundland than St. Johns. In 1828, he came a second time to Nova Scotia; and after seven years, he removed to Canada, where five more years of his useful life were spent in the same delightful employment of calling sinners to repentance. In the year 1838, he came again to Nova Scotia, and continued to labor until the year 1851, when infirmity compelled him to retire from active work and take a supernumerary position. After he became a supernumerary he preached occasionally as his strength enabled him. The last sermon he ever preached was on Sabbath, December 31st, 1851, from James iv. 14, — "For what is your life? It is even a vapor that appeareth for a little time, and then vanisheth away." Shortly after returning from the house of God he was seized with paralysis, which seemed to keep him on the verge of eternity for several months. From the severity of this attack, however, he rallied, but his feebleness was very great. He bore his sufferings with much patience and serenity of mind; he felt abiding peace; praise dwelt upon his lips, and his conversation invariably turned upon the things of God; the salvation of God was his only theme, and the blood of Christ his only hope. On the night of the 20th of August, 1859, he fell asleep in Jesus, in the seventy-first year of his age and the fiftieth of his ministry.

Mr. Croscombe successively occupied the chairmanship of the Newfoundland, Nova Scotia, and Canada districts; and while his prudence and integrity secured for him the full confidence of the missionary committee, his gentlemanly deportment and his Christian kindness gained for him the love of all his brethren, and the esteem of the people. He was a faithful and kind friend, cheerful in his manner; his piety was simple and ardent, and he conscientiously endeavored to enjoy all those blessings and that full salvation which he preached to others.

He labored much to make his pulpit duties acceptable to his congregation, and he seldom failed in his object. His preaching was plain, scriptural, and earnest. Pastoral visitation was his delight, and by it he endeared himself to all classes who attended his ministry. He was more or less successful in every circuit where he travelled, and in several places extensive revivals were the result of his faithful and zealous labors.

2. Simeon Noall was a native of Cornwall, entered the Wesleyan ministry at the conference of 1824, and

came out a missionary to Newfoundland. He labored
on the island for five years with very great acceptance.
He was kind and affectionate in his manner, faithful,
zealous, and successful in his pastoral duties; he was a
good platform speaker; his preaching was plain, yet
eloquent, earnest, and highly scriptural; his sermons
were rich in evangelical truth, often delivered with
telling power, and in prayer he was truly mighty. In
the youth of our church he felt deep interest, and was
incessant in his efforts to instruct them and lead them
to God. Many were the seals to his ministry in different parts of the island; but his constitution was
too feeble to endure the hardships attendant upon a
missionary life; he therefore returned to England in
the year 1829. By breathing his native air, his health
was much improved; so that he labored in different
circuits for nineteen years with the same esteem and
success that he had in Newfoundland. He became a
supernumerary in 1848, in the Hayle Circuit. He
continued to employ his remaining strength, until he
was suddenly called away from suffering to rest, on the
4th of August, 1850, in the fifty-sixth year of his age,
and the 26th of his ministry.

3. Charles Bate was received on trial a Wesleyan
minister at the conference of 1824, and came to Newfoundland in the autumn of that year. He labored
on the island for nine years, and in 1833, he removed
to St. Kitts' one of the West India Islands, and in
the Antigua District. He labored in the West Indies
eight years, and died in great peace at Tortola on the
16th of December, 1841.

In the above list of stations there are thirteen names,
but the reader must understand there were not thirteen
preachers then on the Newfoundland District. Mr.

Barr was removing, and his English appointment was not then fixed ; and one man was retained in order to supply the Labrador. The number of our men and the number of our stations were eleven ; the same in 1825 as they were in 1817.

Of the preachers who constituted the Newfoundland District in 1825, the death-roll records seven ; two are laid aside by infirmity, and four only are now (1864) in the active work. The men who are still spared to labor in their Master's vineyard are John Boyd, John Corlett, George Ellidge,* and the writer.

We have previously spoken of John Boyd, and of the two other brethren we give the following information : —

George Ellidge was received on trial as a Wesleyan minister in the year 1822; he travelled two years in England when he was appointed to labor in Newfoundland. He continued on that mission for twenty-four years, and returned to England in the year 1848 ; since which time he has continued to labor in his native land. In 1863, his name stands as superintendent of the Attleborough and New Buckenham Circuit in the Norwich and Lynn District.

John Corlett commenced the itinerant in 1824, and was stationed at Kendal, in the Carlisle District. He came to Newfoundland in 1825, and labored there with much acceptance for five years.

In the summer of 1826, Mr. Corle t made a mission tour to the north, and visited Green's Pond, which lies some forty miles to the north of Bonavista, and was then our most northern station. That region of country was then in a fearful state of demoralization.

---

* Since writing the above, notice has been received of the death of the Rev. George Ellidge.

There was indeed an Episcopal Church, and one of the readers belonging to the Society for the Propagation of the Gospel in Foreign Parts ; but swearing, drunkenness, Sabbath-breaking, and gross immorality were carried to such an extent that Green's Pond was often called the Sodom of the North. Mr. Corlett in the journal of his visit says, — Sunday, July 2, 1826, —

" We landed this morning at Green's Pond, about four o'clock ; after lying down to rest for an hour and a half, I was quite refreshed, and went to inform the principal inhabitants of Green's Pond what were my intentions in visiting them. I walked through the harbor to see what the people were doing, and found as I had previously heard that the merchant's stores were all open. I saw some purchasing shoes, others, fishing-materials, provisions, &c. In a word, I found that Sunday is what may emphatically be called the market day at Green's Pond. The people are not, however, so abandoned as with *one consent* to prosecute the fishery on the Sabbath day ; although there are individuals who send their boats out on Sunday, as they say, to be ready on Monday. I was informed by the most respectable persons residing in Pond, that during the winter season it is a very common and almost general thing to go shooting seals and birds on the Sabbath day. The people who were not employed were standing or lying on the rocks, rehearsing the news, and the children in groups playing, — in truth and reality, without any person to care for their souls. I resolved, as I could not preach in the church, that I would preach at the church-door as the people came out. But there was no church service. I presume the person who read the prayers, had been counselled to dispense with praying on that day. The weather proving unfavorable, I therefore preached in one of Mr. Garland's stores. A more tumultuous company I never saw assembled together. I almost despaired of arresting their attention ; but after singing a few verses, I prayed and received no further interruption except from a few sons of Bacchus, who were within ; and a few of the ' baser sort,' who stood without blaspheming. When retiring, a few who knew not what spirit they were of reviled and swore, and said I should be thrown into the water."

Mr. Corlett closes his interesting journal with the following observations : —

"Green's Pond is in great want of a missionary. There are about five hundred Protestants, and one hundred Catholics; besides there are Protestants at the following places, which may be early visited, with the happiest effects, several times a year, as most of them are contiguous to the Pond, and all have intercourse with it: Middle-Bill Cove, Pinchard's Island, Swain's Island, Fool's Island, Gooseberry Island, and Pouch Island, — on most of which many Protestant families reside who rarely hear the glad tidings of salvation."

Of the state of public feeling he says : —

"I plainly perceive that, owing to various circumstances, they are greatly prejudiced against us. Those who have formed illicit connections are against us, and those who enrich themselves by the ignorance of the poor are against us. The poor themselves are against us, because, say they, 'they do not allow of killing birds, hunting seals, or going fishing on Sabbath days; neither do they approve of having dances, singing songs,' &c.; and, besides, they say, 'we are no Christians, though we were christened long since.' The Prince of Darkness, whose empire this is at present, will, I have no doubt, take the field against us; but yet, were the door providentially opened to us, none of these things need move us."

After a lapse of thirty-six years, Mr. Corlett's hopes in reference to Green's Pond have been realized. In our minutes for 1861, we read, "Green's Pond to be supplied." The next year it received an appointment; for in the station-sheet we read, "Green's Pond, John S. Allen;" and in the minutes for last year (1863), Green's Pond returns twenty members in society, and twenty-four on trial, and four dollars as its first contribution toward the mission fund.

In the year 1824, Mr. Corlett left Newfoundland, and has ever since been laboring very successfully in different islands of the West Indies.

In the minutes for 1863, his name is down as super-intendent of the Spanish-town and Linstead Circuit, in the Jamaica District.

Before proceeding with our narrative, we may be allowed here to give a short account of the merciful preservation of the writer from perishing on the ice, during a journey in Trinity Bay, Saturday, Feb. 9, 1822. From my journal : —

"Wednesday last was the day for me to have left this place (Old Perlican) for Hants' Harbor, but was prevented by a snow-storm. Toward night, the storm increased, and the thermometer fell to about 16° below zero. On Thursday morning, the storm was at its height; severe was the cold, fearfully howled the wind, and the snow was raised in such suffocating clouds that it was dangerous to go out of the house. Toward night, however, the weather had considerably moderated. Friday was calm; the sun rose with great brilliancy, and the day throughout was fine. In the evening, a man called upon me to say that several persons were going up the bay in the morning, and I had better hold myself in readiness to accompany them; for, although we could not get along on the land because of the heavy snow-drifts, yet we could get up the bay on the ice. We left Perlican, at daylight, in three companies, thirteen persons in all, one of whom was a female. We struck off directly for the headland near Hants' Harbor. The morning was clear and calm, and there was every probability of getting to our journey's end early in the afternoon. About nine o'clock, a light breeze of wind sprung up from the west, and a haze came on the land, but not sufficient to hide it from our view. As we were passing a deep indent in the land, I chanced to look toward a point of land that we had passed an hour before, and were then only just abreast of it, and called the attention of my company to the fact. We halted, and immediately saw that the whole mass of ice was moving down the Bay, at about the same rate that we were walking up; and that we must reach the shore, or be carried into the open ocean and perish.

"Our company, consisting of four persons, was nearest the land; we fired a gun as a signal to the next company, and they repeated the signal to the outer company, with which company was the female.

We made for a prominent point of land, but soon found we had formed a very large angle to the eastward and could not fetch it, and must strike the land a long way below the point. As we got near the shore, the ice began to separate into small pans, and, as it consisted of but little more than the frozen snow, formed during the late storm, it often gave way under our feet, and but for our gaffs, we must have been drowned. The ice did not reach the shore, so that, with our gaffs, we had each to get a pan of ice for himself and push himself, toward the land. But no pan of ice would bear a second person. It always broke under him. Our party reached the shore safely, although very wet; and we watched, with deep anxiety, the arrival of our companions. The second party reached the shore with but little more difficulty than we had experienced; but, by the time the third party had arrived, the ice was quite gone from the shore, and they had to go down the shore a considerable distance before they dared attempt to land. The poor woman, exhausted and much alarmed, fell into the water repeatedly, but was rescued, and all reached the shore through the kind providence of our heavenly Father. We now kindled a fire by the seaside, and endeavored to dry ourselves; but the west wind was cold, and our clothes froze on us, notwithstanding our fire. The day was fast advancing, and we had to leave our encampment, and proceed on our journey. We reached Hants' Harbor a little after dark, very cold and excessively fatigued, but thankful that we had thus been saved from drowning, or perishing on the ice."

All our winter journeys were not like the above, for ofttimes they were very pleasant: it was so with my return from Hants' Harbor. My journal contains the following entry, Wednesday, February 15th: —

" Left Hants' Harbor for Island Cove, distance eighteen miles, at nine o'clock. The day was calm, the weather beautiful, and the walking excellent. Passing through the Hants' Harbor woods, we came to a lake seven miles long, called Pitten's Pond, crossed it, and a few miles further, we came to high table-land, from whence we had a most commanding view of the whole surrounding country. Our course was east-north-east, the sun was a little past his meridian altitude, and therefore on our right hand, in looking along the ridge of the land, it was an extended barren covered with its mantle of snow; numerous ponds were to be seen in every direction, with here and there a ' droke ' of woods; and the thick forest skirting the seashore. To the south were the waters of Conception Bay, calm and placid, with the high lands on the shore reflecting the sun's rays from their snow-capped summits; to the north-west the waters of Trinity Bay, and the whole margin of its northern shore presented a similar appearance, although the reflecting of light was less brilliant, owing to the different position of the sun ; while directly in our front the rocky and desolate island of· Bacalieu, dividing the waters of these two great bays, was distinctly visible ; and far in the distant horizon were the waters of the great western ocean, without a billow or breeze to agitate its glassy surface. We untied our ' nunny-bags ' and took our repast on this elevated land, and, after enjoying the scenery for some two or three hours, began to descend toward the shore of Conception Bay, when this beautiful panorama view vanished, leaving us the only pleasure of a retrospect and telling to other people the scenery we had beheld, and the pleasant journey we had had."

In the minutes for 1828, the Newfoundland station-sheet reads thus : —

ST. JOHN'S — John Pickavant.
CARBONEAR — John Haigh.
HARBOR GRACE — John Corlett.
BLACK-HEAD AND WESTERN BAY — Richard Knight.
ISLAND COVE, AND PERLICAN — Charles Bates.
PORT DE GRAVE — William Ellis.
BRIGUS — John Boyd.
TRINITY BAY — Simeon Noall.
BONAVISTA AND CATALINA — John Tomkins.
GRAND BANK AND FORTUNE BAY — A. Nightingale.
BURIN — George Ellidge.
HANTS' HARBOR — John Smithies.
INDIAN MISSION, MISSION ESQUIMAUX BAY, ON THE LABRADOR COAST — William Wilson.

Of the Esquimau Mission we have already given a full account, and there is no need of any repetition on that subject.

Two names occur in the above list, to which the attention of the reader has not been before directed.

1. John Tomkins commenced to travel in the year 1827, and his first appointment was Hants' Harbor. He continued to labor in different circuits on the island until the year 1833; when he removed to Canada and was appointed to Quebec. Canada then was all included in one district, with only ten preachers, and 2,094 members. Brother Tomkins still lives and labors in Canada, and he has witnessed its progress for thirty years, during which time, from the above small " foreign district," it has become a mighty independent connection, with twenty-five districts, five hundred and thirteen ministers, a membership of near sixty thousand, and carrying the light of the glorious gospel as far west as the shores of the Pacific Ocean.

John Smithies commenced to travel at the conference of 1828; and also was first appointed to Hants' Harbor. He labored on the island nine years, when in 1837 he removed to Abaco, in the West Indies; and after two years he was appointed to Swan River, Western Australia. He labored in Australia for twenty-four years. During that time our cause in Australia and Van Dieman's has increased, from three districts with thirty-five ministers and a membership of 1,878, until it, like Canada, has also become a great, independent conference, with seven districts, one hundred and seventy-two ministers and preachers on trial, and with a membership of more than 30,000. Besides it has seven local preachers; it has also its academic and collegiate institutions, a book-room, two official journals, and a missionary ship. In 1859, John Smithies stood on the minutes, for Langford, in Tasmania.

The missionary income for this year was £43,235 7s. 9d. Our total missionary membership was 34,892.

Two years before this, the British conference, and almost the whole connection, had to mourn the loss of one of its noblest and best laymen, in the death of Joseph Butterworth, Esq., of London. Mr. Butterworth had long served his country as member of Parliament. For thirty years he had been a class leader, and a great promoter of Sabbath schools; he was treasurer of our missionary society, and connected with all the great religious and philanthropic movements of the day. At the time of his funeral, which took place in London, the city of Dover, which he had represented in Parliament, and which is seventy miles distant, closed all its shops as on the Sabbath, and tolled its bells the chief part of the day. In the minutes of the conference for 1826, when speaking of the death of Mr. Butterworth, we read the following : —

" Nor was there anything which related to the stability, extension, or success of the Wesleyan missions, into which he did not enter with an affectionate and constant interest. Great is the loss which our missionary society has sustained by this bereavement. But it becomes us to bow with submission to the dispensations of Almighty God, and to commit his great cause, in all its departments, by a renewed act of faith, to his special care ; trusting in his promises, and remembering, that while the strong are not efficient without him, the weak, in his hand, shall become as the ' angel of the Lord.' "

A few years before the death of Mr. Butterworth, the Episcopal clergy of Newfoundland tried to get an imperial act of Parliament that should exclude the Wesleyan ministers from the right to celebrate marriage, and it was by the influence of that gentleman in the House of Commons, that this design was frustrated.

In the autumn of 1827, the official circular of the committee reached Newfoundland; a copy of which now lies before me, and bears the signatures, — " George Morley, James Townley, John James."

Two of these names occur here for the first time in our narrative. James Townley, D. D., was educated by the Rev. David Simpson, author of the "Plea for Religion." He commenced his labor as an itinerant preacher in 1796, and travelled for thirty-six years. He was missionary secretary five years, and filled the office of president at the conference of 1829. He was a most amiable and learned man. His literary character was very respectable. He was master of several languages, and was noted as a great biblical scholar. His literary attainments gained for him the title of D. D. He died in peace, and in the full triumph of faith, on the 12th December, 1833.

John James filled the office of secretary also for five years. The minutes of conference say of him: " He was distinguished through life by steady and fervent piety and inflexible integrity, united to great affability, cheerfulness, and generosity. As a preacher he was at once eloquent, sound, ardent, and exceedingly useful. He died suddenly on the 6th of November, 1832, in the 47th year of his age, and the 26th of his ministry.

The year 1832 was a year of great mortality among the advocates and managers of our missionary society. The committee in the conclusion of their report for this year say: " Two of the general secretaries, and two other members of the committee, have been removed in the short space of a few months from the scene of their labors to their everlasting reward." First on the list stands the name of the Rev. Dr. Adam Clarke ; he died on the 30th of Sept., aged seventy-two years. The second was the Rev. Thomas Stanley. "In him," says the report, "the society has lost a steady friend, while the church has been deprived of a faithful minister and pastor. His attention to business, his judicious counsel, and his affable manners secured for him the esteem and affection of the committee." He died on the 9th of October. The third was the Rev. John James, who died as already stated on the 6th of November. The fourth was the Rev. Richard Watson, who died Jan. 8th, 1833.

As the funeral knell of these servants of the Lord, these supporters of our missionary cause, sounded across the Atlantic Ocean, and along our rock-bound shores of Newfoundland, deep sorrow took possession of the minds of the missionaries, as they remembered the kindness they had each received from those departed saints, and the Christian and fatherly advice contained in those annual circulars which from year to year were sent by them for our guidance ; as well as for the interest they took in our concerns, and for the manner in which they regarded our requests and supplied our necessities.

These provinces at that time began to feel their duty in reference to the mission fund. The report made up to December 31st, credits Nova Scotia with £305 13s. 3d. ; New Brunswick with £329 13s. 8d. ; Newfoundland with £103 6s. 7d. missionary money. These moneys were raised in these provinces mostly by subscription, although the public collections were included. In Newfoundland there were only seven subscribers besides the missionaries. Of the £103 13s. 3d., £74 16s. 4d. were raised in five public collections, as follows :

St. John's, £24 13s. Harbor Grace, £15 9s. Carbonear, £15 11s. 4d. Port de Grave, £8 14s; Brigus,
£13 9s. These were noble collections, and now that
subscriptions are taken up over the district, as well as
collections, the missionary income of Newfoundland is
more than four times as much in 1863 as in 1828. And
it will yet increase.

CHAPTER XIV.

IN the instructions to the Wesleyan missionaries, given to them at their ordination, and published in every annual missionary report down to the present day, is found the following : —

"Instruction VIII. It is peremptorily required of every missionary in our connection to keep a journal and send home frequently such copious extracts of it as may give a full and particular account of his labors, success, and prospects. He is also required to give such details of a religious kind as may be generally interesting to the friends of missions at home ; particularly, accounts of conversions. Only we recommend to you, not to allow yourselves, under the influence of religious joy, to give any *high coloring* of facts, but always write such accounts as you would not dislike to see return in print to the place where the facts reported may have occurred."

The writer felt himself absolutely bound to this instruction, and he therefore commenced his journal with the very commencement of his missionary life. That journal now lies before him, and from its pages, as well as from his remembrance of past events, he now begs to give the reader some miscellaneous information in reference to Newfoundland.

TRAVELLING IN NEWFOUNDLAND.

In a country where all the inhabitants were engaged

in maritime pursuits, where agriculture as a business
was not followed, where a horse was but seldom seen,
and where roads had never been made, the Christian
missionary, like the people, would have a life of great
exposure and toil. Such was the case when the writer,
in 1821, received his first appointment to an out-harbor
circuit. In removing to our stations, our conveyance
was a fishing-boat, our luggage would be stowed in the
fish-lockers, and covered with a tarpaulin to keep it
from the wet; our females and children would, in a
storm, crowd into the *cuddy*, — a sort of cabin, aft, of
about six feet long, in which standing was out of the
question, but in which we could sit upright by taking
the floor as a stool. The preacher himself generally
took his stand in the *after* standing-room, alongside the
skipper, where he would be exposed to all the weather,
where the *spray* from the weather bow would strike
him, and wet him to the skin. If he were not sick,
passing a fishing-boat, or a headland, the white sail of
a square-rigged vessel, as seen in the distance, a flock
of sea-birds, the blowing of a whale, or the sluggish
rolling along of " sea-hog " or porpoise, would excite
his attention, and beguile his weary moments, and his
hand would be upon the *belaying-pin*, ready to haul in
or slack out the main-sheet, as occasion might require.
But if he or his family were sea-sick, as was almost
sure to be the case, then every mountain wave that
arose, every time the fragile bark would be hurled into
the trough of the sea, every time a reef was taken in
the sails or let out, every time the boat was hove to or
bore away, every shift of wind or change of course,
every creak of the rudder, and, above all, every time
the sea would strike the boat, fresh nausea would be
produced, some want would be expressed in the cuddy

by his crying children or his suffering wife, to which he could not attend, while his shivering limbs and personal weakness would prompt him often to ask, Skipper, is the wind free? Does it blow as hard as it did? Is the sea abating? and When shall we reach the harbor?

This is not a fancy picture, but the result of many years' experience; for often has the writer been for days and nights in a situation like that described above; and once in particular he made a passage from Burin to St. Johns in a fishing-boat, when we were driven out of sight of land in a gale of wind; while his family were prisoners in a wretched *cuddy*, which, for size and comfort, might, like the old Papist prison, be termed " Little Ease," himself was for four days and five nights in succession, under the open canopy of heaven, exposed to the wind, the rain, and snow, of the latter of which in one night there fell three inches.

SUMMER TRAVELLING IN THE CIRCUITS.

This was very laborious, as we had to climb high hills, wade the streams, and plunge through the mire of the marshes, with our bundles on a stick, and carried upon the left shoulder, while our persons were denuded of coat, sometimes of vest and neck-cloth likewise; and, when wearied or hungry, we would doff our bundles, partake of the collation therein contained, drink from the purling brook, and, after resting for a time under the shade of some tree, would again pursue our journey toward its terminus. As our mission stations were mostly on the necks of land that separate the large bays from each other, the streams in our way were fordable in summer, for the water shed on those necks is not sufficiently extensive to produce navigable rivers. Brook was always the term used for our streams; but late in the fall, we would sometimes be breast high in fording these brooks.

In travelling, we never wore boots ; for they were useless to keep us dry, as we would always get over the tops of any boots we could put on when wading our numerous brooks. We were always careful to have good soles on our shoes, to keep the feet from injury by the rocks, over which we had to walk ; but a small hole in the side of the shoe we would rather have than not, as it allowed the water to escape when we got on the hard land, and thus prevented friction in walking. When we arrived at our place of destination, and entered the house, the kind hostess, who knew that we were fatigued and wet and often very hungry, always met us with a smile. The hospitalities of her house were offered to us, and the kindness of her heart was shown by addressing us with, " I am glad to see you ; come, walk in, sit down ; take off your shoes and stockings, and I will get a cup of tea in a few minutes." Thus did kindness make us forget our fatigue, and lead us to exclaim, " What would we not do, and what labor would we not undertake, for those who so kindly receive us, and who listen, with so much attention, to the gospel of salvation which we have come hither to preach ? "

WINTER TRAVELLING.

To understand this, we would remind the reader that the term woods was used in a threefold sense : thus, a hat of woods meant a small, isolated patch of woods in a barren ; a droke of woods meant a piece of wood, whether large or small, on the sides of two opposite hills, with a valley between them ; but the term woods, when used alone, has no reference to situation or extent.

The barrens are a sort of table-land, elevated from

six hundred to one thousand feet above the level of the sea. Over these dreary barrens we had to travel in the winter season, with the thermometer often 15° below zero ; and, as in these journeys we had to walk over a trackless country, and there was a possibility of our being out all night, we usually made preparation to meet contingencies. 1. We went in company of from two to four persons ; seldom did one travel alone. 2. Each man had a nunny-bag, which is a kind of knapsack, made of seal-skin, with the two fore-fippers passing over the shoulders, and tied across the breast with a piece of cod-line. In our nunny-bag, we carried dry stockings, a change of linen, with any papers we might require. We also had in our nunny-bag two days' provisions ; and, as lucifer matches were not then known, we carried the old-fashioned tinder-box, with flint and steel, also an extinguished firebrand, so as to facilitate the kindling of a fire if necessary. 3. We had each a pair of *rackets*, or Indian snow-shoes, with Indian moccasins on our feet, and buskins on our legs. 4. We had a hatchet to cut wood for our fire, and one or two guns, in case we met with any deer or other game. Thus equipped, with the addition of a pocket-compass, we would commence our journey. Often would each man's load be upward of twenty pounds in weight. We generally selected a moonlight night as the time for crossing the country, and generally left at four o'clock in the morning. After going on some wood-path to its end, we took the woods, and climbed the hills, the nearest way to the barrens. If it were early in the season, so that we had frost without snow, or very late, so that the driven snow was sufficiently hard to bear us, in either case our journey was generally pleasant, because we could go in a straight line to our place of

destination. But, if it were stormy, the journey would
be a long one, and often attended with danger.

A journey like this, the writer once made, while on
the Grand Bank Circuit. He had been to Burin to
visit brother Ellis, and, in company with three men,
was returning home, a distance of some forty miles.
On arriving on the barrens, we found the snow very
deep ; so that, notwithstanding our rackets, or snow-·
shoes, we often sank to our knees in snow. To go
across the country the whole distance to Grand Bank
was impossible. We, therefore, strove to reach the
shore of Fortune Bay, somewhere in the vicinity of
Great Garnish. The distance to this place was some
twelve miles ; and one mile an hour was the most we
could accomplish with our snow-shoes. A little before
sunset, we came to a hat of woods, under the lee of
which, we untied our nunny-bags ; and, after taking
some refreshment, we held a consultation as to whether
we should try to reach the shore, still some miles distant, or kindle a fire and remain in this hat of woods
for the night. Our pilot gave it as his opinion that
we should have a severe storm before morning ; so we
determined to proceed, and reached the shore about six
o'clock. It was on the 27th of January, long after
dark, and the moon was not up. We then directed
our way down the shore, in expectation of finding
some place inhabited by human beings. We had gone
but a short distance before one of my companions
refused to travel any further, and threw away his gun.
I took his gun, and threw away my rackets ; and,
after some remonstrance, urged him to make another
effort to proceed. Soon another of the company laid
himself down to sleep. I shook him violently. "Let
me sleep," said he, "only a few minutes and I will go

on." I said, " No, you shall not sleep at all, for if you
sleep, you will never wake again." Presently he was
aroused, and we moved on to a point of land where
we met the coming storm in all its fury. We retreated
for shelter under a high bank, when one of my company, in utter despair, said, " I will lie down here and
die, for we shall perish before the morning." We now
tried to fire off our guns, but the powder was wet.
We strove to make a fire, but our tinder was wet.
Still, there was one alternative: we might be quite
near some dwelling, and if we made a shout, our voice
might reach some ear that would come to our relief.
We were led to this by seeing, as we thought, a reflection in the atmosphere as from a fire. Three of us
shouted together, when, to our great joy, a human
voice, in reply, was heard from the thick bush just
over our head ; and immediately two men made
their appearance, each with a flaming firebrand, and
gave us a hearty welcome to the hospitalities of their
winter tilt. Supper was soon prepared, although
then about twelve o'clock ; most of our party were too
much exhausted to be roused, so they slept until the
morning. We had been in the tilt, but a short time,
before the storm became terrific ; and, had we not obtained a shelter, it was scarcely possible we could have
survived. We were much fatigued, and my feet were
much chafed with the rackets, and my face and my right
ear severely frozen.

In the winter of 1833, two of our ministers nearly
perished in one of those winter journeys, — Messrs.
Knight and Tomkins. They left Heart's Content for
Carbonear, and as the distance was only a few hours'
walk, and the weather seemed favorable, they left without
a guide, a gun, or a pair of rackets, and with but a scanty

supply of provision. When they reached the barrens, it became foggy; then a "*snow-dwie*," that is, a slight snow-shower, came on; another, and another "dwie" followed, until it became a heavy snow-storm. They were now lost; but they wandered on, and about night-fall they came to woods, but what woods they knew not. In the dark they strove hard to pass the woods and get on some shore; but all was in vain,—brother Tomkins could proceed no further. They had no means of making a fire, and their food was all used. The snow was up to their hips, but they found a level spot of some thirty feet in length; there they trod a path, on which they continued to walk to and fro for the space of more than twelve hours. The night was dark and cold, their clothes were torn to rags in getting through the "tuckemore bushes," the storm howled fearfully, the trees were falling around them in every direction by the violence of the wind, and they were exhausted with wet, cold, and hunger; repeatedly did Mr. Tomkins sit or fall to the ground, and request his companion to allow him to take rest on the snow-clad ground, if but for a few minutes. Mr. Knight, who possessed great powers of endurance, a strong muscular frame, and a corresponding vigorous mind, could not grant that request, but shook him, rubbed his limbs, and sometimes dragged him along, knowing as he did, that if his brother slept there, he would wake no more until the "last trump should wake the slumbering dead." Frequently, during the slowly revolving hours of that memorable night, did these servants of the Lord "pray and make supplication to the God of heaven," knowing that he would interpose in their behalf, and deliver them from their perilous position. He heard their prayer, he preserved them during the darkness of the night; and just as the dawn of the next day broke from the eastern skies, the crowing of a cock told them of their proximity to a human dwelling, which if they could reach, they were sure the hand of relief would be extended to them, shelter would be cheerfully given them, and their wants supplied according to the circumstances of whomsoever should be found as occupants of that sylvan abode. They took courage, plunged through the snow and thicket, and reached this " winter tilt," about eight o'clock, just as the storm was subsiding, and the sun, now orient in his course and glorious in his splendor, was bringing the blessings of another day to the inhabitants of the land. In this tilt they obtained food; but what was to them of greater importance, they had a good fire, and took a good rest. After some hours of repose, they procured some articles of clothing from the host, and then directed their steps along a beaten path, thankful and happy, although suffering in their limbs from the effects of the frost, toward that now more than ever endeared home, where smiling countenances would welcome them, the prattling of the little ones would dissipate sorrow, and the heaving heart would rejoice for such a preservation and such a deliverance.

I will mention one more case, illustrative of the difficulties of winter travelling by our missionaries in days of yore. The missionary notice for December, 1820, contains an extract from the journal of the Rev. James Hickson, giving an account of his journey from Old Perlican to Hants' Harbor. It reads thus : —

" Feb. 9. Walked to Hants' Harbor, the snow very deep, the cold intense, having six men in company, some of whom, having recently found mercy, went purposely to tell their friends that they had found the Lord. Just before I got there, I was quite ready

to make my bed in the snow, and give up the ghost. But through
mercy I was strengthened to finish my twenty miles' journey by
taking a morsel of bread which one of the company happened to
have in his pocket.   If my journey had been much further, the
consequence would have been, that I must either have perished
in the woods, or have been carried out by my tired company.
With their remaining strength they were willing to do this if required and possible.   A part of my feet were so ' *frost-burnt*,' (a
phrase used for frost-bitten, or frozen) that when I came to my
friend Mr. Tilley's, I had to sit some time by the fire before the ice
could be sufficiently thawed to take my shoes off.   I could do nothing
that night though much wanted, but strive to rest my weary limbs.

" Wednesday, 23.   To day I went half way to Perlican, and
spent the night in the woods among the ' Tilts,' where several of
the inhabitants reside for the convenience of getting fire-wood
in winter, and materials for the use of the fishery in summer.   In
one of these tilts, I held a prayer-meeting ; and, though small, it
will be remembered by some who were present, when they have
spent ages in eternity.   On the 24th I went on to Perlican, and on
the morning following had six men to break a path for me through
the snow to Island Cove."

Newfoundland is now quite a different place. It now
has fine roads along the shores of its principal bays,
and across several of its necks ; it has fine horses, with
carriages and sleighs, — comforts which the fathers of
the present generation never knew. Our ministers, too,
have good times of it.   They can remove to their circuits in large vessels or steamers. They can travel
their circuits on horseback, and are in consequence
exempt from those exhausting journeys which the pioneers of Methodism had to perform.

We congratulate the inhabitants on this great improvement in their country, and hope it will continue
to improve ; and we congratulate our brethren on the
comparative ease with which their circuit labor can be
performed, and the leisure they have for study and
for pastoral duties, and pray their improvement may be
obvious, and " their profiting may appear to all."

CHAPTER XV.

EVERYTHING was brought to the " stage-head "
in boats, and as there were no carts and but very
few horses, human muscular power would have to do
the trucking. The dry fish would be carried down from
the fish-house in the hand-barrow ; and the oil-casks filled
in the oil-house were rolled to the stage-head and parbuckled into the boat. The parbuckle is a double
rope passed round a cask, one end of which is made
fast, and the other end is hauled upon, by which the
cask is made to roll either up or down the stage-head.
Salt is hauled up with a block and tackle and carried
in a hand-barrow. Molasses is parbuckled up the
stage-head, then rolled to the store. Coals are hauled
and carried in a covel, — that is, a barrel with a strong
stake passed through or near the upper hoops. Flour
is parbuckled up, and then slung upon a stake and carried between two men. Lumber and wood are handed
up and carried upon men's shoulders.

DRINKING HABITS.

Fifty years ago spirituous liquor, particularly rum,
was considered almost a necessary of life. The fisherman could not do without it. How could he stand
" the pitiless pelting of the storm," without a little

drop of rum to keep the cold out? When he went off to the fishing-ground, he must have a little for good luck; when he came in with a good "put of fish," he must take a *horn* for joy. If it were a warm day, he could not take a drink of water, because it would make 'him sick, and to avoid such a catastrophe in the fishing season, he must put a little rum in the water, or take a drink of *calebogus*, which is rum and spruce beer. This was his favorite drink. If he were about to take a journey in the winter, he must take a little before he left, to keep the cold out, and a *pocket pistol* (a small bottle) he must take with him, lest he should be overtaken in a snow-storm and perish; and if he got frozen, there was nothing like rum to wash the part with. If a tradesman were employed, he must have *three drinks* a day; or what he called his *morning*, his *eleven*, and his *evening*. If there was a house-raising, or even a church-raising, there must be rum. If a friend called, he must take a drink; and if he called upon his friend, the act was reciprocated. Rum was plentifully supplied at weddings, and almost equally so at funerals. Wines and spirits were in every house, and in many of the merchants' houses they were used in great profusion. One man, an agent in a northern harbor, used to say, that he allowed a puncheon of rum a year for the use of his own household. To the west, the merchants and agents would sometimes, as they were wont to express it, "give each other a benefit:" that meant, to invite a number of gentlemen to the house, and try which could drink most before he was drunk. One of these dissipated men once told the writer, "what a benefit he had given his friends recently." "I would drink," said he, "go out, be sick, return, drink again, so that

I soon laid them under table, while I could do my business as usual." But let it be recorded, that this man died in the prime of life from the effects of his dissipated habits.

Vessels from Newfoundland traded with most of the countries where inebriating drinks were manufactured, and brought them to the island in large quantities. Rich wines were brought from Madeira and Oporto; sweet wine from Malaga; cordials from Hamburg; rum from the West Indies; French brandy from St. Peter's; besides all that was imported from Great Britain and Ireland. Such importation had a fearful hold upon the community. *Moderate drinking* no one thought wrong at that time; absolute drunkenness was indeed condemned, but it was always palliated with the expression, " He has got a little drop too much, — never mind him."

Twice was the writer in danger from the use of rum on the part of drunken skippers. The following entries appear on his journal : —

" Nov. 11, 1820. Left Harbor Grace at 8 o'clock for Portugal Cove; it blew a gale of wind from the S. W. Our skipper was much under the influence of strong drink, when he came on board. When about half passage he took more rum, which totally unfitted him for managing the boat. We arrived off the eastern end of Belle Isle, when it blew a perfect hurricane. Portugal Cove was full in view, but our skipper swore it was Belle Isle, and he put the helm up to go round it. Our danger was now imminent; the men refused to obey their skipper, the sea was beating over us and filling our boat, and we were rapidly driving out toward the ocean. A young man, a passenger, ran aft, and pretended to join in opinion with the skipper, when he adroitly pushed his hand from the tiller; he rolled to ' leeward;' and, being helpless, was unable to rise. In the mean time we ' hauled our wind,' and 'fetched the Cove.' Thus, by the kind providence of our heavenly Father, were we all saved from a watery grave.

30

" August 14th, 1826.   Left Burin for the Flat Islands at six o'clock.   The boat's crew consisted of only two men, both Roman Catholics.   There were a bottle of rum on board and a keg of spruce beer.   When we got out into the bay, the men began to mix the rum and spruce beer, and drink freely of this cale-bogus.   The wind began to freshen, and we were running among the reefs.   One of the men said to me, ' Parson, you don't drink with us ; you had better take a drop of calebogus to keep out the cold.'   In an instant the thought struck me what to do.   I replied, ' Thank you ; have you any rum in the bottle ? '   ' Oh, yes, there is plenty for your reverence.'   I stooped down and emptied the bottle into the bilge-water ; poured some spruce beer into the basin, stood up, and with the usual, ' Here is a good time to us,' boldly took my drink of spruce beer.   Soon my companions were either cold or thirsty again, but the rum was all gone, so they had to drink the spruce beer alone.   But they could not think of that. Presently one of the men, arousing from a sort of revery, said : ' Pat, the merchants in Burin are great rogues ; they sell their rum too high, so that we could only get one bottle for our trip.   I think one or two of us had better join and get a puncheon of rum, and then we should have plenty.   But it is no use talking ; here is a terrible night coming on, and we have not a drop of rum on board ; let us haul our wind, and get into Paradise ; we will get some rum there.'   I remonstrated ; besides, I added, ' Paradise is a rather singular place to look for rum ; ' but remonstrance was useless ; my companions could not think of perishing for a drop of rum, when they might get their wants supplied in Paradise, which we could reach with but little effort.   We made the effort, but just as we got to the entrance of the harbor, the wind blew so violently, that we were obliged to bear up, and run into the Flat Islands' Harbor in the night, where we struck upon a sand-bank, and the ebb tide left us dry.   The next flood took us off, and through mercy we landed in safety."

The use of exhilarating drink was then a universal practice ; and fond parents often unthinkingly taught their children the habit, by giving them a little drop in a teaspoon when they were in their infancy.   Cowper translates a passage from Homer's Iliad, which describes

this custom exactly. Phœnix is represented as addressing Achilles in the following words : —

> " Nor wouldst thou taste thy food at home, till first
> I placed thee on my knees, with my own hand
> Thy viands carved, and fed thee, and the wine
> Held to thy lips; and many a time in fits
> Of infant frowardness, the purple juice
> Rejecting, thou hast deluged all my vest
> And filled my bosom."

The evil was a shocking enormity. We have seen
the fond parent present the wine or diluted spirits to
the infant lips, which, as in the case of Achilles, was
at first rejected, but afterwards was drunk with avidity.
We have seen the parent himself, only a moderate
drinker, teach his youthful son to take a little in mod-
eration, and we have seen that youth, when arrived at
manhood, become a confirmed drunkard, and when
reproved by his father, now heartbroken because of
his son's delinquencies, would reply : " It is your
fault; you taught me the habit of drinking, and the
guilt is yours." We have seen the young man of
education and promise, — one who had already employed
his talent in public speaking, and seemed likely, at no
great distance of time, to fill a high judicial position in
his native land ; but his once temperate habit gave
way to excess, and while yet a youth he was brought to
a drunkard's grave. We have seen the talented medical man, who was well acquainted with the chemical
properties of alcoholic drinks ; who would forbid their
use to his parents ; but he took a little to stimulate him
when under fatigue, the habit grew upon him, until
taken with delirum tremens, when he died in agony
and despair. And we have known the Christian minister of acknowledged piety, and commanding talent ;
he at first took a simple glass with a friend ; the habit

gained upon him, until at last he forfeited his station in the ministry, brought disgrace upon the cause of religion, became a stumbling-block to many, was expelled from the church of which he had once been the revered pastor, with no prospect before him, but wretchedness, ruin, misery, and death.

With this gigantic evil Wesleyan ministers had to contend in all parts of Newfoundland. In thousands of instances the victory was on the part of religion and truth. We are thankful that a different state of things now exists, and different views are entertained by large portions of the population in Newfoundland; that our hardy fishermen there now see that rum is not good either to keep the cold out, or the heat out; that it is an evil as a beverage, and injurious as a stimulant; that more work can be done without it than with it; that its use at funerals is a cruelty, and at weddings an absurdity; and that the drinking habits of society are an unmitigated evil, and ought universally to be abandoned. We congratulate our friends in Newfoundland upon the change in public opinion as to the supposed utility of inebriating stimulants.

Moderate drinking often leads to drunkenness, which has brought more poverty into helpless families, been the fruitful source of more crimes, hurled down more men from rank and influence, has filled more jails and lunatic asylums, brought more dishonor upon Christian ministers and Christian churches, has brought more human beings to a premature grave, sunk more men and women into the gulf of fire, than has any other single crime of which human nature has ever been guilty.

HOUSES.

The houses in the out-harbor were all built of

wood; the better sort were neatly shingled; the common houses, or tilts, were covered with boards, or spruce rinds. In entering the house, on the one hand was a neat parlor, and on the other hand a kitchen with a very large fireplace called the " chimney-corner." A neat carpet would cover the parlor, but the kitchen-floor would be covered with a blue sand taken from the sea-shore, and prettily drawn into diagonal lines, with a broom, by the skill of the industrious housewife. One or two sleeping-rooms would be found on the ground floor; but the dormitories for the family would generally be upstairs. The furniture was plain, and the beds always clean and comfortable. The merchants' houses were good buildings, well finished and well furnished.

Cooking-stoves were then unknown. The fire was made upon the hearth, and the wood supported by dog-irons. If the fire required a second tier of wood, it was supported upon the lower tier, by small sticks called triggers, which were placed crossways. A large stick was placed against the back, a smaller one in front, and a lesser one still in the middle. The wood was sometimes quite green, and hence making a fire was quite an art, and required back-junks, fore-junks, middle-junks, triggers, splits, and brands; and the fishermen would sometimes say whoever can build a good fire with green fir can build a boat.

Across the chimney, some seven or eight feet from the hearth, was a bar of wood or iron, called the pot-bar. On this pot-bar was hung the cotterall and pot-hooks, which sustained the vessels used for culinary purposes. Nobody had an oven, but baking was all done in the bake-pot. The food would not always satisfy the appetite of the epicure, but it was generally

30 *

substantial and good.   In the winter we would get
fresh beef, but in' the summer season, salt meat was
generally used.   Bread, that is, sea biscuit, was always
on the table, and soft bread, or the raised loaf, was
used when the mistress had time to bake it.   Fish,
cooked in some way, was used at almost every meal,
but the toasted fish was truly delicious.   Spruce beer
was in every house, and was freely used by the people.
The absence of scurvy in the country may perhaps, in
part, be attributed to the free use of the black-spruce
beer.

Here let me bear my sincere and unreserved testimony to the universal kindness and hospitality of the
Newfoundlanders.   I never heard of a Newfoundlander closing his door to the stranger, refusing the
contents of his larder to the hungry, or tying his purse-
strings when the calls of religion and humanity were
made upon him.   He is liberal according to his means,
and I have seen in a case of famine, which I shall
hereafter mention, a poor man and a poor widow shar-
ing their last morsel with their necessitous and starving
neighbors.   To their ministers they were always kind.
If any little nicety came into their possession, it was
sure to be kept until the preacher came ; and for the
fourteen years that I travelled there, I never paid a
cent for travelling expenses, except in the packet across
Conception Bay.

GARDENS.

Near the house is the garden, enclosed either with a
picket or a wattle fence.   The garden seldom contains much variety; potatoes and other culinary vegetables, with a few currants and gooseberries, would generally fill the catalogue.   The women do most of the

cultivation, and they have but little time from the business of the fishery. In most of the settlements there
were some few persons who kept a cow or cows, and
made a little butter ; but goats' milk was used to a
great extent.

WEDDINGS.

A wedding in an out-harbor was quite an affair.
Neither a license nor the publication of banns was required for the performance of marriage ; and frequently
the minister knew nothing about it, until the party
arrived at the mission-house. The ceremony was
usually performed in the church, when the flag would
be hoisted, at which signal almost the whole community
would assemble to see the "couple made happy."
As soon as the party came out of church, a number
of guns would be fired over the heads of the bride and
bridegroom, and also over the head of the parson, as a
salute, which would be occasionally repeated until we
reached the house. Here the invitation would be
given to dinner, which would sometimes be so general
as to include all hands. At the dinner there were great
profusion and drinking, as was then the custom ; but
rioting and disturbance of the public peace were not
known. It was not the habit of the Newfoundlanders
to insult or annoy any person ; much less would they
do so in the presence of their minister.

FUNERALS

Were always attended by large bodies of people ;
and particularly was this the case if the deceased were
an aged person, or much respected in the community.
Spirits and sweet-cake were given at the house. The
corpse was always taken into the church, where two

lessons and the whole funeral service were read, and the
entire matter made as ceremonious and as imposing as
possible.   A funeral sermon must always be preached;
and however the person might have lived and died, it
was expected the preacher would preach him into
heaven.   And, in order to secure this, some one would
go to the preacher just before he entered the church,
and tell him, what perhaps neither he nor any one else
ever knew before, about the goodness of the deceased,
what he did and what he said while sick, and expect
all this and a great deal more in praise of the dead
would be repeated from the pulpit.   Sometimes the
party calling upon the preacher would have very low
views of experimental religion, or what was compre-
hended in " dying in the Lord."   Once the writer was
called upon by a man to attend the obsequies of his
wife, and he wished a very good character to be given
of the deceased; but all the information he gave was
she had been a good wife, had diligently attended to her
domestic concerns, and had taken care of his property.
Not feeling much disposed to repeat this in the pulpit,
because he doubted its truth, the bereaved husband
in the exuberance of his conjugal affection, repeatedly
and very audibly exclaimed while the service was going
on, "Oh, she was a good wife, she never robbed me, nor
plundered me, and besides she was such a fine hand
for the garden!"

Funeral sermons are preached all over these provinces, as well as in Newfoundland; and the practice
seems to have originated when the population was
sparse, and when the preacher's visits were like angels'
visits, " few and far between."   When the scattered
inhabitants were collected at the funeral of a friend, it
was certainly both a wise and good arrangement to

preach to them the words of life and salvation. But in places where ministers are regularly stationed, the same necessity does not now exist; yet the same practice is still followed. If the deceased had been eminently pious, or died very happy, it is a delightful duty for the minister to tell the congregation how that soul was saved, and went triumphant home to God; but if the individual had notoriously lived without religion, had died in sin, or had given no satisfactory evidence of having experimental converting grace, what can the preacher say? To tell the people he believes the deceased had gone to heaven would be contrary to his conscientious conviction; and to point thereto as a warning to others, would be to offer an insult to the whole family connection. When the minister does say anything about the dead, it sometimes happens that one party will complain, " The preacher did not say as much about my friend as he might have said;" while another party would tauntingly reply, " If the preacher had known as much as I know, he would not have said what he did." Would it not be better, as a general thing, to call preaching, at such times, sermons at funerals, rather than funeral sermons?

In the year 1786, — the very year John McGeary was appointed missionary to Newfoundland, — Mr. Wesley gave the following advice to the preachers, which, having been sanctioned by the conference, is our Methodistic law : —

"Never preach a funeral sermon, but for an eminently holy person; nor then without consulting the Assistant. Preach none for hire. Beware of panegyric, particularly in London." [1]

[1] Minutes of Conference for 1786.

LITERATURE.

Of this we cannot say much in reference to the times of which we are writing. The adult population in the out-harbors had not in their youth the educational advantages which are experienced by children in the present day. They had come from the rural population of England, Ireland, and Scotland, and the Channel Islands; and, while those countries were then, as now, the land of light and knowledge to the wealthy, yet they presented but few opportunities for the poor to acquire even the commonest branches of education. It were folly to expect anything else than that those uneducated British emigrants would bring with them their national peculiarities, and their provincial dialects, which nothing but education could remove. But it is questionable, after all, whether their ignorance was more palpable than was the ignorance of the peasantry in the districts from whence they emigrated; and certain it is, the pronunciation of the English language by the fishermen is no way inferior to the pronunciation as heard in many country places in their father-land. There was a fault somewhere. That fault was not in the people. They could not educate themselves; and, when by their hard labor and industry they had acquired means to pay for the education of their children, the teachers were not within their reach. Neither religion nor learning is innate in the human mind. Every child born into our world is both ignorant and wicked; so that both learning and religion are to be acquired. And, as Newfoundland then had no teachers of her own, they must be found elsewhere; yea, they must come from the very country from whence the people themselves had emigrated.

In the early history of the country, one cause of fault was in the English merchants, who, while they gained almost boundless wealth through their Newfoundland trade, yet would not pay one penny for the moral or intellectual improvement of the people, but whose maxim seems to have been, " Keep the fishermen unlettered and in ignorance, then we can rule them, and profit by our trade." The other cause of fault was the supineness of the Christian church in Britain, who, while the children of their land had through necessity been compelled to seek the means of gaining a living by the toils of a Newfoundland fishery, had totally neglected to supply them with the benefits of an evangelical ministry, or send them teachers for the education of their children.

The Newfoundland mind is the English mind; and many of the sons of our hardy fishermen, if they had the opportunity, would master the whole curriculum of university study, and matriculate with as much honor as any recluse of Oxford or Cambridge.

A fisherman in Trinity Bay, in his childhood, had been taught but little more than the alphabet ; but he taught himself to read. He read theology, biography, history, and poetry. With Milton, Young, Cowper, Thomson, Pollock, and other English poets, he was very familiar; and, without a teacher, he acquired a knowledge of arithmetic, geography, astronomy, trigonometry, and navigation ; and, had classical books and books on other sciences been within his reach, he would have mastered them also.

As few people could then read, books were scarce, but what books were found were always of an instructive and useful character. Among our own people where books were found, we were sure to see Wesley's

Appeal, Wesley's journals, or his sermons ; sometimes the whole of his works. Also, Fletcher's Appeal, his Checks, or the whole of his works. Mrs. Stretton, the relict of the gentleman whose name has previously oc- curred in this narrative, had a very excellent library. She had the whole of Wesley's works in sixteen volumes, his Christian Library, in fifty duodecimo vol- umes, his philosophical works ; also, Fletcher's works complete, all our magazines, with some autograph letters from Mr. Wesley, together with a choice col- lection of history, travels, biography, and other books of a similar character and tendency.

Forty years since there were two newspapers pub- lished in St. John, " The Royal Gazette," and " The Public Ledger." Mr. Winton, the editor of " The Pub- lic Ledger," was an intelligent, and a courageous man, and for his courage in exposing some of the doings of the Roman Catholic priesthood, he was waylaid be- tween Harbor Grace and Carbonear, by a number of men in masks, who knocked him down and cut off both his ears close to his head, and left him weltering in his blood. He recovered, however, and attacked the evils, to which he had previously called the pub- lic attention, with more determination than he had ever done. He wore a pair of artificial ears, made of velvet, after this event. Several other papers have come into existence, since 1825, and are generally con- ducted with considerable tact and talent.

EDUCATION.

The first movement to obtain a seminary of learning under Wesleyan influence, and for the benefit of the youth connected with the Wesleyan church in the lower provinces, was at the Nova Scotia District meeting, held in Windsor in the month of May, 1828, when it was unanimously resolved, to establish a seminary of learning under the auspices of the Wesleyan Society, for the accommodation of the children of their numerous friends in this and the neighboring provinces, and a committee was appointed to select a suitable place for the institution.

This committee met at Halifax on the 21st of May following (1829), and the circular on the subject reached Newfoundland early in the autumn. From this circular we learn, that the committee consisted of the Rev. Messrs. Black, Croscombe, and Young, also John A. Barry and John L. Starr, Esqs., with Messrs. Martin G. Black and John Harvis, as corresponding secretaries. The committee contemplated the establishment of an institution that should be competent to impart a thorough classical education, and that at a charge within the means of persons of moderate income. But the site of this academy was soon an insurmountable difficulty; gentlemen from Halifax, from Horton, Bridgetown, and Amherst, all claimed to have it in their respective localities. Thus the object was frustrated and the matter of a Wesleyan Seminary was kept in abeyance ten years longer, until God put it into the heart of the noble-minded, and sainted Charles F. Allison, of Sackville, in the Province of New Brunswick, to give a large portion of his property to found an institution exactly like that which had been contemplated by the Nova Scotia preachers.

That excellent man expended *four thousand pounds* in the erection of an academical institution, which for convenience, for chasteness of architecture, and beauty of situation, is unsurpassed by any similar institutions in these provinces; and munificently deeded the whole

31

with seven acres of land to trustees forever, for educational purposes.

As the Sackville institutions are now so identified
with the well working of Methodism in these provinces,
we shall be excused if we give an account of them
more in detail.

The Sackville Academy was properly a *Centenary
Gift*, for it was presented in the year 1839. The following is a copy of the letter of presentation : —

"To the Chairman of the New Brunswick District.

"St. John, N. B., Jan. 4th, 1839.

"*Rev. and dear Sir*, — My mind has of late been much impressed with the great importance of that admonition of the wise
man, ' Train up a child in the way he should go ; and when he is
old, he will not depart from it.' The establishment of the schools
in which *pure* religion is not only taught, but *constantly* brought
before the youthful mind, and represented to it as the basis and
groundwork of all the happiness which man is capable of enjoying on earth, and eminently calculated to form the most perfect
character, is I think, one of the most efficient means, in the order
of Divine Providence, to bring about the happy result spoken of
by the wise man.

"It is therefore, under this impression, connected with a persua-
sion of my accountability to that gracious Being, whom I would
ever recognize as the source of all the good that is done in the
earth, that I now propose through you to the British Conference,
and to the Wesleyan missionaries in the Provinces of New Brunswick and Nova Scotia, to purchase an eligible site, and erect suitable buildings in Sackville, in the County of Westmoreland, for
the establishment of a school of the description mentioned, in
which not only the elementary but the higher branches of education may be taught ; and to be altogether under the management
and control of the British Conference, in connection with the
Wesleyan missionaries in these provinces. If my proposal should
be approved of, and the offer I now make, accepted, I will proceed at once to make preparation, so that the buildings may be
erected in the course of the next year ; and I will as a further
inducement, by the blessing of God, give toward the support of
the school, one hundred pounds per annum for ten years.

" I shall be glad to hear that my offer is accepted, and to have the earliest information of your decision on the subject.

" I am, Rev. and dear Sir,

" Yours sincerely,

" REV. W. TEMPLE."   " C. F. ALLISON."

The above letter was laid before the New Brunswick District Meeting, held in St. John in May, 1839; and Mr. Allison appeared personally before the Nova Scotia District and made the same proposition. Both districts thankfully accepted the gift.

Several months passed before all the preliminaries were arranged, and the plan of the building determined. But on the 17th, of January, 1840, all these matters were decided, and a plan of a neat building, one hundred and fifty feet in length, forty-five in breadth, and, including the basement story, four stories high, was laid before the building committee, and fully adopted.

On the 9th day of June, 1840, a very large concourse of people assembled at Sackville to witness the ceremony of laying the corner-stone of the Wesleyan Academy. The religious service was commenced by the Rev. William Temple, Chairman of the District, by giving out the 526th hymn: " Except the Lord conduct the plan;" after which prayer was offered by the Rev. Richard Knight. Mr. Temple then delivered the introductory address, when the congregation joined in singing the 737th hymn: " Thou, who hast in Zion laid." The stone was now placed in its proper position, when Charles F. Allison spoke as follows: —

" The foundation-stone of this building I now proceed to lay in the name of the Holy Trinity, Father, Son, and Holy Ghost, and may the education ever to be furnished by the institution be conducted on Wesleyan principles, to the glory of God, and the extension of his cause. Amen!"

The excellent lady of Mr. Allison, then a bride, gave her approval of her husband's act, by giving the stone a final blow with the workman's hammer. Hymn 736 was given out, and prayer offered by the Rev. W. Croscombe; after which, short addresses were given by Rev. Samson Busby, William Croscombe, George Miller, and William Wilson; and this most delightful service closed with the Doxology.

On the 19th of January, 1843, Sackville Academy was first opened, and its career of usefulness commenced. It was the day of small things. One of the class-rooms held the whole company. There were five ministers present, as follows: Richard Williams, William Wilson, Richard Shepherd, Samuel D. Rice, and Humphrey Pickard, also C. F. Allison and lady. These, with a very few other persons as visitors, constituted the entire assembly. An hour was spent in religious exercises, when special prayer was offered for the prosperity of the institution. After the close of these services, the names of the students were taken down, when only *seven* persons recorded their names.

With *seven* students did the Rev. Humphrey Pickard commence his academical toil as Principal of the Institution, which by his constant and indefatigable attention, and judicious management, for more than twenty-one years, has been raised to its present eminence.

But the number of students rapidly increased, so that by the month of April thirty names were found upon the list of the institution. Another and a more formal opening of the academy was determined upon, which took place on the 29th of June following. Upon this occasion, the company assembled in the spacious lecture-room, which was nearly filled. Besides the noble founder, C. F. Allison, were also present, the Hon. Messrs. Botsford, Crane, and Chandler of New Brunswick, the Hon. Mr. Prescott, of Nova Scotia, with a large number of ladies and gentlemen, who now began to feel an interest in the prosperity of the institution.

At ten o'clock, the Rev. Albert Desbrisay, the governor, and chaplain, and the Rev. H. Pickard, the principal, entered, followed by the English master, the French tutor, and the students. After singing, and prayer by Rev. R. Knight, the inaugural address was delivered by the principal, — an address characterized by the simplicity of its language, the elegance of its style and its Christian spirit, — and at once convinced the public that a master-mind was at the head of the Sackville Academy, and that, under the guidance of its principal, it must and it would prosper.

Addresses were also delivered by Rev. C. Churchill, of Yarmouth, Rev. A. McNutt, of Sackville, Rev. W. Croscombe, of Halifax, Rev. R. Knight, chairman of the Nova Scotia District, Rev. S. Busby, of Point de Bute, and Rev. W. Wilson, of Wallace. The tide of prosperity for Sackville Academy began to flow at the close of its first term, in the year 1843, and it has had no ebb down to the present time, 1864, but has continued each year to give full satisfaction to its patrons, and constantly to gain favor in the estimation of the intelligent of all the lower provinces. Its generous founder, C. F. Allison, besides his original gift, and his continued pecuniary aid, also assisted its board of trustees with his wise counsels, and employed a large portion of his time in promoting the objects of the institution, until the year 1859, when it pleased our heavenly Father to call him to his reward. He died

31 *

in great peace, and the benefit he has conferred upon
these provinces will never die, but his name will be
cherished, and his generous, act will be kept in grateful
remembrance by unborn generations. The wise man
has said, " The memory of the just *is* blessed ; " and a
" voice from heaven," has proclaimed, " Blessed *are* the
dead which die in the Lord from henceforth : yea saith
the Spirit, that they may rest from their labors ; and
their works do follow them."

It is due to the learned principal, to say, that from
the very commencement of the institution, he has had
the charge, and has toiled through all the years of its
existence ; he has been constantly at his post ; has
plodded on under many difficulties and discouragements ; he has justly merited for himself the honorable title of D. D. ; he has educated and trained the
minds of hundreds of our youths many of whom are
now filling highly important and respectable positions
in society. Several are in the Christian ministry, and
several have died happy, whose minds were first religiously impressed while under his care, and Dr. Pickard
still lives and labors in the same position. May his
life be long spared, and his efforts to diffuse sound
education and correct moral principles be yet more
abundantly owned of God.

In literary matters Sackville has progressed to astonishment. After the male academy had been in successful operation for a few years, the friends contemplated a like institution for the young ladies, toward
which large subscriptions were raised and the desired
object was soon attained. At this present time there
is in the beautiful village of Sackville, beside the male
academy, and nearly opposite to it, a female academy.
The building is spacious, the rooms are high and well-

furnished, and where a hundred young ladies can be comfortably accommodated with board and lodging. Near the female academy is an elegant building, called Lingley Hall. Here is a rich and well-toned organ, on each side of which hangs a full-length portrait, — one of Dr. Beecham, the first president of the Eastern British American Conference, the other of C. F. Allison, Esq., the founder of these institutions. In the rear of these buildings, stands Mount Allison College, a more recent erection, where its faculty have power to confer degrees, and the curriculum of which will in no way be inferior to that of any other collegiate institution in the provinces. Beside this, there is a theological professor to train the minds of those young men who may hereafter be employed in the important work of the Christian ministry.

Thus has our youthful connection the apparatus and appliances for imparting a thorough education to our youth of both sexes, and of giving to our church in future years an enlightened as well as a converted ministry, certainly not inferior to that possessed by any affiliated conference within the whole range of Methodism.

In the benefits of the Sackville institution, many of the Newfoundland youth have participated, as they received their education there. Now, however, they have academic institutions in their own country, so that their youth will not need so generally to leave their native land to acquire the elements of a sound and thorough education. Thus Newfoundland is rapidly rising in her literary reputation, and although there is still much of ignorance remaining, yet she has made a great step in the right direction. She now has her academies, and can train her own teachers ; she has

her day schools established in very many places. She
has her native legislators, her native lawyers, and is
beginning to supply a native ministry; and we hope
the time is not far distant when every inhabited cove
shall have its church and its school-house, and when
every child shall be instructed and educated.

In St. Johns there is a very excellent and prosperous Wesleyan Academy; a public examination of which
took place in the month of June last, — and with very
great pleasure we transfer to our pages, from the " Provincial Wesleyan," an account of that examination as
given by a visitor who signs his name VERITAS.

" On Friday last, the 17th inst., we were favored with another
opportunity of witnessing the advancement and prosperity of the
Wesleyan Academy in this town, that day being set apart for the
annual examination of the classes; and, when it is taken into
consideration that, although the academy has been in existence
but *four and a half years*, one hundred and sixty-one pupils have
been educated wholly or in part within it, — the attendance for
the past year sixty-eight, — nearly one hundred of whom are
scattered in different parts of the colony, some filling positions in
mercantile establishments, others engaged in the onerous and
equally important duty of teaching, surely it is a cause of great
encouragement. With respect to the *examination*, I take the following from our local papers: —

" ' The annual examination of the pupils of the Wesleyan
Academy was held yesterday, in presence of the Revs. P. Prestwood and C. Ladner, the directors, and a number of the parents
and relatives of the pupils, and other friends of education. About
sixty pupils were present, and their orderly and attentive de-
meanor, and the intelligent interest they manifested in the proceedings of the day, indicated the character of the institution as
one in which the training is intellectual throughout, and not merely
mechanical, as was the case in too many schools of a former generation. Classes were examined in Arithmetic, Geography, Latin,
French, and Spanish.

" ' At the close of the examinations, both forenoon and afternoon, several pieces, original and selected, were recited with good effect, in accordance with the subjoined programme : —

"' FORENOON. — ORIGINAL PIECES.

"' The Relation of Man to the External World.' By David H. Sclater.

"' The Character of the Ancient Romans.' By James C. Rogerson.

"'A Dialogue.' (Selected.) By John H. LeMessurier, Richard White, Edward G. Hunter, and Thomas N. Gaden.

"' The Present State of the World.' By Campbell McPherson.

"' Examples of Illustrious Men.' By Stephen R. March.

"' A Dialogue. (Selected.) By John H. Birkett, Jonathan Sheppard, Thomas P. Pine, and Edwin B. Woods.

"' Rich and Poor.' By Miss Jessie S. Winter.

"' What are We ?' By Miss Mary E. Woods.

"' AFTERNOON. — ORIGINAL PIECES.

"' Thoughts on Leaving School.' By Thomas C. Duder.

"' Decision of Character.' By Samuel W. Pelley, Pupil Teacher.

"' A French Dialogue.' (Selected.) By Stephen R. March, Campbell McPherson, N. Munden Norman, David H. Sclater, John H. Stuart, and Hugh J. Ferneaux.

"' Perform well thy Mission.' By Miss Fanny M. Smith.

"' Nature the True Source of Poetic Inspiration.' By Miss Alice M. Reid.

"' Earth's Battlefields.' By Miss Maria S. Peach.

"' Moral Superior to Physical Triumphs, with Valedictory Addresses.' By Miss Hannah L. Bemister.

"' We are glad to state that it is the intention of the directors of the academy to institute, with the commencement of the next academic term, an English or elementary department, to be conducted in the lower room of the building by a competent teacher, and to be under the control and supervision of the principal, Mr. Reid ; the fees, to be made much lower than those of the academic branches, will place within the reach of all classes of Wesleyans the means of obtaining for their children a sound, thorough, English education at a cost that will be within the means of the poorest and humblest.'

" Government votes annually the sum of £750 sterling, or

about $3462, for training 'Pupil Teachers,' — each receiving £25 sterling, or about $115. Several have been trained in the Wesleyan Academy, and have gone forth to their respective spheres of labor. Five were present at the examination, one of whom has since taken charge of a school in the vicinity of Carbonear. What influence these trained teachers will yet wield in the moral and intellectual training of our youth, time only can develop! The annual government grant for the encouragement of education in this colony is about $62,885, — one seventh of the revenue in ordinary years, — and it may not be uninteresting to your readers to know that provision is made for the support of four academies in this place; two grammar schools or academies in Harbor Grace and Carbonear; twenty-seven commercial schools in the principal outports, and two hundred and thirty board or elementary schools; beside an annual appropriation of $3065 for schools under the control and direction of the Roman Catholic Bishops, $2808 to the Church School Society, and $1404 to the Wesleyan School Society, for their schools. In the town of Carbonear, the Wesleyan portion of the population, not having confidence in the principal of the Government Grammar School, or satisfied with its working, have sustained, at their own expense, an academy, second to none out of St. Johns, under the careful superintendence of a gentleman from your province. Our government officials, the speaker of the House of Assembly, and ablest men within it, our leading barristers (and we hope to say yet our judges and magistrates), are natives of this land.

VERITAS.

"ST. JOHNS, NEWFOUNDLAND, June 22, 1864." [1]

[1] Provincial Wesleyan, July 10, 1864.

CHURCHES.

OUR churches were plain wooden buildings, and as to size they were generally well proportioned to the wants of the place. In many of the out-harbors the whole Protestant population called themselves Wesleyans, when our congregations would be large; and in those places where the Episcopalians had establishments, a goodly number always attended the Methodist church. I have mentioned the Episcopalians, because there were no other Protestant bodies but them and the Wesleyans in any out-harbor in the island. Several of our churches were without stoves, so that in very severe weather we would be obliged to have a very short service, or dispense with our service altogether.

Preaching the gospel is the divinely instituted means for the illumination of the human mind, and for teaching universal man the way to happiness and heaven. Therefore, while the people come to the house of God to be instructed, and have a right to be disappointed if they are not there instructed, it is necessary, on the one hand, that the preacher should read much, pray much, study much, and always strive so to present the truths of the Bible to his hearers, that they may at the same

(371)

time rightly influence their judgment, duly affect their
hearts, and lead them to Christ.   On the other hand,
those who hear should remember that it is the word
of God; and, while their ideas may be expanded
by the erudition of the speaker, or they may be charmed
by his eloquence, let them never forget that for their
reception or rejection of the solemn verities of the gospel, they must give an account at that "day in which
he will judge the world in righteousness."

One of our more intelligent Newfoundland friends
would often, when going to the house of God on the
Sabbath day, quote with much accuracy and earnestness, the following very apposite lines from the poet
Cowper : —

> "The pulpit, therefore (and I name it filled
> With solemn awe, that bids me well beware
> With what intent I touch that holy thing), —
> The pulpit (when the satirist has at last,
> Strutting and vaporing in an empty school,
> Spent all his force, and made no proselyte), —
> I say the pulpit (in the sober use
> Of its legitimate, peculiar powers),
> Must stand acknowledged, while the world shall stand,
> The most important and effectual guard,
> Support, and ornament of virtue's cause.
> There stands the messenger of truth : there stands
> The legate of the skies ! — his theme divine,
> His office sacred, his credentials clear ;
> By him the violated law speaks out
> Its thunders ; and by him, in strains as sweet
> As angels use, the gospel whispers peace."

The Newfoundlanders were generally a church-going
people, so that in the different stations occupied by our
missionaries you would rarely find a person absent
from church on Sabbath, unless he were unwell.   It
used to be a matter of regret that some people outside
the church would occasionally, on Sabbath morning,

discuss the affairs of the fishery; but when they entered the church, they were always orderly and well-behaved. They loved their ministers and they received with gladness the word of life from their lips. They at all times heard with attention, and although, as a general thing, they had not learning so as to examine the Bible for themselves, yet they had good memories, and were not forgetful hearers, but carefully treasured up in their minds the truths they heard from the pulpit.

SINGING

Has formed an important part of divine worship from time immemorial, and, whenever practicable, that singing has been accompanied with musical instruments. But in old time music was all melody, and it is said harmony has not yet been known in the world three hundred years. The writer has in his possession an English Bible in black letter, published in 1625, with which is connected the Book of Common Prayer, and a number of examples of church-music as used in those times. Among those examples is the song of "The Three Children," "The Song of Zacharias," the Creed of Athanasius, the Lord's Prayer, and several other pieces set to music; and the music also is arranged for several of the psalms. This music is all one part; it is only melody. There is no mark for the time or the mood; there are no bars, the C cleft only is used, and the notes are all square.

A very excellent paper, entitled "Thoughts on Music," was published by Mr. Wesley in the "Arminian Magazine" for 1781, from which we beg to note the following extracts: —

"We are told the ancient Greek musicians in particular were able to excite whatever passions they pleased; to inspire love or

32

hate, joy or sorrow, hope or fear, courage, fury, or despair ; yea, to
raise these one after another, and to vary the passion just according
to the variation of the music. Nay, we read of an instance, even in
modern history, of the power of music not inferior to this. A
musician being brought to the king of Denmark, and asked whether he could excite any passion, answered in the affirmative, and
was commanded to make the trial on the king himself. Presently
the monarch was all in tears ; and, upon the musician's changing
his mood, he was quickly roused into such fury, that, snatching a
sword from one of his assistants' hands, he immediately killed him,
and would have killed all in the room, had he not been forcibly
withheld. But why is it that modern music in general has no
such effect upon the hearers ? The grand reason seems to be no
other than this : the whole nature and design of music is altered.
The ancient composers studied melody alone, — the due arrangement of single notes, — and it was by melody alone that they
wrought such wonderful effects. In this respect modern music
has no connection with common sense, any more than with the
passions. In another it is glaringly, undeniably contrary to common sense ; namely, in allowing, yea, appointing different words
to be sung by different persons at the same time ! What can be
more shocking to a man of understanding than this ? Pray
which of those sentences am I to attend to ? I can attend to
only one sentence at once ; and I hear three or four at one and
the same instant ! And, to complete the matter, this astonishing
jargon has found a place even in the worship of God ! It runs
through (O pity ! O shame !) the greatest part of our church
music ! It is found even in the finest of our anthems, and in the
most solemn parts of our public worship ! Let any impartial, any
unprejudiced person say whether there can be a more direct mock-
ery of God."

John Wesley had a fine musical ear, as well as a
truly devotional heart; and he used his utmost
efforts to make the church, over which in the order
of Divine Providence he was called to preside, a musical as well as a devotional people. As early as the
year 1742, which was two years before the forming of
the first conference, he issued a collection of tunes as

sung at the foundry. He enjoined his preachers to learn the science of music, and to preach frequently on singing; not to suffer the people to sing too slow, and let the women sing their parts alone ; let no man sing with them, unless he understands the notes and sings the bass.   Again he says, " Exhort every one to sing ; and in every large society let them learn to sing. Recommend our tune-book everywhere."

The Methodists soon became, as might be expected, a musical people ; and their hymns and music or singing took a high stand, and was heard with emotion all over the united kingdom.   Handel found in the Methdist hymns a poetry worthy of his own grand genius, and he set to music those hymns beginning, " Sinners, obey the gospel word ; " " O Love Divine, how sweet thou art ; " and " Rejoice ! the Lord is King." [1]

The Wesleyan singing was a source of great power to our societies in those early times.   Mr. Wesley, as he travelled in Ireland, heard his own hymns or tunes sung or whistled by Catholic children ; and hundreds of people, who cared nothing about preaching, were charmed to Methodist assemblies by the music.

· In the autobiography of Duncan Wright, a sergeant in the tenth regiment of foot, as published in the " Arminian Magazine " for 1785, we have an amusing instance of the effect of old Methodist music upon the Irish mind.   In the county of Wexford the society was much annoyed by popish mobs, and had to hold their meetings in a barn with closed doors.   The mob wished to know what was done at the private meetings of the Methodists.   To accomplish this they put one of their party into a sack and laid him quietly behind the door, with instructions to come out of the sack at

[1] Stevens' History of Methodism, vol. ii. p. 503.

the proper time, and open the door to his companions.
The society came as usual, fastened the door, and took
no notice of the sack. The singing commenced, and
honest Pat was so charmed with the music that he
thought he would hear it out before he disturbed the
meeting. The singing being so good, he thought he
would hear how they prayed. The mob outside began
to shout to their friend to open the door and let them
in ; but poor Pat could not get out of the sack, and
lay bawling for some one to help him out. He roared
lustily until the people thought *Old Nick* himself was in
the sack. At length, one had courage to go and open
the sack, when, lo! a man was seen there who had
come to annoy them, but now he was a weeping penitent. He confessed the whole matter, and began to
cry to God for pardon.

Duncan Wright, the narrator of this anecdote, afterward became a travelling preacher, and was very
useful both in Ireland and Scotland.

The first missionaries to Newfoundland were all
good singers, and they introduced the same tunes and
the same style of singing those tunes as was practised
by our venerable founder and the first Methodist preachers in England ; hence our people instinctively acquired
a love for old Methodist music, and the missionaries,
while they spread the sublime poetry with which the
Wesleyan body is so amply supplied, broadcast over
the land, also taught the people everywhere to
sing those hymns in the soul-stirring strains of Handel,
Haydn, Leach, Arnold, Rippon, Walker, and other
musical composers of the same class ; and so thoroughly was this done that our people could sing all
our hymns ; and when the hymn was announced, no
matter what was the metre, without any unnatural

gesture on the part of the precentor, calling up people from different parts of the church, or even sounding the key-note, a tune was at once struck in every way suitable both in style and accent.

In some places, as St. Johns, Carbonear, and Brigus, the singing was most superior and highly scientific; which for correctness of time, propriety of accent, and mellifluence of sound, could not be exceeded. Beside the singing was everywhere congregational, every one thought it his duty and privilege to join publicly in singing the praises of God. With all this, there were none of those nocturnal meetings called "singing schools;" nor was any one employed in the capacity of a "singing-master," — many of whom care very little about what kind of singing there is in the church, and who never use our music-books, or habituate our youth to the use of the Methodist Hymn Book. There were generally a few persons in each place who knew the notes, and these taught the rest, who learned to sing by ear. Our own hymns were always used at practice meetings, so that in learning a tune, they also learned a hymn; hence, when the hymn was named from the pulpit, at the class-meeting or prayer-meeting, a tune was ready, in which all could and generally did unite. At those times we had no organ in any church on the island; and the melodeon, that fine imitator of the organ, had not been invented. Our church instruments were the violin and a bass-viol. In some places we had two violins and a bass-viol, and occasionally a flute would accompany these instruments.

It is to be regretted that in these lower provinces, where singing-masters abound, and every village has its singing-school, our ministers can seldom give out

32 *

any hymn except long, common, short metre, or six lines eights, without being told, " Sir, we cannot sing that hymn : we have no tune for it ; " and an organist will sometimes send a message to the pulpit, requesting the preacher to give out some other hymn than the one he had selected in his study, it might have been on his knees, " because we have got no tune for it." Thus many, very many of our best hymns are never sung by us ; and our people lose the benefit which our forefathers enjoyed as they mentally luxuriated in their heavenly strains, which they sang to those Christ-honoring and soul-comforting verses. It is a disgrace to us that we as Wesleyans cannot sing every hymn in the Wesleyan hymn-book.

SABBATH SCHOOLS.

The minutes of the Newfoundland Sabbath schools for 1825, reported 1200 children, and a number of adults, who were receiving instruction in these institutions. In these schools, many children obtained all the learning they ever had, and had there learned to read and to a considerable extent understand the Scriptures of truth. In Bonavista, five boys and three girls learned, and repeated before the congregation with great accuracy, the whole of our Lord's sermon on the Mount; and fifteen of the children had become the subjects of converting grace, and regularly met in class. Our Sabbath schools in Newfoundland, as well as in most of our country circuits in these provinces, were discontinued during the winter season, because of the severity of the weather ; but, during the summer season, they were well attended, and orderly.

In the year 1824, Newfoundland received its first importation of Conference Catechisms. The whole series of these invaluable compilations of Scripture truth were from the pen of the noble and learned Richard Watson, who, at the time of writing them, was one of our missionary secretaries.

Some time in the year 1822, Mr. Watson, under the direction of conference, compiled two Catechisms on Scripture doctrine and history; the first for very young children, the second for children who were able to read the Bible. In these, considerable use is made of the Catechism of the Church of England, — that of the assembly of Westminister divines, — and also of Mr. Wesley's instructions for children. In the spring of 1823, Mr. Watson published a third Catechism, which completed the series. This letter was entitled, " A Catechism of the Evidences of Christianity, and the Truth of the Holy Scriptures." This is entirely an original work ; it states with great clearness and force the evidences of revealed religion, and meets in a masterly manner the arguments which infidels of all grades have brought against the Bible. The series was submitted to the careful examination of a committee of the conference, approved and sanctioned by that body, and hence designated the Wesleyan Catechisms. These Catechisms have been sent forth by tens of thousands, — have been translated in whole, or in part, into the language of every people where Wesleyan missionaries labor, and are found in every part of the earth where the English language is spoken. By these Catechisms the labor of our Sabbath-school teachers has been considerably lightened ; multitudes of children have thereby acquired the first principles of evangelical truth ; have been trained up in the faith of the Bible, and in the knowledge of its truths ; and thus have been saved from the withering blasts of heterodoxy, or the soul-deceiving fallacies of covert or open infidelity.

The children in our Sabbath schools in Newfoundland have these Catechisms ; large portions of which have been committed to memory, and the children there are not behind the children in our Sabbath schools elsewhere in their knowledge of the Bible history, of evangelical doctrine, and the arguments for the truth of revealed religion.

Prayer-meetings were well attended, and were often very lively. In 1823, in Grand Bank we had several interesting young men, who, when they had to cruise for fish, as they sometimes did to the distance of sixty or seventy leagues, were accustomed so to arrange their matters as to meet together on Sabbath days in harbors, where there were no places of worship, and hold prayer-meetings ashore, read the Scriptures, and distribute tracts, to the great delight of the people of those destitute places. Thus our fishermen themselves became missionaries, and were instrumental of doing much good.

The religious state of our societies was satisfactory and encouraging. Revivals had taken place in several circuits ; our prayer-meetings, class-meetings, love-feasts, and sacraments were times of " refreshing from the presence of the Lord." The brethren often had wearisome journeys by land, and dangerous voyages by sea ; but they found comfort and pleasure in their work, in that they saw and felt that the soil they were endeavoring to cultivate would in time yield abundant fruit, and that their labor was not in vain in the Lord.

Newfoundland, while it had its toils, and its disadvantages, also had its advantages and its pleasures. Many of our wealthy planters, and a good sprinkling of our princely merchants, had become favorable to Methodism, and some of them had become members of the Wesleyan church; the connection had gained a large influence in the community, and was the most numerous Protestant body in the island. Methodist preachers were everywhere received with kindness, treated with great respect; they had a home in every house, a seat at every table, and a place in the affections of every heart.

In several of our circuits there had been revivals of religion particularly at St. Johns, Harbor Grace, Island Cove, and Bonavista. The English " Wesleyan Magazine " for 1827, in its obituary department, records the death of three persons in one place, who went triumphantly " home to God," within a few weeks of each other. In English Harbor, in the Trinity Circuit, was a family of the name of Ivamy, nearly all the adult members of which, were the subjects of converting grace. In the year 1826, three members of this interesting family were called away by death. They were all young persons. Ann Burns, whose maiden name was Ivamy, was brought to God under the ministry of Mr. Ellis, in 1817, and for ten years lived in the enjoyment of the favor of God, and when dying said to her weeping friends, " I feel a solid peace;" " I feel peace with God, through our Lord Jesus Christ." She died Feb. 23, 1826, aged 27 years.

Martin Ivamy, aged 21 years. He was brought to God also under the preaching of Mr. Ellis. When on his death-bed, he said to his mother, " My pain is severe, but I shall soon be where there is no more sickness or pain; where tears are wiped from all faces." To his class-leader he said, " In my fishing-boat I have many times sung those words : —

> " ' They sing the Lamb in hymns above,
>   And we in hymns below.'

" Now I am going to join the heavenly choir, to sing the song of Moses and the lamb forever. Oh, the goodness of God! His works praise him, and his saints bless him." Thus he continued until his happy spirit took its flight to the land of rest.

George Ivamy, aged 22 years. He also was brought to God under the ministry of Mr. Ellis. He was an exemplary young man through his whole Christian course, and his last affliction, which was consumption, and very protracted, he bore with true Christian fortitude. He had a good voice, which he employed in singing the praises of God. Once, after a severe paroxysm of suffering, and feeling a little recovered, he broke forth singing : —

> " Be it weariness and pain
>   To slothful flesh and blood ;
> Yet we will the cross sustain
>   And bless the welcome load."

To his mother he said, " Oh, my dear mother, rejoice on my account. Death is gain to me. I am going to Jesus, and you will soon follow." He died in perfect peace.

In 1830 our membership in Newfoundland was 1,287 ; the missionary membership through the world was 41,186 ; the number of our missionaries, 189, and our missionary income, £51,299 18s. 3d.

Our stations were as follows : —

St. John — John Haigh.
Harbor Grace — John Pickavant.
Carbonear — Richard Knight.
Blackhead — John Boyd.
Western Bay — Adam Nightingale.

ISLAND COVE AND PERLICAN — John Smithies.
PORT DE GRAVE — William Ellis.
BRIGUS — George Ellidge.
TRINITY BAY — John Tomkins.
BONAVISTA AND CATALINA — William Wilson.
GRAND BANK AND FORTUNE BAY — Richard Shepherd.
HANTS' HARBOR — William Faulkner.

William Faulkner was admitted on trial in 1829, and came to St. Johns. He labored with acceptance in different circuits for twenty years, when he left the island, and returned to his native land. In the minutes of 1863, his name stands for " Ashton-under-Lyne" Circuit, in the Manchester and Bolton District.

At this time several parts of Newfoundland suffered severely from the failure of the fishery. Island Cove, Old Perlican, and Bonavista all suffered from this cause. In the last-named place the catch of fish during the summer was estimated at not more than half sufficient to pay the expense of the voyage; therefore, as the fall came on, poverty was felt in almost every family, and a deep gloom sat upon every countenance. In a population of two thousand, it was ascertained that there were eight hundred and eighty-seven individuals, who had no means of subsistence whatever, except the potatoes produced in their own gardens, and these it was evident would fail before the next spring. Application was therefore made to his excellency Sir Thomas Cochran, the governor, who promptly sent seven hundred and fifty barrels of potatoes for the relief of the suffering poor. These potatoes, with a number of seals that were taken during the winter and spring, saved many from starvation.

In the midst of this poverty, a fearful epidemic broke out in Bonavista and Bird Island Cove. It was the ulcerated sore throat, *Cynanche maligna*, which seems to have been identical with what is now known as *Diphtheria*. Many fell victims to this dire disease. The journal of the writer supplies the following particulars in reference to the family of Mr. George Crew, one of our leaders in Bird Island Cove, who lost three members of his family by this disease in twenty-one days : —

"July 8, 1830. This afternoon I interred two children; both died on the same day of the prevailing epidemic, one little boy, four years of age, was the son of Mr. George Crew, one of our leaders.

" July 17. Saturday, Mary Minty, a married daughter of brother Crew, was taken alarmingly ill with sore throat.

" July 19. Susannah, a girl of twelve years of age, second daughter of brother Crew, was taken with the same complaint.

" July 24. Saturday, Joseph, a son of the same person; a young man, 18 years of age, was seized with the sore throat.

" July 27. The girl Susannah died on Sabbath morning, and was interred to-day. On entering the room, what a sight! The coffin containing the corpse of Susannah lay on the table, near which was her sister Mary Minty, struggling in the agonies of death, and in the interim of her pain, shouting ' Glory to God.' In another part of the room, sat Joseph, suffering severely, and apprehending the fatal result of his disease; in an adjoining apartment, was the poor mother, — whose feelings can much better be conceived than described, — bewailing the loss of two of her children, and expecting every moment to see a third expire, while a fourth was in a very dangerous and critical state. But in the midst of this scene of suffering, stood the father, who seems to have been endowed with a more than ordinary supply of grace, — giving up one child after another with a father's feeling, but with a Christian's fortitude. Now turning to his dying daughter, he would exhort her to exercise strong faith in the Redeemer's blood, and take courage, inasmuch as a few more groans, a few more struggles, would terminate all her sufferings, when her happy spirit would wing its way to worlds on high, where suffering is never known. Then he would speak to his son, and exhort and entreat him to seek for a clear sense of pardoning mercy, that he also might be prepared for the awful change. After the funeral, when returning home: ' What a house have I to go to!—two children in the grave in so short a space of time, and perhaps another dead before I reach home ; — how can I endure it?' exclaimed the disconsolate mother. ' Wife,' replied the pious father; 'cannot you give up your children when the Lord calls for them ? I can. The Lord knows best what he is about to do with us, and, severe as is our affliction, it becomes us not to murmur.'"

To the writer, our friend George Crew said : —

"The Lord gave me my children, and I can freely give them up at his command; and I do this, because I believe they have gone to heaven. Of Thomas (the little boy), 1 can have no doubt, as he died so young. Of Susannah I was anxious to get something satisfactory, as she was old enough to understand and enjoy religion. ' She told me,' said this pious man, ' she was not afraid to die.' ' I feel,' said she, ' that Jesus has loved me, and I shall soon be with him in heaven.' ' Mary,' continued he, ' has long been a professor of religion, and she now testifies to all around her that she is personally interested in the blood of Christ; that she has no doubt of her acceptance with God, and she will soon join the blood-washed throng in the realms of light and rest.'"

When we reached the house, we found Mary still alive, but in fearful agony; the sloughs in her throat were causing strangulation. One present said to her, " Mary, you suffer much in body, but how is the state of your mind?" She replied, " I do suffer much ; but bless God I am happy ; death is disarmed of its sting ; I feel I am pardoned ; I feel — I feel " — Here a fit of coughing came on with such violence, that all present thought suffocation would be the immediate result. On recovering a little, she said, " I feel Christ is precious, but I cannot converse ; good-by, I shall soon be in heaven." Very shortly after this conversation, she expired in the full triumph of faith.

33

For more than a year, did this fearful plague, "Malignant Quinsy," rage in Bonavista and Bird Island Cove. It seemed for a time as though it would depopulate the place; its victims were numerous; it seized persons of all ages, and no constitution was proof against its attacks. At length it pleased our heavenly Father to stay his chastening hand, when the complaint entirely disappeared from the people.

Bonavista first appeared on our minutes in 1815, and that excellent man, James Hickson, was the preacher. The only religious service the people then had, was reading the church prayers on Sabbath afternoon, by a man who filled the office of store-keeper to a large mercantile firm; and who usually opened his store on the morning of the sacred Sabbath. But the labors of Mr. Hickson and his successors were greatly owned of God in the conversion of souls.

In Bird Island Cove, at that time, there was no kind of religious service whatever, and when it was visited by Methodist preachers, which was the case soon after Bonavista appeared on our station-sheet, the people treated the preachers with every kind of contempt and insult. The moral character of the people was awful. They were accustomed to boast that they belonged to the "established Church of England," and would, indeed, sometimes walk over to Bonavista, to hear the prayers read on Sabbath afternoon, and return home drunk. In Bonavista, Methodism had more opposition, and this opposition offered for a greater length of time, than in any other part of Newfoundland. The Bird Island Cove people therefore, by mixing with their friends in Bonavista, would generally get something new to increase their ire against these new preachers. One man, after his conversion to God, declared to the writer, that he had many times reflected upon the government of England for tolerating such men as Methodist preachers, and for not allowing any one who chose to *shoot them;* and, he added, " I would have shot them if I had dared, and have thought in so doing I should have rendered service to the church and to the state."

Bird Island Cove was for a long time a barren soil; so that in eight years we had only five members in society. But in the year 1824, God poured out his Spirit upon the people, and our society was increased to fifty-four. Now a considerable alarm was excited at the spread of Methodism, and something must be done, or all the wicked people would be converted to God, forsake the " religion of their fathers," and become Methodists. The store-keeper *parson* of Bonavista was now dead, and he was succeeded by a man who had been a sea-captain, who was zealously opposed to Methodist preachers. By his influence a person, who could read only with difficulty, got an appointment to read prayers in Bird Island Cove, so as to prevent the further spread of Methodism in that place. The Bird Island Cove *parson* was familiarly known as " Skipper Joe." But this effort to stop the revival was a failure. There was then a good choir of singers, who, with Skipper Joe, were for a time very zealous for the church. Now that the place had a little church of its own, a parson and choir, surely there was no motive for the people to go to Methodist meeting. But still they went there; and some of the singers went to make sport at the bad singing in the Methodist prayer-meetings. But soon one of these singers became awakened, and cried out for mercy; another and another became similarly affected, until the whole choir was powerfully wrought upon; several found peace with God, and

all joined the Methodist Church. Skipper Joe, the
parson, also, the church clerk, and several of the inhabitants, were all thought to be quite proof against
the influence of Methodism. But not so; for soon the
clerk went to the Methodist prayer-meetings, was
awakened there, and joined the Methodist Church :
and further, Skipper Joe could not keep away from
these meetings, and his mind, after a while, became
seriously impressed with the necessity of experiencing
the converting grace of God. Our nautical friend of
Bonavista, who acted in this locality as a sort of rural
dean, now got alarmed; he went over to Bird Island
Cove, and made some strong remarks about the enthusiasm of the Methodists, and the people going mad. To
which, Skipper Joe replied : " Mr. G., I think your
remarks are very unkind, and quite uncalled for ; I
have been to their meetings, and have seen nothing im-
proper there. It is a solemn thing to die, and to die
unpardoned, and in one's sins ; as I feel is the case
with me." " What do you mean ? " was the indignant
remark of our Bonavista parson ; " you have a salary
from the society,[1] and if you go among these Methodists you will certainly lose it." " I cannot help that,"
he replied, " but I must seek the salvation of my soul."
" Oh, " said Mr. G., " if you leave us, the church will
go down here. I say, do you be firm, Skipper Joe."
" I will *if I can*," said Skipper Joe. " Throw the
can away, and be firm to the religion of your fathers,"
was the remark of our Bonavista friend. Before the
close of the next week this man became a subject of
the grace of God, and cast his lot among the despised
Methodists of the place.

---

[1] He received ten pounds per annum from the " Society for the Propagation of the Gospel in Foreign Parts."

If service was to be held in Bird Island Cove church
at all now, nothing remained but for our nautical captain to go there in person and read prayers. This he
did faithfully as long as he could. There was at that
time a serious woman, who was still faithful to the
church, and who became deeply impressed with the ne-
cesity of experiencing the converting grace of God.
" I believe," said she, " what the Methodists say about
a change of heart is true; but I do not think it is necessary to leave the church in order to get that blessing.
I am determined to seek it in earnest; but I will be a
church woman still." She became in earnest, for several days was a deep penitent, and ceased not night and
day to cry to God for mercy. At length, one Sabbath
morning, as the captain was reading prayers, light broke
upon her mind, and the Spirit of God was given to her;
and she was enabled to cry, "Abba, Father." She arose
to tell the congregation what God had done for her;
but it was an indecorum there. " Woman," called the
captain, " sit down." At first she did not observe the
remark; and it was the least of her thoughts to disturb
the congregation; but the mandate was repeated, and
was promptly observed by her, for she sat down without a word. But, strange, our captain-parson thought
his reproof was not yet sufficient; he therefore, the
next day, sent a note to this good woman, in which he
threatened to " bind her over to keep the king's peace,
if she ever again so disturbed him while he was performing divine worship." In relating this matter to
the writer, she said, " Thus was I driven from the
church, and compelled to be a Methodist; and, oh if I
can keep the peace I have, I shall be happy."

We will mention one more incident connected with
the revival in Bird Island Cove. As our friend the

captain could not sing, and all the choir had joined the Wesleyan Church, he deemed it necessary to take some one with him from Bonavista who could repeat the responses and sing a psalm. He found such a person, who repeatedly accompanied him on his mission to reclaim the Methodists from the error of their ways. But one dark night this new clerk stepped between two stones, on his way home, and very seriously sprained his ankle; his companion could render him but little help, and while help was coming to him, he lay on the ground in agonies; and when at length assistance came to him, and a little rum was given to him, — which was at that time the universal panacea, — he began to curse the Methodists, and amongst other strange things, Frank exclaimed, "If these Methodists will perish they must, for I will not go any more to save them."

After this, Methodism met with but little opposition in Bird Island Cove. Many have been brought to God in that place, and our cause there still continues to prosper.

THE FAMINE.

We must again return to the temporal circumstances of the people in Bonavista and Bird Island Cove· at this very trying time. No sooner did that terrible epidemic subside, which had raged for so many months, and had made such gaps in family circles, than great want and pinching poverty began to stare the people in the face, which continued with increasing severity until absolute famine was the result.

At that time the seal-fishery was only very partially prosecuted in Bonavista, as three schooners, employing about seventy men, constituted their entire spring fleet. There were then no farms, no manufactories, no public works of any kind; the people had to depend upon

the cod-fishery as the only means of obtaining a subsistence. In that northern and exposed station the cod-
fishery does not commence until May, and closes early
in October, so that five months was all the time the
men could be employed in earning a livelihood for
themselves and families for the whole year. If, however, the fishery were good, and the price of the fish
at a medium rate, these five months' labor would supply
ample means for this purpose. But the summers of
1830 and 1831 had been remarkable for the failure of
the cod-fishery in these parts, and particularly was this
the case in the latter year, as, at the close of the season,
the catch of fish was only one half the average, and
the price had fallen, at rates ranging from twenty to
forty shillings per quintal, to twelve. The winter set
in with unusual severity early in November, and for
weeks together the thermometer ranged from 15° to
18° below zero. Moreover, the great northern jam
of ice did not leave the coast until the nineteenth day
of June; so that the spring supplies, which are usually
received in April, did not arrive till near the last of
June. One of the severest snow-storms during the
season was on the fifth of May; and the ground continued frozen until near the month of June. A number
of cattle died for want of food, and, during the night of
the third of June, nine horses died from the same cause.

After the usual time for obtaining supplies had
passed, the most appalling distress began to be felt
among the inhabitants, and particularly was this the
case during the latter part of the month of May and
June. There were no provisions in the merchants'
stores, and no amount of money could purchase a barrel of flour or a bag of bread. Men of wealth had to
dole out food to their families with most parsimonious

care, and the writer with his family was restricted to
two meals a day for three weeks. The ice on the coast
prevented the arrival of vessels; the seals had gone; and
the heavy ice, large masses of which grounded in deep
water, kept the cod-fish from coming near the shore.
A severe famine was felt among the inhabitants; several families subsisted on nothing but potatoes and salt.
Early in June nearly all the flour and bread (sea biscuit) was exhausted, and the cry for bread ceased because it was not to be had; but the mournful cry, " For
God's sake give me a few potatoes to save my children
from starvation," continued to be uttered with the
most heart-rending vehemence. Individuals have passed
the whole day without tasting food, and strong men
were seen staggering through the streets, as if inebri-
ated, as the effect of starvation.

On the 4th of June, some of the crew of a schooner
which had been jammed in the ice for a long time, in
sight of the harbor, came on shore, and reported that
their companions on board were almost perishing from
cold and hunger. On the 11th of June a party of men
came over the ice from Keels, a place about fifteen
miles' distant, and reported that one woman and three
children had died through hunger. The following is
an extract from the journal of the writer : —

" June 11, 1832. — I this morning called upon a poor widow
with six children, who were known to be in a state bordering upon
starvation ; when, after communicating to her the painful information, that no further help could be rendered to her, whatever
might be the result, I desired her to tell me plainly what food she
had, and what were her prospects of living through the famine.
' I will do so,' she replied. She then uncovered a barrel containing two or three buckets of potatoes. ' This is all the food I have,
and all I ever expect to have, unless the Lord in mercy should see
fit to give us a change of wind, so as to take the ice from our

shores.' She had been a stout, healthy woman, but is reduced almost to a skeleton for want of food; but now with tremulous hand, with tottering limb, and sunken eye she stood before me, and said, 'When my children get up in the morning, I send them round to beg a potato from the neighbors; if they succeed I am thankful, and it saves my own stock; if they do not succeed, I roast two or three potatoes for each of my children, both morning and evening. I fear to boil them, because of waste; and I find by this means the lives of my children can be saved until my potatoes are all exhausted; when my heavenly Father may yet smile upon us and send us deliverance. But I am resigned to his blessed will. He knows what is best for me. I am happy in his love; and if he is about to take me away by famine, I know he will take me to heaven. I will praise him for all his mercies.' "

Two days after the above was written, when a deep gloom sat upon every countenance, and nothing but starvation seemed to be the fate of the people, suddenly a messenger arrived bringing the joyful news that forty bags of bread, twenty quintals of dry fish, and fifty gallons of molasses, were already in Catalina, ten miles off, for the relief of the poor. Had it rained bread from heaven, it could not have come more unexpectedly. Food in Catalina! how did it come there? The mystery was soon explained. The news of distress had reached St. Johns, — when the government promptly sent an officer round the head of both Conception and Trinity Bay, to Trinity Harbor, to the magistrates there, with orders to send supplies to Bonavista. Just then a light north-west wind slacked the ice from the north shore of Trinity Bay, by which a boat got from Trinity to Catalina, with the above supplies, and in less than half an hour after the arrival of the boat, the ice again came in and stopped all navigation for ten days more. The next morning, more than one hundred men walked over to Catalina to receive rations, — when the above articles of provisions were divided according to their respective families. One hundred and seventy-six families, comprising nine hundred and fourteen individuals, were thus relieved. At length a south-west wind sprung up, which increased to a gale, by which the coast was cleared of ice, and supplies were brought for the relief of the inhabitants.

REVIVALS.

About this time several of the circuits were visited with gracious revivals of religion. In Carbonear the Lord poured out his Spirit upon the people, and in the year 1829, our church received an increase of one hundred and eighty-five members. In the month of October, 1839, Mr. Smithies wrote the committee from Harbor Grace, in which letter he says: " The good work of God is prospering in an astonishing manner in this bay. The fire of heavenly love is burning rapidly and brightly throughout the whole of our stations. More than five hundred souls have been brought out of the world into the church since the district meeting, most of whom are savingly converted to God." In the month of April, 1831, Mr. Nightingale from Western Bay wrote : " Since last July, one hundred and sixty-four persons have been added to our society, one hundred of whom have found ' redemption in the blood of Christ, the forgiveness of sins.' The greater part of these are young persons, some of whom are considerably gifted, and manifest a deep interest in the welfare of their fellow-creatures. In our prayer-meetings during the last winter they have rendered us considerable service." The following letter from the pen of Dr. Knight, will be read with deep interest : —

"BLACKHEAD, June 25, 1830.

"The Blackhead station is in many respects an important one. Its population, for a thinly inhabited and insulated country, as Newfoundland is well known in general to be, is considerable. It contains not less than 2000 souls, three fourths of whom are Protestants, who have received their religious instruction entirely from our missionaries. They are almost without exception ardently attached to Methodism, and manifest a readiness to support the gospel as far as their poverty will allow. It forms a most delightful field for missionary exertion, — extending over a line of twelve miles of the sea-coast of Conception Bay. It has two good places of worship, and is dissected into seven harbors or coves, in which the services of the sanctuary are regularly performed. The geographical extent of this station may appear very limited, and consequently the performance of its required duties may appear to be easy. The reverse of this, however, is the case. The extreme difficulty of walking, the necessity of travelling it so frequently, the absence of assistance from any local preacher, and almost the whole of official exertion devolving upon the missionary, render it in truth a most laborious circuit. Often have I gone as far as strength and time would admit, and have yet fallen short in the accomplishment of what has been further necessary. These toils have, however, been relieved and rendered sweet, from the spiritual advantages which have resulted to the people of our charge. Hundreds, having found redemption in the blood of Jesus, have sped their flight to the mansions of God from this circuit. They now walk in high salvation in the climes of bliss, and hundreds more are journeying thither. This station received no small share of the labors of those zealous missionaries, Messrs. Coughlan, Black, Thoresby, and Smith, and was in no small degree benefited by their ministry ; as also by that of those who have from time to time succeeded them, and are now laboring in the parent country, and in other parts of the mission-field. But during the past year it has pleased the Great Head of the church to pour down upon us the plenitude of his grace, in a more remarkable manner than ever was previously witnessed."[1]

In this revival, which was very extensive, several old members were quickened, many backsliders were

[1] "Methodist Magazine," 1634, p. 61.

restored ; and one hundred and thirty persons were added to the society. The centre of the revival was the north shore of Conception Bay, yet every circuit in the district, from Bonavista to Grand Bank, felt its influence.

In the minutes of Conference for 1829, our returns show an increase of 99 members ; in 1830, an increase of 128 ; and in 1831, our increase was 561. In 1829, our number was 1133, and in 1831, we returned 1848 members ; showing an increase in our membership in three years, of 715 persons. The history of Methodism in previous times can supply no such returns for the Newfoundland District. The blessed effects of this revival were felt for many years, and some are still living who were brought to God at the time of which we are now writing.

CHAPTER XVII.

IN the year 1834, the writer removed to Prince
Edward Island; and on the 28th of June, the
following entry was made in his journal: —

" I have this day left Newfoundland for another sphere of labor.
On that island I spent fourteen years, one month, and seven days.
I have walked many hundreds of miles on its rough shores, sailed
along its rock-bound coasts at almost all seasons of the year; have
been extensively acquainted with its inhabitants; have seen many
souls converted to God, and witnessed the piety of hundreds;
have experienced the kindness and partaken of the hospitality
for which the Newfoundlanders are so characteristic, from Fortune Bay to Bonavista; have labored in eight of its circuits. I
leave hundreds of affectionate friends and fellow-travellers to Zion,
with whom my soul is united, and with whom I could live and die.
Farewell, Newfoundland, farewell, dear friends, — we shall not
again meet on earth, but let us resolve to meet in heaven.

> " There all the ship's company meet,
>   Who sailed with the Saviour beneath ;
>   With shouting each other they greet,
>   And triumph o'er trouble and death.

> " The voyage of life 's at an end,
>   The mortal affliction is past ;

The age that in heaven they spend,
Forever and ever shall last."

For the year 1835, the following were the stations for the Newfoundland District, as they appear on the printed minutes : —

ST. JOHNS — John Smithies.
HARBOR GRACE — John Haigh.
CARBONEAR — George Ellidge.
BLACKHEAD, WESTERN BAY, AND ISLAND COVE —
William Faulkner, Ingham Sutcliff.
PERLICAN AND HANTS' HARBOR — Joseph F. Bent.
PORT DE GRAVE — Thomas Angwin.
BRIGUS AND CUBITS — John Pickavant.
TRINITY BAY — William Ellis.
BONAVISTA AND CATALINA — Adam Nightingale.
GRAND BANK — William Murray.
BURIN — James G. Hennigar.

From this time, the change of ministers between Newfoundland and these provinces became very frequent and included a number of brethren who are still our fellow-laborers; for which reason we shall not attempt to sketch any character except those who have been called to their reward.

Beside those of our departed brethren whom we have previously noticed, the name of William Murry is now on our death-roll. As we had no personal acquaintance with brother Murry, we shall transcribe the obituary notice of him as found in the minutes of the British conference : —

" William Murry was a native of Barnard Castle, Durham, and in early life was made a subject of saving grace. Soon after his conversion, under a conviction of duty to God and his church, he offered himself as a candidate for our mission work, and was accepted by the conference. For several years he labored in New Brunswick and Nova Scotia, with benefit to many souls. In 1834, he was appointed to the Newfoundland District, where he preached the gospel with zeal and acceptance in the Harbor Grace and Port De Grave Circuits. During his stay in the latter circuit, his health became so impaired that his immediate removal from the island was necessary. After visiting his native land and the West Indies, without any improvement in his health, his afflictions were augmented by the death of his beloved wife, who exchanged mortality for life, in St. Johns, New Brunswick. From that time his affliction increased; but his consolation in the Lord became strong. To many of his brethren he gave satisfactory evidence of his well-grounded hope in his Redeemer; and terminated his extreme sufferings on the 16th of January, 1840."

The year 1835 was a time of great agitation and anxiety to the Wesleyan connection, owing to the attempts of Dr. Warren and a body of men calling themselves the " Grand Central Association," who, because their views on certain subjects were not adopted and carried out, sought to divide our societies and thereby destroy the whole influence of Methodism. For a time a gloom hung over the connection, and the friends of the missionary cause, in some cases, began to despair, lest their finances would be so interfered with that many mission stations would have to be abandoned and the glory of Methodism as a great missionary church thus fade and pass away. But our Great Captain would not thus abandon his followers. On the contrary, this agitation was overruled for good; the members of our church became more firm and decided; there was an increase in our societies the very next year of 2,144, in Great Britain, and on the mission-stations of 7,577; and our missionary income for the year ending in April, 1836, was £70,996 1s. 11d. Our members in Newfoundland now numbered 1,747, and our total missionary membership was 61,803.

From the year 1816 to 1840, a period of twenty-five years, the number of our missionaries, and the number and locality of our mission-stations, continued nearly the same ; which was sometimes eleven stations, sometimes twelve, accordingly as eleven or twelve men were appointed to the district. But in the year 1841, our mission began to extend by the appointment of William Marshall as a visiting missionary to that extensive tract of country between Fortune Bay and Cape Ray, called the Western Shore. " Visiting missionary " was then almost a new phrase in the nomenclature of Newfoundland Methodism ; but it was a wise arrangement to visit certain harbors during the summer season, and preach the gospel to people, many of whom had never heard a sermon or seen a Protestant minister during their whole life.

Of this important mission, the committee, in their report for 1841, page 106, make the following statement : —

" Fifty-two harbors have been visited, in several of which the inhabitants are deeply sunk in ignorance, superstition, and depravity. Nor is this to be wondered at, when it is considered that many of them were never visited before by any Christian minister within the memory of the oldest settlers ; while in every one of them there is a great destitution of the means of religious improvement. With the exception of one school, which was formed by the missionary during his visit, and perhaps one or two others, there is no provision made for the education of the rising generation along the entire extent of the western shore (a distance of about one hundred miles). 'There are,' the visiting missionary writes, 'several harbors in which there is not a single individual that can read, nor a copy of the sacred volume to be found ; and these are Protestants, and chiefly the descendants of Englishmen.' These poor neglected sheep of the Redeemer, whom he hath purchased with his blood, received the agent of the society gladly into their humble dwellings ; they listened with breathless attention and many tears to the message of mercy which he delivered ; and on his leaving them, their earnest inquiry was, ' Oh ! when shall we see another minister.' The committee trust that the time is not distant, when, by means of British benevolence, not only the occupants of Hermitage Bay and the coast to the west, but the inhabitants of all the hitherto neglected harbors of that Island, will have faithful Christian pastors settled amongst them, faithfully ' warning and teaching them in all wisdom.' "

The next year John S. Addy was appointed visiting missionary to Green Bay. Thus by means of these visiting missionaries the extreme points of British Newfoundland were reached, — for the western shore reaches to Cape Ray where the French shore commences ; and the District of Green Bay extends northeast to Cape John, where it terminates.

The mission to Green Bay was very successful, for in the minutes of 1844, 45 members are returned for the Green Bay Circuit. William Marshall, who was then stationed at Green Bay, in a letter to the committee, dated Twillingate, December 6th, 1844, says : —

" The conduct of our members in the circuit generally, but in this place in particular, is unimpeachable ; they are enabled by grace, to walk as becometh the gospel. One has exchanged mortality for life. He died joyfully triumphing over the last enemy. A few have been added to our number, one of whom had been a violent persecutor. His wife has been a member of our society for the last eighteen months, but was much opposed by him ; she stood firm in the hour of trial, and now her prayers are answered in his salvation. We give God the glory."

In several circuits on the island there were revivals of religion, and the brethren had great cause for thanksgiving to God and much encouragement in their work.

In 1845, the Wesleyan Missionary Society had greatly extended, so that its income reached the large amount of £110,462 9s. 10d. ; the number of its missionaries was 382 ; its other paid agents, 1,608 ; children in our Sabbath schools, 65,431 ; and our missionary membership was 102,750.

34 *

In Newfoundland we had fifteen circuits and thirteen missionaries. The printed station-sheet reads as follows : —

ST. JOHNS — Richard Williams, John Brewster.
HARBOR GRACE — William Faulkner.
CARBONEAR — John Snowball.
BLACKHEAD — James England.
ISLAND COVE, — James Norris.
PERLICAN — William Marshall.
PORT DE GRAVE, — George Ellidge.
BRIGUS — John S. Addy.
BONAVISTA — Jabez Ingham.
BURIN — Samuel W. Sprague.
GRAND BANK — Adam Nightingale.
HERMITAGE COVE — One wanted.
TRINITY BAY — John Peach.
GREEN BAY — Thomas Angwin.
HANTS' HARBOR — One wanted.
RICHARD WILLIAMS, Chairman of District

Of the missionaries in the above list, the brethren Faulkner, Ellidge, and Nightingale, we have before spoken. Jabez Ingham is now laboring in England, and in 1863, was stationed at Howden, in the Hull District. James Norris removed to Canada in 1854; and in 1863, his station was Stouffville, in the Whitby District. John Snowball and Thomas Angwin have retired from the work as supernumeraries; John Brewster, James England, John S. Addy, and Samuel W. Sprague are laboring in these provinces; while the brethren Marshall and Williams have gone to their reward.

William Marshall was born in 1811, and entered the ministry in 1838. He was a man of great devotion to his work, and the holiness of his life was proverbial. He was "instant in season and out of season." But his ministerial course was short. He labored for some time on the western shore, then removed to the other

, extremity of the island, Green Bay, where his labors were especially owned of God. He closed his public labors with the watch-night services, and died on the 9th of January, 1846, in the thirty-fifth year of his life, and the eighth of his ministry. The minutes make this record of this excellent young man : —

" His memory is embalmed in the hearts of an affectionate people, who have been brought to God chiefly through his instrumentality. In the judgment of his brethren, excessive labors and privations injured his constitution, and hastened his end."

His remains lie interred in Twillingate, awaiting the trump of the Archangel, which shall " wake the slumbering dead."

Richard Williams was born in the year 1789. His parents were members of the Episcopal Church, and he was brought up within its pale. When about sixteen years of age, under the preaching of Wesleyan ministers, he was led to see himself a sinner, who must experience the pardoning mercy of God or perish forever. He was directed to look to the " Lamb of God who taketh away the sin of the world." He looked by faith ; his sins were forgiven, and he was made a new creature. He entered the itinerant work in 1813. He labored two years in England, when he offered himself for the missionary work, and was appointed to Quebec. He labored ten years in Canada, when the missionary committee appointed him, in 1825, to St. John, New Brunswick. Methodism, in that city, was then in a languishing and almost a paralyzed condition, owing to certain untoward circumstances which had occurred the previous year. The firm and judicious manner of Mr. Williams tended greatly to allay the still existing excitement, to preserve our cause there, and give it a new impetus. For several years Mr.

Williams was chairman of the New Brunswick District. He went to England in 1840, and labored two years in the Helstone Circuit, in the Cornwall District. He returned to New Brunswick in 1842, and was stationed at Frederickton; and the next year he was appointed chairman of the Newfoundland District. This important position he held for five years, until his numerous infirmities compelled him to retire from the regular work. He removed to Nova Scotia, and resided five years as a supernumerary in the village of Bridgetown, in the Annapolis District. Through the whole of his ministerial life his character was irreproachable. Firm and inflexible was his attachment to all parts of Methodism; and in carrying out its discipline, his manner was thought, by some, to be austere, if not stubborn; but his judgment was generally correct, and his decision was made in accordance with the strictest integrity, and the most conscientious conviction of law and rectitude. He was a good divine; and his preaching was always rich in evangelical truth, characterized by a clear exposition of our doctrines, particularly by the prominence which he gave to those great scriptural doctrines, justification by faith and entire holiness. His death was very sudden. It was his frequent prayer that he might labor to the end of his life, and he would often express his desire in the words of our poet: —

> " Oh, that without a lingering groan,
> I may the welcome word receive;
> My body with my charge lay down,
> And cease at once to work and live ! "

His prayer was answered, for he preached, on the Sabbath previous to his death, at Tupperville, from Isaiah xl. 31. On Thursday afternoon he was observed to be unusually cheerful, and retired to rest without any apparent change in his health. About midnight he complained of cold; when a light was procured, the sweat of death was upon him; he raised his eyes to heaven as if in devotion, fell back upon his pillow, and expired without a sigh or groan. He died August 1st, 1856, in the sixty-seventh year of his age, and the forty-fifth of his ministry.

LABRADOR.

It is the practice of many wealthy planters in New-foundland, who own schooners, when those schooners have returned from the ice in the spring, to refit, and send them to the coast of Labrador for the summer fishing. In these vessels many entire families and hundreds of individuals go to prosecute their business, and are thus absent for months from the means of grace, and from all religious instruction. Many persons also go there from Nova Scotia, and the United States, for the purpose of fishing; besides which, a motley group of traders, settlers, sailors, and Indians, are found in the different harbors of those distant shores, who make no profession of religion, take no notice whatever of the holy Sabbath, and who spend what leisure they may have, in dancing, drinking, and other acts of dissipation and crime. Many members of our church were among these itinerant fishermen, who deeply felt their loss and destitution; and not a few of them yielded to the temptations by which they were surrounded, and fell from the way of religion and truth.

For many years had the missionaries deplored this state of things, and mourned over those backsliders who were so frequently produced thereby. But what to do, or how to apply a remedy, they could not tell, until the " Visiting Missionary " system came into operation, when it was soon seen that this would meet the case exactly. Therefore, after trying the experiment with success at the western shore, the coast of Labrador was taken up as a proper place where one of the brethren might be usefully employed in preaching the gospel during the summer months. Accordingly, in the summer of 1845, a visiting missionary was sent there and held religious services, as class-meetings, prayer-meetings, and preaching the gospel, in fourteen different places along the coast. This most important missionary work is still carried on with vigor by the brethren of the Newfoundland District.

In Canada the mission work had greatly extended. The first Wesleyan appointment to that country was in 1814, when John Strong, was sent to Quebec, and the number of our members in all Canada was thirty-two. In 1847, the mission stations in Canada were organized into a separate conference, with Robert Alder, D. D., President, and Matthew Richey, A. M., co-delegate. The Canada Conference was the first of the " affiliated conferences," and at its commencement it had six districts, 88 circuits, 181 ministers, and supernumeraries, and 21,749 members.

NEWFOUNDLAND BIBLE SOCIETY.

For many years had " the British and Foreign Bible Society " liberally supplied copies of the Holy Scriptures to the people " without money and without price ; " but at length the Christian public of St. Johns felt it was their duty for themselves to become subscribers, and assist the parent body in their noble effort to supply every human being with a copy of the word

of God. Accordingly, in the month of March, 1846, a
few individuals met together to talk the matter over,
and to make arrangements for the formation of an
auxiliary Bible Society for the Island of Newfoundland. In the month of May following, a public
meeting was held in the Commercial Room, when the
Bible Society was organized, of which the Honorable
William Thomas was chosen the first president. The
friends of the Bible Society now began zealously to
solicit subscriptions in order to promote the objects of
the society, when their efforts received a severe check
by a great fire, which occurred on the 9th of June,
and which laid a great part of the town in ashes.
Before the people had recovered from the shock and
suffering occasioned by this conflagration, another fearful catastrophe happened; it was a violent hurricane
with which the eastern coast was visited on the 19th
of September. The wind was from the north-east,
and blew directly upon the shore; many fishing-boats,
and several larger vessels were driven ashore, and near
twenty persons were known to have found a watery
grave. Fishing-nets and fishing-stages were destroyed
by the undertow; fishing-flakes were blown down, the
fish scattered on the ground, and the means the poor
fishermen had of purchasing their winter's supplies
were thus taken away. In the forest many trees were
torn up by the roots. In the town of St. Johns, the
new Episcopal Church, although not thrown down, was
moved from its foundation; a large hall, which had
afforded shelter to many whose houses were destroyed
in the late fire, was blown down, and several persons
buried in the ruins; two were killed on the spot, and
others were seriously injured; many houses were
injured and some were destroyed. Added to this, the

potato crop failed, and starvation drove many persons
from the out-harbor to the metropolis to seek for assistance to enable them to pass the coming winter.

In the midst of all this suffering, the friends of the
Bible Society in St. Johns, while they gave amply of
their means to support the poor, also gave liberally to
the funds of the society. The first anniversary of the
Newfoundland Auxiliary Bible Society was held on
Wednesday, March 24, 1847, at which were present
all the ministers of the non-conforming bodies, and
many of the most pious and most respectable laymen
on the island. The parent society in their published
report for that year, acknowledge the receipt from St.
Johns, Newfoundland, of the sum of £125 sterling, as
a free contribution; besides which Bibles and testa-
ments were ordered for sale, to the amount of
£121 16s. 1d. sterling.

In the year 1849, commenced what was called the
" Fly-Sheet " agitation; by which the connection in
various parts of England was seriously disturbed.
These " fly-sheets " were anonymous publications,
issued either by certain ministers of the conference,
or with their connivance and knowledge. No. 1 of
these hostile publications came from the press in either
1844, or 1845. No. 2 was published in 1846; and
No. 3, in 1847. These papers were characterized by
intense bitterness of feeling in reference to certain excellent ministers who were their brethren, and whom
they described as "indolent," "selfish," "artful,"
"ambitious," and "tyrannical;" and also by other
personalities so grossly offensive and libellous, that the
parties issuing them did not dare to affix the name of
either the printer or publisher. And further: " they
declared that the resources of the connection were per-

verted to uphold a system of favoritism, oppression, and extravagance; that many of the public acts of the conference proceeded from corrupt motives, or were of a mischievous tendency; and while suggesting extensive changes in its system of proceeding, and representing the members of the conference as enslaved, and longing for emancipation, they exhorted them to vigorous and united efforts to shake off the unhallowed yoke." [1]

No well regulated body could long exist if its members were thus allowed to insult and assail each other; hence it became a matter of justice as well as of necessity to bring the discipline of the body to bear against the offending parties. The result was that three ministers were expelled from the connection, and three others were formally censured. But the agitation continued, and although the minutes of 1850 report an increase in Great Britain of 10,000 members; yet the minutes of 1851 show a decrease of 46,068; and the minutes of 1852 show a further decrease of 20,946; in 1853, the decrease was 10,298; in 1854, 6,797; in 1855, 3,310. The total loss of members during these five years was 97,858; so that while our members in 1850 were 358,277, in 1855, they were only 260,858. Here the ebb ceased, and there has been constant increase of members to our church in Great Britain every year since. Many of our people after a time returned; many thousands never returned; but great numbers returned to the world and to their former evil ways. Terrible as were these trials, they had their benefits, for they removed from us the contentious and disaffected, and the connection has had peace ever since. Another benefit was, they led to a full ex-

---

[1] Minutes of Conference for 1849, p. 166.

35

planation of some of our rules, which many persons considered as not sufficiently explicit. Thus the agitation of Dr. Warren led to a clear and explicit view of Methodistic law as to the trial of private members and their right of appeal. This is explained in the minutes of 1835. The "fly-sheet" agitation led to a clear " definition of Quarterly Meetings," as to their composition, " regulations concerning memorials to the conference," and the mode of "trial of a trustee." This is found in the minutes of 1852.

While the Methodist Church in England was passing through this great ordeal, and their numbers were decreased by nearly one hundred thousand members, the malcontents tried to "stop the supplies," and in particular the missionary " supplies ;" yet, God blessed and prospered the missionary work to an extent that excited the astonishment and gratitude of the whole connection. The income of the society for 1852 was £102,730 19s. 9d. ; the number of missionaries, 476 ; and our missionary membership, 108,078.

This same year a second affiliated conference was formed. It was the French Conference. It was indeed small; its circuits were only nine in number ; its ministers, nineteen ; and its members, eight hundred and nineteen. Our membership in Newfoundland was now two thousand four hundred and forty-two.

The year 1855 will be noticed by Wesleyan historians in future time as the year when two affiliated conferences were organized : —

I. The Australasian Wesleyan Methodist Conference.

The first session of this conference was held in Sidney; it commenced on the 18th of January, under the presidency of the Rev. William Binnington Boyce. It began under auspicious circumstances. It had one hundred and sixteen ministers, besides a number of native assistant missionaries, nearly eight hundred chapels and other preaching places, nineteen thousand eight hundred and ninety-seven church members, with one thousand nine hundred and fifty-six on trial.

II. The Conference of the Wesleyan Methodist Connection, or Church of Eastern British America.

The first session of this conference commenced in Halifax, Nova Scotia, July 17, 1855, under the presidency of the Rev. John Beecham, D. D. Co-Delegate, Rev. Matthew Richey, D. D. Secretary, Rev. William Temple.

This conference embraces the Provinces of Nova Scotia, New Brunswick, Prince Edward Island, Newfoundland, and Bermuda. Our statistics will be understood by the following table:—

Tabular view of the Wesleyan Church of E. B. A., at its first conference.

No. of Circuits.	Ministers and Supernumeraries.	Local Preachers.	Chapels.	Other places preaching.	Day Schools.	Day School Scholars.	Sabbath Schools.	Teachers.	Scholars.	Members.	No. who attend Public Worship.
70	88	102	222	393	16	1162	160	1138	9114	13,136	65,690

The Newfoundland membership was two thousand five hundred and eighty-six; and of the sixteen day schools under the care of the conference, fifteen of

them, containing nine hundred and twenty-two scholars, were in Newfoundland.

The formation of the districts in the lower provinces into a distinct and independent conference, had
been expected for several years; and by most of the
ministers was much desired, as in their judgment it
would tend to consolidate and extend the work among
our widely scattered and rapidly increasing population.

Perhaps there was not a man in the British conference more fit to arrange, and carry out this important
measure, than the now sainted John Beecham, who
presided upon that occasion. Thoroughly acquainted
with all the minutiæ of Methodism, he could promptly
reply to every inquiry; and while with us his labors
were untiring, and in his official position he evinced
the wisdom of the sage, the firmness of the judge, the
accuracy of the mathematician, the urbanity of the
gentleman, and, above all, the kindness of a Christian
brother. But his work was almost done; he reached
England a little before the close of conference, and
early in the ensuing spring he was called to his reward.
From the death-roll of the British Conference we
make the following extract: —

"John Beecham, D. D., was born at Bartholdy-le-Beck,
Lincolnshire, in 1787, and entered the ministry in 1815. In
early life he acquired a good store of theological knowledge, and
of useful and diversified information, and he was habitually a
diligent and humble student of the sacred oracles; so that, both by
public and private labors, he fed the people of his charge 'with
knowledge and understanding.' The purity of his character,
together with his assiduous and punctual discharge of every duty,
and fidelity to every obligation, gave weight to his utterances, and
won the confidence and respect of all who were acquainted with
him; while the habitual kindness of his heart endeared him to the
poor and the afflicted, to whom, as a pastor, he was constantly

attentive. In 1831, he was appointed one of the general secretaries of our missionary society. For the long space of twenty-four years, he labored incessantly and devoutly in that office to promote the work of God; and he had the gratification of witnessing its gradual advancement to a state of prosperity far beyond his anticipations. In the latter years of his life, he was much occupied in the constituting of affiliated conferences, with a view to the extension of the work of God in different parts of the world; and his labors in pursuance of this object were eminently successful. Having witnessed the formation of such bodies in France, Australasia, and Canada, he undertook to visit the Eastern Provinces of British America, and, having presided over a new conference held in Nova Scotia, returned to Leeds, just before the close of the last British Conference. His account of that mission displayed a peculiar aptitude for such an undertaking, and led many who heard it once more to glorify God in him. His last days were eminently peaceful. Finding his health fail, he sought to recruit it by a month's quiet at the sea-side; but having taken cold there, he returned home much worse, and in six days after his return passed to an eternal rest. No vain regrets or harassing anxieties disturbed his last hours. All was quietness and assurance. 'Do you know that you are dying sir?' said one to him a few moments before he passed away. 'No,' said he, 'but all is well.' To another he said, 'There are the shining ones. They are waiting for me. I shall soon be with them. There is a sharp, thorny bridge to pass, but it will soon be over.' He died on the 22d of April, 1856, in the sixty-ninth year of his age."

The stations for the Newfoundland District, at the first conference, were as follows: —

St. Johns — Thomas Angwin, Samuel W. Sprague.
Harbor Grace — one to be sent.
Carbonear — William E. Shenston.
Brigus — John E. Phinney.
Port de Grave — Adam Nightingale.
Blackhead — John S. Addy.
Island Cove — One to be sent.
Perlican — One to be sent.
Hants' Harbor — Paul Prestwood.

TRINITY — Vacant.

BONAVISTA — Thomas Smith.

GREEN BAY — Under the care of the chairman.

BURIN — Elias Brettle.

GRAND BANK — John S. Peach.

THOMAS ANGWIN, Chairman of the District.

CHAPTER XVIII.

THE total population, within the bounds of the
"Eastern British American Conference," is computed at seven hundred and fifty thousand souls; about
one-tenth of whom are under the direct teaching and
influence of the Wesleyan ministry. During the
first year of our conference the missionary committee showed great kindness by sending out two
additional missionaries to Newfoundland. These were
Charles Comben and James Dove. This same year,
Robert A. Chesley was appointed to St. Johns; but
he was in his new station little more than three months,
before he was called to his reward. The death-roll of
conference for 1857, contains the following obituary
notice: —

"Robert Ainslie Chesley was born at Granville, Nova Scotia,
in the year 1816, and died at St. Johns, Newfoundland, on
Thursday, November 27, 1856, in the fortieth year of his age, and
the fourteenth of his ministry. At the age of twenty-three, he
was brought to an experimental knowledge of the truth, and
became 'a new creature in Christ Jesus.' From the time of his

(415)

conversion he felt an ardent love for souls, and sought to render himself useful and to glorify God by assisting to hold prayer-meetings, and afterwards exercised his talents as a local preacher. Believing he had a divine call to the sacred office of the ministry, he offered himself for the great work with much fear and trembling; and being approved and received, entered upon the duties of the Christian ministry in the year 1843. As a Christian, he was eminently devoted and exemplary, and sought to adorn the doctrine of God his Saviour in all things He was an Israelite indeed, in whom there was no guile. He walked with God, and his path shone brighter and brighter unto the perfect day. In the discharge of his sacred functions, he was faithful, zealous, and unwearied. Whatsoever his hand found to do, he did it with his might. As a preacher of the gospel, he affectionately, clearly, and successfully propounded its saving truths, giving prominence in his public ministrations to the all-important doctrine of holiness and entire consecration to Christ. His labors were abundantly owned and blessed. Many were the seals to his ministry in the various circuits upon which he labored as an ambassador for Christ. To pastoral visitation he paid strict and constant attention, and his amiability, benevolence, sympathy, and solicitude for the good of others, endeared him to the flocks over which he watched with pastoral care. At the last conference he was appointed to the superintendency of the St. Johns' circuit. He went to his new sphere of labor with enlarged expectations, and entered upon his duties with assiduity and earnestness. During his brief sojourn in St. Johns, he gained the affections of all with whom he became acquainted, and was rendered very useful in his work of faith and labor of love. The illness which terminated in his death was caused by exposure and excessive toil during the prosecution of his sacred duties. The disease, which so speedily resulted in his unexpected and lamented decease, was of that nature which prevented him from conversing much upon divine subjects; but his mind was kept in peace, and with resignation he was enabled to commit the keeping of his body and soul to God, knowing in whom he had believed. Those holy truths which he had so long proclaimed were his comfort and support during his last hours. After only seven days' sickness he departed this life in possession of a sure and certain hope of immortal blessedness. Great, indeed, is the loss of the church of

Christ and his afflicted family and friends, by the sudden and mysterious removal of one so talented and eminently qualified for extensive usefulness. But their loss is his eternal gain."

In the summer of 1857, James A. Duke was sent out by the committee as a missionary for the shores of Labrador, and a free passage was given him from England to St. Johns, in a vessel belonging to the Hon. Mr. Rogerson. Mr. Duke, however, did not arrive in time to proceed to Labrador that summer, in consequence of which, he was stationed in Carbonear, under the superintendency of Christopher Lockhart.

In the month of January, 1858, the new chapel in St. Johns was opened, and on the sixth of that month, Henry Daniel, the chairman of the district, wrote to the committee in which he says: — "At present nearly all the sittings are engaged. Our congregations are large and the spiritual state of our society is encouraging. We need your sympathy and prayers. Popery has an awful grasp on this community, and Puseyism, a second edition of it, spreads a deadly blight over the largest portion. Methodism has a great mission to this island. The Lord make us faithful and zealous." An interesting account of the Green Bay Circuit was given at this time by Mr. Prestwood, from which we make the following extract: —

"This circuit is extensive and important; nearly two thousand people, according to the census taken this year, belong to us either as members or hearers; they are scattered almost all round the shores of this large bay, and many more would gladly attend our ministry had they the privilege. Of these some do not hear a sermon preached more than once or twice a year. They are anxious to obtain another preacher in this circuit, and intend to apply for one. For some time past a gracious revival of religion

has been experienced in different parts of the circuit, especially
during the last winter.   At Twillingate, last spring, many were
converted to God, and, we are thankful to say, hold fast the
profession of their faith, and prove the reality of their conversion
by a consistent walk and conduct.   The state of the society is encouraging; the members are sincere, and anxious for the salvation
of their souls.   Most heartily do they thank God for the gospel,
and for the appointment of the Wesleyan missionaries, whom they
term 'men after God's own heart.' "

In the year 1859, the first missions of conference of
Eastern British America are mentioned in the minutes.
They were three in number, and all stood connected
with the Newfoundland District.   They stand thus : —

MISSIONS OF CONFERENCE.

LABRADOR — Supplied during the summer months by Charles
  Comben.
PETITES AND WESTERN SHORE — To be supplied by the
  Chairman.
EXPLOITS AND LITTLE BAY ISLANDS — James A. Duke.

The ministers of the conference were so impressed
with the importance of the Labrador Mission, that they
unanimously passed the following resolution : —

MISSION TO LABRADOR.

" *Resolved*, That the conference recognizes its obligation to sus-
tain the mission to Labrador to the utmost extent of its ability,
and the brethren are directed that when the collection for the
' Home Mission and Contingent Fund' is taken up, the claims of
this mission be urged upon the attention of our friends, and that
they be requested to contribute liberally to the fund, in order
that this important mission may be well sustained."

Mr. Comben went to Labrador in June, and an-
chored in Red Bay on the 30th of the month.   Here he
found eighty persons resident, and about forty more who
were there during the summer.   Most of these were Wes-

leyans from Newfoundland. These people brought
their religion with them, and in consequence held religious services as prayer-meetings and class-meetings, and
also held a Sabbath school. He met a class of thirteen
persons, six of whom were from Carbonear. Thirty
miles from Red Bay are Henly Harbor and Cha-
teaux. In the former place he found some friends resident, and about eighty persons who were there for the
summer; in the latter about fifty Wesleyan residents,
and near a hundred summer visitors, all from Newfoundland, besides a number of persons from Nova
Scotia. A class-meeting was regularly held in one
of these places, and prayer-meetings were held in both.
He next visited Cape Charles Harbor, in the 52d degree of north latitude. There he found one hundred
and forty Wesleyans from Newfoundland, besides a
number of Episcopalians, and likewise a number of
persons from Nova Scotia. Here he had a congregation
of two hundred persons. He visited about twelve or
fourteen harbors, in most of which he found some Wesleyans, and in all he was received with great kindness;
and the universal wish was, that as business called
them to those shores, they would not be left as sheep
without a shepherd, but that our ministers would yearly visit them in their distant wanderings, and preach to
them the words of life and salvation.

The brethren of the Newfoundland district deserve
all honor for carrying out so fully the resolution of the
conference in reference to the Labrador Mission; and
the missionary committee in London were so well satisfied with the measure, that they published the journal
of Mr. Comben's visit in *extenso* in their large report
for the year 1860.

In the summer of 1860, the Rev. Thomas Fox visited Labrador. He arrived at Cape Charles Harbor on the 17th of June, and laid out, as his missionary tour, an extent of coast of from two hundred to two hundred and fifty miles, for all that distance is considered as within the bounds of the mission. He visited twenty-four harbors and coves, and preached to congregations composed of Newfoundlanders, Nova Scotians, Englishmen, Americans, and Indians, including both the Esquimaux and Mountaineers.

The next year Mr. Fox went again to Labrador, and at Cape Charles he says : " Here I met with a welcome at the house of Mr. and Mrs. Hayward Taylor of Carbonear. Stayed nearly a week, held services and visited the people." It was not surprising that Mr. Fox should be received with a welcome by Mr. Taylor and his kind lady, for the house of Mr. Taylor, of Carbonear, has been a home for Wesleyan ministers for more than half a century. During this mission tour, Mr. Fox sailed over four hundred miles along the coast, visited between twenty and thirty harbors, preached about sixty times, held a number of prayer-meetings and class-meetings, read the Scriptures and prayed from house to house, baptized a number of children, and called the attention of the people to the erection of six chapels. He was everywhere received with kindness, heard with attention, and his visits were made a blessing to the people.

The Labrador mission is a very important one, and it is to be desired that one or more ministers will soon be sent to reside on the coast, particularly as we have between forty and fifty Wesleyan families already resident there.

MR. GOODISON'S MISSION.

In 1862, John Goodison was sent to Labrador by

the brethren of the Newfoundland District. He sailed in the government cutter Duck. Owing to rough weather, the great quantity of field-ice, and the numerous icebergs, he did not reach Labrador until the 5th of July. He coasted in a whale-boat, and during the summer sailed over three hundred miles, visited some hundreds of families in the different harbors, preached many times, got several Sabbath schools in operation, and distributed some thousands of books and tracts. In reference to the result of his mission he says : —

"I have seen many souls converted to God, some few backsliders reclaimed, and believers in Christ filled with divine love. One chapel has been erected, the frames of two others are ready to be put up, and next summer it is expected that at Cape Charles, another will be reared."

The Labrador Mission continues to engage the attention of the brethren of Newfoundland and of the conference.

In 1861, the conference of Eastern British America was honored in having, as its president, the Rev. William B. Boyce, one of the secretaries of the Wesleyan Methodist Missionary Society.

Before the conference, Mr. Boyce visited Nova Scotia, Prince Edward Island, Cape Breton, and Newfoundland. Of this last mentioned island he reported as follows : —

"The religious value of this mission cannot be too highly estimated. Here we do battle with popery in the very gateway of America, and by the blessing of God, Methodism has saved the Protestantism of the island; for it is a remarkable fact that in the districts where our first missionaries labored, the people remain Protestant; elsewhere they are mainly Papists, and unless we follow the population the new settlements will become popish also, — a merely nominal Protestantism being no

defence against the Man of Sin. The population[1] of Newfoundland, in 1857, was 119,304; of which 20,144 are returned as
Methodists, being little more than one-sixth of the whole, — a larger
proportion I think, than is found in any other mission-field except, perhaps, some of the West Indian colonies. The Romanists
are 55,309; but the Protestants of the several denominations,
Episcopal, Methodist, Presbyterian, and others outnumber them
by about 10,000. The Romanism of the island is of the most
virulent sort, and is felt, even by those who do not look at the
question religiously, to be a social and political evil of no common magnitude. Vexed questions of local politics cannot altogether be avoided, as, where popish intolerance is rampant, it
becomes the duty even of Christians to resist it by every constitutional means. I arrived in Newfoundland in the midst of
a great reactionary movement against popish political influence,
which is going on in all our American colonies, and found our
people taking a warm part on the Protestant side. There is
some danger in this, yet how can it be avoided? One might as
well blame the rebuilders of Jerusalem for going armed to their
sacred and patriotic work.

"On the Labrador Mission, I will merely remark, that it is grate-
fully recognized as a boon to hundreds of families in Newfoundland, whose husbands, brothers, or fathers are cared for by
it, when far distant from home, and exposed to great dangers
and temptations. It is an enterprise of the purest mercy and
love."[2]

This conference (1861) had to record the death of
another Newfoundland missionary, Mr. Thomas Gaetz,
a young man of piety and promise. The record reads
thus : —

"Thomas Gaetz was born at Musquodobit Harbor, Nova
Scotia, on the fifth of October, 1831. He was thoughtful and
studious when a child, and at twelve years was soundly converted to God. Very soon after his conversion he felt a strong

[1] This was exclusive of the British population on the French shore, where
there are resident 3,334 British subjects, making the total British population, 122,638. See the table of population, p. 96.
[2] Report of Methodist Missionary Society, 1862, p. 180.

desire for the salvation of sinners; and feeling that he ·was called of God to preach the gospel, he was at an early age engaged as a local preacher; but, desiring to devote himself fully to the work of God, he became a candidate for the ministry among us in the year 1851; since which time he has labored with acceptance and success in Nova Scotia, Prince Edward Island, and Newfoundland.

"In the Grand Bank Circuit his labors were greatly owned of God. His name is, and long will be, a household word. He never spared himself, but often labored beyond his strength, such was his anxiety to do good. He was appointed by the last conference to the Old Perlican Circuit. Immediately on his arrival he commenced his labor with great zeal, yea, intense ardor; and although with this people so short a time, yet he was endeared to them, greatly beloved by them, and his death was deeply lamented. When told he could not recover without some speedy alteration, he exclaimed, 'Well, my peace is made with God.' His last words were, 'Jesus is my love!' after which he fell asleep in Christ on the 24th of October, 1860, in the 29th year of his age, and the 10th year of his ministry."

The death-roll of our conference for 1862 records another laborer in Newfoundland, — Mr. William Samuel Shenstone, son of the Rev. W. E. Shenstone, who had been a travelling minister for nearly forty years. Both father and son were travelling in Newfoundland. The father was stationed at Port de Grave, and the son at Hants' Harbor. Mr. Shenstone, Jun., was a pious, zealous, prayerful young man, and there was much probability that he would be very useful as a Christian minister. But he was called away to a better land.

When the question was asked " What ministers have died since the last conference?" four names were given. The first was Mr. Shenstone. The minute reads: —

" William Samuel Shenstone, who was born at Three Rivers,

Canada East, in the year 1838. He feared the Lord from his youth. Amiability of disposition, dutifulness to his parents, fraternal affection, intense love of study, and aptness to accumulate mental stores, were marked elements in his character. At the age of sixteen, he was convinced of the need of divine forgiveness, and a change of heart, and sought, by humble confession of sin and trust in the atonement of Christ, the great salvation; and in him was fulfilled the promise, then shall they find me, ' when they search for me with their whole heart.'

" He obtained peace through believing. At the conference of 1858, he was accepted as a candidate for our ministry, and was appointed to the Bonavista Circuit, where he labored with great acceptance and success. He was subsequently appointed to the Carbonear Circuit, where his Divine Master blessed him, and made him a blessing. He received such a baptism of the Holy Spirit, as to lead him to a closer walk with God. At the conference of 1861, he was appointed to the Hants' Harbor Circuit, where he entered upon his labors with much prayer, a deep sense of responsibility, and a holy resolution to consecrate his energies to the great work of seeking the salvation of souls, and the edification of the church. But he had only labored about a week when he was stricken down by affliction which baffled medical skill; and, after about three weeks of severe suffering, during which his trust in Christ was firm and unshaken, God took him to an early rest in heaven. His last words were ' The best of it is God is with us.' He died in peace, August 31st, 1861, in the 25th year of his age, and the fourth of his ministry."

The year 1863 was a time of great rejoicing to the whole Wesleyan connection. It was the jubilee of the Wesleyan Missionary Society. That society, as we have seen, was formed in 1813; and, during these fifty years of its existence, God has prospered it to an extent that was never anticipated by its most sanguine friends. In 1813, our missionary sphere was limited: we had twenty-six missionaries in the West Indies, one in Bermuda, thirteen in Nova Scotia and New Brunswick, and three in Newfoundland; making a total of forty-three missionaries. Our missionary membership was then only 17,025. In 1863, our ministers and assistant missionaries numbered 889, and our missionary membership was 142,789, besides 13,804 on trial.

In 1813, we had no missionaries in France, Italy, Africa, China, Australasia, Polynesia or Canada; nor had we a printing-press out of the United Kingdom. But in 1863, we had ministers in all the above places, with eight printing-presses, four affiliated conferences, and 146,457 children in our different Sabbath schools. The annual income for missionary purposes, down to 1813, was seldom much more than £4000, but the balance sheet of the society, for 1863, shows an income of £141,638 16s. 8d.

In gratitude for this great success, the friends of missions in England determined to hold a jubilee, and, by an extra exertion, to raise a fund to be called the Jubilee Fund; the object being to assist the general missionary fund, by providing a college for training missionary candidates; to provide for disabled missionaries, and for widows and orphans of deceased missionaries; also to assist the work in France, Italy, India, China, and in various ways to promote the extension of missionary operations, and the conversion of the world from sin to God.

The first blast of the jubilee-trumpet was heard in Leeds, where, fifty years before, the missionary society had been formed. But oh, the ravages of death! but few were present at the jubilee that witnessed the formation of the society. Those pious and zealous ministers, George Morley and James Buckley, have long gone to their reward; the erudite Richard Watson and the profoundly eloquent Jabez Bunting are now with the " hymning multitude," receiving the reward of

36 *

their faithful labors while on earth. Thomas Thompson, the chairman and Methodist local preacher, who was neither afraid nor ashamed to advocate the cause of righteousness and religion before the British senate, has realized the promise, " Whosoever, therefore, shall confess me before men, him will I confess also before my Father which is in heaven." But we must not regret, for he who took those men from the church militant is still with us, and we have received the fulfilment of that assurance, which he gave by the mouth of his servant David, " Instead of thy fathers, shall be thy children, whom thou mayest make princes in all the earth." The missionary spirit of 1813 has fallen on the church, in 1863, to an extent that was never before seen ; the benefit of which unknown nations shall realize, and by which unborn generations shall be blessed. The public jubilee meeting was preceded by numerous religious exercises, as special sermons, special prayer-meetings, and special love-feasts, besides the many petitions that ascended to the throne of grace from the closet, and from the family altar for success in the enterprise. Prayer was heard, and a spirit of liberality was evinced by the Wesleyan church that has surprised the whole Christian world. The money subscribed in one week was £35,000.

The jubilee movement thus inaugurated at Leeds, in the month of October, was speedily followed by corresponding action in every district and in every circuit throughout the United Kingdom ; it extended to all the affiliated conferences, and to all the mission-stations ; in fact, a similar spirit to that which influenced the meeting in Leeds seems to have permeated every heart through the entire range of British Methodism. The financial result is not yet known.

The jubilee movement did not commence in the conference of Eastern British America until the month of July, 1864.

Newfoundland, which is never behind in any good thing, has taken an important part. To that country the time was most inauspicious. Both the seal-fishery in the spring, and the cod-fishery in the summer, had failed, and pinching poverty stared multitudes directly in the face. Some thought it unwise and impolitic to attempt any special effort for pecuniary purposes and that a postponement would be the better plan. Amidst many discouragements a public meeting was held in St. Johns and the noble sum of $1600 or £400 was subscribed. The following sums were also expected to be raised: from Carbonear, $240, Harbor Grace, $400, and Brigus, $300; making a total for the island, of $2540; and this in a season of almost unparalleled failure and distress. The Lord will surely bless that people.

Our conference of 1864 was again honored with a representative from the British Conference, in the person of the Rev. William L. Thornton, M. A., accompanied by the Rev. Robinson Scott, a representative from the Irish Conference. The wise counsels of these excellent brethren, their ardent zeal, their earnest prayers, their Christian courtesy, their pulpit services, — and to mention one case, the address of Mr. Thornton to the young men who were received into full connection, — were of a character that will endear their names to them while life shall last, and can never be erased from the minds and memories of those who had the privilege of being present.

At this conference the Newfoundland District numbered fourteen circuits, eight mission stations, and twenty-two ministers.

The following are the stations for the present year, 1864–5.

> ST. JOHNS — P. Prestwood, A. W. Turner, Joseph Gaetz, Adam Nightingale, Supernumerary.
>
> HARBOR GRACE — James Dove.
>
> CARBONEAR — J. Winterbotham, John Allen.
>
> BRIGUS — Thomas Harris.
>
> PORT DE GRAVE — Joseph Pascoe.
>
> BLACKHEAD — John Waterhouse.
>
> ISLAND COVE — W. E. Shenstone.
>
> OLD PERLICAN — John S. Peach.
>
> HANTS' HARBOR — One to be sent.
>
> TRINITY — Charles Ladner.
>
> BONAVISTA — Charles Comben, J. Goodison.
>
> TWILLINGATE — James A. Duke.
>
> BURIN — S. T. Teed.
>
> GRAND BANK — John S. Phinney.

MISSIONS.

> LABRADOR — John Allen, for the summer months.
>
> PETITES — John M. Pike.
>
> CHANNEL — Isaac Howie.
>
> EXPLOITS — J. A. Rogers.
>
> FOGO AND CHANGE ISLANDS — Thomas Fox.
>
> LITTLE BAY ISLANDS — To be supplied by the chairman.
>
> GREEN'S POND — One wanted.
>
> SPENCER'S POND — One wanted.
>
> JOHN S. PEACH, Chairman.
>
> JAMES DOVE, Fin. Sec.

From the following table it will be seen that, by the mercy of God, we have a total membership of four thousand persons on the island of Newfoundland and its dependencies. Its contributions to the mission fund, for the last year, were $2,243,64, and the adherents to Methodism upwards of twenty thousand souls.

Our membership stands thus : —

	Members.	On Trial.	Total.
St. Johns	304	248	552
Harbor Grace . . .	102		102
Carbonear	501	17	518
Brigus	126	10	136
Port de Grave	50	20	70
Blackhead	435	2	437
Island Cove	128		128
Old Perlican	280	30	310
Hants' Harbor	150	36	186
Trinity	90	6	96
Bonavista	302	25	327
Twillingate	225	20	245
Burin	250	131	381
Grand Bank	197	47	244
Petites	55	20	75
Channel	11		11
Exploits	95	50	145
Fogo	33	47	80
Green's Pond	30	26	56
	3364	735	4099

Such is the state of our church in Newfoundland, in this the centenary year of its existence. We have reached at least one-third of the Protestant population, and one-sixth of the entire population of the island. And if the labors of the few agents, which Methodism had for a large part of the last century, have been so much blessed, what may we not expect in future, with her greatly increased agency, and the appliances she now has at command? We truly have cause to thank God, and take courage, and will heartily join in the prayer of Moses, the man of God : —

" Let thy work appear unto thy servants, and thy glory unto their children.   And let the beauty of the Lord our God be upon us ; and establish thou the work of our hands upon us, yea, the work of our hands, establish thou it."

CONCLUSION.

DURING the past century, the Methodist ministers who have labored in Newfoundland have toiled through many difficulties, and suffered many privations; but those difficulties mostly arose from the physical state of the country, or from men who were influenced by a morbid theology; never from the opposition of the people. A Newfoundlander scarcely knows how to be inhospitable or unkind to strangers; and for Christian ministers he feels a deep respect. The Congregational church in St. Johns, which for many years was the only non-conforming body beside ourselves, always showed much of brotherly kindness; and the Presbyterians, whose churches have been comparatively recently formed, do the same to this day. Roman Catholics, however they may hate heretics, have offered but little opposition to Methodism in a direct way. The opposition we have been called to meet was from men who called themselves Protestants; who pompously claim to be the church; who denounce other ministers as " unauthorized guides," and deny their right, either to preach the gospel or administer the sacraments, because they have not re-ceived ordination from the hands of a diocesan bishop. We can indeed afford to smile at these ostentatious pretensions, yet we would remind these gentlemen that, but for Methodist preachers and their labors before these claimants for " apostolical succession " came to the island, many places where themselves now labor would have been uncheered with the light and truths of the gospel, or have been brought under the power and direct influence of the Church of Rome. We hope and pray that these men may see and act differently; but whether so or not, it is the fixed purpose of Wesleyan ministers to labor on with diligence in their Master's work, give themselves to the "ministry of the word and to prayer," knowing that in "due season we shall reap, if we faint not."

The progress of our mission in Newfoundland has never been rapid; still, from its commencement, it has been gradual and continuous. For a time it was located in and near Harbor Grace; then it commenced in Old Perlican; from Harbor Grace it extended down the North Shore, and from Perlican it was carried to Island Cove and across the bay to Trinity. Next it commenced in St. Johns, and, not long after, it went as far north as Bonavista. After several years, it took a long stretch to the west, and planted itself in Burin and Fortune Bay. Another stationary period came, after which it rolled on north to Green's Pond and Twillingate, and in another direction went to the Western Shore; and, finally, it extended to the coast of Labrador, and as far north on that coast as our hardy fishermen, in the prosecution of their wearisome and dangerous toil, deem it prudent to proceed.

There is no one place that the missionaries have labored, in which they have not had success. In several places they are the only Protestant ministers; and in others they have an influence over the larger portion of the community. Thousands have gone to heaven from Newfoundland, who never sat under any other than the Wesleyan ministry; and thousands are now living in the enjoyment of religion, who, but for Methodism, would be ignorant of God and walking in the ways of sin.

The physical difficulties of the country have to a great extent been overcome. When Lawrence Coughlan landed at Harbor Grace, and for sixty years after, there was not a road to travel on, or a horse to ride; the plough was unknown; the land was uncultivated except what was done with the narrow Irish spade. Now in many places they have good roads and bridges, horses, carriages, packets, steamboats, ploughs, and various other agricultural implements. Hence travelling can now be performed with comfort, and the land cultivated with comparative ease. Moreover, many thousands of acres of rich arable land have been discovered in a country denounced as universally barren, and mines and minerals have also been found of sufficient richness and in localities of such convenience as will repay the capitalist and employ laborers to a great extent; which, with the inexhaustible shoals of fish on its shores, the countless multitude of seals that annually come on its coast, and the rich furs of its interior, will raise Newfoundland, at no great distance of time, to great wealth and prosperity.

In arriving at its present civil position, and acquiring its present political constitution, Newfoundland has had many a struggle, and has sometimes been placed in a position that was humiliating and oppressive. For many years she was without any government whatever; and what in that country was first called a government, which was the " fishing-admiral " system, was only another name for anarchy. The administration of law, by either floating or resident surrogates, was incongruous to every principle which an Englishman would consider as righteous and equitable; and when the question of self-government by a provincial house of assembly was mooted, the measure was stoutly opposed, — the idea was ridiculed. It was said the barren character of the country would not warrant such measure; the ignorance that prevailed in the out-harbors was so great that the people could not be made to understand it; and that there were not men enough of sufficient intelligence to occupy those official positions which, as members in a colonial parliament, they would of necessity be required to fill. When the charter was granted and the constitutional government formed, instead of being a great boon, it for several years was a great bane; for there were not sufficient guards in reference either to the elective suffrage, or the qualification of members. The government, therefore, was soon thrown into the power of the Roman priesthood, and, although nominally a civil government, was practically a hierarchy. For eight years did the Protestants of Newfoundland groan under this oppressive tyranny; but this difficulty was in time overcome, for on the 26th of April, 1841, Captain Prescott, the then governor of the island, dismissed the assembly, and dissolved the charter. A new charter was afterwards granted, more adapted to the wants and circumstances of the people. Under this charter they are now governed. These oppressive acts the Newfoundlanders bore with great patience. There was nothing rebellious in them; they are firmly attached to the British Crown, and they have never sought redress for their grievances, except in a constitutional manner. The papal power still strives to govern the island, as in fact, it does everywhere; yet, the increasing intelligence of the Protestant population, their numbers, and their wealth, are such, that while they will readily concede to Roman Catholics their religious privileges in their full extent, and their just share in the government of the country, they will never again allow the priesthood to rule, or their own privileges, civil or religious, to be taken from them.

In the preceding pages it is shown, that the laboring people often suffer extreme poverty, arising from the failure of the fishery, or the small number of seals which come on the coast in the spring. This is deeply to be deplored. The cause is, these people follow no business but the fishery; they do not cultivate the land to the extent it must be done before this state of things can be entirely altered. There is indeed a great difficulty in the way; for the months of May and June are in general the best months for fishing, and that is the only time to plough and plant the ground. Still, by a judicious arrangement, time may be found to plant a portion of ground before the fishery commences, to cut the hay in the slack time between the caplin and squid scull, and gather, in the autumn, both the fruits of earth and of the sea.

Education is now being extensively diffused and has already been a great blessing to the people. For want of this, in bygone years the Newfoundlanders were often the subjects of banter and burlesque. It was with them as it used to be with the British sailor. When the mariner-would return from his long voyage, and reach his native shore, instead of providing him with a comfortable home, with means of mental culture and religious instruction, he would be left to the tender mercies of the rumseller, the crimp, and the most profligate of human beings; and when, through the influence of strong drink, he would swear like a demon, or act like a maniac, the passers-by would smile, and exclaim, " Never mind him, — he is only a sailor." So it was with the Newfoundlander ; when from lack of education his language would not be grammatical, his accent be that of his forefathers, or he would use terms or phrases which, however expressive at one time, are now old-fashioned and obsolete, those who heard him would smile, and say, " Oh, he is only an ignorant fisherman."

A reproach like this will soon cease to be heard. For Newfoundland now has her academies of learning, her training-schools for teachers, and her elementary schools scattered over the whole island. She has also her institutions for science, literature, her public libraries, botanic gardens, and other means of improvement. She has her public lecturers, her orators, and her divines ; and another generation will not pass away ere her fishermen will be quite as well educated as are the peasantry of any province in this hemisphere.

In the Sabbath schools the children are taught the facts of the Bible, and instructed in its doctrines, while every effort is made to lead them to an experimental acquaintance with the religion of Jesus. The teachers in these Sabbath schools have been rewarded for their past labors, in seeing the benefit the children have received ; while the instances are not few where little children have died happy, through and by means of the instructions received in the Sabbath school.

The ministers of the Wesleyan Church have great cause for thankfulness for the manner and the extent to which their labors have been blessed to this people.

Newfoundland was the first missionary ground ever occupied by the Methodist Church; and Methodism was the first evangelical teaching the people of that island ever enjoyed. For one entire century have they toiled along its shores and preached among its people the words of life and salvation. Their labor has not been in vain. They have been instrumental in the conversion of many. For this they are thankful. But Newfoundland is not yet evangelized; there are many coves and harbors where as yet we have no establishments. Popery still governs nearly one half of the population, and the little less withering influence of Puseyism guides thousands who boast of being called Protestants; while in our Wesleyan communities and congregations there are many who are yet unsaved and in their sins.

Consistent with its character and mission, Methodism cannot remain an idle spectator of the moral evil that is in the world. Her business is to enlighten the minds of men and pluck poor sinners as brands from the burning. For this she was called into existence, and by a chain of providential interpositions, has been placed in her present commanding position; and were she now recreant to her trust, she would lose her glory, be laid aside, and another or others would take her place. With all evangelical churches she cherishes the most fraternal feeling; but with Popery and her young sister Puseyism she is in antagonism, and will never retire from the conflict until those systems are no more. The circulation of the Holy Scriptures, the right training of children, the faithful preaching of Christ crucified, with prayer and faith, are the weapons we employ, and by these shall error be overthrown and the whole be won to Christ.

Let us then labor on until not only every part of the island of Newfoundland be truly evangelized, but until the light of divine truth shines in every land and among every people upon earth. In the word of God we are assured that such shall be the case; for it is therein written, "The earth shall be full of the knowledge of the Lord, as the waters cover the sea."

CHRONOLOGICAL TABLE

AND

INDEX.

CHRONOLOGICAL TABLE.

1497. Newfoundland discovered by John Cabot, June 24th.

1500. Gasper Corteral visited the coast and landed at Portugal Cove.

1502. Portuguese commenced fishing on the coast.

1517. British, French, Spaniards, and Portuguese, collectively, had forty vessels engaged in the fisheries.

1534. Jacques Cartier landed in Catalina Harbor.

1536. British attempted to colonize the Island, under "Master Robert Hore," a merchant of London, but failed, and the colonists nearly perished.

1549. An Act of Parliament passed for the better encouragement of the fisheries of Newfoundland.

1583. Sir Humphrey Gilbert took formal possession of Newfoundland, on Monday, August 5th, in the name of Queen Elizabeth.

1610. First settlers came out to Conception Bay, under Mr. Guy, a merchant, of Bristol.

1612. Guy partially surveyed the coast, and held friendly intercourse with the Red Indians.

1615. Captain Whitbourne sent out to correct abuses.

1623. Second party of English settlers came, under Lord Baltimore, and settled in Ferriland.

1633. First laws promulgated in reference to Newfoundland.
" Fishing Admiral System commenced.

1635. Permission granted to the French to cure fish on the land.

1675. Colonists displanted by royal authority, when many houses were destroyed and much suffering caused among the people.

1676. The order revoked.

1696. St. Johns captured by the French, under Admiral Brouillen.

1705. French destroy a number of British settlements on the coast.

1708. St. Johns captured a second time by the French, under St. Ovide.

1713. Treaty of Utrecht.

1729. Newfoundland separated from the government of Nova Scotia. Captain Henry Osborne, R. N., the first governor. He erected the first court-house and jail, instituted surrogate courts, and appointed magistrates.

1741. Court of Vice Admiralty established.

1751. Captain Drake established a court of oyer and terminer.

1762. St. Johns captured a third time by the French Admiral de Ternay.

1763. Labrador annexed to the government of Newfoundland.

"   Treaty of Paris.

1764. Custom-house established by Sir Hugh Pelliser, and navigation laws extended to Newfoundland.

1765. Rev. Lawrence Coughlan arrives in Harbor Grace, and introduces Methodism.

1770. John Stretton arrives in Harbor Grace.

1772. Lawrence Coughlan returns to England.

1774. John Haskins arrives in Newfoundland.

1775. Year of the great storm.

"   Copper mine opened in Shoal Bay, near St. Johns.

1786. John M'Geary arrives in Newfoundland.

1789. Court of Common Pleas established by Admiral Milbanke.

1791. Rev. William Black visits Newfoundland.

1796. A large French fleet appeared off St. Johns, and burnt Bay Bulls

1807. First newspaper issued in St. Johns.

1815. Mission stations in Newfoundland organized into a district.

1816. Great fire in St. Johns, Feb. 12. Property destroyed to the amount of £100,000.

1817. A second great fire, Nov. 7 ; thirteen mercantile establishments and one hundred and forty houses destroyed.

"   The winter of the " Rals."

1819. Mary March, a red Indian woman, brought to St. Johns.

1823. Mr. Cormach crossed the island ·from Random Sound to St. George's Bay.

" Three Indian females brought to St. Johns, — the last red Indians that have been seen.

1826. Surrogate Court abolished, and Supreme Court established.

1833. First session of the legislature opened Jan. 1, by Sir Thomas Cochran.

1839. Geological survey of the island, by J. B. Jukes, Esq., M. A. F.; G. S.

1840. First steamer arrives in St. Johns

1846. St. Johns again nearly destroyed by fire.

1855. The Wesleyan districts in the lower provinces united, and formed into distinct connection, called THE CONFERENCE OF EASTERN BRITISH AMERICA.

1859. First missions of the Conference formed.

1860. The Prince of Wales visits Newfoundland.

1865. The centenary year of Methodism in British America.

—

INDEX.

www.ingramcontent.com/pod-product-compliance
Lightning Source LLC
Chambersburg PA
CBHW031058110726
47900CB00003B/976